BLOODSPELL

BLOODSPELL

Amalie Howard

LANGDON STREET PRESS
212 3ʳᵈ AVENUE NORTH, SUITE 290
MINNEAPOLIS, MN 55401
612.455.2293

WWW.LANGDONSTREETPRESS.COM

THE TEXT OF THIS BOOK WAS SET IN 11.5-POINT MINION
COVER DESIGN BY ALAN PRANKE

ISBN-13: 978-1-936782-11-6
LCCN: 2011925039

DISTRIBUTED BY ITASCA BOOKS

PRINTED IN THE UNITED STATES OF AMERICA

for Connor, Noah, and Olivia
the lights of my life
and
for Cam
who has my heart

Never shall a Vampyre consort, befriend, or choose for a mate any Witch, Wizard, Warlock, or any creature harboring sorcerous abilities or knowledge of magicks, save if such relations have been warranted and sanctioned as crucial by the Vampyre Council, and only in the combined and unanimous interest of the Seven Vampyre Houses.

Henceforth under the Peace Treaties of the Great War, never shall a Vampyre attack, kill, or consume the blood of any such persons or creatures under penalty of immediate conviction and sentencing by the Vampyre High Council.

To break this Covenant shall be punishable by exile or execution in accordance with Vampyre Law.

Vampyre Covenant XVI, The Book of Reii

ONE

Metamorphosis

"HEY FREAK, YOU lost? The hobo section is on the other side of the cafeteria!"

Victoria shuffled past a crowded table keeping her eyes on the scuffed toes of her sneakers as the table's occupants burst into laughter.

"By the way, the Salvation Army called, they're having a sale!" A foot blocked her path and her stomach tensed.

No, no, no. Not now. Keep it together, Tori!

Her fingers hovered over the volume dial on her iPod as she stepped over the foot without looking up and moved faster, away from the table. The rush of music in her ears did nothing to dissipate the jeers. She tucked her hands deeper into the pockets of her black hoodie and swallowed the knot in her throat. Just a few more steps and she'd be out of their reach. Junior year was almost over, and the last thing she needed was a scene in the crowded school cafeteria.

She could usually handle the Stepfords, but she wasn't herself today. Since earlier that morning, everything had seemed off, unpredictable. Volatile. After another mostly sleepless night, she'd woken up soaked in sweat and with such achy muscles that it'd taken almost a half hour just to get out of bed. A cold shower had done nothing to calm the heat inside her. If she hadn't had her Calculus final, she'd have stayed home.

A large hand crossed her peripheral vision and before she could guess its owner's intent, her headphones were ripped from her ears.

"So what's with all the black? Somebody die?" Victoria raised blank eyes to the boy who'd spoken. Brett Halloway. Captain of the football team and king of the popular crowd at St. Xavier's, he had a ruthless reputation. He was flanked by two cheerleaders, both blond, blue-eyed, and leggy. They eyed her with identical expressions of undisguised disdain. Victoria felt anger flood to the tips of her toenails.

Stay calm. Stay calm. Stay calm.

"I'm sorry, I didn't realize where I was," she said in a careful monotone.

"You bet you didn't. Otherwise we might think you wanted to try out for cheerleading." Brett laughed and turned to his friends. "What do you think, boys? She could do it. She's got a nice pair … of legs." His eyes settled on her chest. Victoria felt a flush steal up her cheeks.

"Very funny, Brett," she said. "Can I have my headphones, please? Then you can go back to figuring out whether you're going to repeat yet another year of high school on daddy's dime." The group at the table erupted in smothered laughter. For a second, something ugly rippled in Brett's eyes before he masked his anger with a smile.

"Sure. Just give me one cheer. Come on, give me a V! Give

me an I! Give me an … R!" Brett taunted. "How do you spell virgin again?"

Victoria scanned the room for help. No teachers or monitors in sight, and everybody else seemed suddenly preoccupied with other things, even though she could still feel their furtive glances. Humiliation scorched her ears.

"Or should we be spelling something else? Give me an S! Give me an L …"

Brett's voice faded into nothingness as pain exploded behind her eyes. A violent surge rushed from her stomach up into her throat, and Victoria knew instantly that if she didn't leave that minute, something terrible was going to happen.

"Give me a U …"

She snatched the ear buds back and rushed past Brett, not bothering to breathe until she reached the wide entry doors. Outside, she felt wetness on her upper lip. A nosebleed. She sank to the ground, pinching the bridge of her nose between her thumb and forefinger to stop the flow. Sweat dripped down her back, her skin impossibly hot, as she shuddered from the terrifying feelings in the pit of her stomach—the ones that had started appearing the minute she'd awakened, the ones that made her feel like she was being gutted from the inside out.

Victoria glanced at her watch. It was almost one o'clock. She still had two hours left before she could go home.

"Screw it," she muttered, running to her car parked behind the west building. She didn't see the two people waiting in the parking lot until she almost crashed into one of them. Her heart sank.

"What do you want, Brett?"

"You think you can talk to me like that and get away with it?"

"What are we, five? Did I hurt your feelings? *You* stopped *me*, remember?" Victoria glanced around quickly. Other than the three of them, the parking lot was deserted, dotted with a handful of empty, silent cars. She tried to move toward her car, but the other boy blocked her way. Victoria recognized him as a burly linebacker named Ryan.

"What do you want, Brett?" she repeated.

"I think I deserve an apology," Brett said. He was smiling, but Victoria knew it was only a performance. She could smell the rage evaporating off him.

"Fine, I'm sorry for whatever it is I did," she said. "You've had your fun. Can you guys get out of my way now?"

"I wouldn't say that I'd had all my fun yet," Brett said, leaning in suggestively. "Rumor is you're … friendly."

"What?" Victoria masked her sudden panic with sarcasm. "Surely you already have enough friends of your own?"

Brett laughed. "Come on, don't be a tease. You know what I mean … *friend.*"

Victoria felt the air around her being sucked into a vortex as if she were a flame burning up all the available oxygen. She was hot again, her rising fury shattering any shred of control she had left. Her green Mini was only one car away, but Ryan still blocked her way, smirking.

"I don't know what you're talking about. Please move …" she gasped, unable to catch her breath. Her hands shook.

"Please what, not-so-virginal-Victoria," said Brett, grabbing her by her arms and pushing her against the nearest car. "I think you need to learn your place at St. Xavier's."

"Get off me," she gritted through clenched teeth, as she jabbed her elbow into his ribs with all the force she could muster. Brett staggered back.

The heat was suffocating now—the rage seething to dangerous levels held together only by the thin barrier of her skin. The thing boiling inside her tore at her eyes and hissed past her cracked lips. Victoria twisted toward Ryan and swung her knee up, connecting with the soft tissue of his groin as she pushed past him. She'd only taken five steps before she felt fingers yanking her hair so hard that her head jerked sideways.

"Where do you think you're going, you crazy witch?" Brett snarled, dragging her by her hair to the passenger door of her car.

"Please, let go!"

"Shut up." His hand cracked against her face, splitting her lip. Dazed, she touched a fingertip to her chin and stared at the blood. For an instant its color was mesmerizing, dark and shimmery, like something alien. The taste of it in her mouth was like burnt molasses, sweet and powerful, the silent catalyst of something beyond her control. An eerie calm descended.

Brett shoved her against the door, his breath sour in her face. "You like being here on your church scholarship? My *daddy* paid for that too, you know. I heard your aunt sent you here because you got kicked out of your last school for being a sl—"

The thing inside her keened, her mouth giving voice to its agony. Victoria didn't even notice as Brett flew backward, his words choked into silence. All she could feel was the frighteningly raw energy burning fiery lines along her veins, stinging her eyelids and tasting like ash on her tongue. Brett stared at her as if she were a monster and scuttled backward like a strange crab, suddenly desperate to get away from her.

"*You need to learn your place,*" the thing hissed with her voice. In the next second, it was as if a sonic explosion hit the parking lot; a *silent* sonic explosion, the only evidence of which was the blood gushing from Brett's eyes and mouth as he lay on the ground clutching his head in agony. Behind her, Ryan screamed then fell silent. Euphoria spun in giddy circles inside of her.

"Hey!" Through a filmy red haze, Victoria could see someone running toward them, one of the Stepfords. The girl slid to cradle Brett's head in her hands, her eyes darting to Ryan's inert body a few feet away. "What did you *do*?"

"I didn't ..." Victoria could hardly finish the sentence. The world was spinning off its axis once more. She couldn't breathe, and all she could see was the expression on the girl's face, fearful and so utterly damning. She felt wetness on her face and her legs, and looked to the clear sky, confused.

Was it *raining*?

It was her last thought before she sank into unconsciousness, something still singing madly, terrifyingly, inside her head.

WHEN VICTORIA AWOKE, she was lying in a spotless hospital room. There were tubes in her arms connected to discordantly beeping machines. Her aunt Holly sat reading in a chair across the room near the window, opposite the empty bed occupying the other half of the room. The white of the walls was blinding.

"W ... water," she croaked. Holly darted to her side.

"Oh honey, you gave us such a fright," she said, holding a cup to Victoria's lips. "How are you feeling?"

"Where am I? What happened?" Victoria felt foggy, as if she'd been asleep for months. Her eyelids were sticky, heavy, but the water was cool against her gums and tongue, which seemed coated with a strange metallic film like she'd sucked on a dirty copper penny.

"We're in the hospital. They brought you in five days ago," Holly said. "You and two other kids."

"Two others?" Holly brushed the strands of hair out of Victoria's face.

"One went home three days ago, and the other is here recovering. But you, my darling, you almost died." Her voice broke on the last word. "What happened, honey? I really don't understand. One of the girls from school said there'd been some kind of a fight."

"I don't … know. I must have blacked out." Victoria blinked, trying futilely to remember. "I've been here five days, Aunt Holly? Why?"

"You really should rest," Holly said, not wanting to overwhelm her.

"No, please tell me." Despite her distress, Victoria was resolute. "Aunt Holly, please. I need to know."

"You lost consciousness at school and they called 911 because of all the blood," Holly began, her fingers twisting in her lap. "By the time you got to the ER, you were losing so much of it that nobody seemed to know what to do at first. Something about the color, it was so dark. They said it was overly de-oxygenated. It was black almost …" She glanced anxiously at Victoria, who nodded for her to continue.

"At first, they thought some kind of rogue strain of leukemia was attacking the blood cells in your bone marrow. That's what they said was the cause of the bleeding, some kind of infection in your nervous system. It seemed as if you were dying and there was nothing anyone could do about it. Then your heart stopped. They tried to resuscitate, but your heart just wouldn't respond. Just when everyone thought it was over, a miracle happened, somehow your heart started beating again, and somehow by God's grace, you came back to us … to me." Holly pulled Victoria into a tight embrace. "I almost lost you, Tori," she choked, then turned her face away and sobbed.

"But you didn't, I'm still here, Aunt Holly, I'm fine," Victoria soothed, her mind whirling. Everything Holly had just said seemed entirely too surreal. "I wish I could remember, but it's all so fuzzy. I remember eating breakfast. I remember going to school but nothing much after that. There was no warning, nothing ..."

Victoria stared at the plastic tubing shackling her wrists. From what Holly had said, it was a miracle that she was even alive. Yet again. A sense of despair crashed like a tide against her and she felt the tears she'd been struggling to hold back coming. She couldn't shake the sense that something terrible had happened, something she'd *done*.

You have to remember! she urged herself. *Think!*

The memories swirled beneath a black fog in her mind but the more she fought against it, the thicker it became. Her head throbbed, accompanied by a dull ache in her stomach. Her hands pressed against it.

"Something else, Tori. Your monthly came," Holly said, her eyes kindly. "The doctors said it was most likely the trauma."

Victoria didn't know whether to feel embarrassed at the circumstances of having her first period or relieved that she'd finally gotten it. She'd started wondering whether she was abnormal after her sixteenth birthday had passed with no womanly fanfare. A visit to Holly's doctor had only confirmed that the range for young women went from as young as nine to as old as eighteen. He'd assured her that it would come in time.

And now that it was here, Victoria felt nothing, just a peculiar sense of anticlimax. On top of everything else, the one event that was supposed to make a girl feel normal only made her feel more odd than ever. She'd blacked out. Had she gotten her period at school? In the cafeteria? In class? In front of everyone?

A hazy recollection of mocking laughter drifted through her mind. She'd be the Carrie White of St. Xavier's, enacting that awful scene from *Carrie* in the girls' bathroom. By now *everyone* would know. Victoria couldn't even begin to imagine what they would all be saying about her. Her stomach heaved.

A clean-shaven young man in a white coat walked into the room carrying her chart. "Ms. Warrick, you're awake. How do you feel?" he said, not looking at her. "I'm Dr. Mills."

I got into a fight at school, bled in front of everyone, almost died, and can't remember a thing. How do you think I feel?

"I feel okay, I guess. A little groggy, and I can't remember anything."

"Yes, well, it's temporary memory loss. The grogginess will wear off; it's the medication. You hit your head quite hard when you fell, so try not to push yourself. It's been a tough few days for that body of yours but you have a very strong will to live."

Victoria glanced from Dr. Mills to Holly's drawn face. Holly's wrinkled fingers were still gently squeezing hers. They were warm, reassuring. Victoria gripped back and voiced the thought at the edge of her mind.

"What's wrong with me?"

"Nothing's wrong with you. In fact, you're a healthy, strong young woman who's recovering very well, but you should try to get some rest." Victoria frowned at the bland response.

"Do I have leukemia?"

A glance. "No. Those tests were inconclusive."

"I don't understand. How can I be absolutely fine if I've been here in a coma for five days?" Her voice sounded petulant even to her.

Dr. Mills hesitated, looking first at Holly. "We have different theories, none one hundred percent conclusive. But your complete recovery in such a short time ... well, there is no way to explain that medically." He paused, and then smiled brightly studying her chart. "The main thing is that you're alive, and recovering. You are a very lucky young woman."

The luck of the devil ...

Her muscles tightened with unexpected dread and for an instant, Victoria felt violently ill. The beeping of the heart monitor matched her escalating heart rate. How does a normal, healthy girl have a blackout and end up in a hospital for five days with no memory? And why wouldn't Dr. Mills *look* at her?

"I just want to go home," she gasped, black spots marring her vision as the cramping feeling in her stomach intensified. The heart-rate monitor beeped erratically.

"We need to keep you just a few more days for observation," Dr. Mills said, pressing the button for the floor nurse.

"Observation?"

Like she was some kind of freak.

A wave of anxiety overcame her. Heat flooded her limbs and she flung the blankets aside, clawing her hospital gown. "It's … too hot in here!"

The day nurse came into the room bearing a tray, and Victoria stared warily as Doctor Mills prepped one of the syringes on it. A drop of pale liquid formed at the needle's tip.

Full-scale panic. "What's that for?"

"It's just something to help you rest," he said, emptying the syringe into the IV connected to her wrist. A cool sensation slithered along the hot veins of her forearm.

Victoria's eyes connected with his deep brown ones. What she saw there made her breath hitch. He looked at her with both fear and fascination, the way she'd once felt after seeing a two-headed snake on the Discovery Channel; an aberration of nature, fascinating yet obscene. Unnatural.

Her eyelids drooped as Doctor Mills faded into the background of the room.

"Aunt Holly?" she heard herself say thickly.

"It'll be okay, darling," Holly said, stroking Victoria's hand gently. "I'm here."

"I don't want to close my eyes. The monsters …"

"I'm right here, sweetheart."

"They're coming …"

TWO

Inheritance

THE NIGHTMARE'S TERRIBLE fingers touched everywhere, holding her prisoner in that space between dream and reality. Flashes of shiny, corrugated metal, the smell of fire and sulfur heavy in the air, and the blood, so much blood, it was everywhere—on the ground, on her clothes, on her hands. Oh God, *her* hands. What had she done? Their faces were gruesome in death, their bloodied arms grasping her, pulling her down into hell with them.

Her body jerked. She was older now, lying in a sterile hospital bed. Molten lava flooded into her body, drowning her. She was imploding, her skin splintering as something unimaginable inside her struggled to get out. She felt it tearing its way through her body, shredding tissue and bone and skin like paper until it was free. The creature turned slowly, agonizingly. Burning red eyes blazed into hers. The demon had her face.

She couldn't stop screaming.

"Tori, wake up," a worried voice said, shaking her. "Victoria! Wake up!"

Her screams dissolved into strangled gasps as she struggled to sit up. A kind, wrinkled face swam into focus. "It's okay, love. It's just a dream. You're safe now."

"Oh God, Aunt Holly, their *faces!*"

"It's okay, it's over now. It was only a dream. Take a deep breath, sweetheart."

"It wasn't just the car crash this time, it was something worse. Did you ever see *The Omen*? Well, in my dream, I was the baby ... I was the devil."

"No one could live through what you've been through and not have terrifying moments," Holly said kindly, stroking Victoria's back with a soothing motion. "Now try to get some sleep, it's early."

"Aunt Holly, I should have died with them. It's just not fair to be so *lucky.*"

"Hush now, darling. You've been through a lot the past few days. Please just get some rest. Things will look better in the morning, I promise. I love you."

"Love you, too."

As Holly left the room, Victoria stared into the darkness. The clock on the nightstand said four a.m. Sleep was an elusive bedmate. Whenever she was able to fall asleep, she had terrible dreams, although none quite as bad as the one she'd just had. Most nights, she lay awake in bed thinking about anything and everything, afraid to close her eyes until the dawn's light chased away the monsters. Tonight was no exception.

Despite occasional flashes, she still couldn't remember everything that had happened in the parking lot, and when she tried to think about it, her head ached as if the memory was blocked by some obstruction. Under Dr. Mills' orders, she hadn't returned to St. Xavier's, and given the circumstances, she'd been excused from the rest of the school year. It'd been a relief not to have to face the

Stepfords or anyone else at the exclusive high school that had for the past two years made her life a living hell.

St. Xavier's had been a special scholarship from their church—one which the benefactors had insisted would give Victoria an edge come college time. A loner by nature, making new friends had always been difficult at best, and after a few months, Victoria had given up, preferring to keep to herself. Then the Stepfords had taken everything to a whole new level as Brett had let it leak that she was his parents' charity case. It had been a nightmare from there on out, and a different Victoria had begun to emerge, one fluent in cynicism, distant and aloof. For the first time in her life, she had become a social outcast.

"I am officially a freak," Victoria murmured out loud. She hugged her middle, her fingers encountering a soft, furry head. Leto. She stroked him and he purred in response.

"Hey, how're you doing?" she whispered, fondling his soft velvet ears.

Leto had been a fixture in her life as long as she could remember. He was the only living memory she had of her parents, and whenever she confided in him, spilling out her secrets, everything always seemed better ... and less lonely. She pulled him unto her chest.

"I've missed you. I hate these nightmares so much ... mom, dad, school, the hospital. It's all so ugly." Leto watched her, unblinking, as Victoria thought of Brett, remembering the way he'd looked at her with such horror, blood covering his face. She shivered. "I wish I knew what happened, but it's like I don't *want* to remember or something inside of me doesn't want me to."

She scratched his head. "You love me, don't you, Leto? At least you don't think I'm a freak, like everyone else does."

She sighed and glanced at the clock. Six a.m. Her body still ached and she sat up slowly, pushing a grumpy Leto aside. Streaks of pale golden light seeped through her bedroom curtains chasing away the shadows of the night.

For a minute, she stood transfixed by the light dancing across the dark material—light into dark, dark into light; hypnotic, a silent metaphor for something she felt but couldn't express. Her eyes burned as she jabbed the backs of her thumbs fiercely into them. She'd promised herself no more tears.

Today is no different than any other day, Victoria told herself. *You're just one year older, nothing more.*

Selecting a black sweatshirt and a pair of black jeans, Victoria finger-combed the snarls out of her thick, dark hair and surveyed her reflection in the mirror. She'd lost more weight since the hospital, and the black clothing only made her look more gaunt than usual. In the dim lighting, even her eyes looked dark. The girl in the mirror smiled at the irony. Black was fitting; it was a day of death after all.

As if on cue, pins and needles surged through her hands and she rubbed them tiredly against her jeans. The tingling hadn't stopped since the hospital, but Dr. Mills had said that it would go away eventually. Leto jumped down from the bed and rubbed his silver-furred body against her legs, yowling as static electricity sparked from her jeans to his fur. His large, green eyes fixed on hers accusingly.

"Oh Leto, I'm so sorry! I'm a live-wire lately." She pulled him into her arms after a last glance at the mirror and scratched his ears as she started toward the stairs. Leto stared at her with oddly knowing eyes and purred loudly, pressing his face into the crook of her arm. Strangely enough, the tingling in her palms lessened.

Victoria peered over the landing. She knew Holly was up to something, especially given how excited and secretive she had been during the days leading up to Victoria's birthday. Although not her real aunt, Holly had been her grandmother's best friend, and when Victoria's parents had died when she was nine, Holly had taken her in and brought her to her home in Millinocket, Maine.

An hour north of Bangor with a population of just five thousand people, Millinocket was the most picturesque town Victoria had ever seen, home to lush forests and pristine rivers and lakes, resting against the backdrop of Mount Katahdin. It was a far cry from the hustle and bustle of Greenwich Village in New York where she had lived with her parents until the tragic accident that had torn her life apart.

Holly's house was located just on the outskirts of the main village and backed onto the thickly wooded forest of the North Maine Woods. It felt safe in a way New York no longer did without her mother and father. The minute she'd set foot on the threshold, it felt like home, and Victoria had found that she didn't want to live anywhere else.

"Don't make a sound," she told Leto, and tiptoed toward the kitchen. It was empty. Sighing with relief, she poured herself a cup of coffee just as a second dizzying wave of queasiness made her double over, pins and needles spearing her entire body. Her back arched backward, hot coffee scalding her hand and flying everywhere.

"Ouch! Son of a—"

As Victoria shook her stinging fingers, her elbow caught the edge of a crystal vase sitting on the counter and tipped it off the side. Time slowed to a crawl and she could foresee the next four seconds of flawless inevitability ending with one of Holly's prized possessions shattered on the floor. Blood thundered in her ears and surged to the tips of her fingers in electric response.

A single word escaped her lips. "No!"

Obediently, time stopped.

Victoria swung around to the right to pluck the vase from

midair milliseconds before it crashed to the floor, her breath harsh in the unnatural stillness. A blink, and the spell was broken. She replaced the vase with shaking fingers and took a deep, calming breath, her blood coursing wildly in her veins. Leto growled softly, his sudden stare insistent, unnerving. She shook her head.

"You imagined it," she said, pressing her hot palms to the cool surface of the countertop. "It's just adrenaline ... excess energy. Breathe, Tori."

She shook her head again, starting to feel that she would be better off returning to bed, when she heard the sound of a car pulling into the driveway. A few minutes later, Holly walked in, beaming as she saw Victoria and towing a bunch of shiny balloons behind her through the kitchen door.

"Happy Birthday, Tori! I've got one for each year! *Seventeen* of them!" she cried. "So, how's my birthday-girl?" Victoria couldn't help smiling.

"I'm not exactly sure. Still waking up, I think," she said, with a glance at her reddened hand.

A concerned look. "Did you manage to get any sleep at all?"

"Not much. The nightmares have been a lot worse lately. But I guess it's just the time of year," she said. "Not every girl has a birthday on the anniversary of her parents' death."

"I know, darling, it's hard. But they would be very proud of you, you know," Holly said, squeezing Victoria in a sympathetic hug before adding briskly, "so let's focus on the positive. How does it feel to be seventeen?"

Victoria smiled at Holly's intensity. Holly pretended to love birthdays, but Victoria knew deep down that Holly only did it so that the happiness of the celebration would eclipse the sadness of what had happened eight years ago. And her thoughtful ploy worked, year after year.

"It's strange, I do feel different. My body feels like it could run a marathon, like I've had six cups of coffee or something. I've had pins and needles all morning. Even Leto won't come near me."

"Sounds like birthday jitters to me," Holly said. "No wonder, seventeen, that's a *big* milestone."

"You said that last year when I was sixteen, remember? 'Sweet sixteen is a big milestone,'" she quoted in a chirpy falsetto.

"Well, it is, and they all are," Holly argued good-naturedly. "And I do not sound like that."

"You do when you get excited," Victoria said, pouring herself a second cup of coffee. "Seriously though, why is it even called sweet sixteen? It's so archaic. It's not even a true coming-of-age anymore. Don't you know eleven is the new sixteen?"

"Very funny," said Holly. "When I grew up, sweet sixteen was about celebrating girlhood into adulthood. I think the saying *sweet* sixteen comes from 'sweet sixteen and never been kissed.'"

"Don't look at me, I'd hardly know. I've never kissed anyone, unless you count Peter from church when I was thirteen. Gross. Anyway, I'm glad *sweet sixteen* is over. I can honestly say there was nothing sweet about it."

"Maybe this will be your sweet seventeen then," Holly said with a wink, and Victoria rolled her eyes. "Your grandmother always said that seventeen was a big deal too, you know, like a rite of passage."

Victoria turned and leveled a suspicious glance in Holly's direction. "Aunt Holly, you haven't gone and done anything crazy, have you?"

"Now, now, Tori, don't get that tone with me, young lady. A young woman deserves something special on her seventeenth birthday, doesn't she? I really think, no … I *insist* that you should have something special! Happy Birthday, Tori!" Holly put two gaily-wrapped boxes in front of Victoria on the table. "Go on, open!"

"Aunt *Holly*! You do too much already!" Victoria said. "You spoil me."

"Don't deny an old lady her joys, darling."

"Old lady? Whatever!" Victoria laughed as she squeezed her thoughtful, infuriating, wonderful aunt in a bear-hug. "But this is the last time, okay. No more," she joked, before removing the wrapping paper carefully and opened the smaller of the two boxes. Inside, nestled on a bed of cotton gauze, was a delicate, golden key. She looked questioningly at Holly who indicated that she should now open the second, larger box.

"Oh no, Aunt Holly, you didn't!" Victoria gasped and pulled the shiny, thin laptop from its plastic wrapping. She held it gingerly in her hands. "It's too much, really it is!"

"Do you like it? Jim at the shop told me it was top of the line, and great for writing or drawing. I know you're always doodling in that notebook of yours, and well, the one I've got is practically extinct as you know." She laughed.

"I love it! It's perfect! You're perfect! I can't believe you got me a Mac! The graphics in these things are amazing! It's got like a super fast processor and stacks of RAM. And look how thin it is! It's so *pretty*!"

"I'm so happy that you're happy, Tori," Holly said. "I don't know about rams and sheep and whatnot, but I'm so glad you like it. Seeing that smile again was worth it. I was worried it wouldn't be the right one, you know how you young people are." She reached for a package beside her. "I still have one more thing for you."

Victoria touched the laptop's shiny surface reverently. "You've already done so much, Aunt Holly. Really."

"Well, this one is indirectly from your grandmother," Holly said, lifting a delicately carved wooden box from beneath several layers of yellowing tissue paper.

"My grandmother?" Victoria repeated, confused. Her grandmother had died when she was eight.

"This was her music box. That's what the golden key is for. Before she died, she told me that I was to pass it to you on your seventeenth birthday. She said it was important, that she meant for you to have it."

With infinite care, Victoria held the music box. It was a warm, worn, cherry-wood interlaid with rosewood, crisscrossed by delicate gold carvings in an intricate design. She squinted closely ... the design looked like some sort of crest. She ran her hands across the top of it and it warmed to her touch.

Feeling strangely expectant, she put the small gold key into the lock and turned the latch. As she opened the top, the faint smell of gardenias drifted up and a haunting melody hummed. It was *Moonlight Sonata* by Beethoven.

Victoria swallowed, her throat tight, and realized that Holly had left the room to give her some privacy. Inside the box was a collection of papers, some yellowed with age, and a small red velvet box. The top piece of paper was folded over and inscribed with her name. She opened it with surprise.

My darling Victoria,

How I wish I could have seen you grow up. You were so full of life and carried so much joy, my beautiful granddaughter. If this box has come to you in the manner I wished, you will be reading this on your seventeenth birthday. This is a special birthday for Warrick women. It marks both an end <u>and</u> a beginning, the end of what we know and the beginning of what we are to become. Don't fear it. Embrace it. You are a Warrick.

All my love,

Your Loving Grandmother, Emmeline Warrick

Victoria read the letter again, savoring the memory of the voice behind the words, then shuffled through the rest of the papers. There were many more letters, some quite old, that appeared to have been written to other Warrick girls on their seventeenth birthdays, all with the same message. She realized that the letters must be some sort of coming of age ritual for the women in her family. They seemed to cling to her hands as if they were part of her, drawn to her mysteriously, and she liked the feeling they gave her. She also found a thin notebook that looked like a journal. She put it aside; she would read it later. The red velvet box beckoned.

She opened it carefully and, with a gasp, removed a delicate amulet on a thin chain. The amulet held a shimmering rose-tinted diamond suspended between the golden threads edging its perimeter in the same triangular design—*crest?*—as the one engraved on the music box. It was breathtaking.

Victoria gently traced the outside of the delicate crest and winced as the sharp bottom edge almost sliced her finger—it was very sharp when held just so, although seemed to be quite safe when flat on her palm. *How strange.*

"Aunt Holly, did you ever see my grandmother wear this amulet?" Holly walked back into the kitchen and examined the necklace.

"Many times. She told me that it was a family heirloom. Your grandmother was convinced that this amulet kept her out of trouble. She called it her lucky charm. And it did too! She always said she had the devil's own luck. You wouldn't believe her escapades and how many times she got away with murder!" She laughed at the memory and fastened the necklace to Victoria's slim neck. "There, it's lovely. Go have a look."

Victoria went to the bathroom mirror and peered at her reflection. Her dark, blue-black hair hung in the same tangled mass as always, but the necklace lent a warm glow to her face. The amulet lay on her chest like it belonged there, its weight heavy and profound. Leto, who had followed her into the bathroom, scratched his front paws against her knees and she bent to pick him up.

"What do you think, Leto? Beautiful, isn't it?"

Leto's green eyes met hers in the mirror. She suddenly felt breathless, unable to look away from the cat's bright gaze.

"Isn't it odd that our eyes are exactly the same color? I don't think I ever noticed," she heard herself say.

The amulet was so bright and so hot that she could feel it nearly burning her chest. Her blood raced beneath it, her breath coming in rapid, shallow pants. Leto's body trembled in her arms, his green eyes blazing.

Embrace it.

She almost dropped him as the words echoed unbidden in her head.

"Leto?" she said. She *was* going crazy. But Leto mewed softly, still holding her gaze. Victoria was so spellbound by the pull of the amulet that her mind felt drunk, her instincts leaden. She was burning hot just like in her nightmares, exploding from the inside out. Underneath the murkiness, she felt something awaken inside of her. Terrified, she grasped Leto so tightly that his claws dug into her forearms.

The more frightened she became, the more her blood seemed to be feasting on her fear. The amulet scorched her chest, and the light she'd felt not ten seconds before disappeared into a thick, suffocating darkness. Dark into light, light into dark. Victoria stared at the mirror.

The demon had her face.

Her nightmare had become reality. Everything suddenly felt as if it were spinning out of control, the floor beneath her feet tilted and bile coated the back of her tongue. Victoria flung Leto aside and ripped the amulet off her chest.

She didn't want it! She didn't want any of it! She thought about her grandmother who'd spent the last years of her life in some sort of psychiatric hospital because she'd been so weird, if not insane. Victoria was already an orphan and an outcast. And after what had happened at school, being anything like her grandmother was exactly what she didn't want or need.

Leto looked up at her and made a sound that was halfway between a hiss and a growl.

Victoria avoided the cat's penetrating gaze. She threw the amulet into the music box and slammed the lid.

"Everything all right, Tori?" asked Holly, coming back into the room and noticing Victoria's wild expression. "You're bleeding!"

Victoria stared blankly at the long, nearly black scratches on the backs of her hands. A strange rusty-sweet odor filled her nostrils. "Just Leto," she said, wiping the blood with the sleeve of her sweatshirt. "It's nothing."

"You're sure everything's okay?"

"I'm fine. I just need some fresh air." Victoria forced a smile to her face and kissed Holly's cheek. "Thank you for a wonderful birthday present, it's exactly what I wanted. I can't wait to set up my laptop."

"What about the necklace?" Holly asked, looking at the music box on the table.

"I don't want it. I'm sorry."

"What happened?" Holly said cautiously. "Was there something in the box?"

"No, nothing important," said Victoria. "I'll see you later, Aunt Holly."

"Do you want me to put it in your room?"

Victoria glanced at the box, and the heat surged in her chest. Her palms tingled painfully and she dug her nails into the soft flesh, looking away with effort.

"I don't care what you do with it. Really. Just give it away."

Leto's sharp hiss was cut off by the door slamming behind her. She stared down in surprise at her throbbing hands and the new streaks of fresh blood seeping from her scratches. They bled, hot and angry.

Something inside her smiled.

THREE

At First Sight

VICTORIA CHEWED HER bottom lip as she drove to the registration building. She didn't know why she was nervous but she was. She had enrolled at Windsor Academy, a private preparatory school about three and a half hours south of Millinocket, where she'd been accepted with a partial scholarship to finish her senior year of high school. Money-wise, it would be hard even with the financial aid, but she'd preferred to scrimp and save, rather than go back to St. Xavier's. The local high school had been an option but the gossip would only follow her there.

Canville was perfect—far enough away but still close to Holly. She was staying with an old friend of Holly's who rented out a tiny apartment in her house. To offset her tuition, she'd secured a job at a local restaurant, the Black Dog, as a waitress and bartender. Luckily, Maine was the only state that allowed bartenders at seventeen, so she'd be able to get more shifts and make more money. Her part-time job as an assistant to the music director would be just enough to cover the rest of her costs.

Despite her recent disturbing tendency to know what people were going to say before they said it, things had been quiet over the summer. She'd spent most of her time working at the local bookstore in Millinocket. All she'd wanted was to be normal—no strange voices, no weird energy, and no mysterious music boxes with hidden family secrets. The strange blood disease and her stay in the hospital had faded into a distant, if troubling, memory. That part of her life—St. Xavier's, the hospital, Brett—was over, and she was determined to forget it. She'd buried her grandmother's music box in a carton full of other unwanted things in a corner of her new apartment.

Victoria hadn't told anyone, not even Holly, that she'd remembered what had happened with Brett. At first, it'd just been bits and pieces over the months, but eventually she'd remembered it all in cold, gruesome detail. She had almost killed him. She also remembered what had happened in the hospital, which was a little harder to come to terms with, because it was in every sense, impossible.

She *died*.

She'd read Dr. Mills' report from the hospital. Her heart had stopped beating for forty-three minutes, enough time for her to be completely brain-dead, and they'd tried everything including a defibrillator at its highest level to resuscitate her. And just as Holly had said, when they'd been about to call it quits, her pulse had resumed of its own accord. No wonder Dr. Mills had looked at her as if she were a freak.

In the end, her regeneration had been so dramatic that within days, despite her blood's atypical dark color, her blood count was back to normal, healthy levels, and the abnormal cells that had supported the initial diagnosis seemed to have disappeared. They'd kept her in a medically induced coma for four days after she'd been admitted, but for all intents and purposes, her recovery had been deemed a medical miracle.

A miracle or the devil's own luck?

Victoria breathed slowly and ignored the errant thought, inhaling through her nose and exhaling through her mouth as she walked to the entrance of the building. That chapter of her life was now closed. Over.

After she'd turned seventeen, things had just felt different. It had felt like she could do anything. Maybe it was the freedom from the chains of St. Xavier's, but at Windsor, Victoria discovered a new lease on life. This was her fresh start—new school, new personality, no craziness. She had even made sure that she looked different. Her hair had been cut in a flattering shoulder length style, and she'd chosen to wear a scarlet sweater, a far cry from the more somber colors she usually favored. She was older and wiser, and things would be different.

"Admissions, please?" she asked the security guard at the entrance. He nodded over his shoulder to the right without even raising his eyes from the magazine he'd been reading. Victoria went into the building and filed the required paperwork with the clerk, receiving her senior class schedule in exchange. She was finished in ten minutes. As she turned to leave the Admissions Office, she collided with someone walking in from outside and her papers went flying.

"Omigod, I am so sorry! That was totally my fault. I wasn't watching where I was going."

"I hardly think you were solely to blame," said a melodic husky voice.

Was that a *French* accent??? Victoria's head whipped up from where she was kneeling to collect her papers, and she immediately banged heads with him again as he knelt down to help her. The single thought that registered before stars blinded her vision was that he didn't look *anything* like the boys she'd known at St. Xavier's! He had strange eyes that were so light they didn't seem to have any color in them. They seemed hard, out of sync with the boyish contours of his face.

"Ouch," she said, suddenly tongue-tied. "That was … me. I'm so sorry." Her eyes met his startling silver ones and her heart almost stopped as he smiled at her. His smile did not quite seem to touch his eyes despite the brilliance of it, and she bent her head quickly.

"Apology accepted. I'm Christian, Christian Devereux." The velvety voice washed over her already overheated senses, and her hands shook as her own voice stuck, paralyzed in her chest. Where she came from, boys did not speak like that, with mellifluous, perfect diction and voices that sounded like butterscotch! It was a voice that was also at odds with the hardness of his eyes. It confused her.

"I'm Tori Warrick. I'm a senior, I mean, I just enrolled … transfer," she said. God, what was wrong with her! He was just a boy, for goodness' sake. Her hands felt clammy as she gathered up her papers. Her heart was hammering heatedly in her chest.

Stop it, she told herself. She couldn't understand the sudden rush of adrenaline deafening her ears, the unexpected liquidity of her limbs. His eyes met hers, and her blood burned in response.

Christian was not what she would consider in conventional terms to be good-looking. His face, though perfect in its symmetry, lacked the softness that would make him handsome. But he was … magnetic. Dark blond waves of hair framed a face of striking sharpness, with strange silver-colored eyes as she'd noticed before. A thin white scar curved into his left eyebrow.

He had long delicate hands, she noticed as he gathered the last of the papers before handing them to her. His mouth was wide, with beautifully shaped lips lending a brief softness to the rest of his face. Beautifully shaped *smiling* lips! Her eyes snapped up guiltily, flushing that he had caught her gawking like an adolescent girl.

"Here you go, this looks like all of them," he said.

Victoria must have imagined his eyes being cold before, for now they glinted a warm silver. He smiled and passed her the sheaf of papers. Every movement was smooth, unaggressive, yet something about him made her feel like prey that knows it is being hunted. Her pulse spiraled and she took a step back.

As he too stepped back, he looked at her with a slightly pained expression as if something had bothered him momentarily, but then he just said carelessly, "Well, see you around, Tori Warrick."

"Um, sure. Thanks for your help ... Christian," she responded, flustered. What was *wrong* with her? She watched his back as he walked away. Strangely enough, the further away he got, the less agitated she became. After several tense moments, she drew a long strangled breath and made her way out of the building.

As VICTORIA EXITED the building's front doors, Christian Devereux turned around and stared, coldly appraising her. He followed her and watched as she drove out of the parking lot, dissecting their meeting methodically in his mind.

Despite her coltish appearance, from the minute they had touched, something had caught and held his attention ... something obscure but potent. Every instinct in him had been drawn toward her, a moth to a flame.

And that was *before* her scent had invaded his already strained senses, her blood racing under the surface of her golden skin and amplifying the scent of her a hundredfold. It had taken almost all of his concentration to maintain his composure and not to bury his face in her neck, losing himself in that bewitching fragrance. He'd stopped breathing instead.

Christian closed his eyes, savoring her lingering scent. It was delicate yet underscored by something thick and heady. It troubled him because he was drawn to it so desperately, yet something else warned him away from her. Self-preservation had become an instinct unfamiliar enough to be completely foreign to him. He found it curious, and unsettling.

He deliberated whether to place the call or not, taking the sleek cell phone out of his pocket and turning it between his fingers. Christian thought about how he'd reached out just before she'd driven off, feather-lightly, attempting to explore her unconscious, and how easily she had blocked him from her thoughts. Her response had been intuitive, in fact, he was sure of it. That could only mean one thing. She had no idea what she was.

Christian frowned. Better safe than sorry, they would find out about her anyway. They always did. He shrugged off the remaining tendrils of her scent and dialed the number.

"Lucian," he said, when the voice on the other end answered. "Witch, mild paranormal strength, blocked me." He could hear the derisive snicker on the other end of the phone and it infuriated him, but he remained calm. "I don't believe it was conscious. It may just be purely instinctive, no need for you to intervene at this point. I will … appraise the situation."

"Anything else?"

"No, that's all."

The phone went dead. Christian fought not to crush it between his fingers as he closed it shut. "Au revoir, mon frère." *Nothing like a warm brotherly conversation*, he thought. Then again, he'd expected nothing more.

Christian didn't like surprises, least of all, his brother's underlings invading his privacy and disrupting the life he had so carefully built over the last few years in this remote Maine town. His preemptive call would take care of that for the moment. His brother's obsession with identifying sources of magical energy and finding paranormal threats had reached new heights, and although Christian thought Lucian was being overly paranoid, he no longer had a say in how things were run in the House of Devereux. That, by his own choice, was now Lucian's realm.

It was just a minor hurdle that Tori Warrick had enrolled at Windsor, one that he would assess for his brother's sake, if not his own. He got into his car and gunned the engine. There was something elusive about this girl; he couldn't quite put his finger on it. He only knew that he *didn't* want Lucian to interfere just yet.

Tori.

The name rolled over his thoughts like honey, and he ruthlessly squashed the memory of her. He wasn't an animal. He wouldn't let one girl destroy the perfect balance and independence he had defied his own world to achieve. He wanted a life of obscurity and quiet. The rules of the Devereux aristocracy no longer applied to him. Christian wanted to keep it that way.

As he drove along the narrow roads at over a hundred miles per hour, the thick forest on either side cloaking the way with long, dappled shadows, he briefly considered returning to Paris but he just as quickly discarded the thought. The urge to run was not his style. It wasn't that he was afraid of her, he was afraid of something far worse. The violent temptation that she had put him through had been momentary, more an accident of fate than anything, yet his loss of control had been staggering. It had taken every ounce of his discipline to hold himself together and not succumb to his darkest urges … the secret that haunted his existence.

Christian Devereux was a vampire.

A vampire, whose mask after almost two centuries, was perfect. He was cultured, urbane, sophisticated. Yet for all that, he'd never been more afraid of *what* he was, than he had been at that single moment when he'd locked eyes with Tori Warrick.

Christian hadn't killed anyone in more than one hundred years; he satiated his thirst and his victims lived, human or not. But with *her*, the most reviled part of himself craved her blood to the last drop, to the death. Already he could imagine the warm, briny taste of it, and his teeth lengthened, his body trembling. He willed himself under control, his jaw tightly clenched.

She was what she was, and he was what he was.

The laws were clear. And he was bound to them.

Christian pulled into the driveway of his house, an old Georgian mansion that he had spent the last few years restoring. It rested on ten acres of flawlessly manicured grounds, fringed by untouched woodland backing onto even more thickly wooded forest. The property afforded him the privacy he needed. He glanced at his watch. It was almost four o'clock. Right now he needed to hunt. He needed to satisfy his hunger, and drown the taste of her from his mouth.

FOUR

Assessment

VICTORIA WALKED ACROSS the open quad between the tall red and white brick buildings, following the student map together with the course assignments she held in her hand. Kramer Hall, it said, for psychology. Oh hell, not five minutes into the day and she was lost already.

Windsor shared the town and its rolling landscape with its sister school, Harland College. Both private institutions, they shared not just the same acreage, but the same benefactors and some of the same facilities, including a library and concert hall. Windsor prided itself on preparing its students for college, and according to the brochure, ninety-eight percent of Windsor graduates went on to a four-year college, with almost a fifth of its graduating seniors matriculating to Harland.

"Okay," Victoria told herself. "Head back to the library, that's the building over there with the big clock, and then start over."

"Hey there! Are you lost? You look confused, and well, you're talking to yourself." Her savior was a pretty girl with tight, reddish brown curls and brown eyes. She was with a dark-haired girl with an extremely sour face. The redhead continued in a friendly manner. "My name is Charla. That's Angie. Are you new? Where are you headed?" It was hard to keep pace with her rapid-fire speech.

"Um, yes, I'm a transfer. I'm looking for Kramer."

"Psych? Yeah, I'm in that building too. Come on, we're headed there. Those maps are the worst, but don't worry, you'll get the hang of it. Only a few hundred students here, so it's not that big of a place and everything's pretty easy to find."

Victoria nodded her thanks and fell into stride beside Charla. The other girl followed and Victoria could feel the heat of her stare burning into her back.

"I'm Tori by the way, Tori Warrick. Thanks so much for stopping. I was getting desperate."

The dark haired girl's sudden hiss of indrawn breath behind her was barely audible, but Victoria heard it and could feel an answering flush heating her cheeks. Before she could turn around, Charla announced that they had arrived. Victoria shook it off. Maybe she had imagined it—or not, as the dark-haired girl rudely pushed past her and tossed an unpleasant look over her shoulder. Victoria ignored her and smiled her thanks again to Charla before heading into the crowded classroom.

The senior class material was the same as what she would have been taking at St. Xavier's, and she took careful notes on her new laptop during the hour-long course, enjoying the feel of being back in a classroom after the summer.

She glanced around and recognized the dark-haired girl, Angie, sitting about ten rows down. As if she had felt the weight of Victoria's glance, she turned around and stared back malevolently, her dark eyes piercing. Victoria refused to look away—she hadn't done anything wrong—and only the teacher rapping his books on the table signaling the end of class broke their eye contact, neither willing to back down.

Victoria shook her head and gathered her things, refusing to let some random girl ruin her day. She quickly checked her schedule. She had a break and then history, which was in another building. People chatted loudly as they exited the room, laughing and talking about their summer holidays. It felt nothing like St. Xavier's, the energy and excitement were infectious. She couldn't help smiling to herself as she walked toward the concert hall to finalize her assistant job before her next class. This time, she found the building easily.

"Five minutes," mouthed a young woman sitting at the outer desk while she wrapped up a phone call. Victoria waited in the small hall area and perused the posters of concerts and events lining the walls. She loved music. Going to Carnegie Hall every weekend with her parents in New York had been one of her favorite pastimes, and remained a fiercely cherished memory. As she walked, the lilting sounds of Beethoven came from a piano down the hall, its haunting melody flawless. Curious, Victoria motioned to the assistant that she'd be right back.

She pushed open the nearest door, noticing a lone, shadowy figure on the stage at one end sitting at a grand piano. His fingers flew over the keys with practiced ease. The music shifted from Beethoven to something that sounded like Chopin's *Fantaisie-Impromptu* piece with its impossibly fast finger-work that made her breathless, and then jerked yet again to a simpler refrain that sounded oddly familiar. The hairs on the back of her neck rose as the pianist's raw emotion flowed through the music, his keystrokes forceful and heated. As he gentled his movement and lowered the key, spacing out each note of the last few bars, Victoria recognized the music. It was Michael Nyman's score from *The Piano*, a piece of music that was as dark as it was sweet, and one that had always moved her. She closed her eyes.

The music faded into silence as the sounds of a stool scraping back filled the void and her eyes shot open. Christian Devereux was staring at her from across the dark room, his gaze impaling her to the wall. In the dim light, she knew he probably couldn't see who she was, but she guessed he knew that someone was there, and had been listening.

"You play very well," she said, then fled, the door swinging shut behind her.

In the hallway, Victoria pretended to stare at the floor as the door swung open, crashing on its hinges as Christian strode out. His brows were drawn together in a scowl and his lips were pressed into a thin, grim, white line. Annoyance emanated from every inch of him, yet even angry, he was as striking as she'd remembered. No doubt she was the cause of his anger, spying on him as she'd done. He looked furious … and attractive in a way that shouldn't be attractive at all.

Her heart raced, jumping into her throat as his strange colorless eyes met hers for an instant, the beginnings of a smile on her mouth faltering and then disappearing altogether from the intensity of his flinty glare. His nostrils flared, his brow snapping together even more tightly, and he looked right through her as if she were not even there.

"*Miss?*" The assistant's voice was sharp as if it were the second or third time she'd asked, and Victoria turned distractedly. "Student identification card, please!"

"Um, yes sorry." She fumbled in her bag and handed over her ID.

"Fill these out." The girl thrust a pile of papers across the desk, which Victoria took mumbling her thanks.

Christian had gone without so much as a word, and his

burning, ominous glare had left her shell-shocked. Swallowing the clogged knot from her throat, Victoria sighed and filled out the paperwork.

"Superb start," she said to herself, as she made her way out of the building and across the quad. She'd managed to somehow alienate two people in the space of three hours and it was only the first day. She couldn't begin to imagine what the rest of the day would bring.

Her history class was interesting enough though, and she met a few more people at the library prior to the class. Before she knew it, she was heading back to the parking lot utterly exhausted. Not really looking where she was going, and more than a little glad that the first day was finally over, she almost tripped over the pair of long denim-clad legs leaning against the side of her car. Her heart double-tapped as her brain drank in the way his gray rugby shirt clung to his shoulders and matched his eyes. His tousled blond hair shone gold in the fading sunlight.

Victoria berated herself for feeling any degree of pleasure upon seeing him after the way he'd treated her earlier but she couldn't disregard the sudden increased tempo of her heart or the sudden trill of her blood. Nonetheless, she tried to project a look of distracted boredom, as she stepped over his legs and unlocked her car.

"Oh, hello. Christian, was it? Are you lost?"

"I guess I deserve that," he said without rancor. "Here, let me help you with those books." Before she could protest, he'd placed her things in the backseat of the car, and then stood up to face her. "I really want to apologize for what happened in the music hall earlier today. I was upset and taking it out on the piano, and then you arrived. I'm sorry. It has nothing to do with you. I was just … frustrated."

"Why?" she said, distracted by his absurdly luxurious lashes as she tilted her head to look up into his face. She was five foot eight inches and still had to arch her neck to look at him properly.

"There's been a change in the funding for my program, and there's a chance that it will be revoked completely," he said. "I'm a student here," he added helpfully.

"In music?" she asked before she could help herself. "I mean, I saw … I heard you playing. You're not bad."

A smile. "Thank you. No, not music, cultural studies."

"Oh. Well, I'm sorry about your program."

"It's one of those wait and see situations."

"I hope it works out then," Victoria said politely, wanting nothing more than to escape his nearness as she reached back to close the passenger door of the car. He reached forward at the same time and their hands met. A jolt of electricity passed between them that made her want to wrench her hand away. Her blood raced as tiny pins and needles surged across her entire body from the one single touch. For a second, she forgot how to breathe.

Christian stared fiercely into her eyes, the warring emotions in hers reflected in his, and she swallowed, hypnotized by something completely outside of herself. She felt her body sway toward him. He took a deep, steadying breath and released her fingers, stepping back at the same time. A practiced, shuttered mask fell into place.

Victoria jerked back, mortified at her body's heated response. She swallowed, her distressed gaze drawn by an imperceptible movement of his mouth. A fleeting vision of what it would feel like to be kissed by him ran through her head and heat ballooned in her chest. Unbearably warm, she too stepped back, staring at his impassive, granite face. Every part of her wanted to read his mind, as she'd done so easily with others earlier in the summer.

What are you thinking?

As if the thought magically translated into action, a part of her subconscious leapt forward to obey the instinctive command.

It was like hitting a brick wall head on.

Christian raised an eyebrow. He had felt it! He'd felt her trying to read him! Emboldened, Victoria accepted the unspoken challenge and *pushed* harder. The wall didn't budge. His mouth twitched, and for some reason, his amused arrogance infuriated her so much that without thinking, she gathered the already agitated energy swirling within her and hurled it toward him.

Christian went flying back three feet before crashing to the hard asphalt. He was on his feet in seconds.

"What the hell was that?" he said. She was frozen in shock.

"I have no idea," she said, then immediately contrite, she asked, "I'm so sorry. Are you hurt?"

"No." His voice was flat, cold.

"Well, you're the one who asked for it," she said, hiding her horror and remorse behind a show of bravado. She wasn't sure whether to kick him or apologize. And now, blast it, he knew that she could do things—strange, freakish things that would no doubt have him running in the opposite direction.

Only he *wasn't* running ... he was staring at her with an odd, appraising expression. He stepped forward, his face relaxed but wary, his fingers barely brushing a tendril of hair that curled into her face.

"Don't worry, Tori, your secret is safe with me." He paused, as if considering his next move. "I'll forgive you on one condition."

"What's that?" she asked, stunned into silence by his gentle caress.

"Dinner. Saturday night."

"You're asking me on a *date*?"

"I would say tomorrow but my back just isn't up to it," he said, deliberately misunderstanding her question and pressing his hands into his lower back. He grimaced. Almost immediately, he saw the guilty flush steal up to her cheeks and he knew she would agree, if only out of misplaced remorse.

"Why?" she asked.

"Because we got off on the wrong foot, and I'd like to make amends."

The velvety tone of his voice was back and Victoria could feel herself melting in response to it. His reflective eyes were intense, compelling. She'd never wanted to say yes so badly to anything in her life! She tore her eyes away. A date, or anything that required proximity, would be disastrous! It wasn't that she didn't trust him, she didn't trust *herself.* Already her legs felt like water.

"I don't think it's such a good idea …" she began.

"Why not?"

"I barely know you."

"So this is a way for us to get to know each other."

"I don't—"

Christian didn't hesitate. "Don't you think you owe me just a little?" She stared at him hard. The expression in his eyes didn't flicker for an instant.

"Fine, Saturday then!" she said, capitulating not at all gracefully, flouncing into her car and slamming the door. As she drove off, she didn't deign to look back but could hear his laughter in her head all the way down to the end of the drive. *Damn him!*

CHRISTIAN WATCHED THE car's retreating lights and smiled. She'd resisted his compulsion easily but he didn't mind doing whatever it took to get what he wanted. In more than a hundred and fifty years no one had been able to catch him off-guard, far less knock him off his feet. If it were as instinctive as he had initially thought, then he had seriously misjudged her abilities. The thought of Lucian rose unbidden in his mind, and he shoved it away. He knew *exactly* what Lucian would do with her.

He took out his cell phone and turned it between his fingers, his face brooding. Christian remembered the touch of her fingers on his own and the electricity that had coursed between them. He'd barely been able to contain himself, and all he could think about was placing his lips in the delicate curve of her neck, taking and taking until he couldn't take any more. The thought of it had almost driven him to his knees. Very deliberately, Christian placed the cell phone back into his pocket.

Everything in him knew that it was a mistake. He should call Lucian, and let him assess the threat, because now he knew without a doubt that there was one. Her power was too raw … too dangerous.

He should walk away before he was pulled any deeper or jeopardized far more than just himself. But still, even as he thought the words, a part of him recognized that it was too late.

Far too late.

They would already know.

FIVE

Discovery

SHE SHOULD HAVE said no. But if she was really being honest with herself, she had wanted to say yes. When they touched, she'd been shocked by the connection between them. Victoria had known there was something there—she'd felt that spark from the moment they had first met that day in the Admissions Office.

Yet, despite the fact that Christian Devereux was so charismatic and made her heart race, something felt wrong. When he looked at her with those eerie light eyes of his, she felt rattled and on edge. Not to mention what she'd done to him just by thinking about it. Her throat tightened at the memory. Her palms tingled and she felt a familiar heaviness stir in the pit of the belly, the same sensations she'd fought months ago, the ones she'd thought were dead and gone.

Embrace it.

Victoria almost jumped out of her skin as the phantom thought invaded her head. Exhaustion was making her remember things that she'd prefer remain ancient history. She shook it off and sighed, leaning back against the sofa and watching Leto lying on the top edge of the cushions. She stroked his ears as he watched her intently out of one eye, and resorted to her familiar means of making sense of her feelings.

"I don't know why I said yes," she murmured to him. "He's arrogant, and rude, and irritating." She sighed, a soft smile on her lips turning onto her side to face Leto. "But you should hear him on the piano, he's amazing. Reminded me of New York." Leto curled his head into her palm. "Mom would have loved hearing him." Her words slowed. "Maybe that's why I said yes. Anyone who plays like that can't be all bad, right?"

Victoria stared out the window behind the sofa and curled her legs beneath her, her fingers still lingering in Leto's fur. She wrestled with her thoughts.

"But that's not the whole reason. I don't know how but"—she hesitated again, a shiver passing through her—"it happened again. And it's just strange that he didn't react like I thought he would … like the others."

Leto's head turned toward her and for a second, she felt a strange sensation as if he'd heard her. She could feel a sense of concern that wasn't her own. She frowned dismissing it, and continued her monologue.

"I mean, he's not stupid. It's unnatural to be able to move whole *people* around without touching them." She studied her hands as if they held the answer, frowning. "It was like invisible hands just reached out of my chest and shoved him backward."

This time there was no mistaking the response. Leto stared at her so hard that every hair on the back of her neck stood at nervous attention.

"Why are you staring at me like that?" she blurted without thinking.

Leto growled, holding her gaze disconcertingly, once again compelling her to grasp at something that was just beyond her reach.

Given the last few months, she shouldn't have been surprised by anything, and after the existentialist episode with Christian, it didn't seem that farfetched to have an animal stare at her as if he understood her every word. *She* could *do* things, unnatural things. A cognitive cat was hardly a stretch.

Victoria bit her lips as a rush of unexpected hysteria filled her, brought on by Leto's stare. She glared at him.

"If you have something to say, just say it already," she snapped.

Her anger faded as abruptly as it had appeared and without waiting for the response that couldn't possibly come, she slumped back on the couch bursting into laughter at her own absurdity. What was she thinking?

Embrace it.

She almost fell off the sofa. That time, the voice had not been a figment of her imagination—it'd been real. But there was no one else in the apartment apart from Leto. She looked at him warily.

"You're imagining things again, Tori," Victoria muttered, closing her eyes.

You know what you are. You've known all along. Embrace it.

She sealed her lips shut against the hysterical panic bubbling behind them. She'd fallen down the rabbit hole into a crazy world where she could topple people over just by thinking about it and where animals could talk. She could feel Leto's glower as if in response to the tune of her thoughts, and she opened her eyes.

He flattened his ears and hissed, staring directly at her. But that was *impossible*! Cats didn't understand people and they certainly couldn't talk back, unless … he was like her, something else … something not entirely natural, not of this world.

"I don't know what you want me to do," she whispered, feeling like a lunatic.

The music box.

The music box? It was a rhetorical question, and in that instant, somehow she understood immediately that the music box held all the answers; it always had.

Victoria rummaged through the cardboard box marked "junk" and found it. It felt the same as it had the first time she'd held it, warm and welcoming. Hers. She removed the amulet from the box, mesmerized by its light. It was undeniably beautiful.

And undeniably terrifying.

Victoria shook her head. "I can't," she said, her hand trembling.

To embrace who you are, you must.

The words were simple but powerful. Victoria understood that she had to know who or what she was even if it meant "embracing" the mad energy that she'd tried to bury inside her. Not knowing was far worse than knowing. She couldn't risk what had happened with Brett ever happening again, or repeating what she'd done with Christian without understanding her strange power. The voice was right—she needed to embrace who she was, but even more, she needed to learn to control this thing inside of her.

Pulling herself together, she took a deep breath and focused inward, finding the sphere of energy, the strange force that she'd used against Christian. Her grandmother's words echoed in her head as she clicked the clasp into place around her neck. "Don't fear it. You are a Warrick."

Victoria closed her eyes, imagining that she was pulling the energy toward her heart near where the amulet rested. To her disbelief, she sensed it follow her bidding. It felt like she had been doing it all her life. The energy responded fluidly, pliant and receptive to her every thought. It was astonishing, and humbling. Victoria breathed out carefully, knowing what she had to do.

With a long indrawn breath, she pulled it into her center and felt it fill every cell in her body. She'd never felt so tall, so full, so *whole*. She feared that she would burst with it until her breath rushed past her lips and the energy rippled inward, resonating into blood and bone and tissue.

She opened her eyes.

The diamond burned the color of blood.

Leto's eyes glittered.

Yes.

"I don't know how to—" Victoria faltered for a moment.

You've talked to me your whole life.

She stared at him. "I didn't exactly … expect a response."

Open yourself. Your power is an extension of you. Push outward, and imagine your mind connecting with mine.

She hesitated, but Leto's eyes compelled her to finish what she had started. Tentatively, Victoria envisioned her mind as a ball of energy and imagined a silver thread linking her mind to his.

Leto …

Victoria.

Curious, she slid alongside his consciousness, exploring it gently. Although he felt catlike, warm and comforting and like family, he didn't quite feel like a cat. She sensed great intelligence, sensitivity, and even humor. In a way, he reminded her of her English teacher in second grade, a twinkly-eyed but bar-no-nonsense kind of person. As an onslaught of memories flooded her mind, she felt Leto cringe and block her out completely.

Shape your thoughts, Leto thought to her. *Then give them form with words. Guard your mind always, even against me.*

Mindful of not hurling a barrage of thoughts and feelings his way, Victoria formed her mental words carefully, releasing them one by one. It felt strange, enunciating each thought as if she were learning to speak a foreign language.

How do I do that? Guard, I mean.

Imagine an impenetrable wall around you, encasing your entire mind. Good. Do you feel me pushing against you? That wall you just imagined is real.

Victoria frowned. *It feels like I have a headache.*

Over time it will become effortless. She met Leto's green eyes.

Was the voice always you?

Yes.

So does this mean I am telepathic?

You are so much more, Victoria. Surely you know that. Leto's look spoke volumes. She considered his words.

I … made those things happen by thinking about them, like Brett … and Chri … the boy from today. It felt different earlier though.

She thought about Brett and remembered how the energy had raced along her veins, rampant. Wild. She'd cowered from it then, running away from it and burying it so deeply that it was no wonder she'd been caught off guard by its reemergence.

Yes, the energy felt different. Now it was responsive, less raw. With Brett, she had reacted to a threat and her unconscious reaction had been explosive, uncontrolled. It had terrified her. But now, the energy felt compliant—she was directing its flow, projecting it with purpose and shaping its response. Even with Christian earlier, her action had been more deliberate. She was controlling it instead of it controlling her. Victoria could feel Leto's approval.

Why couldn't I control it then?

Perhaps you were not yet ready.

And I am now?

Only you know the answer to that question. She eyed him curiously.

So what are you?

I'm … your friend. Leto settled back onto his haunches, his brilliant green eyes twinkled. *Technically, a familiar,* he clarified.

Victoria swallowed. A flicker of *Sabrina, the Teenage Witch* flashed through her head. *Like Salem in Sabrina?* She thought the words aloud before she could think twice.

His immediate disdain was eloquent. *Victoria, that is a television show. But yes, if you must make the comparison, although this form is just a shape, a vessel.*

Her mouth hung open. If he was a familiar, then that would make her …

And … me? Am I … a … witch? She almost choked on the last word, feeling stranger with each passing second. She could swear that Leto was laughing at her. His thoughts felt distinctly amused.

You already know the answer to that, Victoria. Of course you are, he said. *Although not in the way you're thinking. You don't use a wand or fly on a broom.* Victoria's face fell. The amused sensation she'd felt earlier from Leto returned. He *was* laughing at her! *But your mind can command energy, you will foresee events, and you can heal yourself.*

Wait. Heal myself?

Yes. If you are hurt, you can call upon your energy to heal yourself, and others too if you will it. However, for most it is finite. At her questioning look, Leto explained. *There's only so much magical energy one can wield at any given time, but there are ways around these limits.*

"What else can I do?" she asked, her normal voice hoarse.

As you have already discovered, you are capable of enhanced strength and you can cure yourself and others at will, but you can also unleash powerful energy blasts. You can teleport, exert powerful levels of telekinesis and telepathy, and you can invoke powerful spells.

Leto stopped as Victoria's mouth formed a small "o" of astonishment. Even as her brain incorporated what he was saying, she was stunned. She was a *witch*! How was that even possible? Her family had been normal. Hadn't they?

My grandmother was a witch. The ponderous thought was not a question.

Yes, Leto agreed, *but not like you.* His tone was enigmatic and he had an expectant expression on his face. It made Victoria feel peculiar, tingly again.

And my father? Did he know about me? Was he like … us?

Your father was human. Sometimes the magic skips a generation. It happens with mixed witch and human bloodlines.

But it didn't skip me?

No. Leto's eyes were intense.

Doesn't that make me half-witch, half-normal then?

No. You are a Warrick witch. Magic remains undiluted from generation to generation. You are as powerful as the very first.

The amulet and her grandmother's words flashed through her memory, "Embrace it. Don't fear it." She grasped the amulet, feeling its familiar warmth in her palm.

Why did the diamond turn red?

Leto paused, seeming to search for words. *It is a part of the amulet's magic but it only reveals its full power when a true descendant of Warrick claims it. The answers you seek are in there.* His glance indicated the open music box, but Victoria wasn't quite finished. She hesitated. There was one more question she needed to ask, one that had haunted her for years.

Leto, is this why I can't … die?

The magic protected you when you needed protecting.

Memories assaulted her: surviving the mangled wreckage of her parents' car crash, falling thirty feet from a tree when she was ten without any broken bones, narrowly escaping a skiing accident without so much as a scratch … there were suddenly too many "narrow escapes" to count. Other than her recent time in the hospital, she couldn't remember being sick a day in her life. The luck of the devil …

Victoria shivered, and changed the subject.

So my grandmother wasn't crazy after all.

No, but her fear for you was misunderstood. She wanted to protect you.

Protect me? From what?

Leto looked uncomfortable. *From yourself. Perhaps it would be better if you read the journal.*

And just like that, the conversation was over as he jumped off the sofa and padded to the bedroom. He glanced back at her once thoughtfully and then disappeared into the room.

Victoria stood, stretching her cramped body, and checked the clock. It was two in the morning but she was wide awake. She had completely forgotten about the journal in her grandmother's music box but she knew she couldn't ignore it anymore. She followed Leto into the bedroom, caressing the top of the warm box with her fingertips. She opened it and the soft melody whirred to life.

Leto lay on the bed, his eyes inscrutable, watching her. She lifted the thin leather-bound journal from the base of the box. The same crest was emblazoned on the front of it with the name "Warrick" inscribed beneath it. She traced it with her fingers, not sure what she was waiting for. She knew that the instant she opened the journal, her life would be forever changed. There would be no going back.

"Who are you, really?" she whispered.

The answers were in the journal. She glanced at Leto. His eyes were closed. The decision was hers alone.

Victoria's trembling fingers turned to the first page, the faint smell of gardenias drifting into the air. The first entry was dated May 21, 1602. The writing was painstakingly precise. She took the journal to her bed and began to read, her blood trilling softly.

Lancaster, England: My name is Brigid Anne Warrick Kensington. I am but fourteen and married to a man I have never met. My father thinks the marriage will unite our families and win the King's favor now that His Majesty, King James, is the King of England. I am told that His Grace, Lord Lancaster, is a young man and some would consider him handsome. Mother, I swear to you that I will be true to our blood! I will honor my new husband though I am a Warrick and will always be a Warrick.

The first few entries described the young girl's life in the home of her new husband, and at first were consistent but then started becoming less and less frequent, until there were gaps as long as a year between entries. The next entry date that interested Victoria came two years later, July 14, 1604. Brigid would have been just sixteen years old.

Lancaster, England. Mother, my son was born last week. He looks like his father, a Lancaster through and through.

Even the tiny scowl on his brow is identical to his sire's. He is a handsome devil. The birth was horrific and painful. I cannot bear to remember it. I shall call him Marcus James Warrick, after his father and our Liege Lord, the King.

There were two other entries, one written on Marcus' birthday, outlining his various accomplishments, learning to walk, talk, first horse, first everything. Her pride and delight in her son were unmistakable. The next entry that concerned Brigid herself wasn't until a year later, dated August 7, 1605.

I have lived seventeen summers today. Something is happening within my body. I can feel the restlessness of my blood. It burns. At night I awake drenched and screaming. Some of the servants think that I am possessed. Mother, I fear I must be. I cut my hand yesterday and the blood was black, shimmering with an unholy luster. It could have been a trick of the candlelight, but it frightened me. There was so much of it, and it bled for hours! I hid my wound for fear of the servants' talk. My Lord Lancaster is worried for my wellbeing. I try to comfort him but it feels like I am dying. I fear he can see through my lies.

Victoria's heart pounded. What she had been through was the same. The next entry followed quickly on the same page, just a day later.

I am so weak. I cannot eat. My body is feverish. Even as I write these words, my hands shake with cold. The servants come in and out of my room, whispering. I keep my wound wrapped because I know they are all watching with their fearful condemning eyes! Mother, I cannot bear it. This blood is a curse! My Lord Lancaster has sent Marcus to the King's court for the celebration of his son Henry's birthday. He refuses to leave my side. O Mother! Help me. My blood is burning.

Victoria noticed that the last words were faint almost as if Brigid had had little remaining strength to pen her thoughts to paper. She could hardly forget the fiery feeling of her blood in her own veins, the same that Brigid had brutally endured, also alone. The next entry was just a year later, written on the anniversary of Brigid's birthday.

Lancaster, England. How things have changed since my last birthday. As you may well discern, I am in perfect health. We are expecting our second beloved child and I am seven months into the pregnancy. I already know that it is a daughter. My Lord Lancaster showers me with his affection. How is it possible to love someone so entirely? He is kind and wonderful. He is my life. Forgive me Mother, but I have told him about my strange new gifts. My Lord Lancaster's love for me remains undiminished and true.

My talents are astonishing. I have many premonitions and visions of the future. Sickness avoids me, and it seems I have developed a Healer's touch. I can also read my beloved's thoughts. I can sense that he is worried about King James. The witch-hunts have grown more vicious in the past few years. He fears for our safety, particularly mine, given my abilities. If King James were to find out, we would surely be condemned.

The next entry came just a month later, on September 14, 1606.

My daughter is dead.

The single abrupt sentence floored Victoria, and she gasped as if the pain were her own. The writing continued a day later, pressed into the paper with angry black strokes. The pages rustled, heavy with tears and stained with splotches of dark ink. Victoria felt her heart wrench in empathy as she continued to read.

I am dead. Elizabeth Marie Warrick Kensington is dead. She came into the world a warrior goddess, bathed in blood, so much black blood, it was terrifying. My cursed blood killed her! The servants crossed themselves every time they entered the birthing chamber. She was so perfect, an angel. I have never known such joy watching her tiny, peaceful face, so divinely beautiful even in death. I curse the God that ripped her from my womb! I curse myself!

The dark splotches of ink shimmered and Victoria realized that they weren't ink at all. They were blood—deep, dark red drops imprinted on the pages forever. The journal trembled in her shaking hands. The amulet pulsed hot on her chest, as if it were reliving memories that scorched it. Victoria's eyes raced over the remaining lines of the passage.

The screams that shake the castle nightly come from my own heart. Lancaster has taken Marcus away as he fears for his safety. So he should. I can feel his fear as he looks at me drowning in my hate. I am lost to him, he cannot save me where I have gone. My devil's blood guides me now. I confess I can do things, demonic things. I sliced my wrist and I swear it healed before my eyes! Over and over I did it, until the black blood barely wept anymore. I bend the servants to my will, taking grotesque pleasure in hurting them. The blood's magic takes control and I willingly go where it leads me, where I am free of consequence. Lancaster was right to take Marcus away. I am unworthy. I am evil.

The amulet was growing so unbearably hot that Victoria dropped the journal and frantically unfastened its clasp, hurling it into the box. The diamond pulsed blood red. She backed away slowly from the music box. Leto opened a sleepy eye and looked at her.

"Leto!" she cried. "The amulet is cursed! I have the same poisoned blood that she did. I am cursed too. I never should have worn it! Why did I listen to you?"

Calm down, Victoria. He began to purr and within a few minutes, Victoria felt less agitated from his calming energy. She sat back down on the bed, staring helplessly at him, her throat tight.

"I can't wear it," she said. "I just can't."

It is your birthright. You are a Warrick witch and the amulet is yours. You are who you are.

Victoria shook her head fervently. "I don't want it. I don't want any of that! I just want to be normal, and have a normal life. And not hurt people!" On the last word, Victoria's voice broke. "I can't be a witch. I wouldn't know what to do, or be … or how … I don't want to become … *her.*"

Then don't, Leto answered simply. Curious, he asked, *did you read the whole journal?*

"How could I?" Victoria said. "I can't bear to read anymore."

Perhaps you will feel differently if you do.

SIX

Friends

VICTORIA WELCOMED THE many distractions of the next week, if anything to avoid thinking about the journal. She had banished it all deep into the recesses of her brain. She worked to fill her days and nights, and kept herself so busy that she wouldn't have time to stop and think about anything, especially about who or *what* she was. She'd done it for the entire summer, and she could do it again. In time, she was determined to forget it completely.

"Tori? Earth to TORI!"

"Sorry, Charla. What did you say?" Victoria asked. They were sitting on a bench outside the cafeteria, waiting for Angie. It was hot for September, and some of Charla's friends had organized an impromptu lake party. Charla was her usual outgoing, affable self, talking non-stop. Victoria liked her openness and felt very comfortable with her, especially because she didn't have to talk that much, just nod occasionally.

"I said … are you going to Marlow's birthday party?" Charla repeated.

"No, probably not."

"Why not? It's one of the biggest parties of the fall!"

Victoria couldn't stop the unwanted blush that stained her cheeks. "I have plans."

"Oh, really?" Charla's eyes brightened. "What kind of plans? Sounds like a date to me. Come on, dish—who with?"

She was saved from having to answer when Angie appeared, her face as usual, sour and tight. It tightened even more when she saw Victoria. Victoria couldn't understand what had made Angie take such a strong dislike to her. She had so much experience blocking people out that it really shouldn't have taken much to ignore Angie, but something about the girl really got under Victoria's skin, made her feel *exposed*.

Earlier that week, she'd seen Angie looking at her surreptitiously … assessing her. But when Victoria made eye contact, Angie had just glared and looked away. She had stopped trying to break the ice with her as Angie either looked right through her or looked away rudely. Though it was tiresome, Charla was oblivious to it all and didn't seem to mind being the link between them.

"So are we going or what?" Charla broke her train of thought once again. Victoria realized they were both looking at her. She nodded.

"I'm driving. Come on!" Charla said. "Gabe's going to be there and I want you to meet him."

"Who's Gabe?" Victoria asked, as they piled into Charla's convertible Jetta.

"He's Angie's brother, and well, he's a great guy … a good friend. He's a senior. You have to meet him." Victoria's doubtful expression made Charla grin.

"Don't worry, I promise you'll like him."

Despite Charla's assurance, Victoria fully expected that Gabe would be a male version of Angie and was already preparing herself for the worst. Something about the way Charla had talked about him showed that Gabe was a lot more than a good friend to her, but Victoria noticed that she had been careful not to say anything that would imply that he was a boyfriend.

They joined the long line of cars heading up to the lake. The weather in Maine was unpredictable—one year it would be December before the temperature dropped below freezing, and the next, it'd be bone-chillingly cold by mid-September. This year, it was still eighty degrees and everyone wanted to get to the lake one last time before autumn arrived.

"How do you like living in Canville? Can't be much different from Millihooha, right?"

"Millinocket."

"Whatever, it's all the same anyway," Charla sighed. "I grew up in Portland, and I cannot wait to get out of here! Angie and Gabe are from New York and they love it. I'm going back with them when I graduate. No Harland for me, I'm only applying to colleges down there. Big city, here I come!"

Victoria was surprised that Angie was from New York, although she knew she shouldn't be, since students at Windsor came from all over the place. But for her, New York was part of a different lifetime, and she didn't bother to correct Charla's mistaken assumption that she was also from Maine.

"Actually, I like Canville a lot. It's peaceful here. And I really love Windsor so far."

"It's a good school, just in the middle of nowhere. You can go a little stir crazy." Charla glanced in the rearview mirror. "Where'd you transfer from again?"

"St. Xavier's." The shape of it was acrid in Victoria's mouth.

Angie caught on quickly. "You didn't like it?" she asked.

Victoria was saved from saying anything at all when Charla interjected with a snort.

"No wonder. My cousin went there. It's snooty as hell. And the cheerleaders are manic. They hunt in packs." Charla made spirit-fingers waggling them across her face and chanted, "Be aggressive! Be, be aggressive!"

"I called them the Stepfords. Robotic cheer dolls," Victoria said dryly.

A guffaw from Charla. "I'm coining that one! Hilarious!"

"So why *did* you leave?" Angie's insistence irked Victoria.

"I got sick and missed a bunch of classes, and I … wanted to go somewhere else."

Angie blinked. "Just like that?"

"No, not 'just like that.' What is your problem?" Victoria snapped. Angie's black eyes remained speculative, a small smile playing around the corners of her mouth. Charla shot Angie a surprised look.

"Jeez, Ange. Chill. Who cares? It's no wonder she had to transfer. I'd probably get expelled in a second if I went there." Charla winked in the rear view mirror. "But enough crazy talk, let's get some tunes going to kick off the weekend, shall we?"

As the sounds of funk-inspired hip-hop filled the car, Victoria leaned back, watching the dark green scenery go by letting its beauty diffuse her irritation. Here and there, some leaves had already begun to redden, hinting that fall was just around the corner. New England's stunning autumn landscapes were unsurpassed. She sighed, enjoying the breeze blowing through her hair.

A silver car heading in the opposite direction caught her eye. The car was fantastic, sleek and foreign, and looked totally out of place in Canville. As it passed by, almost in slow motion, she could see the familiar, striking face through the windshield.

Christian Devereux …

His eyes caught and held hers, and for a moment, they were both frozen, time and space passing around them. She tore her eyes away from his as they drove past, resisting the urge to turn around in her seat and stare. One look, and it felt as if she were dissipating, like fragments of paper on water.

"Is Christian Devereux hot or what?" Charla said, breaking her trance. "And that car! What I wouldn't give to get a ride in that!" She laughed. Angie rolled her eyes.

"Does he go to Windsor?" Victoria blurted out. "I mean I saw him at Admission's."

"Harland. But he's involved with a class at Windsor," Charla said. "Seriously, I couldn't stand to take AP Epistemology. I would be like freaking out the whole time."

"AP *what*?" Victoria said.

"Epistemology," Charla said with a grin. "Mouthful, right?"

"That's a class?"

Angie surprised Victoria by commenting in a dry voice. "It's an elective class, part of a new program—the study of knowledge and truth and what people believe in, things like that. It's a new major at Harland, one of the first in the state I think, and they want to gauge high school student interest. Everyone freaks out when he comes to class. It's totally ridiculous." Quietly under her breath, she added, "as if they even know what he is." Victoria heard her and the words were out of her mouth before she could stop herself.

"What do you mean? What is he?"

Angie was quiet for a minute, and Victoria thought she was going to ignore her as usual but Angie surprised her by turning around. "You know, he's some kind of foreign prodigy slumming, but you'd think he was a celebrity the way everyone gets." Her tone was as disgusted as if she had something awful in her mouth.

Victoria wasn't sure if that was because she was addressing her or because she was talking about Christian Devereux.

"Well, I don't care!" Charla said. "Slumming prodigy or not, I would do *anything* to get in that car. I would look so hot in there!" For some reason, Charla's words infuriated Victoria but she stifled the blistering response that rose in her chest and plastered a smile on her face instead. Charla grinned in the rearview mirror. "Here we are!"

The lake was encircled by thick green woodland. They parked and walked down a wooded trail to the water's edge where a long, gray pier jutted out. The water was crystal clear and the sun hung low on the horizon, casting a golden tinge across it. There were throngs of people milling about, many of whom she didn't know, but Victoria didn't mind as the coolness of the water on her toes and the smell of the clean, warm air were more than enough to make her forget about everything else.

A floating dock out in the middle of the lake looked inviting and Victoria thought she would swim to it. She stripped off her jeans and was just tugging on her T-shirt when she heard her name.

"Tori," a high-pitched voice shrieked. Victoria turned to see Charla dragging along a cocky-looking young man. "This is Gabriel. Everyone calls him Gabe. Gabe, meet Tori. She's with us."

At first glance, Victoria could see why Charla was head over heels for Gabriel. He was good-looking with black curling hair and dark, flashing eyes. His skin was tanned and his body athletically muscular. He looked like a gypsy. Victoria could see the strong resemblance to Angie, and the only real difference between them was her perpetually sulky mouth and his smiling one. He stuck out his hand and took Tori's in a warm grasp.

"Nice to meet you, Gabriel. So you're Angie's brother?"

"Funny, how can you tell?" he said. He smiled conspiratorially and a slight overbite kept his face from being too perfect. "So how do you like Windsor so far?"

"I actually really like it, thanks." His eyes were intense.

The way he looked at her as if he were really interested in hearing what she had to say was refreshing. After all, she had only met Charla, who didn't really care what anyone else had to say as she could more than capably say it *for* them; Angie, who never had anything to say; and Christian, who infuriated her to the point that she couldn't say anything at all.

"Do you swim?" he asked, nodding toward the floating dock.

Victoria's smile was genuine as she moved toward the end of the pier. "Race you!" She pulled off her T-shirt in mid-run and dove neatly into the crisp, clear water. The coolness enveloped her skin and she remained under for several strokes, enjoying the feel of the cold water before cutting the surface. She extended her arms in a competent free-style and sliced through the water. She was an excellent swimmer and knew she could give Gabriel a run for his money. As she pulled herself up, a hand reached down to help pull her out the rest of the way, followed by a laughing, dripping Gabriel.

"How did you …?" she said. "You must be part fish!"

"Too slow!" he said, laughing as she struggled to catch her breath. "Okay, I confess, I'm captain of the Windsor Swim Team."

Victoria's laughter echoed across the water. It was wonderful to feel so at ease and relaxed with someone she had just met. She lay back.

"So where are you from? You didn't get that skin color from living in Maine, right?" Gabriel asked.

"Not so much." She grinned. "I get my permanent tan from my mother's side of the family, Persian ancestry I think. I lived in New York for most of my childhood and then I moved to Millinocket with my aunt when I was nine."

"Well, I'm glad you did," he said. Victoria blushed.

"It's so beautiful here," she said looking around, awed by the natural beauty of the lake with its thick wooded shores and pristine waters. "I mean New York is great but there's just nothing like this anywhere else, you know? This is perfection."

"Spent my whole life in the city, but since I've been here for three years, I can't imagine being anywhere else. I know exactly what you mean when you say that it's perfection."

They lay in companionable silence, watching the sun slide slowly behind the horizon. The air was still warm, and it was starting to get quiet as the voices on the far shore faded. Victoria never felt more at peace than at that moment. She turned on her side toward Gabriel, and realized that he was looking at her intently.

"What?" she asked, "do I have something on my face?"

"No." Gabriel smiled. "I was wondering about something." He hesitated for a second. "I was wondering how someone like you ends up hanging out with Charla, the chatterbox, and my social leper of a sister. I mean, how does that happen? Was there a sign that said 'sign up here to commit social suicide' when you enrolled? Did they pay you?" He kept a straight face but Victoria was laughing by the time he got to the end.

"Charla's, well, Charla. I like listening to her talk, because I don't have to," Victoria said. "And your sister is not a social leper." She hesitated. "I like Angie."

Gabriel burst out laughing. "You know, if you hadn't choked on the 'like' part of that, I could have actually fallen for it!" He grinned at her chagrin. "Don't worry, she can be a little … abrasive. Let's just say that we don't get along that well even though we are related." Gabriel got to his feet, and pulled Victoria up beside him. "Okay, if I give you a five stroke head-start, you think you can put up a better show than you did last time getting out here?"

"You're on!" Victoria swam for all she was worth toward the shore. She almost swallowed a mouthful of water when she saw Gabriel's lithe form coming up beside her. He was a powerful swimmer and something about the way he moved in the water seemed effortless. Breathless, they waded up the pebbly shore toward Charla and Angie who were sitting on a picnic table with two other friends.

"I think we can call that one a tie!" she said.

He gave her an incredulous look. "Maybe I'll give you that one, new girl, as a gesture of goodwill, but that was no tie." He grinned mischievously as he threw one arm across her shoulders. "We'll have to have a rematch one of these days."

Victoria noticed Charla's eyes narrow, and brushed Gabriel's arm off hurriedly by pretending to grab a towel. He didn't pay any attention and sauntered over to Angie, ruffling her hair. Her face, if possible, got even tighter and angrier, and she flinched from his touch as if he had slapped her. Victoria frowned, puzzled at her reaction. Gabriel said something to her, laughed his deep laugh and walked away. Angie's face looked like she was going to explode, throw up, or do both.

"Later, Charls! See you around, Tori," Gabriel said over his shoulder. He ignored his sister, which Victoria thought was odd, but understandable given the dynamic she had just witnessed between them.

They headed out soon after and the drive back was even more magnificent. The sky was a riot of color—red, gold and orange streaking across a deepening blue canvas. Victoria couldn't get over the purity of the landscape. Its beauty was everywhere she looked, in the trees, in the sky, in the lake, in the air. Even the houses were perfectly picturesque in the scenic setting. Victoria sighed. This was what she loved best about Maine; it was as if she were living in a

Monet landscape where everything was vibrantly alive. She drank it all in, and it wasn't long before they got back to the campus parking lot where she'd left her car.

"See you on Monday then, Tori, if you're not at Marlow's tomorrow," Charla said. "Have fun on your date."

"It's not a date," Victoria said, but they had already driven off.

Reluctantly, she headed back to her apartment. The minute she walked in, like a siren, the music box on her dresser drew her attention. She'd had some time to decompress on the drive home, and looking at it no longer made her feel like burying it at the bottom of the lake.

Though she'd pushed the journal from her mind, some part of her subconscious had still processed its essential meaning—one, the Duchess of Warrick was her great, great, great, great grandmother; two, Victoria had inherited her blood from a line that stretched back at least three hundred years; and three, she was a witch, a very powerful witch.

She was less edgy for some reason, probably because she was worn out after her swim. Maybe she should go for a run—it was still early enough. *Or read the rest of the journal,* her sneaky inner voice whispered. The sudden rush of blood in her ears made her hesitate.

"Oh, get over it," she told herself, and walked over to the box, opening it. Beethoven switched on as she turned to the last page that she had read.

The next entry was dated October 31, 1616, ten years after the last. The tone was dispassionate and cold just like its prior entries. The strokes of ink were hard and bitter.

London, England. My abilities are endless. As I learned with Elizabeth, when my Change happened during my seventeenth year, my new blood foreshadowed death. I did not write about it in my last message to you, but all the servants at her birth ... and death, died from poisoning of the blood. Such poetic irony. Still, I have discovered something about myself. I can change it. I can control it. You would not believe the things I can do!

Victoria shuddered but forced herself to keep reading and finish the passage. Every fiber of her being wanted to toss the journal as far away from her as possible, away from the grotesquely cold sense of delight that emerged from its pages, but a quietly insistent part of her needed to *know* who she was. *What* she was. She continued to read.

Lancaster was the first. I tried to reach him when he took Marcus away. And I found him. My mind found his so easily, almost like he had called me to him. I could still feel his love for me as he pleaded for me to leave our son with him. "You are lost, Brigid," he said, "do not lose us too." My heart cleaved in two as I heard those words. But still I felt the war within myself, my heart and my blood dueling. Lancaster could feel our love losing. Blood always won. "Then you will need to take me," he said, "for I will never let him go." My eyes burned black as my blood boiled in fury, and in my anger, I crushed the life from his body with a single word! The blood's cursed magic rejoiced and I felt the castle walls shudder as a part of me died with him. Lancaster was right. I am lost! I murdered him. But still, that was not the end of it, I could not help myself, I searched for Marcus too. And for my life, I could not, still cannot, see him. I am amazed he can block himself so easily from me. My son, after all.

Victoria continued to read, the next entry again a year later in 1617.

London, England. I have found Marcus. But perhaps as Lancaster intended, he is in the safest place he can be in King James' court. I don't believe Lancaster ever betrayed me to King James, but I can hear their frightened thoughts easily. My stillborn Elizabeth and now Lancaster's death were pieces of a simple puzzle, and James is ruthless in his pursuit against witchcraft. Confessed or proven, the penalty under his rule is death. I can sense he knows the truth of what I am.

There were only a few entries left in the thin journal, the next written almost nine years later, in March of 1626. The script was hurried, obviously written in great haste. But as with all of Brigid's entries, Victoria knew she wrote only because it had meant something to her or had some significance in her life. Victoria quickly calculated her ancestor's age. Brigid would have been thirty-seven years old.

Newcastle, England. My power is boundless now, taking its price in blood, running in my veins unbidden and overflowing. All manner of night creatures serve my desires, even the dark fey who serve none. I am the queen of darkness, the harbinger of death.

The Witch Clans seek an alliance, for they fear me.

The Warlocks compete for my favor for they desire dominion above all else. As a high witch, if I choose to take a consort, he will rule at my side. But I have no interest in ruling the Clans or the Warlocks, nor do I wish to control the Wolf-beasts, the Fey or the Undead or any matter of dark creature. I have made that abundantly clear. The only thing my blood knows is death, and I crave it like the Undead crave the essence of human life. I am a slave to it, forever serving, forever bound.

Valerius, a Vampire Ancient, sought an audience today. The threat of war is looming and they question my intent. The answer is simple—do not rise against me to take what isn't yours to take. The look of pity in his eyes as I struggled with the demands of the blood almost made me kill him. The Reii, the Ancient Undead, are powerful ... he would be so delicious. And the blood was so thirsty, so demanding, clamoring for him. But for some reason, I resisted. Perhaps it was because I saw a little of my own Lancaster in him. Perhaps it was that very look of pity that saved him, that sorrowful understanding in those penetrating eyes.

Somehow he knew. I banished my desire, even though to flaunt the forbidden would have been so entertaining—a witch queen and a vampire consort. It would unmake laws, defy legions, unhinge everything. But there is no time. The attack is imminent. I let him go. Four others died in his stead, no sacrifice was too great, and the blood was so hungry ... always wanting more.

As sure as I can foresee tomorrow's events, it will be a bloodbath. The Clans will attack, and united with the Warlocks, they will be strong, but still no match. The payment in blood will be consummate and my power will revel in the inevitable sacrifice. My eyes bleed black from the blood that oppresses me—its possession of me is nearly complete.

Victoria's throat was dry. The journal felt heavy in her hands, like a stone pulling her down into uncharted, treacherous waters. She could feel the blood churning within her, recognizing itself in the journal, and she couldn't suppress the surge of fear that made the tendons in her neck ache—the fear that inside, maybe she was just like Brigid.

Blood always won.

SEVEN

First Date

VICTORIA DRESSED SLOWLY. She had just been for a five-mile run on the ring road around the town. The exercise had been exactly what she'd needed after finishing the journal the night before. She hadn't slept a wink. It had been overwhelming—the casual mention of witches and fey and vampires, not to mention so much death and bloodshed. She'd felt even more like Alice thrust down an ever-deepening rabbit hole. The magnitude of her birthright and the shadowy path of her future hung like twin nooses around her neck.

Who was she, really?

She shook her head and tried to pull herself together for her date with Christian. Apart from seeing him for those brief seconds driving past each other yesterday en route to the lake, she hadn't seen him all week. She should have felt relieved but instead, she'd felt strangely depressed. The ringing of the telephone made her jump.

"Hello?"

"Tori, it's Christian," he said without preamble. "I realize I didn't mention where we were going." His velvety voice was husky, and Victoria's throat tightened in automatic response.

"I was wondering about that," she said.

"The Portland Museum of Art has an exhibit that I've been looking forward to seeing, and I was thinking we could get dinner afterward, if you'd like?"

Victoria's heart lurched. Portland? An hour's drive each way with him in a car alone! Impossible. She didn't even want to think about him sitting in such close proximity! She needed to give her hands something to do, find something for her mind to focus on; she already knew how distracted she became whenever he was around. There was no way she could sit in the passenger seat of his car for an hour!

"Portland?" she asked. "Can't we go somewhere local? Like the Dog?" Somewhere local and *safe*.

"I already have the tickets," he interjected smoothly. "Trust me, it's a beautiful exhibit, you'll enjoy it."

As her stomach began a slow free-fall, inspiration struck. "Christian, would you mind terribly if I drove? I … I … get … carsick on long drives," she said. She could hear the silence on the phone and knew instantly that he would probably see right through her. She didn't care. If she were driving, she'd have to pay attention to the road, not to him.

"Sure, no problem. I'll be at your place in a half hour." Victoria swore she could hear him laughing under his breath.

It was still unseasonably warm, so she chose a simple sundress embroidered with pink flowers and tiny green vines. She toyed with a braided green necklace, and then tossed it aside before opening the music box to the tinny sounds of *Moonlight Sonata*. Her fingers brushed over the red velvet case and she felt the amulet's magnetic pull. She hadn't worn it since that day she'd started reading the journal. She held it in her fingers, watching the light dance off its facets. She remembered Leto's words.

You are who you are.

Everything she'd read in the journal had terrified her. Despite her underlying apprehension, with a deep breath, Victoria fastened the clasp and felt the amulet drop to rest against her chest. There was no doubt in her mind—she felt complete.

The buzzer rang, and she tucked the diamond into the bodice of her dress, giving herself a cursory look in the bathroom mirror. Her hair fell in soft waves past her shoulders and with the exception of some gloss and mascara, her face was bare. Victoria frowned. She looked like she was thirteen but it was too late to go for a more sophisticated look. Christian Devereux was a courtesy date, nothing more. She slipped on some ballet flats and made her way downstairs.

Christian stood leaning against her car across the street, looking boyishly casual in his dark blue Diesel jeans and a fitted black T-shirt. She forced herself to not stare at him as she unlocked the car doors. Once again, she felt her heart flip-flop as she realized he was staring at her. Its pace tripled. Did all girls react this foolishly to him? His smile was warm as he opened her door, and then let himself in on the other side. It was ridiculous how flustered he made her feel. He wasn't even her type! The amulet flared but her skin was already so warm, she barely even felt it.

"So carsickness, was it?" A hint of a smile curved his lips, and Victoria swallowed guiltily as she started driving.

"Yes, it's very bad," she said, proud of the conviction in her voice.

"I thought that usually happens in the back seat?"

"Um, yes, usually, but mine is … unusual." Her mouth twitched. She refused to look at him and could feel her ears burning hot.

"So tell me something about yourself, Tori. You are quite the mysterious one."

She shot a sideways glance at him to see if he was joking. His body was angled as far away from her as possible against the door but he was watching her expectantly. His eyes were twinkling with amusement so she relaxed.

"You mean apart from knocking people over just by thinking about it?" she said.

"We could start with that if you want." His voice was amused but there was an edge to it.

"Well, I've never actually done that before ... I mean as in meaning to do it. You know, not to hurt you, but to do it." Her words were halting and flustered. "I mean something like it happened before but I think it was instinctive. Sorry, what I mean is that I wasn't thinking about doing it at the time." She glanced at him, embarrassed.

But Christian just nodded, his expression carefully neutral. Victoria peeked at him again. He was staring at her thoughtfully, his lower lip between his teeth. He had that look in his eyes again, the one that made her feel like a fly caught in a spider's web.

She looked away and kept driving with her eyes on the road. It was a straightforward trip on I-95 to Portland and after a while, they made easy small talk to pass the time. She told him about her childhood in New York, and how she had ended up in Millinocket with Holly after the accident. For some reason, she even told him about her time at St. Xavier's, which she hadn't really talked about with anyone, and glossed over the bits she felt didn't really need explaining.

"You were protecting yourself, that's all," he said, after she'd told him what had happened with Brett. "He got off lucky." His lips had thinned, and if Victoria didn't know better, she'd guess that her story had made him angry on her behalf. His odd reaction made her feel flustered and warm again. The rest of the drive passed quickly and before long, they were at the museum.

They walked leisurely through the exhibit—Landscapes from the Age of Impressionism—enjoying the featured *en plein air* easel paintings of Monet, Boudin, and Childe Hassam. Christian explained that the tradition of working outdoors with changing light conditions, typical of the Impressionism Movement, meant that colors, textures, shadows and shapes changed from moment to moment, creating subtle differences in the end result of the works. He knew a lot about the artists and of the period in general, and his anecdotes about each of the various paintings made the experience an enlightening and memorable one for Victoria.

"I love Monet. He is one of my favorite painters … sometimes I imagine myself escaping into his landscapes." She said it so quietly that it was almost a whisper, but Christian still heard her as they finished up the exhibit.

"He was very talented, and was happiest at his home in Giverny. Some of his best work came from painting his own gardens, like *Water Lilies*," he said. His voice was nostalgic.

"You almost sound like you knew him," Victoria said.

"You could say that my family knew his," he said, ushering her out to the street. "Why don't we walk? There are a couple of good restaurants just around the corner. It's not far. Are you cold?"

The night air had cooled considerably and Christian moved closer to her, putting his arm lightly on her shoulders. His body was not that much warmer than hers but she could feel the heat flood her body at his touch. She didn't have to look at him to know that he was smiling at her as the color bloomed across her shoulders. The scent of gardenias permeated the air. Victoria felt incredibly self-conscious, and she pulled her hair around her shoulders in a protective shroud.

"By the way, I forgot to tell you that you look very … nice," she heard him say.

"Thank you," she said. Victoria was absurdly flattered by the compliment, and then scolded herself in the same breath for feeling anything at all.

"I am really happy that you decided to come here with me."

"Did I really have a choice?" she asked with a dry look. He had the grace to look sheepish.

"No, I guess not," he agreed.

"I came to Portland once with my Aunt Holly for my birthday, years ago."

"So when is your birthday?"

"Was. Back in May."

"Well, happy belated. So let me guess, seventeen? Eighteen? You hu … kids look older and older these days."

"Seventeen," she replied automatically, and then stared at him. "Us, kids? Come on, you're hardly that much older than I am!"

"I am wise beyond my years," he quipped. "Here we are."

The Italian restaurant was small and cozy, and they could see the water from their table. Victoria studied Christian openly as he enjoyed the view. His skin was youthful and his body toned, but something about his eyes did make him seem older, more mature. His pale compelling face was like a Botticelli painting, and his ridiculously long lashes lent a certain innocence to his face, which was in severe contrast with the danger she sensed lurking beneath the surface whenever she was with him. Victoria had to admit she was very curious about Christian Devereux. He seemed to have so many secrets hidden behind those enigmatic eyes.

She took the plunge. "So Christian, what's your story?"

"What would you like to know?" Although his eyes remained

warm, she couldn't help noticing that his tone grew noticeably cooler.

"Well, what brought you to the thriving metropolis of Canville, Maine for one?" she said, leaning forward in a journalistic pose. "Where did you grow up? Do you have any brothers and sisters? How were you able to get up and walk away after what I did?" She had slipped in that last question so smoothly that Christian almost didn't notice. Almost. Victoria was staring at him intently, but his face remained a carefully composed mask, giving away nothing. She sighed theatrically. A ghost of a smile appeared.

"I was born in New York but I spent most of my life in Paris, including my childhood and early teenage years. I have a"—Christian hesitated, then continued in an almost dispassionate tone—"twin brother, he is still there." Victoria's eyes widened as she digested that information. He rushed on as if he just wanted to get it out in one go. "My parents are dead although I have a few cousins and other extended family still in France. Then I moved to America to study, moved around here and there, and pretty much ended up here at Harland with my program. Et voilà." He spread his hands and inclined his head in the mockery of a bow.

"That was the fastest synopsis of someone's life I have ever heard! And you managed to tell me absolutely nothing. Saying just enough without saying too much so perfectly—it's an art!" Her voice was nonchalant despite the amulet burning a hole in her chest.

"Why would you say that?"

"I don't even know you. You could be dangerous."

Her cheeks flooded with violent color at her blunt comment, and Christian leaned forward in magnetic impulse. His jaw tightened and pain shadowed his face for an instant before he changed the subject abruptly.

"Tell me more about the hospital." His tone was brusque and

Victoria stiffened but welcomed the change of topic.

"Not much to tell." She unconsciously echoed his curt tone. "I told you that I had some sort of blood poisoning, which the doctors thought was a form of acute leukemia when some abnormal cells tried to take over."

"Did they?"

"Did they what?"

"Take over?" Christian's tone was light but he was watching her carefully.

"I recovered, didn't I?" Victoria could be evasive too. After reading the journal, she knew she had to be more careful. She could play the offense as well. "Tell me how you managed not to get hurt when I threw you."

Christian smiled a slow, lazy smile that didn't quite reach his eyes. "Perhaps I am like you," he said.

"I sincerely doubt that!"

From that point on, their conversation began to degenerate into an evasive verbal exchange. They circled each other like two alpha lions, each waiting for the other to make the first move and neither willing to trust the other. Before long, their check arrived, and they walked to the car. The ride back was quiet, with long awkward silences, and Christian spent most of the time looking out the window, preoccupied.

Victoria focused on driving as she pulled off the exit, her own thoughts chaotic from the strangely charged dynamic between them. She jumped as his soft voice broke the silence.

"It's just up here on the right."

She pulled into a curving driveway lit with ornamental lights that led to the front of a majestic house.

Victoria switched the engine off and turned to face him. Admittedly, she didn't want the night to end, even if the ride back had been uncomfortable. A part of her didn't want him to leave, the insistent part that was drawn to the danger lurking just beneath the surface, like a moth to a flame. She wanted ... her gaze dropped to his lips and she hastily averted it ... she didn't know what she wanted!

She focused her attention on his house. "Your home is beautiful."

"Thank you. Would you like to come in?" he asked.

"No, thanks. It's late and I should be getting back." Without thinking, she leaned over and pressed a soft kiss to his cheek, a silent apology for her part in what the rest of the evening had become.

Christian froze as her lips grazed his skin, his body a statue. A muscle ticked in his jaw as if he were fighting to control himself, his eyes like pieces of flint, dark and furious. Victoria pulled back, a flash of hurt lancing through her at his response.

"I'm sorry. I didn't—"

The words stuck in her throat as Christian unclenched his jaw and forced himself to face her, gently grasping her shoulders. Liquid silver stared into molten jade, and he touched his lips to hers, the kiss tentative at first, as if he were afraid to give himself over to it. But as the warmth within her bloomed, decimating walls and reason, his lips sank into the softness of hers with desperate urgency. Victoria dug her fingers into his arms, caught. It felt as though her life began and ended in that kiss.

Her lips parted in a silent gasp against his mouth and Christian's body jerked as the warm rush of her breath tore through him. He pulled away with sublime regret, a tortured look in his eyes. His voice was a harsh rasp.

"What am I *doing*? It's ... forbidden."

Victoria felt his bunched muscles shift restlessly under his shirtsleeves where her fingers still gripped, and although her mind felt fuzzy, his words still registered. She ripped her hands away in silent shame. His arms remained wrapped around her.

"Let me go," she said thickly. Her eyes were panicked.

Christian released her. He looked like he was in pain, his lips a thin, grim line. "I'm … sorry."

"I need to go," she said, shoving the memory of his lips away, and forcing herself not to look at his mouth. How could she have thrown herself at him like that? She was mortified. Christian shifted and she tensed automatically.

"Please, I won't—" *hurt you.*

"You won't what?" She turned to face him, her eyes glacial. "Do it again? Don't worry, that was a mistake for both of us."

Christian stepped out of the car, his earlier warmth replaced by a shuttered, careful expression. "It was a mistake. I'm sorry."

Though they were hers, the words stung.

She did not look at him. She couldn't look at him.

"See you around then." The tears didn't come until she reached the end of the driveway.

CHRISTIAN STARED THOUGHTFULLY down the driveway long after she'd left. After that kiss, he knew without a doubt that he was playing with fire. The ferocious hunger in his belly had almost consumed him, just from the single taste of her lips. Even then, his body continued its slow metamorphosis as he struggled to calm himself—his muscles bunching spasmodically, readying themselves for the chase, his teeth distending, adrenaline flowing wildly in his veins.

Christian steadied himself, for the first time in over a hundred and fifty odd years, having the difficulty he would expect of a far younger vampire. The effort was futile.

The only *safe* place for her would be in a world where she'd never met him.

As the bloodlust filled his eyes, all he could see was her face.

EIGHT

Falling

OVER THE NEXT few days, Victoria busied herself with classes and getting settled into a manageable routine. Charla had taken her under her wing, and Victoria didn't protest too much even though she sometimes felt like Charla's new prize show pet. She was grateful to Charla for bringing her into her circle of friends and for making the transition a lot smoother than she could have hoped for. Senior year at Windsor actually had the makings of a good year.

She hadn't read anymore of the journal, ignoring its pull every time she looked at the music box, but she'd kept wearing the amulet. Every day following her acceptance of her power, she'd felt the magic grow more and more inside of her. Yet Victoria still found herself reticent to explore it. The power scared her, and the fear of being like Brigid terrified her. She held on to "staying normal" like a lifeline, and for the most part, Leto seemed to understand her desperate need for normalcy.

On top of that, it had been almost two weeks since her shattering kiss with Christian. Even the mere thought of him sent her heart into a panicked whirlwind and made her bones feel like they were made of rubber. She couldn't fathom how someone could make her feel so conflicted—wanting to see him yet dreading it at the same time, and then being disappointed if she didn't. It was exhausting!

She'd found herself breathless on several occasions when she'd seen someone who looked like him walking across the campus or in the town. But it was never Christian and she'd always felt curiously deflated. Victoria was sure that something was wrong with her.

She found herself thinking about him again as she walked toward the music hall between classes and gave herself a mental shake. "Get a grip, Tori," she told herself. "Christian Devereux is not part of your life and you are better off without someone like him. Forget him." She took a deep breath in support of her declaration, and walked into the building.

Her job as an assistant to Windsor's Junior Youth Orchestra kept her busy, and included assisting with attendance paperwork and coordinating rehearsals for the band. So far, she liked it. Charla called it her "Band Geek Job" but Victoria didn't mind. Being around music was therapeutic.

An alumnus of Julliard, her mother had been a concert pianist and Victoria's childhood had been filled with music. She'd learned to play the piano at the same time she'd learned to talk. Despite her natural talents, she'd stopped playing the day her parents died.

"Hey Tori!" a young man with a tuba called out waving. She turned to wave back making her way to the front office and crashed into someone on his way out. She fell straight back into an ungainly heap on the floor.

"We really have to stop meeting like this," a wry voice said, extending a hand to help her up. "At least this time it's not me on the ground."

Victoria grimaced from the pain shooting up her backside and ignored Christian Devereux's proffered hand. She pulled herself up and glared at him.

"What are you doing here?" she snapped, glancing at him out of the corner of her eye as he stuffed his hand back into his pocket. His face was expressionless, guarded, and still as compelling as she'd remembered. Her gaze flicked to the floor.

"Rehearsing."

"But you're not in the band. You don't even attend Windsor."

"I'm a guest soloist for the performance," he said, moving past her and brushing her arm as he stooped to pick something up off the floor. Almost immediately she could feel the flush start in her toes and work its way all the way up the backs of her knees to her ears. "You dropped this," he said, and handed her a clipboard.

"Thanks," she said, concentrating on the fabric of his sweater and not the way it hugged his body beneath it, which was an entirely hopeless effort. Her eyes swung to his face, avoiding his eyes and fluttering to his lips instead. Her chest flared. Focusing on a point on the opposite wall, Victoria gritted her teeth, ears flaming and pushed past him, suddenly desperate to escape him. "Well, okay, see you."

"See you." His response was soft, and something lingering in the two words tugged at her. She ignored it and after a few minutes he walked away.

Victoria felt her heartbeat calm after heaving several large gulps of air into her lungs. Her arm still burned where his shoulder had grazed against it, and she rubbed at it furiously as if trying to erase his touch. It brought back feelings and words she didn't want to think about—the sound of him saying that kissing her had been a mistake and the humiliation she'd felt that was now returning in hot, violent waves.

Get it together, Victoria. It's over and done with. Ignore him. You have a job to do, so do it, she told herself fiercely.

Christian wasn't at the rehearsal and Victoria assumed that he was off practicing in another room. The band shifted on the stage for a new song, and Victoria distributed the sheet music. She heard the music director call her name.

"Can you give Christian a folder, please?" he asked.

"Sure." Christian walked over and she handed him a booklet with the piano sheet music.

"Violin," he said.

"What? But you play the pi—"

"It's a violin solo," he said gently, reaching for another folder lying on the table next to her.

Victoria shot him a dubious look. He couldn't possibly play the violin as well as she'd heard him play the piano. But she was wrong. When Christian drew the bow over the strings, it was as if everything else in the room just disappeared and the music took over. Victoria had never heard a violin played with so much effortless grace, and she was sure her mouth hung open.

She didn't want to look at him but couldn't help herself. Christian was staring right at her as he played, and she felt her breath stop as their gazes collided. For an unguarded second, his eyes held an impossible longing, communicated only by the fluency of the wooden bow and violin under his chin. But before she could blink, it disappeared and the music came to a resonant halt. The hall erupted in spontaneous applause.

Dumbly, Victoria clapped along with the others, certain she'd misread their shared glance. Christian didn't want anything to do with her; he'd made that very clear.

Jake, the boy with the tuba, elbowed her. "He's amazing," he said, his voice awed. She nodded, an automatic response, and stood, making her way out of the room pretending to collect discarded sheet music. She felt Christian's eyes on her again, but kept walking until she reached the office.

She took a deep breath, focusing on the energy inside of her and calmed her racing heart, beat by beat. The magic helped to soothe her frantic spirit. And she was grateful.

After that, when Victoria saw Christian at rehearsal, it was as if the interlude during his first violin solo had become a figment of her imagination. He ignored her most of the time, and seemed to take special care to not be in the same room when she was. Sometimes it was inevitable, and during those times, he treated her with a casual indifference that hurt more than anything, but after a while, she became adept at concealing her hurt behind a façade of activity.

If she concentrated hard enough, the sensation of him seemed to fade into the background like a dull buzz. She had no idea if what she was doing was a part of her magic but it helped, and that was all she cared about. The amulet became a source of comfort as she found that whenever she held it, she found clarity, and with it strength. And each day it became easier to avoid and even ignore Christian Devereux.

Along with Christian's violin solo, he was also doing a piano duet with another girl in the orchestra; one who stared at him with such lovesick eyes, it was a wonder that she could even play sitting next to him. The choice of music was a beautiful piece, a four-hand piano arrangement of Tchaikovsky's *The Sleeping Beauty Suite*.

Despite not having played for years, Victoria loved it so much that one day after rehearsal she sat at the piano and just let her fingers drift over the keys. Her playing was halting at first and then grew more confident. It was only a one-sided rendition of a piece meant to be played by two people but the music still soothed that place in her heart occupied by memories of her mother. When she finished, she let the tears come and was so lost in her thoughts that at first she didn't hear the soft voice beside her.

"Are you all right?" Christian asked, as she wiped her eyes hastily. He hadn't spoken more than two words to her in two weeks and suddenly he cared why she was crying? Victoria wanted to tell him to go away, but a part of her was so desperate for comfort that she found herself sitting with him and telling him about her parents and her mother's life-long love affair with music.

"I stopped playing after they died," she told him. "She loved Tchaikovsky, this piece in particular. I'd forgotten how much I loved it … her …"

Then she cried again, and he stayed with her talking until the custodian came to clean the building. He told her funny stories about his brother when they lived in France as children and some of the pranks they'd played on each other.

"Lucian was a trickster. I was always the one who got away, being my mother's favorite. No one could tell us apart but even when we switched identities, she always knew," he said.

"Were you close? You and Lucian?" Victoria asked.

"We were inseparable." Sadness thickened his voice. "I remember when we were ten," he said with a nostalgic smile, "we'd gone sailing and as we often did, got into a scrape about something. I don't even remember what it'd been about. But one thing led to another and we both fell in. In those days … winter," he said, after a glance at her, "clothes were thick and heavy. I pushed him out first, but then I started sinking. He jumped right back in to save me, and in the end, we both had to be rescued. That's how it always was. We protected each other even if it meant hurting ourselves to do it."

"Sounds like you loved each other very much."

"Yes." His eyes were far away then, but his hand gripped hers tightly. She squeezed it sympathetically.

"So, why *did* you go sailing in winter?" He sent a startled smile her way. "That sounds like something I would do."

They talked for hours and Victoria found herself telling him things that she'd never told anyone else. Memories of her parents and living in New York, mundane but beautiful things she missed about the city, about them, about her life.

"My father was quiet," she told him. "My mother was not. They were polar opposites, but you'd think they were a match made in heaven the way he loved her and she, him. He'd sit and listen to her play for hours like it was their special language. I miss that the most, their music. It made me feel … part of something beautiful."

Christian was understanding and sweet and funny, making her sadness disappear, and despite their earlier interaction, it seemed like they could be friends.

"Thank you," she said to him after he'd walked her to her car. "You didn't have to give up your entire evening for me."

"I wanted to."

"I feel like I should apologize for thinking you were a bad person," she confessed, as she got into her car. "I misjudged you, and I'm sorry for that. I'd really like it if we were friends."

He stared at her then, his light eyes unfathomable. Victoria felt them on her long after she'd driven away and was out of his sight.

THE NEXT DAY Christian reverted to his other personality, the one who couldn't bear to look at her or be near her. It was as if someone had flipped a switch inside of him and the night before had never existed. He was agitated and angry, snapping at her when she brought him the wrong music, until finally she lost her patience with him and yelled, not caring who heard. "It's pretty obvious we can't be friends. You don't like me, and I don't like you. And you can get your own music!"

Over the next few days, Victoria stayed as far away from him as possible during rehearsal, and when he performed his solos, she usually tried to find something else to do in the office. His music undermined every strong thought she had against him, flowing into her as powerful as actual words. It left her weak. And he knew it. Those were the times that she left practice running for her car, desperate to escape his presence, the amulet in a death grip between her fingers.

Once they ran into each other at Willard's, the local diner in town, and despite their attempt to be civil to each other, the conversation was forced and fake. He wasn't even able to look at her. Even Charla gave her a quizzical look over Christian's obvious rudeness.

"What's with you and hot-French-boy?" she asked.

"Nothing. He's doing a solo for the orchestra, and he's a prima donna," Victoria responded, still smarting from his coldness.

"Devereux is a *band geek*?" she laughed. "That's just rich."

Angie surprised Victoria by commenting in a sour voice. "He's not a band geek, he does solos every year at Windsor and Harland. My parents said he played at Carnegie Hall last year for some charity benefit."

Victoria and Charla stared at her with twin expressions of astonishment.

"What? I'm just saying," Angie said, ducking her head.

"Why're you keeping tabs on him if you don't like him?" Charla exclaimed with a wink at Victoria.

"Not keeping tabs, and I *don't* like him. He's good at music, that's all," Angie said. "There's a reason for that but it's not like anyone cares," she muttered under her breath. Victoria frowned. That was the second time Angie had made a snide comment about Christian Devereux.

"What's that?" Victoria asked.

A glare from Angie. She answered Victoria's question with a question of her own. "Doesn't it strike you as weird that he so good at everything?"

"Gabe's like that too though," Victoria pointed out.

Charla smirked. "Two words. Silver spoon. He's like the British princes, doing the works—boarding school, etiquette classes, clarinets, and polo. I wonder what else he's good at." She wiggled her eyebrows suggestively.

Angie stared at her, a shocked giggle transforming her dour face. "Char, *you* did all those things at boarding school," Angie said, still smiling before her tone soured. "And Christian Devereux does not date girls at Windsor. Remember sophomore year?"

"Oh right," Charla said. She turned to Victoria. "I almost got expelled."

"Because of Christian?" Victoria said.

"He was a senior here. Some girl was flirting with Gabriel and Charla was all over Christian to make him jealous. But Christian made it clear that he wasn't interested so Charla knocked the girl's teeth out instead." Victoria gaped at Charla who wore an unperturbed expression.

"You punched someone?"

"She *knocked* her *teeth* out," Angie emphasized dryly. "Charla's a black belt."

Victoria stared at Charla's slight figure, skeptical. She looked like an anime doll with her red spirals and huge brown eyes. *A black belt?*

Charla shrugged. "I had a lot of aggression issues as a child," she said mildly, as if that explained it all. "Therapy and Taekwondo."

"Remind me never to mess with you," Victoria said, half-joking.

Charla turned toward her, her stare measured. "Just stay away from Gabriel, and you and I will be just peachy." Her tone was mild and she'd said it with a smile but Victoria couldn't help but sense the menace underscoring her words. An odd coldness settled across her shoulders.

"I would never—"

"I know."

NINE

Angst

To keep herself busy, Victoria went straight from classes to rehearsal to the Black Dog. Her days merged into a carbon copy of the day before; wash, rinse, and repeat. But she didn't mind the predictable monotony. It helped her to not think about anything other than what she was doing at the time—not her strange gifts, which she'd ignored since her discussion with Leto, and certainly not Christian Devereux.

She saw Gabriel once at a football game that Charla had dragged her to, and he had asked her to a party at his friend's house. Victoria had declined. Although she liked Gabriel, he was too fast for her and given Charla's obsessive-compulsive behavior where he was concerned, she didn't even want to be around him. Gabriel had seemed disappointed but hadn't pushed. After what had happened with Christian, Victoria wasn't sure that she wanted to get involved with anyone at all, not even someone who would help her to forget him.

She'd briefly wondered about what Angie had said about

Christian not dating anyone at Windsor even when he'd gone there, and it didn't surprise her. He seemed far too self-assured to have a girlfriend, which made his bizarre reaction to her even more extraordinary. It overwhelmed Victoria to even try to understand him. He had a Jekyll and Hyde complex that was beyond her comprehension. So she'd decided to just pretend he didn't exist. And apparently, he'd decided to do the same. Despite her relief, her disappointment must have been transparent because Charla had caught on to it.

"What's with you lately?" she asked, when they were hanging out after class at Willard's. "You're all jumpy one minute and mopey the next. If I didn't know better, I'd say you were in love."

"What? No!"

"Okay, now that's definitely a sign. Jumpy, and mopey, and defensive." Charla leaned over the counter of the booth pushing her plate of blueberry pie to the side and patting her flat stomach. "Stuffed. So come on, spill it. Who is he?"

"It's no one. Really." Victoria flushed, shoveling a piece of pastry in her mouth to avoid talking.

"And the fourth sign is denial," Charla said dryly. "Trust me, I am an aficionado of boys and boy behavior. You, my dear, are in the first stages of boy fever."

"Don't be ridiculous," Victoria said, her mouth full with another bite. "Look there's Angie. Hey Angie, over here!" She waved to Angie, who shot her a mystified scowl but made her way over to their booth.

"Hey," she said warily, eyeing Victoria and sliding in next to Charla. "What's up?"

"Not much except that Tori has a crush on someone and is totally holding out on me," Charla said, scooting over. She turned back to Victoria. "Speaking of, didn't you have a date like three weeks ago?"

"I don't have a crush, and my date was with a boy named ... John."

"John?" Charla tapped the side of her head and then shook it decidedly. "I don't know any Johns."

"Come on, there's at least five of them in our senior class," Victoria protested.

"None worth crushing over," she said, winking. "And you got saved, because here comes my crush right now. But don't think you're getting away, I'm on to you." She waved to Gabriel who'd entered the restaurant with four other football players.

Gabriel sauntered over, once again completely ignoring Angie to say hello to Charla and Victoria, and leaned against the table. He had his shirtsleeves rolled back and his tanned forearms were taut with muscle. His smile was lazy and confident.

"Hey Tori, is my girl getting you into trouble?" Charla blushed prettily.

"No more than usual," Victoria joked back.

"There's a party tonight at Jake's place. His parents are away and it'll be fun. You guys in?"

"Sure," Charla said. "Ange?" She turned to Angie who hadn't moved an inch since Gabriel had stopped to talk. Victoria didn't see anything but she could have sworn that Angie trembled slightly and shut her eyes almost like she had a sudden sharp headache. Her fingers clutched the books in her arms with a death-white grip. Victoria was astonished at the abrupt change.

"I ... I have to study. So no." Angie's voice was a dry rasp.

"Ange, it's Friday! And I need my buddy!"

"So take her," Angie said, jerking her head in Victoria's direction.

"Tori, you should totally come. It'll be fun," Gabriel said, as if

Angie hadn't spoken and pushed off the table. "We'll make sure you have a great time." He grinned, his teeth white and perfect. "See you later!"

Angie rounded on Charla the minute he walked away. "Seriously, Charla? You know he doesn't want me to come, why did you even ask with him right there? Sometimes you are so clueless, I can't even imagine how you function." Victoria gaped at Angie in complete confusion as she gathered her things and left without another word. Charla rolled her eyes.

"Don't worry about her. It's probably PMS."

Victoria shot her a disbelieving look. "Hardly. She looked like she was going to faint when he came over. What's with the story with the two of them?"

"They've always been like that. Like oil and water ever since I met them."

"Are they twins?" Victoria asked, curious.

A laugh. "No but they could certainly pass for it, right? They're like ten months apart, Gabriel's older, but Angie skipped a grade in junior high." Charla glanced over at Gabriel standing at the sit-down counter near the front of the diner talking to two juniors and frowned. "She told me once that it had something to do with their parents but never elaborated. And as much as you probably won't believe me, I didn't pry." She grinned and then sighed, pushing her hair off her face and resting her chin into the crook of her arm across the table. She kept darting furtive black looks in Gabriel's direction.

"Is Gabe your boyfriend?" Victoria asked, noticing what drew her attention. Charla's eyes clouded over and she wished she could take back the question.

"Ever heard of friend-with-benefits?" Without waiting for Victoria's answer, she continued. "Well, that's what I am. It's always about what Gabe wants. I wish he'd just commit, but we've been on and off for the last two years. So no, not exactly my boyfriend."

Victoria didn't know what to say. From the expression on Charla's face, it was clear that she was obsessed with Gabe. She couldn't imagine anything harder than watching a boy you liked flirt with other girls, just as Gabriel was doing with the two pretty juniors. The thought of Christian flashed through her head and she thought for a second what it would be like to see him smiling or flirting or kissing someone else. Her stomach curled. They weren't even together and she knew it would be torture.

"I'm sorry," she said to Charla for lack of something better to say.

"Don't be," Charla said brightly, with a forced smile. "That's why I have you. I plan to live vicariously through your love-life, and see you married and with child within the year."

"Great, a knocked-up teen bride. Every girl's fantasy." Victoria rolled her eyes and they shared a laugh.

"So I'll pick you up tonight then?" Charla made a beseeching face. "You have to save me from making a complete fool of myself over him. Or at the very least, save those two unsuspecting tramps who're flirting with him. I can get a little Ted Bundy crazy where Gabe's concerned."

Charla must have seen her expression at the obscure serial killer reference because she made a face and said, "I'm just kidding. I pretty much just yell at everyone, and then cry, and then he comforts me. So everyone wins. No random strangling, I promise," she said, throwing her palms up in mock surrender.

"Or punching girls in the teeth?" Victoria said, smiling at her antics.

"Well, there's always Taekwondo. You can't say I don't keep things interesting."

Victoria glanced at her watch. "I just have to stop by the music hall first. One of the guys in the band today left his wallet in one of the rooms. And I have to finish an assignment. But I promise I'll come later, okay?"

They said their goodbyes at Willard's and headed back to Windsor where Charla dropped her off. "Say hi to the band geeks! See you later!" she shouted, driving off.

VICTORIA RETRIEVED THE wallet and walked past the hall with the grand piano. She saw that the lights were on and the piano lid was open with sheets of music strewn across the top. Someone must have forgotten to turn them off and put the music away. She was just gathering the sheet music when she heard a noise behind her. She whirled around, panicked, her hand to her throat.

"Sorry, I didn't mean to scare you," Christian said softly.

Even when recognition set in, Victoria didn't relax. Her body remained tense, poised for flight. "That's okay. I didn't know anyone was here."

"I was just … practicing."

"Oh. Well, I'll let you get back to it." She eased past him.

"Tori? Will you play? With me this time?" His voice and eyes were gentle. Victoria stepped back, the automatic "no" on the tip of her tongue. "Please?"

Victoria's throat tightened. She could only nod despite the warning spark of her amulet, his nearness and startling sweetness overwhelming.

Reading the sheet music for *The Sleeping Beauty*, she played the introductory chords. She was clumsy at first, and what had come so easily the last time she'd played it seemed to take a lot more effort, but Christian was patient. Soon they fell into a harmonized rhythm and made it through to the end without too many jarring mistakes on her part.

"I think I've made you worse," she said.

"Let's try it again."

They played it again and after a while, she let the music take over as her fingers glided across the keys. Mindless of Christian sitting beside her, his fingers moving in accord with hers, she became lost in the melody, letting the memories sweep her away—back to Greenwich Village, back to her apartment and sitting beside her mother at the piano, back to when she was laughing and smiling and alive. She played until her knuckles—and her heart—ached.

"Beautiful," he said, breaking the spell that held her. "You're a natural."

"Thank you. I forgot how good it feels," Victoria admitted, as her fingers performed a scale exercise up and down the keyboard. "I'm nowhere as good as you are though."

"Years of practice. I actually don't really like the piano," he confided. She shot him an incredulous look. "Listen for a second and you'll see what I mean." Christian stood and leaned over near the side of the piano to take his violin from its case. "Pick something. Any composer you like."

"Vivaldi."

Without hesitation, he plunged into a rendition of Winter I, *Allegro Non Molto*. His eyes were closed as he started the beginning notes tapping the bow against the strings. Then the muscles in his forearm and neck clenched as he whipped the bow across the strings with such a driving, passionate intensity that she felt it in her fingernails. The bow was a blur until its pace slowed, and then built once more. Victoria felt the hairs on her arms raise as the music swept her along with it rushing toward its final conclusion. Her chest felt like it was ballooning into her throat.

When Christian stopped, she could only stare at him in silent awe. He was good at the piano, but he was astounding with the violin. It was nothing like she'd heard *anyone* play before. With the piece for the orchestra, she only now understood just how much he'd been holding back. She shook her head in disbelief and after a minute breathed, "I see what you mean." A self-conscious smile touched his lips as he replaced the violin.

"So what's your favorite music?" he asked, pushing back the hair that had fallen into his face and sitting on the bench next to her once more. She shot him another incredulous look at his blasé nonchalance.

"You should be at Julliard or in a concert hall in New York somewhere."

"I don't like the spotlight." His words were quietly spoken, and Victoria got the feeling that he wasn't just talking about music. She didn't want to pry, so she answered his earlier question.

"For classical piano, Chopin hands down. Vivaldi as you may have guessed. But on the flip side of that, I'm a big fan of popular music, movie soundtracks, Broadway, that kind of thing. And for violin, don't laugh," she told him, "but I love the *Bond* girls."

"*Bond*?" He flashed perfect white teeth. "They're pretty good … looking."

Victoria rolled her eyes skyward. "I guess the fact that they're four hot, half-naked girls playing strings doesn't hurt. But I like the fusion of classical and electronic. It's cool."

"Shall we?" he asked, notching an eyebrow toward the piano keys. "So Broadway? How about this one?" He struck the opening chords to *Phantom of the Opera*, and she grinned, her fingers recalling the notes of the song's upper register as he played the lower.

"Fitting," she said, and he laughed, a full-throated sound that made something inside of her tremble.

"I should be offended. You think I am some deformed, ugly

guy behind a white mask stalking you."

"I don't think you're ugly!" Victoria blurted out, and then blushed as his silver light eyes found hers. Embarrassed, her gaze dropped to her fingers as warmth flooded her body from tip to toe.

"I don't think you're ugly either," he said softly. Victoria could feel the side of his thigh plastered to hers on the short piano bench, and the nearness of him was suddenly overpowering. She held every part of her, except her hands, perfectly still.

They played in silence, the music the only sound reverberating between them. After a few bars, Christian reached over her hands to the right and started improvising. He was so close that she could see the slow pulse in his neck beneath the thin sheen of sweat from his fiery violin performance. Distracted, she faltered, her fingers fluttering and then going still.

Christian pulled his arm away and she saw something desperate flash in his eyes before he grinned, and brought his fingers down on the keys in a swift version of *Chopsticks*. He raised his eyebrows with a challenging smile, and she joined in laughing at his over the top performance. He played faster and faster, and she kept up with him, their fingers moving at an incredible, unbelievable pace, until Christian was the one to stop, begging for mercy. Exhilarated, Victoria threw back her head and laughed out loud.

"Quitter!" she teased.

"You are a pianochist."

Another laugh. "That's not even a word."

"Pianist meets masochist. I think it's appropriate."

Victoria gave him a playful shove with her shoulder. And instantly regretted the action as the length of her arm came into contact with the lean muscle of his. His face hung inches from hers. In that single moment, they were back in her car sitting in his driveway and the laughter in his eyes transformed into something else, something liquid and unsettling. Her eyes glued to his, she leaned toward him in unconscious response, the amulet scorching her skin beneath her shirt.

He met her halfway and then froze, his lips a hair's breadth away from hers, almost unwilling to bridge the last remaining space between them. Her pulse leapt, uncontrolled. Christian's cool breath fanned against her lips until she saw it in his eyes, the familiar coldness emerging and then shutting her out as the planes of his face transformed into a furious rigidity. He pulled away and Victoria jerked back as if she'd been burned.

"I can't," he said through clenched teeth, standing and backing away from the piano to put as much space between them as possible. "I'm sorry." Those two words eclipsed any sense of hurt she felt and she scowled at him.

"What is your *problem*?"

"I'm sorry, it's complicated and—"

"Save it," Victoria said, easing herself off the bench and gathering her things. She was proud of the firmness of her voice. "I heard you the first three times so the message is pretty clear. Fool me once, shame on you. Fool me twice, shame on me. I get it."

"Tori—"

"If you don't like me, just stay away from me. Go play your mind-games with someone else!"

She kept walking until she got to her car. Victoria couldn't understand Christian Devereux. He was like a human rollercoaster. One minute, they were laughing and having a great time, and then the next, he was angry and withdrawn, the latter usually after being in close proximity to her. He'd wanted to kiss her too—every instinct inside her had known that. But just like the other times, he'd let her get close and then pull away leaving her jolted and confused, and utterly devastated.

CHRISTIAN SAT ON the piano stool, feeling like a total cad. All the laughter in the room had left with her. He sat in the silence, his body shaking as the hunger ripped through him, razor-sharp. His control had been iron-clad until the moment she'd leaned into him, her natural appeal impossible to resist and his lips had almost been touching hers when he'd felt the points of his teeth pressing against the inside of his mouth. Reality had come swiftly—and violently—after that.

Victoria couldn't be more wrong; it wasn't that he didn't like her. He liked her far *too* much. He could recall every part of her face as if it had been etched into his mind—the wide, slanted emerald-green eyes, the dimple that flashed in her right cheek when she succumbed to a full-fledged smile, her inky, blue-black hair flashing tortuous glimpses of the long neck that dipped sinuously into the curve of her collarbone. She walked with the provocative grace of a dancer, and when she stepped into a room, he could think of little else.

Christian knew he was being reckless when it came to Tori Warrick. But for some reason he couldn't control himself when he was around her. He hadn't felt his human age in years but something about her made him feel like a fumbling awkward teenager. The moment she'd stared at him with those eyes on the piano stool, it was all he could do not to take her in his arms and do, well, what it was that he did. It had taken every ounce of his strength to step away.

Every vampire instinct in him wanted her with a savagery so intense it was decimating, and the only way he could control it had been to stay as far away from her as possible. But fate had not cooperated with his intentions, throwing them together at every turn. And despite his repeated avowals to stay away, each time he failed, drawn like a moth to a flame mindless of its own destruction.

When he'd seen her crying the last time, something in him had been desperate to comfort her and for a time, like her, he'd actually thought they could be friends. After she'd left, he'd run twenty miles just to get her out of his head, and even then she'd lingered, driving him to hunt with a ruthless violence he'd long since forgotten. This time, he knew with certainty that giving into his impulsive desire to be around her had been a mistake ... a terrible, irreversible, *stupid* mistake.

TEN

Secrets Revealed

VICTORIA WAS LOOKING forward to getting away, if only for a few days, over Columbus Day weekend with Holly in Millinocket. After the last episode with Dr. Jekyll and Mr. Idiot, she'd busied herself with classes and hours at the Black Dog, even taking on extra weekly shifts just so she wouldn't have to think. She'd caught up with Charla and Angie a few times, but for the most part she had just stayed on her own after classes.

Charla had jokingly told her that "hiding" was the fifth stage of lovesickness, and had vowed to find out Victoria's mystery crush. The threat of that alone had made Victoria hide even more to the point that she grew sick of her own company. So when Holly called to check in, Victoria had jumped at the chance to take some time and just get away from the source of all her stress.

She put Leto in his carrier and drove over to campus to return a book before she left. On her way back to her car, she noticed Angie sitting off to one side leaning on the stone balustrade of the library steps, chewing an apple and looking at her. Angie hadn't actually gotten any friendlier over the last few weeks, but at least now she deigned to converse with her—there was some sort of understanding that they were both friends of Charla's and although that didn't mean that *they* had to be friends, they could still be somewhat civil to each other.

"Hey," Angie said. "Have you seen Charla?" Victoria almost laughed. Everything had to be related back to Charla, like they couldn't have a normal conversation without it tying back to her in some ridiculous inane way.

"No, I haven't. Not since Wednesday." Victoria was trying to figure out how to leave without being rude, and then noticed the book that Angie had face down on the step next to her. "I didn't realize that you were interested in Wicca," she said before she could help herself.

Angie's smile was strained, more like a grimace. "I'm not," she said. She chewed a nail while still looking up at Victoria, conflicting emotions playing across her dour face. "Are *you*?" Victoria's eyes snapped to hers, shaken by her meaningful tone. Angie's face was calm but she looked almost smug. "I can always tell, you know. It's my gift."

"Tell what?" Victoria tried to keep her face expressionless, but her heart felt like it was lodged in her throat. Surely Angie couldn't possibly know what she was.

Angie rolled her dark eyes. "That you're a witch." She drawled the last word, rolling it insolently on her tongue. Victoria stared at her expressionlessly, waiting for her to continue. Angie didn't disappoint. "I'm not one, if that's what you're wondering. I can just see it in others."

"But how can you—"

"Colors." Angie cut her off, anticipating the question, and not even acknowledging that Victoria hadn't denied the statement. In

Angie's world, what she saw was absolute. "I see colors in the air around you, an aura I guess. Everyone has one, something like a unique signature. Like I said, it's my gift, although not something I'd ever ask for."

"Why are you telling me this, Angie?"

Victoria was curious. It wasn't as if they had spoken more than two words to each other on any given day, and now they were having a bizarre supernatural conversation that had come out of nowhere. The amulet began to heat up, smoldering under the light sweater she was wearing. She shifted uncomfortably.

"Well, I thought you should know," said Angie, "that I know, I mean. After all, I'm sure it's not something you want other people to know about."

"Wait a second! I never said—"

Angie interrupted Victoria before she could finish.

"Like I said, you don't have to. I know what I see." Angie's voice was authoritative and calm. Victoria sat heavily on the step and Angie continued to chew her nails, her eyes dark and fathomless. "Don't worry, I haven't told Charla."

After a while, Victoria asked quietly, "How do you know what the colors mean?" It was the first time that she had ever seen some kind of life come over Angie. Her eyes lit up and her face became animated. She looked like a different person, and Victoria was stunned at the transformation. Angie's tone remained guarded, but her whole manner was different.

"I don't know exactly, but, well, normal people look the same. Their colors are a little different but basically have the same patterns." She smiled a little proudly. "I can even tell what kind of people they are by the color differences. Yours on the other hand has a lot of shimmery reds and purples in it, with wavy black lines. The pattern is very distinct, luminous. I taught myself how to figure out what the colors mean. I'm almost never wrong."

"Does Gabe—"

"Gabriel's ... not like me," Angie said quickly. She seemed to be choosing her words carefully. "Don't worry." Victoria relaxed a little but she was still dazed by the conversation they were having. She felt vulnerable and uncomfortable that Angie of all people knew what she was, or at least claimed to know what she was.

"So do you see in neon all the time?" she asked, desperate to sound nonchalant. Angie actually laughed, a full-throated chuckle that made her normally severe face seem even pretty.

"No, only when I want to, like I'm doing with you now," she replied. "I have to focus."

Just that moment, out of the corner of her eye, Victoria was distracted by a tall lanky figure walking across the quad, and her heart raced uncontrollably. It was ridiculous the effect he had on her still! She tried to squish herself back into the cold stone of the staircase as if she wanted to make herself as invisible as possible, and noticed Angie's quizzical expression.

"What's with you? Your colors just went all fiery red and blotchy!" Angie unfocused her eyes and peered at Victoria's face. "Your face is super red, too." Then she looked around and noticed the cause of Victoria's reaction. "Oh," she said. Victoria stared at Angie helplessly and saw comprehension dawn, along with an imperceptible hardening of her eyes.

"Him," she said in distaste. "I really don't know what Charla sees in him either. He's colorless." She gathered up her book, apple core, and satchel and stood up. "I have to get to class. If you see Charla, tell her I was looking for her."

There it was again, the unfailing tieback to Charla. It made it seem as if their entire conversation had never even happened. Victoria nodded tightly, her throat dry. She was trying to force herself to not look at Christian. But unable to help herself, her eyes turned to him. Sensing her gaze, their eyes connected in an infinite split-second, but then he looked away and kept walking. Victoria felt like he had punched her in the stomach. She almost didn't hear the quiet voice beside her say, "I told you he was empty." She didn't even notice when Angie walked away.

Victoria didn't know how long she stayed on the steps, her eyes burning from the sting of unshed tears. It felt like she was crying about everything lately! After days of not even seeing him at rehearsal, she didn't know what she had expected, but it certainly wasn't him looking coldly through her as if she didn't exist. She should have known better, and trusted her instincts where he was concerned!

She ran to her car, stopped to get gas, and started on the three-hour trip, turning up the music as loud as she could stand and letting it drown out her pathetic thoughts. Leto mewed unhappily in his carrier from the chaos but she ignored his complaints, trying to think about anything but *him*.

She focused on the conversation she'd had with Angie and her uncanny ability to see people's "colors." When Angie had started talking about the colors, she had been genuinely animated and had looked *happy*! Still, Victoria was worried. They weren't really friends, and it wasn't like they were going to be now that Angie knew what she knew. Perhaps that was what the amulet sensed when it had grown hot, or maybe the heat had been a manifestation of her own fear. Either way, she knew she would have to be more careful around her.

Despite her efforts, her thoughts inevitably wound their way back to Christian. Victoria wondered what Angie had meant when she had said that he was "colorless." Was that a metaphor of some sort indicating that he was boring, or worse, incapable of being a nice human being? It had sounded like that, especially when she had said that he was empty.

Either way, despite his recent coldness, colorless would have been the last word that Victoria would have used to describe him. No matter what she did or how hard she tried to push him from her mind, she couldn't stop thinking about him. She wanted to hate him, to not think about the feel of his lips on hers or his gentleness when she'd cried about her parents or his inimitable grace with the violin. After two weeks, she thought her feelings would have diminished, but they had only gotten stronger. She needed to banish Christian Devereux from her head! He had obviously banished her from his.

Victoria pulled into Holly's driveway, and immediately felt better, the weight of everything from the past few weeks falling off her shoulders. Holly raced from the house and embraced her. Their reunion was delirious and they talked for hours. Holly filled Victoria in on all the local gossip. Victoria told Holly about Christian, except for certain pertinent details, and had a good cry, getting it out of her system. A dose of Holly was exactly what she'd needed.

The time went by quickly, and after just a couple days, Victoria was well rested. She'd taken long walks, enjoying the peace and quiet, and spent time exploring her abilities in more detail. After her unexpected run-in with Angie, Victoria realized that they only way she could protect herself from harm would be to learn about her gifts and be prepared to *use* them.

Leto was patient, teaching her simple spells and the words that were used to give the spells form and dimension. She discovered that as a familiar, he could not perform magic on his own, but he was a veritable treasure trove of magical lore. Under his tutelage, she learned quickly.

Try this one, he told her. MUTO CAPILLUS. *It's a glamour.*

"MUTO CAPILLUS," she said, and watched as her hair shimmered into a pale blonde. "That's amazing! How do I go back to normal?"

RECURRO CAPILLUS.

Victoria parroted his words and her hair reassumed its natural color. She frowned thoughtfully.

"But why do I need the words, Leto? I've performed magic without them. If I think hard enough I can do a glamour without any words." She stared at him intently and watched as his silver-colored fur metamorphosed into black and white polka dots. "See?"

You're not like most witches, Victoria. Most others have to use words to shape the magic or it won't respond. Even though your own magic is not defined by words, they can still help to increase the potency of your spells.

"That's good to know."

Wonderful. Now change me back.

The magic came easily to Victoria, and it made her feel better than she had in weeks. It felt good knowing that she was learning to control the strange and sometimes overwhelming power inside of her. She couldn't change who she was, but if she learned enough, maybe one day, she'd be able to control the demands of the blood and not end up like her ancestor, Brigid. Despite her fear, that had been the tipping point—Victoria vowed that she would *never* become a slave to the blood.

The amulet, too, felt as if it were harmonized to her every feeling, like a mood ring she'd worn when she was younger. She was fascinated by its unerring ability to warn against danger, and as much as she tried to outwit it, she found that it always flared hot whenever she endangered herself. Each time she mastered a new spell, the amulet warmed with approval.

It was heady and frightening at the same time.

She became adept at moving things with a simple command, "effero," and bending others to her will, which Leto definitely did not like, especially when she made him walk into the ice-cold spring in the back yard. He retaliated with a vicious swipe of his paw on her leg, which healed on its own at an unspoken command, "curo," from her mind.

Shall we try teleporting? Leto asked her one afternoon while Holly was out grocery shopping.

"Didn't you say it was really difficult? As in things-can-go-terribly-wrong difficult?" Victoria said, frowning.

It's an important spell. I'd rather you get hurt now than later.

She backed away warily. "Hurt? I don't—"

Leto hissed in her direction. *See that tree over there near the spring? Clear your mind and focus on a spot near it. Say "transeo" when you are ready. The destination* must *be clear.*

Victoria scowled at his tone but took a deep breath and focused on the spot he'd said, envisioning it clearly in her head.

"TRANSEO!"

It felt like everything was being sucked into her belly button and then all of a sudden she was standing near the tree, the wind knocked out of her. Momentarily disoriented, she felt exhilarated with success until pain jackhammered through her leg. She looked down. A fallen branch skewered her calf, blood spurting everywhere. Lightheaded, she crumpled to the dirt, and gingerly tugged it from her leg.

"CURO," she gritted through clenched teeth, and watched as

the wound healed before her eyes.

That was relatively painless, Leto said. *Let's try it again when you're ready.*

Victoria made a choked noise. "Relatively *painless*? You're a sadist, Leto."

At least you didn't get fused to the tree trunk. Victoria blanched. *Trust me, I've seen far worse.*

After some practice, Victoria grew to understand the nuances needed to successfully teleport. Leto explained it succinctly.

It's physics. Mass and matter displacement, he thought to her. *Certain materials will give to support a teleported object. In other cases, the reverse is true. With the tree branch, blood and tissue gave.*

Victoria learned quickly, moving inanimate and animate things alike, seemingly without effort, and a few times, she'd almost slipped up with Holly.

Once, Holly walked into the kitchen when Victoria was pouring herself a cup of coffee, only from the *other* side of the room. She'd coughed loudly to distract Holly, and set the cup down gently.

Later that same night in her room, Leto confided something she'd wondered herself.

I think she knows the truth of what we are. Victoria was startled.

Of what we are?

His green eyes glittered. *I have something to confess. I also belonged to your grandmother.* Victoria stared at him, frowning.

But that would make you over eighty years old! How long do familiars live? You could be five thousand years old for all I know, no wonder you're so grumpy half the time, she said with a grin.

Leto paused giving her a sidelong glance. *Not that old. But back to the start of the conversation, I think Holly knew about Emmeline.*

Should we ask her?

Perhaps you can look first, he said pointedly.

"Leto, I can't just go into her head! She's family and that's intruding! I do have a few principles," Victoria said aloud. "While we're on the subject, there has to be rules. What's to stop me from controlling someone's mind completely?"

Nothing. You could if you so wished, Leto said, nonchalant.

Her eyes flicked to his. "Then that makes me just like Brigid," she said. Her eyes remained on Leto. *I will not use this power at the expense of everything I cherish and love, against what I know is right. I won't.*

Leto's expression did not change as she left the room but she could sense something like disappointment radiating from his thoughts. It puzzled her. Did he *want* her to control people? To use her powers in a way that went against everything good inside of her?

For the first time, Victoria understood that the gray area between right and wrong had become larger, and more indistinct. Things, once simple, were more complicated. Black and white blurred into each other, and with this strange power of hers, intent wouldn't always be enough, it could always be twisted.

Was she strong enough? Or would she succumb to the dark side of her power that terrified her? Would she become Brigid? She could still feel the weight of Leto's thoughts pressing in upon her. Victoria fled from his presence but his thoughts still followed.

Don't be afraid of who you are. You cannot hope to control your power if you do not understand it and who you are. You must protect yourself at all costs, even against those you … love. He hesitated lost for a moment, and Victoria felt his thoughts flicker briefly into a strange nothingness before moving back to the consciousness she recognized. His words were hard. *Love is a breeding ground for betrayal. Guard against it.*

Unable to bear any more, she closed her mind to him.

At dinner that night, she stared furtively at Holly, wondering how and whether she could broach the subject.

"Darling, if you slice that chicken any more, you won't need to chew it." Victoria stared down at her plate and laughed at the pile of shredded food.

"Sorry, just distracted about something."

"What is it, dear?"

"Aunt Holly, did you … did my grandmother ever tell you anything about her?"

"Like what?"

"Things about her past? Who she was? Did you ever notice anything different or strange about her?"

"Darling, is something wrong?" Holly looked concerned. "Why don't you just tell me what's bothering you? Did you find something of Emmeline's in your music box?"

"I think my grandmother had secrets, a lot of secrets that she kept hidden, things like the music box and the amulet, and … I was just wondering if you … knew anything," she finished lamely.

Victoria paused, maybe Leto was right, a flash of Holly's consciousness would be easier, and safer—No!—she would try to be more specific. "Did you ever see her *do* anything? Make things happen, you know, as if by magic?" She stared at her plate, flushed from saying it aloud. "Forget about it, it's nothing."

The sound of Holly's laughter filled the room, and Victoria's head snapped up. "I was wondering when you'd get around to asking me about Emmeline's abilities." Holly stood and walked over to sit on the chair nearest Victoria, and grasped her hands in hers.

"You *knew*? All this time and you never said anything?"

"I couldn't. She made me promise, only until you came to

me," Holly said with a sad smile. "I don't know everything, just what Emmeline told me. About what she was, and what you are. When she died ..." Holly choked, "she made me swear to always look out for you, and for Leto."

"Leto?"

"Yes, didn't he tell you?"

Betrayed by those you love? she hissed mentally, pushing her savage feelings out toward Leto and feeling him recoil from their force. *You* knew! *Was it another one of your tests? Was it?* Her words thrust themselves into his mind like daggers. She could feel him blocking her but she tore past his defenses. *You want me to be cruel, use my power to control ... to hurt! How does it feel? How* does *it* feel?

I was also bound, Victoria. I am sorry. Leto's words were gasps, and belatedly, Victoria realized that she was crushing him so terribly with the force of her own mind that he was barely conscious. She released him with a strangled cry. Holly reached for her automatically.

"No," Victoria said in a hoarse voice. "Don't touch me. I'm monstrous."

"Tori, darling, you are not," Holly said. "You have every right to be upset. It's human to be angry. But you must pull yourself in. You must control your anger—it is the one thing that you cannot afford to give in to." Holly held Victoria's shoulders firmly, her voice urgent. "Victoria? Do you understand?"

"Yes." *The blood.* Victoria could feel it uncoiling like a giant snake within her, flexing ... testing the walls of her all-too fragile control of it. She heaved several breaths into her body, her fingers reaching for the amulet, hot against her chest. The word flashed into her brain.

Soporo, she thought. Everything slowed and calmed. Her

eyes caught Holly's and she managed a wan smile. "I'm okay now," she said, releasing her death grip on the amulet. Holly touched the pendant, thoughtful, before brushing a stray strand of hair out of Victoria's face.

"Emmeline told me that you must never ever take off this amulet. She said that it is the only thing that can protect you when all else fails. It is the key to controlling your magic. She also told me that I must tell you not to underestimate those who would covet this power of yours."

Victoria's stare was guarded. "So you know? What … I am?"

A gentle nod. "Yes."

"I don't want this, any of this," Victoria whispered.

"Oh my darling, not everyone wants what they are born with. One person's gift is another's curse. But you are who you are, Tori, and who you choose to become is entirely up to you."

"Did you know all this, all along, when I was in the hospital?"

"Yes … no … I did but … no …" Holly stopped, confused. Leto came to her aid.

She knew, but only when you asked about Emmeline's secrets was she able to remember, he explained.

A spell?

Yes, to protect not just you, but also Holly. Emmeline was very … protective of both of you. Leto's thoughts felt weak, and Victoria cringed, knowing how terribly she'd hurt him. It was so easy to let power become undermined by emotions—far too easy.

To Holly, she said, "Leto says it was a spell to protect us." To Leto, she sent her naked regret and as if that wasn't enough, she followed it with the words.

I'm so sorry, Leto. Forgive me.

Forgiven, child.

Victoria turned to Holly, unable to find the words to say to this wonderful, generous, amazing woman who'd looked after her so selflessly, and carried such a terrible burden of knowledge for the sake of her friend's granddaughter. Overwhelmed, she hugged Holly tightly.

"Will you tell me about her?"

Holly smiled. "I thought you'd never ask."

ELEVEN

Eye for an Eye

WHEN VICTORIA RETURNED to Windsor, it was just after seven o'clock. She had a message on her answering machine from Tony at the Black Dog checking to see if she could work a short shift that night. She wasn't tired so she unpacked her overnight bag, got right back into the Mini and headed down Main Street to the Dog. She also wanted something mundane to take her mind off of everything she'd just learned about Holly, her grandmother, and her own powers. She wanted *normal* for a couple hours, and then she'd allow herself to dissect it into manageable pieces.

For a Monday, the place was packed. Students from both Windsor and Harland frequented the Black Dog, and it wasn't a surprise that there weren't many free seats in the place. She waved to Charla, Angie, and several of their friends as she walked to the bar. The time passed quickly and the bar was still pumping at midnight with no signs of slowing down. A familiar face drew her attention and she smiled.

"Hi Gabriel, what can I get you?" she said.

"Sara's twenty-one! What's her drink?" Gabriel said, grinning.

It had become an in-house Black Dog tradition during the last few weeks to have Victoria Warrick, bartender extraordinaire, pick out the special birthday drink for anyone celebrating a birthday at the Black Dog. The trick was to predict their choice of drink, and given her abilities, she was unfailingly perfect at it. She rationalized her brief intrusion in their minds with the excuse that they were going to order the drink anyway, so she wasn't really prying, and it was just a harmless game.

Victoria didn't hesitate to place a Sex-on-the-Beach cocktail on the bar, and everyone dissolved into laughter, including Gabriel. It wouldn't have been so funny if Sara didn't run the "Abstinence Until Marriage" coalition at Harland. Out of the corner of her eye, Victoria caught Angie's knowing smile but she ignored it despite her immediate unease. Sara accepted both the drink and the jibes with good humor.

"If I'm going to wait, I may as well enjoy the drink, right?" Sara said with a laugh. "Thanks, Tori!"

Personally Victoria didn't think that Sara was as crazy as most of the other girls seemed to think she was—she hadn't done "the deed" either. Ever since Brett, she had a healthy fear of losing control, and frankly, sex wasn't something that interested her. A fleeting vision of Christian came to her, and she felt her ears grow hot. Well, maybe it interested her a little. Or not! She banished the traitorous thought with a fierce frown. Not with him anyway, Christian Devereux meant *nothing* to her.

"Whatever it is, I don't think it has much time to live," said a dry voice.

"What?" Victoria said.

"Whatever you're glowering at like it's the devil," Gabriel said.

"No, I'm fine, just distracted about something silly, not even worth worrying about." She smiled brightly at him.

"Well, let me know if I can help. I'm a good listener."

"Thanks Gabe, I will."

"So, can I ask you something?" he asked. "How do you do it, Tori? The drink thing? How do you get it right every time? Is it like ESP?"

"I wish," she said. "I'm only right half of the time really. It's just a logical guessing game based on what they've had in the past." She avoided his eyes and pasted a vacuous expression on her face. He frowned.

"You've been right every time I've been here."

"I'm sure I get it wrong a lot actually, but I think people just play along for fun."

At that moment, Charla and Angie came over to say hello, and Gabriel left after shooting a nasty look at Angie. Victoria was grateful for the interruption. Lying always made her nervous.

The girls ordered two sodas, which Victoria gave them on the house despite a dark look from Tony. Charla was her talkative self as usual, going on and on about her weekend in Boston, and Angie spoke in monosyllables, giving no indication that they'd had more than a civil conversation just a few days before.

In the midst of listening to Charla's breakdown of a guy she had met in Boston at a baseball game, Victoria felt him come in even before she saw him. She kept her face calm—a fair feat, given the fact that her body felt like it was on fire. She was already red-faced from the heat of the bar and hoped that Angie wasn't using her "second sight." She refused to acknowledge him and busied herself serving a round of drinks to the people at the far end of the bar.

Christian Devereux means nothing to me.

Victoria saw him nod to a few people he knew, waiting and

watching her openly. She tried to ignore him but his heavy-lidded stare made her feel cornered like she was in some cat-and-mouse game she didn't really understand. He tore his gaze from her lips when she glared rudely at him and stomped down toward his end of the bar. As she approached, she heard his attempt at casual conversation. "I hear there's a birthday special here." She instantly tried to turn around and duck out the back, but it was too late as the chanting began, sung by the overzealous bar patrons.

"Birthday! Birthday! BIRTHDAY!"

"Okay, fine," Victoria said. "Last one tonight though, okay?" She looked at Christian, and fought an involuntary urge to flee. In that single glance, she could see his remorse, but instinct together with the amulet scorching her skin, warned her not to give in. Victoria knew she could not fall prey to whatever lay behind those compelling eyes.

"Stop looking at me like that," she hissed under her breath.

"Like what?"

"You know exactly well like what! Like ... like I'm ... something to *eat*!" His smile deepened, transforming the austere planes of his face and catching her by surprise.

"Is that so bad?"

"Is it really even your birthday?" she countered, ignoring the question that had started a slow burn in her chest.

"Tori, what happened a few weeks ago, it's not what you think." His voice was quiet, for her ears only. She resisted its velvet undertones.

"Wait, don't answer that," she said. "I don't care."

She steeled herself against his gaze and focused her mind toward his. She was met with the same brick wall as before. Without a second thought, she looked at him head on and released the full force of her power, engaging everything she'd learned about herself and her magic over the last few weeks. Christian's lips parted and his eyes widened in astonishment. Within seconds, it was over and she deftly mixed a drink, placing a Bloody Mary on the table in front of him.

"It was the closest thing we had to what you wanted, and you're underage so virgin it is."

An amused smile crossed his face but he picked up the drink and inclined his head toward her. Everyone cheered. He sipped it as she disappeared out the back yelling to Tony that she was going to take a few minutes to herself.

Victoria sat in the small break room holding a glass of water and took a deep calming breath. The Bloody Mary had been a wild guess, because for some reason, she couldn't get past the feeling that he wanted a drink with the word blood in it. She cast her thoughts back. She wasn't sure how she'd done it, but when she had pushed past Christian's initial defenses, she'd seen a lot.

What had really surprised her was the barely discernable energy she had sensed, as if he possessed special abilities himself. Something told her that he was hiding more, deeper still, because just as she'd withdrawn, she'd felt something else, but it was so brief she wasn't sure what it'd been.

She'd also seen his regret for how he'd behaved but he'd been wearing that on his sleeve the minute he had walked through the door. It had gone some way to mollifying her hurt, until she understood something else inside his head, something that had made the breath whoosh out of her in a painful rush; a thought he'd wanted to keep hidden but still flashed loud and clear—they could never be together.

Enough is enough, she told herself fiercely. *You have your answer. Move on.*

When she came back out to the front, she felt Christian

watching her, but she deliberately did not look at him and walked down to the opposite end of the bar where Charla and Angie were saying their goodbyes.

"You guys heading out?" Victoria said to Angie.

"Charla has an assignment due tomorrow, so we're going to call it a night."

"Can I ask you something?" Victoria whispered, leaning in. When Angie nodded surprised, she continued. "When we were talking last week, you said something about Christian Devereux being colorless. What did you mean by that?"

"That's what I meant. Colorless." Victoria's blank stare made Angie clarify. "As in no color at all. As in dead," she said. Angie leaned closer to Victoria, her stringent face anxious. "He's not good for you, Tori."

Victoria was so stunned by the fact that Angie had called her Tori that she barely took in the fact that Angie was warning her off.

"Wait, I don't understand what you mean by dead."

"He's not human."

As if she'd said too much, Angie gave her a searching look and left without another word. Victoria could feel Christian's eyes boring into her.

Not human. Not human. Not human.

The words drummed in time with her chaotic pulse, making her palms clammy.

Tori, look at me. The silent command was inviting, compelling. Victoria's heart raced even as her brain registered that his words had been spoken inside her head.

Why should I? So I can serve as your punching bag some more? She felt his sadness. *I am sorry. It's … complicated.*

How complicated can it be, Christian? You've made it pretty clear how you feel about me every time you are near me. It's exhausting. I just want you to stay away from me.

I ... cannot.

I am not doing this with you. I won't. I can feel every part of you pushing me way. If I'm that horrible, then just leave me alone.

Tori, look at me. She clenched her teeth as he opened himself to her, the raw feelings he conveyed undermining her will far more than any words could. She steeled herself. She'd *seen* all of his excuses, all the reasons why he couldn't allow himself to feel anything for her. She didn't understand why, but it'd been as clear as day—he was not meant for her.

Please, Tori, he said.

No.

You must. She felt the surge of his compelling magnetism. She brushed it aside like a troublesome fly, turning to look him directly in the eye.

I don't know who or what you are, but try that again, and I will hurt you. Get out of my head, Christian! She held his gaze before her final push. *You are not meant for me.*

Although she knew he was prepared, especially after the last time she'd knocked him over, it gave her great satisfaction to see his eyes widen as she forcefully shoved him out, erecting an impenetrable fortress around her mind. She moved further down the bar to put as much distance between them as possible and gravitated recklessly toward a familiar face.

"Hi Gabe!" she said over-brightly, throwing caution to the wind. Her tone was warm and flirtatious.

Gabriel leaned forward, his tanned forearms pressing on the bar, giving her a charming smile of his own. "So if I said it was my birthday, what would be my drink of choice?" His tone matched hers, and Victoria was too agitated to listen to the voice of reason in her head. She gave him a coy smile, leaning forward.

"Is it your birthday, Gabriel?"

"No, but I was hoping for a freebie."

The bar erupted in cheers, and took up the chant of "Freebie!" with uproarious glee. Victoria put her hands on her hips, playing along shamelessly, putting into play all of the feminine wiles she had been born with, but had never been a fan of using.

Until then.

"It looks like … you want …" People leaned forward in anticipation. She peeked through her lashes toward the end of the bar, registering the expression of contempt on Christian's face as he glared at Gabriel.

Gabriel raised his eyebrows in cool challenge, and Victoria didn't hesitate, an instinctive response born out of wanting to make Christian *react* just a little bit, to make him pay for the hurt she'd suffered at his hands.

"I'm just not quite sure whether you want it …" She paused for dramatic effect. "Shaken or stirred." Then she leaned forward and planted a light kiss on Gabriel's lips.

She didn't hear the snarl, she *felt* it, but before she could react, the crowd erupted, clapping Gabriel on the back and laughing noisily. Gabriel looked at her and winked, ordered a Coke, and then headed back over to his friends who were laughing and cheering like idiots.

Victoria waited a couple minutes as a wave of embarrassment overcame her, and felt a stab of disappointment as she saw the empty seat. She felt strangely drained and stupid. She'd wanted to teach Christian a lesson, to show him that his kiss and his thoughts had meant little to her, but it had only backfired. She felt worse than ever.

CHRISTIAN STOOD OUTSIDE the bar, his clenched fists drawing blood in his palms. He wanted to destroy something, anything to offset the fury that consumed him. Having skipped rehearsals, the need to see her had been tormenting, its ache relentless, and he'd come to the bar because nothing else could assuage it. He had tortured himself watching her flirt with Gabriel, watching the long line of her neck bend toward him, watching her long fingers on the cusp of her hips as she leaned back provocatively, watching her lips press onto his in agonizing slow motion, and worst of all, her doing those things *knowing* that he had been watching.

Losing control was a risk that he simply could not afford. He couldn't fathom how she made him so uncontrollable, so violent with just a look or a word. His usual defenses were like paper before her, not just because she was an accomplished witch, but because she was *her*. If he had stayed one more second, he wouldn't have been able to control his actions, and he would have torn that boy to pieces, along with everyone else in that bar.

And the clincher, her words—*you are not meant for me.* She'd taken them straight from his head, straight from the laws that bound him. How could she possibly understand what they meant? All she'd seen were the words themselves and believed them to be his. Explaining that law to a human would mean breaking another law.

He leaned his head against the cool stone of the wall, suddenly weary. The way she'd looked at him when she'd given him the drink had stunned him. She'd looked at him as if she recognized something, and it had made him feel very uncomfortable. He couldn't remember the last time something had made him uneasy, but he was slowly getting used to the unpredictable emotions that Victoria, more often than not, was able to arouse within him.

As he stood in the cold alleyway, all he could think about was the feel of her lips on his and her imperious voice telling him to get out of her head. Christian raked his hands through his hair. It had been a long time since he'd thought about self-preservation, but this was like nothing he had ever experienced—this feeling was like acid, eating away at his very essence. He'd never felt such terror or joy in equal abundance.

He closed his eyes, barely able to admit the truth to himself.

She was already in his blood.

TWELVE

Revelation

VICTORIA SPENT THE next two weeks buried in midterms and trying to figure out how she could have possibly made such a mess of things. She hadn't seen Christian since the disaster in the bar. He'd either stopped rehearsing or he was careful to be at the music hall whenever she wasn't there. She'd found herself playing the Tchaikovsky piece more than once after rehearsal, hoping despite herself that he'd show up to partner her. But he never did.

Harland could have been on the other side of the state for all she saw of him. Victoria was certain it was deliberate. She didn't blame him one bit. She wanted to apologize for her appalling behavior but she didn't know what she would say if she did see him. As the days turned into weeks, eventually she stopped looking for him.

After a particularly punishing midterm following a predawn study session, she'd caught up with Angie and Charla at the cafeteria, where she had immediately zoned out, eating a salad and letting Charla's chatter resonate in the background. She was exhausted. On top of everything, they'd had their first dusting of snow, and it had grown unexpectedly cold in the space of a few days, so all in all, not really a perfect day.

Suddenly, Charla jumped up and Victoria's eyes snapped open.

"Oh, no! Gotta run, catch you girls later. Don't forget the ski trip, okay, Tori?"

Ski trip? Victoria blinked seeing a bleary vision of Charla moving away.

Charla was always running late for something, but rather than being annoying, it was part of what made her Charla. Angie and Victoria shared a look and rolled their eyes at the same time. As they both came back to reality, the moment of camaraderie dissolved and they stared at each other in uncomfortable silence.

Angie went back to writing in her notebook, and Victoria continued eating. She didn't mind the silence. Truth was, she was starting to like Angie. Victoria liked her natural quietness and the way Angie hadn't treated her, Victoria, like she was a freak when she had discovered what she was. Not that Angie would, given what *she* was, but just that she hadn't. Still, that didn't make them best friends, but it was enough for them to be civil.

Victoria finished her salad as Angie doodled absently on a page from her binder, and what had started out as an awkward silence changed into a fairly relaxed one as they sat, each preoccupied with her own thoughts.

"You can ask me if you want to, Tori," Angie said, without looking up. Victoria swallowed and took a sip of her Diet Pepsi.

"Why did you say what you did about him?"

"Because that's what I saw." Angie leaned forward, real anxiety in her face. "He's dangerous, Tori." She hesitated as if she wanted to say more but clamped her lips shut, doodling fiercely.

Victoria sighed. She looked at Angie and quickly squashed the wave of guilt she felt before she did a quick flash of Angie's mind.

In the milliseconds it took, Victoria confirmed exactly what Angie had said down to the smallest detail. She really was straightforward; everything was just there in simple black and white. No more, no less. As she relaxed, Angie looked up at her with a quizzical expression.

"What?" Victoria asked guiltily.

"Nothing. Your black lines got really dark for a second. It was weird."

Victoria flushed. "I think I'm getting a migraine. On top of midterms, I'm studying for the PSAT. My brain is going to explode."

"So use magic."

Victoria choked and almost spat a mouthful of Pepsi all over the table. "What?" she spluttered.

"I would, that's all. See, it's pretty simple to me. If you have a talent that makes you do something better, you'd use it, wouldn't you? Well, you should ... use your talent, I mean."

"Why don't you use *your* talent?" Victoria shot back, suddenly disoriented at the conversation's turn. Angie gave her a measured look before leaning forward.

"I don't think it's the same thing, but okay, I'll play. Look around you. What do you see?"

Victoria glanced around the crowed cafeteria. It looked the same as it did every other day—the jocks in one corner, the blondes at the table next to them, the nerds in another corner. It was like every other high school cafeteria.

"I see kids eating." She looked at Angie. "What's your point?"

"Know what I see?" she asked, gesturing with an open palm toward the other tables. Victoria frowned, deducing what Angie was going to say even before she said it, and started shaking her head.

"I see you understand already," Angie said. "We're not exactly the only *different* people at Windsor."

"What do you mean, different?"

An exasperated look. "Did you think we were the only ones? Not all of these students are human. Hang on a sec." Victoria watched in incredulous surprise as Angie stared around the crowded cafeteria, and unfocused her eyes, invoking her special Sight. She pointed to three tables over from where they were sitting. "Over there I see a fairy eating with a team of football players, and over by the drinks, a werewolf."

Victoria glanced at the boy getting a soda. She recognized him as a quiet, slight boy from her calculus class.

"Matthew?" And then a thought occurred to her. "Hold up a second, did you just say you saw a *fairy* eating with *football* players?" Angie nodded, turning to her as they both collapsed into shared mirth.

"You're making it up!" Victoria giggled.

"I'm not kidding. He's a fairy as shimmery as they come with wings and everything. Cute, if you like sparkles." Angie's unexpected drollness took Victoria by surprise but she grinned back.

She remained unconvinced as she stared at the burly linebacker, but Angie had known she was a witch when no one had. It stood to reason that if she, Victoria existed then other ... things did as well. Brigid's journal entries of fey and werewolves and vampires filled her thoughts. She reassessed Angie's unruffled expression.

She leaned toward Angie, her smile fading. "You're *not* kidding? Are you?"

"I wish. They're everywhere. Some have glamours and look like you and me. Others don't, they're invisible to the human eye."

"Are they everywhere you look?"

"Pretty much. I don't know what it is but supernatural things love it here in Canville. Maybe it's the woods. They're everywhere. Things that belong in books like goblins, and shape-shifters, and trolls with fur and scales, thorns and curled horns." Angie shivered as if the mere memory of them terrified her. "You wouldn't believe some of the things I've seen." Her eyes clouded. "Sometimes they hurt each other. Badly."

"I'm sorry," Victoria said, at a loss for words. Angie would have to be a spectacular actress to look *that* afraid of something just in her head.

Angie went quiet for a minute. "I used to wish I was blind. I wanted to cut my own eyes out," she whispered. "I think I even tried one time. But what can you do? You are who you are, right? So I'm careful. And I only have one rule."

"What's that?"

"Never, ever let them see me looking."

Angie shrugged at the horrified expression Victoria knew she must have on her face. "Don't worry, they're not that bad," she said, and then paused, reconsidering her words. "Most of them, anyway. They tend to stick with their own kind, like what you'd usually see, the jocks and the Mathletes and the—what do you call them again? Oh right, the Stepfords."

The thought of where Christian would fit in flashed through Victoria's mind. Her question was tentative, but she wanted to know. "Angie? When you said that Christian wasn't human, what did you mean? What, exactly, *is* he?"

Before Angie could answer, someone stopping at their table interrupted their quiet conversation. It was the boy who'd been over by the drinks. Victoria saw Angie blanch.

"Hey Tori, you heading to class?" Wolfboy's voice was guttural despite his slight appearance. Victoria glanced at Angie who'd gone perfectly still. Her fear, though veiled, was real.

"Hey Matt. Sure," Victoria said. "I'll catch you later, Angie."

As she gathered her things, Victoria hesitated. Maybe there

was a way she could see as Angie did. Without looking at Matthew, she pushed her senses out toward him as unobtrusively as possible, the reverse of what she'd done with Christian. Holding her breath, Victoria peeled past Matthew's human glamour and slid into his mind.

It felt … raw, and distinctly not human. The amulet flared against her skin. She pushed deeper and then recoiled in immediate horror as the truth of what he was flashed into her consciousness in terrifying, gruesome, graphic detail. She stepped back, her eyes snapping to Angie's. Angie glared at her and Victoria remembered what she'd said about being careful.

"You ready?" Wolfboy asked. Victoria let the glamour slip back into place. She tried to focus on his boyish face and ignore the fact that he was a ferocious beast who could tear anyone limb from limb in seconds.

"R … ready?"

"For the test?" Matt raised thin blond eyebrows questioningly but all Victoria saw was the memory of callused ridges of hairy flesh above a flattened, elongated snout, and orange-hued lightless eyes. She fought back a shudder.

"As ready as I can be." For a second, Victoria wasn't sure whether she was talking about the midterm or something else entirely.

She felt Angie's eyes on them the entire way out of the building.

THE AFTERNOON HAD turned into a dark, cold evening by the time Victoria finished her final midterm for Calculus, and she pulled her jacket tighter as she walked down the library steps to the parking lot. Charla had called earlier asking her to meet up for dinner, but she was far too tired. Her brain was still spinning with a nauseating combination of derivatives, limits and quotients, and fairies, werewolves and witches. She just wanted to get back to her apartment, eat some takeout, and go to bed.

She unlocked and started her car with a single unspoken command to warm the engine and get the heat going, and almost jumped out of her skin when she saw Christian leaning against the hood of his silver car parked opposite hers. Her heart hammered to life.

"Impressive," he said. Victoria stared at him silently. Everything else in her head disappeared but him. There was so much she wanted to say, to apologize for. She knew that she had hurt him by kissing Gabe and no matter what had happened between them or what she'd seen in his thoughts, he hadn't deserved it.

"Christian ..." she began.

"Have dinner with me, Tori," he said. His face was haunted, his eyes shadowed but inviting. Victoria knew that she couldn't refuse him, and even as tired as she was and despite everything she'd learned from Angie, she only wanted to be near him again. So she nodded and relocked her car.

The ride to Christian's house was silent, and other than the soft background noise, the only sound in the car was their breathing. He looked tired, his angular face made even sharper by the shadows under his eyes, but still her pulse raced at his closeness. She felt her breath stop when he quietly slid his hand into hers as they pulled into his curving driveway.

They walked into the foyer of the house and Victoria bit back a gasp. It was as magnificent on the inside as it had appeared from the outside. Warm, rich mahogany floors led into a large entrance hall with two sweeping curved staircases winged out on either side. Beautiful cathedral ceilings opened up to a prism-like sky light in the foyer.

Christian, still silent, pulled her into his arms and buried his face in her hair. It wasn't at all what she'd expected. Her heart drummed a familiar tune in her chest, a tune that every logical part of her fought futilely against. She didn't want him to be this way— she preferred him arrogant or hateful, not soft and contrite as he was now. It made it too difficult to be indifferent and to not give in to her bewildering feelings for him.

He moved, pressing his cool cheek against her hair.

"Christian, I'm so sorry," she whispered. "I didn't mean—"

"It's forgotten. I was the cause, I see that now."

"But you didn't deserve—"

He pressed his thumb over her lips quieting her, and brushed it back and forth, his face strained and unreadable, but warm.

"Why don't we start over?" he said. "I'm Christian."

"Tori," she whispered.

"Enchanté, Tori." He kissed her on both cheeks in the French custom and Victoria felt as if her knees were melting.

She hesitated, still wary, but didn't move until Christian took her hand and led her toward the back of the house where there was a large, comfortable den. As they sat down, a tiny Asian man appeared, carrying a tray of food along with a bottle of red wine, which he placed on the coffee table. He left as silently as he had come in.

Victoria hadn't realized how ravenous she was and she inhaled the simple meal. She noticed that Christian didn't eat. He only sipped a bit of the wine while she ate, and when she looked inquiringly at him, he assured her that he had eaten earlier. When she was full, she sat back into the cushions and curled her feet beneath her.

"Tori," Christian began, his voice husky, "I have tried to escape this thing between us, to push you out of my mind, but I can't. The truth is that you haunt my dreams and my every waking moment."

"Is that so bad?" she said, echoing his words at the bar.

"Yes." He sighed. "I brought you here to talk to you, Tori. You should stay away from me. It's for your own good. What you saw before inside my mind was real—I *am* bound by a covenant to stay away from you."

"I don't understand. I thought—"

"In my world, for us to be together has terrible consequences. There are laws in place that forbid it."

"What laws? What *world*?"

"The laws of my world." He stared at her, understanding her confusion; she didn't know what he was. "And it's not fair to you because you don't know … what …" He looked away as if the words were choking him.

"What?" she said. "Christian, please just tell me."

"What I am," he finished. "It's better if you see. I won't block you Tori, but please promise me one thing."

"Anything," she said, as he raised a palm for her to listen.

"Promise me that you will give me a chance to explain." Victoria stared at him, startled by what sounded like fear in his voice.

"Okay?" he said. She nodded. His smile was strained as he clasped her hands.

Victoria cleared her mind and took a deep breath, her clammy fingers grasping his tightly. She reached forward tentatively and entered his mind, his walls gone. What she found was, Christian, his sensitivity, his sharp intelligence, his bare uncluttered feelings for her. She wanted to bask in them, bask in the feelings she now understood as mirroring her own.

Keep going, please. You must know it all, he thought to her. *You must see me.*

She forced herself go further, glimpsing his childhood, his

adolescence and his older years. And further still, so many images in the older years that she became confused, something was off about the timing and the way he looked so *consistent* in all of the images. She went deeper still, following the shadows down, down, down, until she found herself on the edge of a cloying darkness— the thing she'd sensed briefly at the bar.

Victoria felt Christian's hands squeeze reassuringly against hers and she pushed against it. Without warning, it shifted into something heavy that enveloped her, her skin crawling as if hundreds of roaches covered every inch of her body. A red-eyed face formed in the darkness. The monster grinned, its distended fangs bloodied and gleaming, and a salty, metallic tanginess coated her tongue. She tasted blood.

Angie's words echoed like thunder in her mind—*not human, not human, not human*. With wild strength Victoria withdrew, wrenching her hand out of Christian's now slackened grip. His expression was unfathomable.

"You're a—" she gasped, incoherent, scooting her body to the far end of the sofa. She tasted the phantom blood again and swallowed the hot bile in her throat along with the words that wouldn't come. Angie was wrong—he'd been human once, just not anymore.

Christian stared at her, his fists clenched in his lap. There was no way he could explain or condone what he was. From her reaction, he was prepared for the worst. It seemed like eons had passed until she finally spoke, her gaze burning into his.

"You're not human." It was not a question.

"No."

"You're a vampire."

"Yes."

Victoria closed her eyes, her breathing harsh in the deafening silence, her heartbeat erratic. Christian was a vampire. *A vampire!* As in a dead thing that needed to drink blood to stay alive. It seemed like an absurdity—the physical beauty of him and the ugly truth of what he was. The knowledge was staggering.

Still, like her, he wielded a terrible power and was capable of committing many horrible things, but that didn't make him a terrible person. The words Brigid had written flooded her mind ... liaisons between witches and vampires, the Undead, were forbidden. How much had he risked to show her what he was? Humbled by his trust, Victoria moved closer and touched his cool face with her palm.

"You're still Christian. Beneath what you are, it's still you." Her hands trembled, the amulet searing into her skin even as the words left her lips.

"Victoria, I am not that boy anymore." Christian's laugh was jarring, the ugly sound echoing in the room. "I'm not him. This"—he gestured at himself—"body is not alive. It's a dead monster that steals life from others. Didn't you see what I *am*?"

"Christian." She said his name so quietly that it gentled him even before she placed both hands on his side of his head. "I know what you are, I saw it. What I am trying to tell you is that I also saw how you feel about me. And I know you would never hurt me."

"But what if—"

"You won't." A smile lit her face. "You may have just met your match. There's no way you could get past my magical defenses!" Then her tone got serious, and she said quietly, "Don't forget what *I* am, Christian." It was the first time that Victoria had ever acknowledged what she was to him, and the act frightened and liberated her all at the same time.

"The laws—" Christian began. She placed a hand against his mouth.

"Some laws need to be broken."

Christian kissed her palm and pulled her into his arms with a smothered laugh, giving in to the silent ache that had been his constant companion for weeks. He brushed the hair off her temple.

"Thank you," he said softly.

"For what?"

"For not running."

"A wise friend once told me, 'you are who you are.'" Victoria traced a line from the scar on the corner of his eyebrow across his cheekbone. "I know what you are, but I also know *who* you are too. And the 'who' is the part that defines us."

Christian stared at her with an enigmatic expression. "You are extraordinary."

Her heart skipped a beat. "Well, I'm not exactly normal either."

Despite her brave words, fear slunk around her insides. Though she refused to reconcile the thing she'd seen with him, a part of her knew that they were one and the same. Deep down, it terrified her. Memories of monsters with sharp teeth and red eyes skulking in the bowels of her closets filled her head. *But that wasn't him*, she told herself fiercely. She knew it wasn't him. Just as what she'd learned about herself, was not all of who she was. Still, she shivered.

"Who was the little man who served us?"

"That's Anton. He's my caretaker, you could say. His wife cleans and he also takes care of the gardens. They live in a small guest house at the far end of the property."

"Do they know?" she asked.

He shrugged. "Yes, I suspect so, after all, it's not like they see me eat food on a regular basis." Christian flashed his perfect white smile at his joke. "Don't worry, their family has worked for my family in France for years."

"So how old are you really then?"

"I was born in 1816, so you could say a couple of centuries give or take a few years."

"Omigod, a geriatric!" Victoria grinned, then sobered. "How did you—" She broke off, unable to phrase the question. Christian nodded; he didn't have to read her thoughts to know what she was asking.

"It's a long story. And you're tired."

"That's okay, I'm comfortable," she said, stifling a yawn.

Christian looked at her once with an enigmatic expression then started his tale.

"My father was Charles Beaumaris, the Duke of Avigny, a cousin to King Louis XVI. In 1792, my family fled France at the direction of Marie Antoinette for fear of assassination. They lived for a while in Austria, and then spent several years in Louisiana, New York, and Boston. Lucian, my brother, and I were born in 1816 in New York. My family returned to France three years after the abdication of Napoleon." Christian took a deep breath and continued, knowing he had just finished the easy part, the easy *human* part.

"Because of my family's connections with Louis-Philippe, who was then king, in the summer of 1835 my brother and I were kidnapped and tortured by the very same people who attempted to assassinate him later that same summer. We were nineteen. They wanted information on his whereabouts and beat us to within an inch of our lives, leaving us for dead in an alley. It was the last thing I remember then, waking up ravenous days later … but not for food …" He looked at Victoria almost apologetically. She motioned for him to continue. "The people who had found us were vampires. They knew who we were and at first, they were only going to take one of us, but in the end they turned us both."

"It was hard for me, but Lucian bore the mantle as if he had been born to their world. He reveled in the changes and became a willing servant of the blood. I did not. I *could* not. We were charismatic, young, and immortal. He wanted to conquer. I wanted to learn and remember what it was like to love, how to be *human*."

Christian opened his mind to Victoria as he delved into his memories and images flooded her mind. She was lost in the pictures of his past, no longer on the couch beside him but in a different world, a different time.

Dressed in riding breeches, boots, and a waist-coat with a smart riding jacket, Christian was a polished young man surveying his estate as a red-orange sun descended beyond a row of hills. The landscape rolled for miles, acres and acres of perfectly manicured gardens. A large L-shaped stone mansion loomed behind him.

Victoria felt herself gasp at its magnificent lushness. *Fontainebleau,* he thought to her. She watched the young Christian climb onto a skittish black horse that calmed the minute he whispered something into her ears. She sensed that the horse was afraid of the monster it carried, but it still gave in to its master's velvet commands.

In his recollection, a girl in a yellow dress approached him. "Your Grace, your brother Lord Devereux sent me to welcome you back home," she told him. Her face was flushed and the young Christian was clearly affected. He turned away but Victoria could feel his aching desire as fresh as it was then.

"Go," he told the girl. It was little more than a growl. "I do not want ... you."

"Please my Lord Duke, he will kill me should I return. Please." Her voice was beseeching as she pulled a yellow scarf from her neck. Blood flowed from a vertical incision already cut deep into her flesh. The smell buckled every restraint within him, just as Lucian had known it would, and he flew off the horse toward the girl in a single leap.

"Will my brother stop at *nothing*?" he snarled, bending the girl's neck to the side. He bent, drawn despite himself, a terrible change ripping through his body. It was only the terrified rearing of the horse beside him that made him snap out of the fog of hunger consuming him. Christian staggered back. "Tell *Lord Devereux* I said go to hell, and I shall be happy to join him there!"

Victoria could feel Christian's self-disgust buried deeply into the memory. She squeezed his hand, and the images dissipated. His regret was suffocating, even now. He turned to her.

"Lucian did that often, and sometimes, too many times to count, I gave in to the horror of what I was ... *am*. There was no way back so eventually I stopped fighting."

"I'm sorry."

"Don't be. I've long made peace with what I am," Christian said. "Before long, Lucian and I were at odds with each other and started to drift apart. He used to say I was too soft. As the first-born twin, I was a Vampire Lord, but I wanted no part of Lucian's regime so I abdicated my rights to him, and left. The House of Devereux is now a very powerful vampire coven and Lucian is feared by many."

"Why?" Victoria asked.

"Let's just say that he is where he is because he takes what he wants, brutally if necessary. Lucian is very, very powerful and very, very ruthless."

"But you don't live by his rules?"

"Yes and no. Yes, because I am bound to protect who we are, the House of Devereux, and he will always be my brother even though I don't agree with his principles. And no, because I am here," he said simply.

"Is it hard being away from your family?"

"Why do you ask?" Christian asked, surprised by her question.

"I don't have anyone but my Aunt Holly. If I did, I'd want to be near them, that's all," she said, shifting as he curled an arm around her. The warmth from the fireplace coupled with her exhaustion, made her eyelids heavy. She leaned into his embrace, forgetting for an instant everything she'd discovered about him, and gave in to the sweetness of just being held. "Family is important, isn't it? And knowing who you are, and where you belong?"

"Yes," he said. "But sometimes we're forced to make choices … hard ones, just for the sake of family. Lucian wanted something I had, and it was easy for me to give it up. The Devereux mantle always meant more to him than it ever did to me."

Christian trailed off, for a moment lost again in his own memories. Victoria left him alone this time, sensing his need for momentary solitude.

AFTER A WHILE, Christian shifted and realized that Victoria had fallen asleep, the warmth of the fireplace and the hypnotic thud of his heartbeat combining to lull her into a fitful slumber. Her breathing was deep and even, her trust in him absolute. Even the threat of shadowy creatures lurking in the darkness hadn't been able to stop her eyes from closing. Christian had felt her heart accelerate ten times in the last hour. She'd been afraid. Yet despite her fear, she had seen something inside of him worth staying for.

Not wanting to wake her, Christian lifted her carefully against his chest and carried her upstairs, watching as she curled into a tiny ball under the sheets. She looked so small in the giant bed. He sat down next to her, brushing the hair off her face and clasping her fingers in his own. She mumbled something and shivered.

"Sleep," he soothed.

What he'd done was unimaginable, unthinkable. He'd broken

laws he was sworn to uphold under penalty of exile, or worse, death. And executing a vampire wasn't as simple or as neat as killing a person. It involved a great deal of pain, and a lot of fanfare designed only to serve the power of the Vampire Council. Punishing a blood traitor was always an event. Punishing Christian Devereux would be a spectacle.

He didn't care. All he knew was what he felt, and Christian had lived long enough to know that what he felt wasn't just fleeting. It was something far more. Despite the risks, everything inside him knew that letting this girl go would be a mistake.

Stay with me, Victoria, he thought, unable to voice the words.

"I will," she said sleepily, squeezing his fingers.

THIRTEEN

Choice and Consequence

VICTORIA AWOKE PANIC-stricken. It was dark as night but she could feel that she was in a bed, and her hands flew to her throat as she dizzily recalled pieces of the previous night and snatches of broken conversation. She remembered that she had been at Christian's but she didn't remember falling asleep in his bed!

She sat up appalled, and groped blindly for a light switch. Her fingertips felt something on the wall near the headboard and pressed it. A whirring noise was followed by a crack of bright white light peeking through the nearest bedroom window. The electronic shutters rose slowly then stopped. It was enough to illuminate the room. She blinked against the daylight and squinted around the room.

It was beautiful, like everything else in the house, with subtle masculine touches of dark wood and elegant style. A large armchair and ottoman sat in one corner, but the massive four-poster bed on which she was sitting dominated the room. A clock on the wall above an elaborate dresser said that it was ten o'clock.

Saving what would undoubtedly be the best for last, Victoria turned her attention to the boy lying next to her on the bed and appeased her blossoming curiosity. He looked so peaceful. She leaned in slowly—he didn't even look like he was breathing!

He was sleeping on his stomach, one arm up around his head, on top of the duvet. Smiling at his propriety, her eyes roved over the angular planes and long hollows of his back disappearing into the waistband of black silk pajama pants. An intricate tattoo that looked like a rope of intertwined silvery-black letters meandered from the base of his skull all the way down his back. It was in a language that she didn't recognize.

Victoria longed to touch the expanse of smooth porcelain skin and she gave in to the temptation, running her fingertips across his shoulders and down the line of the silvery writing. He didn't move. His skin felt smooth and hard like it was stretched taut over granite; the muscles didn't even jump reflexively at her soft caress.

"Christian," she whispered. He didn't move. "Christian, are you awake?" she said more loudly. Nothing. It was as if he were dead. Victoria laughed to herself, given what he actually was, that was understandable. She leaned closer and moved her lips to his ear, one hand pressing down onto his right shoulder blade to support herself.

In the space of half a second, Victoria found herself flipped roughly onto her back, a snarling face inches from her own. He had her arms pinned to her side and she stared in horror at the familiar face she could barely recognize. His eyes were slits, his face twisted in a ferocious grimace, and his teeth! Long, white and deadly. She felt the amulet blaze.

"Christian!" she said, her throat thick with terror. "Stop it. Stop IT!"

He was somewhere else. She shouldn't have touched him, she realized too late, and now he was milliseconds away from her throat. Even in its transformation, his face was savagely beautiful. Despite her shock, she felt an unfamiliar warmth settle in her chest.

Victoria had two choices: the first was to hurl him away but she knew that his death grip on her arms meant that she could go flying with him; the second was to teleport herself to another place in the room.

Calling on her power, she felt the magic begin to flow in her veins as she focused her energy. If only she had more experience with teleporting! She fought her rising panic and the spell faltered. As she felt his hot breath on her face, Victoria knew she had no choice.

"TRANSEO!" she shouted.

She focused on the dresser across the room and in a split second she was at the other side of the room. Dizziness made her knees buckle, causing her head to collide with the dresser's sharp top edge. At the same time, the furious growl of a predator deprived of his prey filled the room. Even in her lightheadedness, Victoria knew the wetness on the side of her face was blood.

The air thickened as Christian flew toward her with lightening speed, pinning her against the wall. Her hands pushed with futile resistance against his chest. His eyes were wild with hunger as his face hung inches from hers. But Christian hesitated, his slitted eyes squinting warily. She could feel him studying the trickle of blood on her cheek but he seemed reluctant, afraid even, to take it. That single split second gave her time to react.

With Herculean strength, she pushed her hands against his chest and slid them up his corded neck. She grasped his face with her hands, her magic lending her strength to keep him still. His eyes were feral. She stared into them, letting him see her, *willing* him to see her. The rampant energy coursed like a river into her hands, suddenly powerful in that moment, and without a doubt, Victoria knew that she could kill him in an instant.

Open to me, she commanded. He resisted.

Victoria gathered her power, and entered his mind. She could see the vampire in him, hungry and wild, pacing like a starving lion.

"Soporo," she said. She felt its recognition, and slowly as her fingers soothed the rigid planes of his face, the beast's wildness ebbed as her magic compelled. After several long moments, she withdrew.

Faced with a different pair of silver-gray eyes, Victoria felt absurdly self-conscious, his expression equal parts of sorrow, fear and awe. His tried to speak but no words came, and he could only stare at her helplessly.

"It's okay," she whispered.

"No it's not. I *attacked* you … like an … animal," he choked. Grief and remorse lined his face and transferred in force from his thoughts in violent waves. How close had he come to hurting her? Hurting *her*!

"Christian, don't."

She understood now that he'd been controlled purely by instinct. Something about her blood had driven him far beyond his own meticulous control of himself. *Something about her blood …*

Ignoring the sour feeling in her stomach, she raised herself on her tiptoes and pressed her lips to his, tenderly kissing the monstrous face that had seconds before been desperate to kill her. Christian's lips tightened against hers, sheathing his sharp white incisors, and he pulled away. He ran his hand down the side of her temple where she had hit her head. She winced. He paused, looking at her carefully. Victoria stared at the ground; she already knew what he was going to ask.

"Is your blood normally that dark?"

"No more than usual. Actually it's dark in here." She couldn't look at him.

Christian tilted her chin up and said, "Tori, look at me." She raised wary eyes to his, wanting so badly to tell him but knowing that she couldn't just yet. She couldn't trust anyone with her family's deep, dark secret. Not after Leto had warned her, and especially not after what she'd just done. She forced herself to look confused, as if she didn't know what he was talking about.

"It isn't just its color, it's the smell of it too." Christian's jaw clenched at the mere thought of it. "It's so *pure*," he said, struggling for the words to describe what he wanted to say, "so untainted. I don't think I'm explaining clearly, but it's like nothing I have ever smelled … like it's not human blood, which I know makes no sense at all."

Victoria pulled away and shrugged, needing to escape the penetrating intensity of his eyes. She settled for telling him a veiled half-truth.

"It may have to do with my blood disease. They gave me a lot of experimental drugs …" Her voice trembled as if it were too much for her to talk about, and it accomplished the goal she wanted— Christian inclined his head as if he were satisfied or willing to let the matter drop, for now. Victoria carefully kept her expression blank so that the intense relief she felt would not be visible, and tried to draw the attention away from herself.

"What does your tattoo mean?" Christian flinched as if the thought of it were painful.

"It's a quote from an English novelist, Baron Lytton, written in the ancient language. It reads, 'What is past is past. There is a future left to all men, who have the virtue to repent and the energy to atone.' It reminds me that there's always hope for redemption."

"Oh." She paused, at a loss for words. "It shimmers."

"Silver dust."

"Isn't silver a bad thing?"

"Painful, but not deadly. It's … a reminder of what I am." He smoothed away the furrowed concern on her brow.

"I'm sorry."

"Don't be. I hardly feel it anymore."

The silence extended like a web between them, sticky and unavoidable. The signs of his earlier change still marred his features, and despite his calm voice, the tendons corded his arms in rigid lines.

"Christian, you need to …" Victoria said, trailing off. "And I should go."

The air between them was charged and heavy. She needed space to process what had happened—his attack, her miraculous ability to control the monster inside of him, everything. Most of all, she needed to escape the intensity of his eyes and the questions she knew he still had about her blood.

She touched his face, suddenly unsure and afraid of what the next day would bring. His expression was unfathomable. "I'll call you later."

BACK AT HER apartment, Victoria took a long shower, soothing the aching tension out of her muscles. The walk from Christian's house to her car on campus had been more than six miles but it had done her a world of good. Leto had given her a strange look as she'd never spent the night away from the apartment but she'd pretended not to notice. She kept her mind carefully closed.

The amulet was still warm—it felt like it had been burning from the moment she'd gone to Christian's place. She felt guilty for not listening to what was an obvious warning but all reason went out the window whenever she was around him. She knew he was dangerous, but that didn't make him any less appealing.

Victoria sighed and her eyes fell on the journal lying on the music box. She had little desire to continue reading it. Its ominous contents were hardly what she needed after everything that had happened, but more than ever, she recognized that she needed to learn about her powers and how much she might actually be capable of.

She opened it to the last entry she'd read. The next entry was dated November 1626, eight months after the last.

London, England. The Undead legions have declared war upon the Clans, what remains of them that is. I suspect that it is part of a strategy to shift the balance of power given the decimation of numbers they suffered at my hands. Atrocity upon atrocity committed throughout history has only cemented the hate of their centuries-old feud—victims raped and disemboweled, corpses butchered and left to rot, untold violence cloaked in secrecy in their never-ending silent battle.

War is the inevitable culmination of their enmity.

Yet I remain unmoved. I choose no side. I cannot. My blood has no allegiance, only its own, and its price in blood does not differentiate from one creature to another. They are all the same. If the Undead legions were to attack me, they would suffer the same consequences as the Clans, but so far, they have been smart. Valerius was well to take my advice to heart.

Valerius ...

The all-too-human pace of my heart doubles. It has been so long since Lancaster. It would be so easy to summon the vampire to me, and he would come, I saw it in his eyes. But all that awaits him once I have given in to my desires is death. The blood will surely exact its price for my weakness, of that I am certain.

Victoria shivered. The sense of cold desolation was almost tangible. The blood was like a parasite that had completely possessed Brigid, who it seemed, had completely lost any will to live or desire to fight for herself and her humanity. *Would the same happen to her?*

Victoria forced herself to finish. There were only three more entries. The next was five months later, April 1627.

London, England. The Great War continues, providing easy prey for a demon like myself who must pay constant blood homage. My transformation is near its end, although I do not know what I will become after the last of my humanity dies nor do I know the fate of those who will remain behind. But I care not. I will be free of my human consciousness ... free of conscience, free of emotion. Free of weak regret. At last.

The next entry was a month later.

London, England. The Vampire Ancient, Valerius, has requested another audience. He must know that death awaits him; he will not escape so easily a second time. The blood will not allow it, and what is left of me is too weak to oppose its demands.

Valerius is as I remembered, and my blood boiled at the girlish fantasies that spun within me. He says that the War is over—they have finally agreed upon a truce, one that will forgive old debts and set the rules for a new peace. I asked him then why he sought an audience, for such trivialities matter not to me.

He replied that he came for me, and also that he was ready to die.

I smiled, a rare thing, and for a moment, I admired his courage, and wished I had the strength to save him. But the offer had already been made. It was over far too quickly, and his body disintegrated like dust in my arms. The blood relished the energy. If it were a person, it would have licked its fingers clean. I am sickened at what I have become but the regret is momentary, fleeting.

For I am the blood.

And in that instant, I know. It is almost over.

Victoria chewed dry lips. It was worse than she'd imagined—vampires and witches had hated each other since the dawn of time. No wonder Christian had been so troubled. She'd had no idea what he had meant, until now. Truce or not, years of deep evolutionary hatred and mistrust would be hard to avoid … or surmount. She thumbed through the last few pages. Brigid's story couldn't possibly end like that. There had to be more … for her own sake!

There was only one remaining entry, three months later that same year. Victoria noticed immediately that the writing and the entire tone of the entry were different. They seemed lighter somehow, as if Brigid had found some sort of impossible absolution.

Her body trembled … she needed something … she needed hope.

Lancaster, England. I have come back home—to end it where it began. Something truly wondrous has happened! Marcus came to me today. I heard his beautiful voice for the first time in twenty years. I see the forgiveness in his heart, the same unconditional love as his father's. He could not contact me for fear of King James. It was the only way he knew to protect his family and me until James' death four years ago. His family, he says! He tells me I have two beautiful granddaughters, one named Brigid and the other Elizabeth. And I am undone. I can see them in his eyes, beautiful and perfect. Angels!

I weep, but it is far too late for me, I feel the blood consuming me, struggling to take what little hope is left in me and with it, my only chance for peace. The cost has been so great but I will not let it take me. Although I embody it, I will die before I become it! My Elizabeth, wait for me. I am coming to you.

Victoria wept as she finished reading the final chapter of Brigid's life. There were no more entries. She closed the journal, and a small sheet of paper fell out. It was yellowed with age and she picked it up gingerly. It read:

My darling Marcus, I leave this journal to you. I beg you, do not think too harshly of me. I bore my curse as best I could. If I had known then what I know now—Marcus, the price of the blood's magic had always been mine to set! In my weakness I let it consume me and in the end I lost everything. I lost sight of the one thing that could have saved me ... love.

Victoria's heart careened into her rib cage. She read the words again—*the price of the blood's magic had always been mine to set*—and for the first time appreciated the precarious edge on which her choices balanced. Ultimately, she was in control of what the consequences were. The knowledge was freeing, and terrifying.

Reading the rest of the letter, Victoria saw that Brigid had also come to the same realization of *choice* and *consequence*.

You have brought me hope, Marcus. And so, I cannot suffer this curse to live, even though every part of me begs to survive now that I have so much to live for. If I die, then my blood shall also die, for I am the only one who can conquer it. My son, it has been so long since I have thought of the meaning of true sacrifice. This will be my last gift to them, your beautiful daughters, and their children, and their children's children!

I leave this amulet to you. This is everything that was best of me. It is my legacy, and your inheritance. It will always protect you and yours. Always know that it was your love that saved me.

I love you now and forever, my son.

Your Mother,

Brigid Anne Warrick Kensington.

And so Brigid chose. She chose to die so those she loved could live.

FOURTEEN

The Attack

"GOD, I AM never going to get this assignment done!" Victoria said to Leto as she paced, frustrated in her apartment. "And what is with this hideous weather!"

She peered out the window at the three feet of snow already on the ground and the billowing wind that made it nearly impossible to see more than a few inches. The world was a sea of white that covered everything, a big white nothing!

Well, it is December in Maine, Tori, Leto said patronizingly. *And if you are so worried about the assignment, just use magic.*

Victoria was horrified at Leto's nonchalant suggestion. "But that would be cheating!" Then when she gave it real consideration. "*Could* I do that?" Leto smiled his strange little cat smile and blinked his large, green eyes.

You wouldn't believe me if I told you some of the things you could do.

"Like what?" Despite being completely appalled at the mere thought of cheating, Victoria was intrigued.

You could not only create that whole paper in an instant, you could predispose your professor to give you an A. You could even see what he plans to set for finals and give yourself a premeditated grade.

"You are a devious little cat, has anyone ever told you that, Leto?" Victoria shook her head in amazement. "But seriously, what would be the point of me even finishing high school, if I didn't do it properly? *Normally*, you know, like everyone else."

Well, you're not exactly like everyone else are you? he replied smugly.

Victoria rolled her eyes, sighed and sat down resignedly at her desk. She kept getting distracted by thoughts of Christian and fussing about the weather was just a pretense to think about something else *other* than him. The last few weeks had been a whirlwind of secret romance, and while she couldn't keep her mind totally closed to Leto without arousing suspicion, she kept her thoughts about Christian carefully compartmentalized.

After finishing the journal, her indecision had only worsened knowing Brigid's story and learning about the ancient enmity between witches and vampires. It didn't erase anything she felt about Christian. If anything, her feelings had become twice as sharp, and twice as difficult to ignore. Despite what she'd read, the truth was she didn't *want* to listen to the rules. She glanced at Leto lounging on the sofa.

"Leto, can I ask you a question? Why are relationships between vampires and witches forbidden?" Leto's eyes shrank to slits, his ears flattening against his head. A hot hiss rippled down his spine.

Why? Did something happen?

"No, no. I was just curious," she said hastily. "I read something in the journal about it, and I wanted to ask you." She cleared her mind as best as she could and pasted an innocent look on her face.

Relations between our worlds are tenuous at best, bound by a strained centuries-old truce. His tone was cold, dispassionate. *We interact with them when we need to, but anything more is expressly prohibited. There are rules, ancient laws in place that prohibit … mingling, like anti-miscegenation laws.*

"That sounds incredibly archaic. Why can't they change? This is the twenty-first century, after all." Leto's stare was hot. Discerning.

Because it is the law. It has always been the way since the Great War. We are probably the only two societies powerful and evenly matched enough to annihilate the other. The werewolves would be a threat if they could unite their packs but they are territorial by nature. The rest, like most of the fey, just care about their own worlds. They don't integrate with humans like we do or the vampires do.

"So the laws don't apply to mingling with humans?"

Humans aren't a threat.

"And the penalty for breaking these laws?" Leto's eyes were slits.

Death. Exile. Worse. Exile for a witch means being stripped of all magical powers and forbidden to wield magic for all time. For witches or wizards, it is a fate far worse than death. Losing your magic is like losing your soul.

"And the vampires?"

The same offense is punishable by death. Burning, or so I've heard.

"Oh."

What they were doing was not only wrong, it was risky. Victoria buried her head in her French textbook, feeling the twin lasers of Leto's eyes boring into her, as the familiar flush invaded her body. She kept her mind blank, refusing to think of anything, least of all Christian, despite her racing heart. Leto was far too perceptive for his own good.

The phone rang, interrupting her concentration and the

heavy, awkward silence that had suddenly invaded the apartment. She lunged for the phone with a relief that she hoped didn't seem desperate.

"Hello?"

"Tori?"

"Oh, hey Gabriel."

"How's your paper coming?" he asked.

"Not bad, I got stuck so I was just taking a break." *One of three hundred breaks*, she admonished herself silently.

"A bunch of us are heading down to the Dog tonight. We all need a break with finals right around the corner. You up for it?"

Victoria sighed inwardly. This was the fifth time Gabriel had asked her out this week, and she was running out of excuses. She glanced at Leto who was still staring at her disconcertingly. Gabriel suddenly seemed like the lesser of two evils.

"You know what Gabe, that sounds like fun," she said. "I'll see you there."

Gabriel over Leto was an easy choice. She would deal with Gabriel if she had to. His attempts to date her had become more persistent in the last few weeks, no doubt because of the bar kiss. She knew that it was her own fault for misleading him and giving him the wrong impression that night at the bar when she'd been trying to make Christian jealous.

Victoria felt a spasm of guilt for the sneaky reconnaissance she'd done when she had flashed Gabriel's mind. What she had seen was what she'd expected, with maybe with a few extra details like his intense dislike for his sister Angie, which had been obvious. Still, the blunt evidence of Gabriel's feelings for her had made her blush.

He really, *really* liked her. Victoria hadn't delved too much deeper. There was a difference between protecting herself by investigating someone's motives and invading their personal privacy. Despite her limitless new powers, she was trying hard to maintain some standards.

By the time Victoria finished her paper and walked to the Dog, it was packed. She secretly hoped she would run into Christian, but she knew it wasn't likely. A few days out of every month, they'd decided it was better—*safer*—for her to stay away from him. Despite her obvious ability to protect herself, the smell of blood, hers in particular, didn't help matters given what Christian was. It was a small but necessary sacrifice each month.

She took a deep breath and headed in to the mob. As she pressed through the noisy jostle of bodies, she was glad that she didn't have to work. She had done three straight nights of six-hour shifts! Hearing her name, she walked over to the large crowd of people on one whole side of the bar near where the Harland college band, "Riot," was playing.

"Hey guys!" she shouted over the music. Charla waved. She was talking animatedly to two football players, and they were all laughing. Angie didn't seem to be around, but she didn't go out much anyway and certainly not when Gabriel was part of the group. She saw him surrounded by his friends and he walked over to say hello.

"Hey Tori," he said. "I'm really glad you came!"

"Me too," she agreed, happy to be out.

Gabriel's energy was infectious and Victoria soon relaxed. He introduced her to some of his friends, other seniors and juniors from the football team. Gabriel was their star quarterback and everyone had high hopes for the team for the divisional playoffs. Harland had already recruited him with a full ride for college.

Starting quarterback in the high-school social world made him an extremely desirable commodity, and Victoria couldn't believe how many people, especially girls, were standing around their table and hanging on Gabriel's every word. She tried to ignore the daggers that were being shot in her direction from some of the other girls desperate for him to notice them.

Out of the blue, she felt a light brush against her thoughts.

You look beautiful.

I didn't know you'd be here!

Program review ran late.

Where are you? she replied, trying not to react as Gabriel was in the middle of an animated byplay of his last game.

Come on Tori, you know you could find me easily if you wanted to.

Victoria focused her energy, sifting through the throng of bodies gyrating to the music. There he was at a booth in the corner over by the front of the bar. She could see that he wasn't looking straight at her and was listening to what the professor he was with was saying, but she could feel him staring at her surreptitiously behind his lashes, the hint of a smile playing about his lips. His glance brushed across her temple, then her cheek, and then back and forth, back and forth across her lips. Her knees turned into jelly.

Stop it!

Why? He continued to mentally caress her lips, and Victoria felt as weak as if he were actually kissing her. It was harmless flirting but she could barely breathe.

I mean it, Christian.

You look even more beautiful when you are blushing.

Victoria nodded to what Gabriel was saying, and focused a sliver of her attention to the corner. Christian's eyebrows rose in challenge, egging her on. She opened her mind to him and vividly imagined kissing his lips. His eyes snapped to hers in immediate response.

She dropped butterfly kisses on his cheeks, down his jaw to

his neck where she bit gently into the soft hollow where his neck met his collarbone. The thought was far more provocative than the act itself, and Christian almost half jumped out of his chair. She watched grinning as he explained himself to his companions. He met her eyes.

Touché.

As Gabriel introduced her to more of his friends, she felt Christian's gentle parting caress and soft whisper that he missed her and couldn't wait to see her. Victoria smiled to herself as she recalled the look of utter shock on his face when she had thought of biting his neck. He had definitely not been expecting *that*!

"Is that smile for me?" Gabriel said, tossing an arm over her shoulders. Victoria rolled her eyes and sneaked a glance at Charla hoping that she was distracted enough not to read anything into Gabriel's amorous attentions. He was laying it on pretty thick!

She chatted to two other seniors for a while, but soon after Victoria started to feel ill, the noise and heat of the bar making her suddenly dizzy. She sat for a minute but a stinging headache had come out of nowhere. She felt disoriented. Even her amulet seemed hot but Victoria wasn't sure if it was the necklace or her body that was burning up. She told Gabriel she needed to go home. After declining his offer of a ride, she insisted that she preferred to walk.

The minute she left the bar, Victoria felt better. The night air was cold but refreshing against her hot skin as she started the two-mile walk to her apartment. The wind sliced across her cheeks, and she pulled her coat tighter around her neck.

It felt good, the icy coldness helping to clear the cobwebs from her head. It was a dark night but she wasn't too worried; street lamps and homes lit most of the way, and there was only one small area that crossed the five-mile loop, which didn't have any lights. She walked briskly before the chill could seep through her coat and settle in her bones. She briefly considered teleporting, and then decided against it—too public, even if the area was deserted.

She pressed on. Halfway through it, she was just starting to regret her decision to take on the subzero temperatures and the wind chill, when out of the corner of her eye, Victoria thought she saw a quick movement, and a chill that had nothing to do with the weather ran up her spine.

She walked faster, wrapping her arms around her body, glancing behind her once or twice but seeing nothing out of the ordinary. The hairs on the nape of her neck were at stiff attention, and suddenly she regretted not taking Gabriel up on his offer of a ride. Movement to her left caught her eye again and she froze, her body tense with coiled fear.

It was a man, a short thin man.

A menacing snarl curled from his throat. Before she could think, he sprung toward her with lethal precision. Victoria felt the blood roaring in her ears and summoned her energy, sledge-hammering it toward the man's body. He flew back twenty feet and crashed into the base of a maple tree but was on his feet in seconds snarling hideously.

Victoria's focus sharpened and the blood rushed in her veins, giving her strength and clearing her brain of everything but self-preservation. The amulet at her breast pulsed hot as her blood pushed her fear into a dizzying frenzy. Another quick movement on her right made her spin around, and in the darkness she could make out another shape, a feminine shape. As her eyes adjusted, she saw a beautiful woman with long, white-blond hair.

All Victoria could think was that somehow she *knew* that face, but the memory eluded her. The woman dropped into a crouch and feinted, ready to attack, and Victoria braced herself, feeling the magic responding to her needs, the energy amassing in her fingertips. The blast rocketed past the woman who spun with inhuman speed to avoid the blow. Victoria shifted to the left keeping the first attacker in sight and realizing that there was a second man, behind her. She didn't have time to hyperventilate. The power surged through her leaving her breathless—she was born for this.

They circled like three sharks that smelled blood in the water. One of the man-things leapt toward her. Words shot through her head and Victoria screamed them without even thinking about where they had come from.

"IGNIS CREMO!"

The curse's fiery arms destroyed the creature in midair. Its shrieks were hideous as it died, and Victoria's blood soared in response, exultant with its success. On her left, she could see the blond woman staring at her uneasily.

Victoria lifted her chin in cool challenge. The woman's answering stare was venomous, and as Victoria fought to grasp the elusive memory of *who* she was, she didn't notice the other man-thing springing toward her from the side. Razor-sharp, serrated fangs tore into the flesh of her right shoulder. Victoria screamed, but before she could react, the thing fell onto the ground and started convulsing in terrible agony and clawing at its face. She stared in horror as its mouth and face blistered off, the rest of it smoldering to slow ashes before her eyes.

Blood congealed into her sweater and coat, its tackiness coating her skin, pungent like corroded rust. Her shoulder stung as if there were powered glass underneath but she ignored it, her burning eyes scanning the area. With some relief, she realized that the woman had disappeared. Her vision clouded as her knees buckled. The earth was cold and wet, and her eyes grew heavy as she lay back on the grass at the side of the road, looking at the black sky and feeling the blood dancing in her veins. It was resonant with victory, but she felt drained. The pain in her shoulder faded to a dull throb as she felt herself slipping into unconsciousness.

Christian …

VICTORIA WAS FLYING. There were tight bands around her arms and her thighs, holding her close. Dizzily, she turned her face and saw the familiar angular profile. He had come for her, just like she had known he would. Her throat stung from the effort of the words.

"Killed v … v … vampire … oh God … I killed it … them …"

Sleep, chérie.

And she did.

CHRISTIAN SHOUTED FOR Anton the minute he arrived at the house with Victoria limp in his arms. Although Anton's special poultice, made for an infected vampire bite, seemed to calm the weeping of the lesions, they still remained angry and raw. Even worse, Victoria was still unconscious.

When she'd called him, Christian had followed her call, the lushly wet scent of her blood like a beacon. Its siren song was nearly impossible to resist. The thought that a vampire had *bitten* her incensed him, and he fought to keep his rage under control as it simmered beneath the surface. He knew *exactly* who had sent it, and his wrath made him reckless. He picked up the phone and punched in a number. No answer.

I know you're there Lucian! he roared mentally.

They rarely communicated telepathically but the unique bond they shared had not diminished with time or immortality. They had always been able to finish each other's sentences as children, and that ability had evolved into something much more unique. Despite its usefulness, it reminded Lucian too much that they were brothers, a fact that he preferred to forget.

Christian's cell phone rang.

"What can I do for you, brother?" Lucian's voice was composed, arrogant.

"Explain."

"Explain what? That you were hiding a witch of immense power? That she killed two of Lena's men in the space of minutes? Or worse, that you thought I wouldn't find out?"

"You sent Lena?" Christian's voice was choked.

"Afraid, brother?"

"She is of no threat to you Lucian!" Christian could scarcely control his fury, he felt like he wanted to rip Lucian apart with his bare hands. He didn't even want to imagine what he would have done if they had been on the same continent. Lucian's response was quiet.

"You forget your duty, Christian," he said. "The Watchers have foreseen it. The prophecy—"

Christian interrupted him fiercely. "She is NOT the one you seek." But even as he said it, Christian doubted himself. *Could* she be?

"No. The Watchers are not infallible. They are trained to detect paranormal threats against the vampire world, but still, their visions aren't set in stone. You know that better than anyone."

"So you admit that there's something, then? A threat?"

"If there is a threat, I'll deal with it. Don't ever send anyone here again," Christian said, "because *brother*, trust me you will not like the result."

"And what if she is the one?"

"Lucian, her power is raw but not extraordinary. She can't be the one from the prophecy. It's impossible." Christian could hear the silence on the other end of the phone as Lucian processed the information. After a while Lucian spoke, curiosity evident in his tone.

"So why do you care so much? Giving in to the temptation of a little forbidden snack?" Lucian's laugh was derisive.

"None of your damned business."

"That's forbidden too, in case you forgot. Not that I don't mind a little witch blood myself from time to time. We always crave the illicit, don't we? I just didn't think my straitlaced, uptight brother would indulge in such criminal inclinations."

"Think what you will, Lucian. Do not send any of your people here again, or I will return them to you in pieces myself. Food or otherwise, the witch is not your concern." Christian's words were final, indicating the subject was closed, and he disconnected the call.

The tension drained out of his body. If Lucian refused to leave Victoria alone, Christian didn't want to think of what he would do. A tendril of unease crawled up his neck—what *did* the Watchers know? What had they said to Lucian? And worse, what did *he* know?

Was Victoria in danger? Was she the one?

FIFTEEN

The Prophecy

W HEN V ICTORIA FINALLY awoke, it was to inky darkness, much like the very first night she had slept in Christian's house. She floundered weakly for the window switch and opened it a crack; no light, which meant nighttime. She closed her eyes and had to take a few minutes before she could focus properly, trying to remember the words Leto had taught her for the spell.

"ILLUSTRO," she rasped, illuminating the lamp in the far corner of the room. Her mouth felt like dry cotton and her eyes hurt as if they had grit in them. When she tried to sit up, the agony that stabbed through her back and neck was excruciating, and she gasped, falling back against the pillows. After a few minutes, she hauled herself up and inched her way into the bathroom.

She looked like hell. Her face was pasty with huge black circles under her eyes and a large purple bruise covered the side of her temple. A thick white bandage encased her shoulder, and she winced as she touched the edges of it. Splashing some cold water on her face, she finger-combed her hair and made her way downstairs where she found Christian sitting in the den, still and in repose, hands clasped against his chest. His lips moved soundlessly. Was he *praying*?

"Hi," she said, startling him.

"How are you feeling?" His voice was rough like sandpaper.

"Like I got hit by a truck." She smiled weakly and sat beside him, grimacing from the effort. "Thank you for coming for me," she said. "I don't know what—"

Christian put a finger against her lips and mindful of her injury, pulled her into a gentle embrace. He felt her familiar curves settle into his body and he swallowed painfully, tensing from the sheer proximity of her elegant, *so* elegant, throat.

Victoria felt his tension and propped herself up, noticing his very pale face and stormy dark slate-colored eyes. There was no light in them, just a latent hunger blackening their edges. His arms were rigid and she could see the muscles bunched tightly beneath his white skin. He looked *hungry*.

"Have you …?" Christian shook his head, and she could see the effort it cost him. He wasn't even breathing.

"I couldn't leave, not while you …"

He was very quiet and her eyes softened as she realized that he hadn't fed because he'd been afraid to leave her side. *But at what cost?* she wondered. He looked haggard, but it only heightened the perfect surreal beauty of his face. Victoria understood in that second why people could fall prey to vampires so easily—their beauty enticed and compelled, *especially* when they were hungry.

"I'll be okay," she told him. "I'll wait. Go." Victoria stood up and literally shoved him out the door. It was snowing again and she watched his lithe body disappear into the trees, their dark evergreen branches heavy with snow.

With Christian gone, Victoria returned to the chair he had

vacated and pulled her mind into focus. Her body ached but her mind felt uncluttered. Even her magic felt more malleable, *different*. Something new had arisen within her, something intense and strong and frightening. It excited and terrified her at the same time.

Who are you, really?

The amulet pulsed as if it held the answer. Victoria held the stone. She knew that she had only survived because of its protective power and magical knowledge. She thought about the fire curse that had incinerated the creature, and her blood boiled in response, the amulet scorching her icy hands. She remembered what Brigid had written in the journal about the inhuman exchange between the blood's magic and sacrifice, and her face paled in horror. In that single moment, everything became crystal clear.

She had *killed* last night!

Victoria closed her eyes and whispered a summoning charm, the music box from her bedside table materializing in her lap. She removed the journal, and found the letter that Brigid had written to Marcus, rereading the lines she wanted, "the price of the blood had always been mine to set" and the piece about the diamond amulet, "this is everything that was best of me."

She set aside the journal and removed the amulet, her brow furrowed as she examined the diamond. One thing was clear: somehow, the amulet had protected her with its own magic of its own volition. Tentative, she pushed her consciousness into the stone, prisms of crimson light dazzling her, and found herself in a blood-red cavern. The air felt heavy as if she were swimming underwater. Drawing her mental hands forward, sifting through it, her fingers left a trail of silvery-blue phosphorescence in their wake, and she stopped fascinated. Magic!

This was the legacy that Brigid had left—a living testament to her fathomless power, a part of her own *consciousness* existing forever in the amulet. The stone undulated, embracing her with familiar strength, and she felt renewed.

Victoria pulled some more of the energy into herself as she withdrew, aware of its colossal strength. She would need it for what she was about to do. She lay back in the chair and closed her eyes. Now for the hard part.

A soft noise interrupted her as Christian strode back into the room.

"Victoria, are you okay?"

"Yes. I just have one thing to do but I'm trying to figure out whether I should do it," she said, smiling at his use of her full name. His skin was flushed as if he'd been running but he looked far more human than when he'd left.

"What's that?"

"The wound. I can heal it myself from the inside out but I'm wondering what would happen if I took it into me instead." She quelled his instant look of concern with a gentle smile. "Trust me, it has been a day of discoveries. It won't hurt me."

"Why would you want to do that?"

"Because I need to understand why it attacked me." She hesitated. "And how it died."

"Do you want me to stay?" Christian asked.

Victoria nodded and leaned forward, clasping his long fingers in her own. With his free hand, Christian removed the gauze bandage, and was shocked at the yellow and red mottled skin. Victoria wrinkled her nose at the slimy odor as she closed her eyes and concentrated on healing the area surrounding the wound.

"CURO," she murmured.

Before his very eyes, Christian watched spellbound as the skin lightened slowly and visibly cleared, the angry color dissipating as Victoria's magic compelled it. Her body shook slightly as her intense concentration created lines of tension in her face. After a minute the skin on her shoulder became unmarked but for a thin half-moon scar, where the teeth had penetrated her skin. After about ten seconds, Victoria relaxed, opened her eyes and smiled fiercely at him. Her expression was triumphant.

"Did it work?" he asked, his thumb stroking her hand.

"Yes, I learned a bit about him and a bit more about what you are." As she said the words, Christian stiffened because even though she already knew what he was, she had now just seen what a truly evil vampire was capable of, and, in truth, what Christian was capable of. She read him easily.

"Christian, stop. I know *who* you are. How I feel about you won't change because I've seen what your kind can do," she said gently. "It would be naïve for you to think that I don't know what a vampire is." She frowned. "He was different though, wasn't he? Not like a man, more like an animal."

"They are trained assassins, more fiend than vampire. They are control fed, only to keep their hunger sharp, to kill. I'm sorry I wasn't there—" Christian's face was tight.

"It doesn't matter. I'm here now with you." She paused, her words cautious. "When you say control fed, you mean starved?"

"Yes, of blood." His voice was strained.

Victoria watched him, speculative. She understood that Christian had to feed, but it was more convenient for her to equate that in her head with the natural act of eating as opposed to the unnatural act of consuming live blood.

Even earlier when he'd returned, it hadn't bothered her. Now that she'd seen into the other vampire hunger-warped consciousness, she understood all too clearly what *feeding* meant.

"You eat food though, I saw you on our date … but you still need … blood or you'll become like them?"

"I can still eat human food although flavors are far more overpowering now, which is why we tend not do it very often. And yes, blood is a necessity." The apology was ever present in his eyes.

"Human blood? Do you ... have to kill?"

"Any blood works really. Human blood tastes different, which mainly has to do with diet, herbivores and carnivores, that sort of thing. And no, *I* don't have to kill." Victoria noticed the emphasis he placed on saying "I" and tilted her head questioningly.

In response to her unspoken query, he explained, "We have an enzyme in our saliva that has special healing properties, so if I need to, I can take blood from someone and they would heal easily. The trick is to know when to stop. You see, a young vampire can barely control the hunger, so early on killing is a natural consequence of feeding. Over time, most learn control."

"But won't you make more vampires by killing people?" Victoria asked, curious. Christian smiled thinly.

"Myth. If that were the case, humans wouldn't exist. We have special rules, more laws actually, for that. Unfortunately there are some vampires who are far more indulgent and enjoy taking a victim's death for the pleasure of it, the thrill of it."

"Is it thrilling?" she asked in morbid fascination. Christian stared at her with those compelling silver eyes and she shivered softly. She changed direction very quickly.

"What about mirrors?" she asked, forcing a teasing note into her voice.

"I look pretty good in them most days," Christian said, rising to her attempt at light banter. Victoria smiled. *More than pretty good*, she thought.

"Can you change into a bat?" A look of involuntary disgust crossed her face and he laughed.

"Mostly myth, although very old vampires can shift forms."

"Crucifixes?"

"I died a Catholic, remember?"

"Hmmm." Victoria pursed her lips racking her brains for some of the other so-called facts she had read in books. "Sunlight's a myth too right, because you walk around in the day?" Christian shook his head.

"Correction, I walk around in the *shade*. Sunlight is actually deadly to us. Not as in incinerate in seconds to dust, but still lethal." He paused, searching for a suitable example and continued. "Imagine the pain you would feel the next day if you lay out in the sun for four hours without any protection? Well, think about that multiplied exponentially in the space of minutes. We can get fatally ill after prolonged exposure. Light clothing and sun block like zinc oxide can help but I just try to stay out of direct sunlight. The older we get, the better the tolerance, you build up immunity."

"Ah ha!" she said. "I've got a good one!" She paused dramatically and then her face fell. "Never mind, I just realized I pretty much slept in bed with you the other night, so probably no coffins, right?"

Christian burst out laughing. "Only you can make *not* sleeping in a coffin sound like a tragedy."

"Garlic?" she asked hopefully.

"Love the smell, hate the taste," he said, his lips twitching.

"Silver!"

"Wrong type of monster, sorry. Although as you know, it hurts if it gets into our blood." She stared at him in sham disappointment.

"Do the movies get *anything* right at all about you people? We have been so misled!"

"Well, we can die from being stabbed in the heart, pretty much any sharp object. We don't age, take my beautiful young effervescent self for example." He earned a punch in the leg for his vanity. Then his voice grew quiet, a sudden rough tenderness to it. "And when we fall in love, it's for forever."

She stared at him, her breath hitching in her throat. "You're falling ... for me?"

"What do you think?"

Victoria couldn't speak as the warmth in his eyes enveloped her. Her blood raced as his lips found hers.

It didn't last long.

Gently disentangling her arms, Christian pulled back. His eyes were excited, his body on edge. He'd explained to her that the feelings that flooded him weren't that different from the ones that ruled him when he was hunting. He wanted her. He wanted her blood. To him, it equated to the same thing ... and that meant he couldn't be trusted.

Christian cleared his throat, searching for a distraction and his eyes fell on the music box resting beside her.

"It's a family heirloom," Victoria said, noticing his gaze.

"It's very beautiful." Christian felt a strange sense of familiarity as he saw the box. The crest on the top of the box tugged at his memory but he couldn't for the life of him place it. But why would he have a memory that was related to a family heirloom of Victoria's?

"It was my great, great, great, great grandmother's box," she said. "Her name was Brigid and she was a duchess, the Duchess of Lancaster."

As she said the name, suddenly something clicked in Christian's head and he almost flew up in astonishment. *Mon Dieu*, Lucian was right! Victoria looked at him quizzically.

"What's the matter?" she asked. Christian searched her face, looking for anything, anything at all that could show that she was deceiving him, but he could see nothing.

"How much do you know about your ancestor, the duchess?" he asked finally.

Victoria deliberated. She wanted to be honest with Christian but she didn't want to betray any family secrets that should remain in confidence. Christian saw her hesitation and understood the reason for it. So he took the plunge and went first.

"Tori, we have a prophecy in the vampire world that goes back centuries. I am talking centuries before I was even born a human. It's based on the legend of a witch, a very powerful witch with amazing, nearly mythical powers." He paused and looked at her carefully expressionless face. Her hands gripped each other so tightly that her fingers were almost bloodless.

He continued, his voice soft, compassionate. "The part of the legend that applies to vampires and other supernatural beings was that she could take away the curse of what they were, make a vampire mortal or a werewolf a man, just by willing it to be so. And she could also make anyone, either mortal or immortal, more powerful than they had ever dreamed, again just from her own power. Her magic was consummate, said to be descended from gods or demons."

Victoria sank back into her chair, her eyes wide. He grasped her hands in his and squeezed reassuringly before continuing. "You see the key to all her vast power was her blood. We call it *Le Sang Noir*, which translates in English to 'black blood.' It was unique, and perfect—the source *and* strength of her power."

"And what happened to her according to your legend?" Her voice was raspy, raw with emotion.

"She disappeared. Some say she died by her own hand because she was unkillable and invincible, but not before she obliterated hundreds of witches, wizards and warlocks who had united to kill her and take her power. She killed anyone who opposed her, including vampires," he said softly.

Christian could barely hear Victoria's voice, it was so quiet. "It was the call of the blood," she whispered. "She couldn't control it."

He could feel her anguish but pushed himself to continue. "It is said that the blood cost to her soul was so great that she gave up her humanity for it. She killed herself in the end."

Victoria stared at Christian her eyes burning, vehemence making her voice shake. "She *sacrificed* herself ... for her family ... for me! She fought the blood. She found something to believe in, and won. She *won!*"

Christian folded her in his arms; her silent sobs shaking her body. He forced himself to finish the prophecy because he knew she had to know.

"Tori, there's something else," he said, tipping her chin up. "The legend was about the duchess, but the prophecy I speak of ... well, it's about ... *you.*"

"W ... what?"

"You remember that day at my house when you were bleeding?" When she nodded, he kept going. "When I smelled the blood, I wanted it. I wanted you, Tori. The scent of it made me insane, I was delirious with it." Christian's eyes went dark with the mere recollection of it. He closed his eyes and breathed deeply, banishing the memory.

"It was all I could think about, and I almost took you. Almost. In the second before I went in for the kill, something stopped me. The colors in your blood were so dark and so luminous that I thought they couldn't possibly be real. And what I realized in that second was that your blood was calling me to my death. And yet, I still *wanted* it!" Christian grasped her face in his hands, his thumb brushing gently across her soft, red lips. His eyes were wild. "I think I knew it was you from that moment, but I refused to reconcile it with what I knew ... what Lucian knew," he breathed.

Victoria felt dazed. There had to be more to this whole story. She wasn't the one he spoke about! She knew she wasn't the one. She couldn't be. She was Victoria ... a loner from Millinocket, a terrible leader if there ever was one, not some fantastic witch in some mystical prophecy. It wasn't true. It couldn't be true!

She pushed Christian away and walked to the window. What he said was impossible. *Wasn't it?* Brigid's words flooded her brain ... the blood, the magic, the power ... the *blood*. Her reflection in the window stared back at her. Her face was pale but the knowledge swirling in her eyes was undeniable. Deep down, Victoria knew exactly what her legacy was.

Christian regarded her silently as she turned back toward him. It was so obvious now that he couldn't believe he hadn't seen it before. She was the descendant of the Duchess of Lancaster, and even if she didn't accept it, he saw it. It was in every curve of her body, every movement of her head ... even the air bowed in deference to her as she walked through it.

It didn't change anything, and it changed *everything*.

"So what do we do now?" she asked. "Are they going to come again in search of this prophecy?"

"I don't think so, not yet," he said.

But they will.

Victoria studied him for a minute, trying to gauge if he had been honest with her all along. She believed him, she had to—otherwise it would make everything that she had lived for during the last four months, and their love, a lie. It was her turn to confess.

"When I killed the vampire," she said, "Christian, you wouldn't believe the pleasure I felt. I knew it was the blood, the Sang Noir, and the sacrifice it demanded. It was awful. And then the one that bit me

…" Her voice trailed off into revolted silence. Christian waited for her to continue.

"It went beyond normal pain …" She struggled to find the right words. "It was like I … wanted it, just like you said, luring the vampire in … and my blood killed it, and I felt the pain of it dying within my own blood, if that makes any sense." Her voice broke. "Christian, that could have been you, and I wouldn't have been able to do a thing to stop it!"

"But it wasn't, so you can't torture yourself thinking about it." He couldn't say anything more because he knew that she was right. Her blood would have killed him instantly.

"Are you okay?" he asked after a few minutes of silence.

"Yes, it's just … a lot to take in."

"Don't worry, chérie, we'll figure something out. I'll talk to the Council next week," he said. She sighed.

"I really wish you didn't have to go to Paris so soon," she said. "Especially now, after—"

"I know. If I could cancel my trip, I would. But you'll be skiing with Charla and the others right after finals. And I'll be back before you know it. I have to go, Tori, now even more so. I need to figure this out and make sure this doesn't happen again." His eyes were fierce.

"I know," she said. "I'll miss you. You'll be careful, won't you?"

"Yes. I'll miss you, too."

Leaving her alone and unprotected while he went to Paris had been one of the hardest decisions he'd ever had to make, now more so after what had just happened. But Christian knew that he didn't have a choice—not only because of what he now knew about Victoria, but because he'd been summoned by the Vampire Council and could not refuse.

He had to see where Lucian's head was, and determine Lena's

involvement. Otherwise, the attacks on Victoria's life would only continue, and there was only one way that he could stop them.

SIXTEEN

Paris

THE LIMOUSINE PULLED to a smooth stop in front of Lucian's apartment in the seventh arrondissement, not far from the Musée D'Orsay. This was one of Paris' most exclusive and wealthy neighborhoods. Lucian had a penchant for expensive things and for indulging himself with the best that life had to offer. His ostentatiously marbled and palatial apartment reminded Christian of a mausoleum. The single thing that he liked about the apartment was the view—a magnificent panorama of the Eiffel Tower over the quarter's rooftops.

Christian had mentally confirmed Lucian's whereabouts as soon as his plane had landed, looking for him at the apartment and at the chateau. The chateau was a sprawling seventeenth century estate seven minutes south of Fontainebleau, but they usually only used it for entertaining. Lucian's version of entertainment differed greatly from Christian's. He used the chateau to host his favorite type of party—hunting parties, only with humans as the prey. It disgusted Christian. And amused Lucian.

"They are people, Lucian," Christian had argued.

"They are food, dear brother. And the sooner you realize that, the sooner you will come to terms with who you are. A *vampire*. A killer."

It had been years since they had spoken about it, but Lucian still mocked Christian's overly tender sensibilities toward humans and had chastised Christian for denying what he was and his place at the top of the food chain. Nonetheless, they had agreed to disagree, and with Christian staying out of the leadership of the House of Devereux, Lucian simply did things his way.

Christian gave his coat to the silent housekeeper as he walked into the foyer. He noticed that she was human, and given the lurid combination of black, purple, brown and yellow bruises on her skin peeking out from beneath her stark uniform, he could see that she also served as the "entertainment" from time to time. It was so easy to attract them. Some humans loved the thrill of it as much as the vampires did, and lived for the chance to become one of them. His lips thinned into a tight hard line.

He hated everything this house represented. As much as he had come to a tenuous peace with what he was, every time he was in Lucian's home, the complete absence of humanity made him tremble with impotent rage at the reality that in the end no matter how much he tried to run from it, inside he was just like them.

As he moved through the coldly elegant rooms, he sensed something different that he couldn't quite put his finger on. The space felt shrouded, cloaked in something dark and shadowy. Christian shrugged it off; Lucian's house always brought out the worst in him.

He walked to the receiving room at the end of the hall. Lucian hated to be alone, so even at this early hour it was filled with a throng of vampires who grew quiet as he entered. Christian scanned the room for his brother.

"Ah," a deep voice drawled, "the prodigal brother has returned." Lucian stood and walked toward Christian, drawing him into a showy embrace and kissing him on both cheeks. He appeared pleased to see his brother but his eyes were dark and guarded.

In spite of their disturbing resemblance, Lucian was thinner than Christian. His face was narrow and gaunt, and the way his blond hair was cut short made his angular features even more skeletal. Like Christian's, Lucian's hooded eyes were gray and spiked with the same luxurious lashes, but they didn't convey the same warmth as Christian's did, especially when coupled with his full, but cruel-looking mouth.

Christian knew that Lucian had considered killing him many times but had never tried for two reasons. In the first place, he wasn't quite sure that he could. Secondly, he didn't want to incur the condemnation of the Council, which established the rules of vampire existence and united the seven Houses under their common laws. It was no secret that Lucian reviled the Council, and they in turn only tolerated him out of fear and because of Christian.

The Council was another topic that he and Lucian disagreed on—Christian believed in the inherent values of the Council and the structure that it brought to the vampire world, even though the Council still condoned the killing of humans and supported old archaic blood rituals that were little more than murder. For Christian, that was a small sacrifice in exchange for the way the Council laws prevented the chaos that would result if the Houses had made the laws themselves or even worse, hadn't followed *any* laws.

Christian looked around the room warily and his gaze fell on the stunning white-blond woman leaning on the wall at the far end of the space. Lena. She returned his look evenly, and tilted her head in an explicitly suggestive invitation, her blue eyes mocking, which he ignored.

"Perhaps we should talk in your study, Lucian." He turned back to his brother and inclined his head toward the audience. "And let your guests enjoy themselves."

As Christian walked out of the room, he noticed another woman standing in the shadows, who avoided looking in his direction. She was human, but held herself with an authority that belied the fact that she was surrounded by vampires who could kill her in an instant. Other than this commanding quality, she was nondescript with short, brown hair and a swarthy complexion.

He noticed that she had the same bruises on her arms as the housekeeper, another of Lucian's toys it seemed, although something seemed strange about her bruises, as if they were over her skin instead of beneath it. He shrugged again and dismissed her from his thoughts, following Lucian down the hallway to the study.

In the dark wood-paneled study, Christian helped himself to a large glass of Louis XIII cognac and sat on the edge of the massive, mahogany desk.

"So what brings you to town?" Lucian was brusque, his manner dismissive. But underneath, Christian knew he was curious. It wasn't like him to show up unannounced.

"I was requested to come before the Council."

"On what grounds?" Lucian asked, feigning indifference.

"On the *grounds* of your actions! You've gone too far this time, Lucian."

Lucian looked completely unfazed by the furious snarl in Christian's tone and stared disinterestedly at his manicure. But inside, his mind was racing. The Council would only have called Christian back to Paris to consider one thing—him assuming control of the House of Devereux because they were threatened by Lucian's recent actions.

As much as Lucian feared his brother's power, the vampires of the House were loyal only to Lucian. Once he found the witch from the prophecy, he believed he would have the power to finally eliminate Christian, and have total control over the Council and the vampire world. The Watchers had felt the shift in flow of magic that heralded the birth of a witch-queen, Lucian just needed to find her and find her quickly.

Christian tried to soften his voice, misinterpreting Lucian's silence. "Lucian, I am serious. This isn't a game anymore. Your flagrant disregard for the rules and our laws will only put the House of Devereux in jeopardy. The witch clans are uniting in retaliation, damn it!" He slammed his fist on the top of the desk in anger, unable to restrain himself. "That's what the Council is afraid of. War. One we cannot afford."

Christian knew that the Council had the power to call him back to France to stay and that they would use it especially under threat of war with others. That was the one thing he did not want. He liked the life he had created for himself, he liked living according to his own rules, and he liked his solitude—away from the very cusp of what made him despise his own nature. Their ways, Lucian's ways, were *not* his ways.

And when he thought of the inevitable danger for Victoria because of Lucian's actions, it only made him further incensed.

"Your torture and murder of people you believe to be witches in search of this ridiculous prophecy. It will be the death of us all."

"Are you finished?" Lucian said.

"I'm just getting started!" He was in Lucian's face now and he could see a muscle starting to tick in Lucian's jaw even as he continued to feign boredom. "The prophecy is a legend, it's a myth!

You're letting Le Sang Noir destroy you in your obsession to find it. Leave it alone Lucian. If this is about you and me, I already gave you my rights to the House of Devereux. It is yours! Don't you understand? I. Don't. Want. It." Christian punctuated the last sentence with sharp jabs on Lucian's chest.

Lucian's eyes flashed fire and his fingernails dug into his palms as he fought to restrain his anger. "How dare you? You have no concept of what is at stake, hiding away as you've been in some desolate little North American town with mortals for companions! The Watchers have foreseen it. *Everyone* is looking for the witch. I'm just taking the necessary steps to find her first!"

His tirade continued, spit flying from his mouth as Christian stared at him in stunned horror. "So what if the witch and warlock clan leaders are approaching the Council in negotiations? After I find Le Sang Noir, it will be a moot point. They will all eventually be under my rule! It's too bad that the Watchers failed to track the witch … her magic has until now concealed her from them, but that doesn't mean they won't find her. It's only a matter of time, *mon cher frère*." He spat the last three words like bullets.

"Is that what this is about? Power?"

"What do you think it's about? You never cared for any of it, for me or for what I wanted—" Lucian broke off as if he'd said too much, and composed himself with a cold smile. "Who cares about those witches anyway? They are just like humans, only they taste a thousand times better. Cattle," he said derisively. His glare was vicious and his next words deliberately provocative. "After all, what do you care? I let your witch live, didn't I? But maybe I need to pay her a personal return visit to see whether you're hiding something from me, to see if she's the one after all—"

"YOU WILL NOT TOUCH HER!"

Christian leapt on top of Lucian, crashing them both into the wall of the study and sending a hundred books flying.

The noise was deafening as the wooden panels split under the force of their bodies. Lucian delivered a vicious kick to Christian's stomach hurling him across the room. As Christian vaulted to his feet, Lucian brandished a wicked-looking cane that was sharpened on one end and tipped with silver. Christian's eyes narrowed.

A loud banging on the door followed by worried shouting ensued. Christian and Lucian slowly circled each other, Christian's jeering expression daring Lucian to call for help. As Lucian passed the doorframe, he shouted that anyone coming through the door would die. He twirled the cane in his hands, irritated that Christian barely looked perturbed by the weapon. Lucian shot forward, the silver tip of the cane piercing Christian's thigh. Christian grimaced.

"Like my little pleasure tool?" Lucian asked. "I use it on vampires who don't know their place." They continued to dance around each other so fast that their movement blurred.

As Lucian slashed the air with the cane, a thin diagonal line of blood welled across the chest of Christian's white shirt. Beneath the torn material, his skin knitted back together in seconds. Christian crouched low and waited for the right moment before feinting left and kicking Lucian's feet from under him. He grabbed the cane out of Lucian's hands, and as Lucian fell back on the floor, Christian was on top of him in a flash, his fists hammering in blind rage. He could feel the bones shattering under the force of his furious blows, and as he felt the rage drain out of him with each successive strike, Lucian's bloodied face swam into focus.

Christian stood up, bringing Lucian up with him and watching as his brother's broken brow bone, nose and jaw mended themselves, the pulverized face reforming perfectly and the broken skin healing before his eyes. In moments, Lucian's features were unmarred except for the blood that remained on his face and spattered on his clothing. His expression was dark with hatred.

Christian stepped away and turned toward the fireplace, his hands falling to his sides. Instinct alone alerted him to the movement behind him and he ducked just as the dagger whizzed past his head, spinning with inhuman speed to bring the heel of his hand into Lucian's exposed neck.

As Lucian buckled, Christian slammed him up against the splintered wall and spat, "Don't even try it, Lucian."

"Or what?" gasped Lucian.

"You will not like the outcome, that, I can assure you. I will deal with the Council and then I will go back home, Lucian. And you, you will respect the rules of the Council, do you understand?"

Christian released his brother and walked away without a backward glance. The room was in complete shambles. As he closed the door behind him, he heard the fifteen hundred dollar bottle of Louis VIII smash into the doorframe followed by a slew of violent curses. Christian walked out to the foyer, past the throngs of Lucian's followers watching him with wonder. They feared him, and rightly so. As he neared the ornate front door, Lena held his coat draped over her arm, her beautiful face expressionless.

"He won't forgive you so easily for that, you know," she said.

"I don't care," Christian said flatly.

He sighed and ran a hand through his hair. He didn't fully understand the relationship between Lucian and Lena, but he could hazard a guess at the nature of it.

Despite her history with Christian, Lucian seemed to trust Lena implicitly. And Lena seemed to have decided that second-best was better than nothing at all. The look in her eyes, if anything, still told him that, even after all these years. But there was a new hardness to her that Christian noticed. Years of committing atrocity after atrocity would eventually take its toll, even on an eternally perfect face. She placed a hand on his arm.

"Christian," she said. "It's good to see you." Again the unspoken invitation was apparent. Perhaps another time Christian would have taken her up on it, but not now.

"Lena, I can't." He saw the glimmer of hope die in her ice blue eyes. Understanding dawned, and the blue sparked with venom.

"It's because of *her*, isn't it? She is a dirty mortal witch, Christian, and not your equal! You degrade yourself by deigning to be seen with her. It is forbidden!"

"Actually, she deigns to be with me," he said, "but I wouldn't expect you to understand." Christian looked at her with some measure of pity despite her malicious words. "You don't understand love Lena, you never could."

"Love?" she spat. "I thought Lucian was out of his mind when he said that you had put a filthy mortal before your duty! But he was right wasn't he?" Lena's eyes flashed fury and disgust and jealousy. "You are not fit for the House of Devereux."

He looked at her coldly and she shrank from the intensity of his frigid glare. "You forget *your* place, Lena. I am a Devereux. I answer to no one. Don't you *ever* forget that!" Christian's voice shook with wrath. His next words were silky. "If you ever challenge me like this again, be prepared to face the consequences. I won't be so forgiving the next time." The door crashed into its frame as it slammed shut behind him.

The limousine pulled away from the curb and Christian leaned back into the seat. He had just succeeded in antagonizing two of the most powerful vampires in the House of Devereux and quite possibly in the whole of Europe, which probably had not been the wisest move. But if it kept his brother from realizing who Victoria was and kept the Council in balance, then it would be worth it.

Christian thought about Lena. She, on the other hand, was

a different story—she was one of the deadliest and most lethal vampires he had ever met. He should know, after all, he had made her.

He stared out the window at the passing shops and restaurants, and thought back to the first time he had met Lena. An Austrian baroness, she had been stunning, mesmerizing, and both Christian and Lucian had been enraptured the minute they had seen her dueling in Vienna. It was in the last decade of the nineteenth century on a day neither of them would ever forget.

Her delicate feminine beauty had belied her strength and furious force of will, not to mention her skilled grace with a rapier. They'd watched her as she fought against three men, two twice her size, her weapon spinning at impossible speed. Her blond hair had whipped free of its covering, and people around them gasped. They'd thought her a boy.

"She's magnificent," Lucian had announced, staring at his brother in unspoken challenge. "I want her." Back then, competition had been a natural force between them—it had made the prize more exciting and much more satisfying when won.

"I want her, too," Christian had said.

And so it began.

They had pursued her relentlessly, fueled by the competition from each other, and fascinated by everything about her; her disregard for propriety, her flagrant disrespect for the rules, and her insatiable appetite to try anything—she did what she wanted when she wanted. She could speak nine languages, fight with all manner of weapons including her fists, having grown up with seven brothers, and she was fearless.

In the end, Christian had been first to petition the Council to allow her to become his companion, and they had granted the request. He'd told Lena the first time he'd taken her to his bed, and afterward, Christian offered Lena the gift of immortality.

"How could I want anything more than to be with you forever," she'd said.

There'd been no mention of love, and Lena had embraced becoming a vampire, and him, with open arms. Lucian had been a gracious loser, but in hindsight, Christian recognized that things had changed between them after that day.

It was during a time in his life when the monotony of immortality had weighed its heaviest and he had been looking for something, someone, *anything*, to offset the incredible sense of emptiness that had plagued him. Lena's uninhibited zest for every part of life had been like a spike of adrenaline to his system.

But despite his being her maker, a true bond between them had never formed and his attraction to her had worn off. He didn't love Lena, and the things that had drawn him to her in the first place, her fearlessness and lust for life, became the very things that he loathed the most. Like Lucian, she reveled in the kill, she reveled in being immortal, being stronger, faster, better, and she was willing to do whatever gave her the biggest thrill. In the end, she couldn't change who she was, a deadly killer who thoroughly enjoyed being one.

So he had left the House without any regrets, and she had stayed with Lucian. Over the years, she had remained eternally beautiful, but had become a thousand times more lethal.

As they drove through the city, Christian caught a glimpse of the gilded top of the Eiffel Tower in the distance, beautiful and majestic, and he felt an urge to just stop and breathe in the magic that was Paris. He instructed the driver to head toward the Arc de Triomphe. He felt like taking a walk.

He got out of the car and dismissed the driver for the night, saying that he would get himself back to St. Germain. The night air was crisp and cold, the Champs-Elysées beautifully lit with trees covered in tiny white lights meandering down either side of the grand avenue. Brightly lit storefronts glittered as far as the eye could see and the occasional glow of headlights pierced the darkness. He loved the sounds and the smell of Paris. It was like old world glory, infusing his blood with the sense of life and warmth that he barely remembered from his mortal existence. He knew it would always be home in his heart even though he only visited once a year.

Perhaps one day he would bring Victoria here. She would love it.

As her name crossed his mind, he felt the familiar stirring in his heart and wondered whether she was thinking about him. Christian had tried to communicate mentally with her but for some reason, he'd been unable to, and when he'd tried to call, it went straight to voicemail. He didn't like not being able to reach her, but there was nothing he could do but keep trying.

He clasped his hands behind his back and walked down the avenue as groups of young people with their ruddy happy faces swirled past, laughing and talking loudly. He watched as a young couple, hands laced, kissed passionately on a bench, and felt the familiar sensation unfurl in his belly. He hadn't fed since arriving in Paris. Normally he could last a week between feedings but the fight with Lucian had drained him more than expected.

His gaze remained relaxed as he slowly swept the area. He didn't have acres of woodland to work with as he did in Canville, but at the end of the day, blood was blood. He supposed he could go to Lucian's, there were enough willing human donors there as he had seen from the housekeeper's lurid bruises, but everything about it repulsed him, making the cattle analogy a little too real for comfort. He kept walking, his predator's mind alert and searching.

Soon, it seemed like hours had passed, and Christian had

considered and just as quickly discarded several handfuls of people passing by. Frustrated, the sensation in his stomach becoming more insistent with each vibrantly alive body, he faced the truth of the matter—he knew exactly what he wanted, someone like *her*. Despite how terrible it seemed, a small part of him wanted in some desperate way to mirror the act, with someone who at least looked liked her. The mere thought of it excited him.

He walked past the Place de la Concorde and into the Jardin des Tuileries, where he sat on a small green metal chair and waited, watchful. Something stroked his awareness and he focused on a girl who had just crossed the far end of the gravel path. She smelled nothing like Victoria, but her long dark hair, coloring and height were enough to make his heart beat faster from a distance. Curiously, she did not appear to be nervous when he approached her, asking if she had the time in flawless French. She smiled coquettishly, attracted despite herself to him, a handsome, mysterious stranger. He had forgotten how naturally the magnetism came to him.

It wasn't difficult to persuade her to accompany him to a wooden bench in the shadow of a small tree, his silver eyes compelling, his vampire power hypnotic and irresistible. She had no chance. They sat and he leaned into her slowly as her hair fell forward in a dark curtain, her neck long and slim and inviting. Warm. Pulsing with life. He felt his jaw tighten, his teeth lengthen, and a single thought crossed his mind … *Victoria*.

To the random passerby, they looked like any other couple in love, sharing a fevered embrace, her expression beatific, arms resting on his shoulders. Christian took what he needed and watched as the puncture wounds healed, facilitated by the enzyme in his saliva until the only sign of entry remaining was a slight, reddening bruise. He thanked her for her assistance and watched as she woozily made her way to the main road. She would not remember the encounter other than a stranger asking her for the time.

Although the blood had satiated his hunger, he felt strangely empty, and the edge of his desire remained, taunting him with its presence. It was a longing that only Victoria herself could assuage.

Christian couldn't sleep and spent half the night sitting on his balcony in the blistering cold, staring out at the night sky. He missed not being able to communicate with Victoria at any moment and his anxiety was getting the better of him. He wanted to call her, knowing that it would only be nine in the evening there but he didn't want to seem obsessive. After all, she hadn't called him either.

After another hour of arguing with himself, he finally picked up his phone and dialed her cell number. It went straight to voicemail and he didn't bother to leave a message. He went back to staring blindly at the dark sky.

SEVENTEEN

The Council

CHRISTIAN TRIED TO call Victoria several times throughout the morning with no success. He decided that he would try the ski lodge once his meeting with the Council was over. It had only been a couple days, but he needed to know that she was all right.

The limousine cut west neatly through the afternoon traffic on the way to La Défense, the business center of Paris. The Council was a powerful body that owned several wealthy corporations and made use of their boardrooms to conduct other business like special Council meetings. Real estate was just another of the perks of immortality.

The limousine pulled to a stop, and the chauffeur opened the door. Looking up briefly at the overcast sky, Christian stepped out, leaving his overcoat in the car and walked briskly over to the Tour Areva, one of the tallest skyscrapers in La Défense. The building was entirely black, fitting for its owners, with dark granite walls and darkly tinted windows, a massive onyx structure rising more than six hundred feet into the air.

Christian walked into the lobby and immediately turned heads. Despite his youth, his height commanded attention, and the authority and confidence he emanated, held it. Dressed in an impeccably tailored charcoal Italian suit, crisp white shirt left open at the neck with no tie, and polished Dior loafers, he certainly looked the part of an executive. He looked young, sophisticated and entirely too dangerous.

Normally Christian preferred a more casual look but at these Council meetings, appearances were everything, especially for someone considered vampire royalty. By human standards, nineteen was young. By vampire standards, a hundred and seventy-five even more so. Still, after so many years, the pretense came naturally to him and his act was flawless.

He took the private elevator to the top floor where a gorgeous brunette showed him into the conference room. Human, with not a mark on her perfect, bronzed skin that he could see. He smiled and was rewarded with a warm look of unmistakable invitation. So maybe the marks were elsewhere. In a delightful breathy voice, she said, "They'll be here soon. Is there anything I can get you?"

Christian smiled again and declined, allowing himself to relax a bit after she left, although he wasn't naïve enough to think that they weren't watching him, so he continued to play the part, lounging in his chair and looking indifferent to being kept waiting.

When the receptionist came back in to let him know that they would be in shortly, he stood up and strode over to the floor to ceiling windows. The city of La Défense stretched in an undulating wave below, and even when he heard the door open behind him, he didn't turn around until he knew they were all there.

"My Lords," he began, using the formal address, "I am here at your request." He stared around the long table, his gaze impassive yet respectful. Despite knowing the part that he was expected to play, he was also well aware of the power at this table. Some of the Elders were thousands of years old. He recognized many of the faces and nodded politely to those he knew. Others were unfamiliar, younger members more recently inducted to the Council. Though Paris was its headquarters, the Council was global, with twenty members from all over the world. Christian also noticed with some surprise that there were now two female members on the Council. Things *were* changing.

On the whole, he did not detect any measure of blatant hostility, although some of the newer faces were wary. Good, that meant that they knew what to expect.

Enhard, one of the Council speakers, stood gesturing for Christian to sit at the last remaining seat at the table. Enhard was handsome, his unlined youthful face belying the fact that he was several hundred centuries old and considered an Elder. Christian sat with a gracious inclination of his head.

"Your Grace, thank you for coming," Enhard said. "As the first matter of business today, we raise the issue of the prophecy. We fear that the actions of your brother, Lord Devereux, will bring war upon us. The witch clans have made claims that he has murdered innocents in his blind desire to discover Le Sang Noir. The worst offense was a thirteen year old witch killed in full view of her entire coven." Enhard paused. Christian's face remained impassive. "There is a centuries-old truce based on a violent past between vampires and witches; we don't hunt them and they don't attack us. Our agreements have been tenuous at best, and our truce is now in jeopardy. His flagrant disrespect of this law, among others, must be addressed."

Enhard stopped, his dark gaze intense. The tension in the room was palpable.

"We respect the power and lineage of the House of Devereux,

and it is in deference to this ancestry that we have come to you. Lucian must be controlled." Enhard's voice was soft, but the veiled warning in it was unmistakable. Other members of the Council nodded their heads in vehement agreement.

"What is it you expect me to do, my Lords?" Christian said coolly. "I will tolerate no attack against my brother."

His manner was deferential yet imperious. There was a muttering as if they hadn't quite expected him to respond in that manner. What they didn't understand was his loyalty. Regardless of what Christian thought of Lucian and his reckless activities, he would never throw him to the wolves of the Council, no matter the cost.

One of the younger council members called Avael spoke. "You must speak to your brother and advise him of the consequences if he chooses to pursue this course of action!"

"And what are the consequences?" The astonished looks he received were almost worth the price of asking the audacious question. He leaned forward in an attitude of expectant inquiry.

"Why, execution, of course," said Avael. Christian's expression hardened. Enhard rushed to amend Avael's overzealous response.

"What Lord Avael means, of course, is that the Council will be forced to take immediate punitive action against Lucian. The massacres he has orchestrated against the witches are bringing undue attention to us. Our society is at risk. He must be stopped," he said.

Christian stood and walked to the wall of glass overlooking the business district, clasping his hands behind his back. He knew it was not considered good manners to turn his back to the Council, but it was a strategic move. He waited several long minutes, feeling the stares boring into his back, before he turned and addressed the Council.

"What of Le Sang Noir?" His simple, direct question sent a ripple of anxiety through the conference room. Christian was resolute. He had to understand what they knew about the fulfillment of the prophecy. Several sputtered as if in shock. He could see that Avael was contemplating saying something rash. He liked to keep them off-balance. They had far too much confidence in their own power.

Enhard responded, as Christian faced them, waiting. "Our Watchers have revealed movement in the magical spheres, something big. We believe that Le Sang Noir has reappeared and caused this disturbance."

"And have you pinpointed its location?"

The Council members murmured and Enhard raised a hand slowly for silence. He knew they believed that he was going too far, sharing this much with Christian Devereux, despite his lineage and status in the vampire world. Enhard knew that if it came down to it, any animosity between Christian Devereux and the Council could only end badly. Even Christian didn't comprehend the full power of his lineage, not his human one, but his vampire lineage. It was the main reason Enhard had petitioned him for help against Lucian. Any other course of action would have meant declaring war against the House of Devereux, all in all, a very foolish proposition.

"Yes," he said, and Christian's heart lurched. "We know that she is somewhere in the Americas."

Christian resumed his position at the table, knowing that the Council would interpret the gesture as a positive action. He placed his elbows on the table forming a steeple with his hands. His body language was non-threatening, and he could feel the Council members relax now that the worst had passed. Or so they thought.

"Regardless, what makes you think I would do anything to hand my brother over to the Council?" he asked. Enhard glanced at him sharply, recognizing his double-edged tone of voice and Christian returned his gaze evenly. "Especially now that you have confirmed the existence of Le Sang Noir."

Several Council members jumped to their feet in angry response, and Christian pushed his chair back deliberately, his long, lithe body signaling danger, forearms braced against the edge of the table. His face was as hard as sculpted marble.

David, another Elder, stood along with Enhard and commanded everyone to sit down. Christian remained standing, his stance uncompromising. David spoke, his ancient voice thready.

"Your Grace, I understand your reluctance to agree, but Lucian is dangerous. His desires outweigh his judgment. All we ask is that you get him to see reason. We simply cannot risk war with the magic world." He hesitated. "You are correct to be wary of Le Sang Noir, but so should we all, for if the witch clans harness its power against us, we are lost."

Although Christian saw the undeniable truth in David's eyes, he wasn't naïve. He knew that if he had given in to the Council about Lucian, they would own them both *and* the House of Devereux. He'd had enough.

"As you wish, I will speak to Lucian," he conceded. "But on my terms."

He inclined his head graciously and walked out of the conference room without a backward glance. He had almost reached the elevator when a voice called out behind him. Christian turned and saw that it was Enhard, whose face was cautious as he approached.

"Thank you, Christian," he said. "I know this must have been hard for you."

"Come on Enhard, you've known Lucian as long as I have. When has *anything* he has done not been hard for me?" Enhard chuckled in response and Christian relaxed.

Enhard had been more like a father to the two of them than he cared to admit. In fact, Enhard had been one of the vampires who had found them on the edge of death. Ever since they had been turned, he'd stayed close as a mentor and guide throughout the years.

Christian clasped Enhard's shoulders and brought him close into an embrace kissing him on both cheeks, as was the French custom. He knew that even in the foyer that he would still be closely watched, and it was always critical to keep up appearances *and* alliances especially with someone as powerful as Enhard. The Council was meticulous in the extreme, and the embrace was as deliberate as were Christian's next words.

"Meet me at L'Echiquier at the Hilton," Christian murmured, as he embraced Enhard. "My warmest regards to your family," he said in a normal voice. Then he entered the elevator, Enhard watching him until the doors closed.

CHRISTIAN SAT IN the bar in a comfortable club chair. He had chosen an out of the way corner which offered a clear line of sight. He ordered a glass of cognac from the flirtatious waitress and sipped it waiting for Enhard. Even though the cognac had little effect on him, he enjoyed the taste of it.

The waitress came by again, her look suggestive and inviting as she asked him if there was anything else she could get for him. It would have been easy enough to consider her explicit invitation with her reddish hair and lush hips, but he politely said that he was fine for just then. She smiled provocatively as she walked past him, and he sighed. It seemed that Paris incited his predatory magnetism.

In Canville, life was a lot simpler. He was an ordinary student, and he liked it that way. He blended in, and tried very hard to make his dark nature invisible. He was certain that he was the only vampire in Canville, and that was why he'd chosen it—obscurity. When he took blood from humans, he had always made sure that it was well away from the small town. Christian had learned early on that his vampire magnetism was a capricious thing. Sometimes the seduced remembered him long after he had satiated himself and sent them on their way, so he preferred to err on the side of caution.

Still, the vampire magnetism had its uses … and benefits. Christian smiled, thinking of Victoria.

"I hope that smile isn't for me," Enhard said, as he sat down on the vacant club chair opposite Christian. Christian shrugged, embarrassed.

"I was just thinking of a friend," he said.

"If she can make you smile like that when she's not around, I shudder to think what you are like when she *is* around," he said. He settled into the chair and leaned forward expectantly.

Christian deliberated momentarily, but then for some reason or perhaps because he just wanted to talk to someone about her, he decided to tell Enhard the truth. Well, the partial truth.

"Her name is Tori. She's beautiful and captivating."

Christian could see Enhard going through the Rolodex in his head, trying to make a match. He waited until he saw Enhard's brows furrow as he struggled to figure it out.

"She's human, Enhard," he said. Enhard's eyes widened because that was possibly the last thing he had expected to hear, given the besotted look he had seen on Christian's face.

"Human?" he echoed dumbly, his expression vacant. Christian wanted to laugh. It wasn't that unheard of! But he knew where Enhard was coming from, the whole royal blood thing, and the fact that any good female vampire would kill to be with a Devereux.

"Christian, there are tons of girls, good *vampire* girls from good families who would be perfect for you," he said predictably.

"Enhard, she's the one. Human or not, it doesn't matter."

Enhard sat back in his chair at a loss for words. The whole mortal/immortal issue was not a trifling one, and the fact was that Christian *had* already made one vampire. Their laws were very specific—a vampire could only be made with the approval of the Council, and in most cases, a vampire was only allowed to make one other vampire. Control of numbers was a critical part of their existence.

"Christian, I am sure you understand my concern. It's not that I haven't had my fair share of female human companions over the years, but those relationships were fleeting, because their *lives* are fleeting," Enhard said after several minutes. "You know the law."

"Yes, I do." Christian's face was impassive and Enhard sighed, leaning back in his chair. He knew when to let the matter drop. "So tell me what the real agenda of the Council is," Christian said bluntly. Enhard's face immediately went serious.

"It's not an agenda, Christian. Lucian's actions have been terrible. I understand what's driving him, but he is risking our way of life for something that may not even exist."

Christian gave him a sidelong sardonic glance. "I thought you said that Le Sang Noir was for real?"

"Yes, we believe so. But it still doesn't mean that he can use it for whatever he thinks he can use it for. It's like an urban legend. No one actually *knows* how it works." Enhard looked at Christian, noticing the suddenly shuttered look in his eyes, and rushed to continue. "Lucian is obsessed with the prophecy, and his pursuit of this obsession is bringing us to the brink of war. You know, Christian, as well as I do, that Lucian is dangerous." He took a long sip of his drink. "The Council wanted to take immediate action against him but many fear him and lack the courage to oppose him."

"Enhard, you know that I want no part of the House of Devereux. Lucian *is* the House of Devereux, not me."

"But you are first-born. It is your birthright, and you are the only one powerful enough to stop him," Enhard said, desperate.

Christian smiled. "My birthright has always been what I choose it to be." He signaled the waitress to bring him another cognac, and leaned back in his chair. "Tell me more about Le Sang Noir," he said. Enhard stared at him.

"We are not a hundred percent certain that it is back, but the movement of magic this year alone has been immeasurable. We've always kept an eye on the witch clans and the ebb and flow of magic over the years, just as they've kept a close watch on our numbers. Recently, the magic index has spiked, indicating the possible reemergence of Le Sang Noir. We're still not sure though. All of our information has been spotty at best as to what exactly is its true power," he said.

He leaned forward, his voice a whisper.

"The Council suspects that Lucian has an alliance with a witch or warlock." At Christian's disbelieving look, Enhard continued. "There are magical wards in place that were not here before. Even our Seers are inhibited by them, they are so powerful." Enhard's handsome face was anxious, and after eight hundred odd years, it took a lot to get him worried.

"Exactly what kind of wards are we talking about?" Christian asked suddenly very alert. He thought back to the strange feeling he'd had when he entered Lucian's house, that odd cloaking feeling. Something started to click into place.

"Dark magic, Christian, I'm sure of it," Enhard said. Christian had never seen the old vampire look so troubled. "They've grown stronger in the last day."

"Enhard, if Lucian discovered Le Sang Noir somehow, what would that mean?"

Enhard hesitated, searching for the right words. "I love Lucian as my own son, as I do you," he said, "but Lucian has become … corrupt. He does not follow the old code. You know we kill if we have to …" Enhard stopped to acknowledge Christian's raised eyebrow, and nodded. "It is our way Christian, even if you disagree. But your brother Lucian kills for pleasure, indiscriminately and even more so in search of Le Sang Noir and the power it holds. He is deliberately careless, and it makes the Elders nervous for our security. We have lived through countless centuries, millennia even, in the proverbial shadows." Enhard seemed amused at his choice of words. "Not like we used to, of course, but metaphorically speaking now." He gestured needlessly at the people swirling around them.

"It's not just the witches, Christian, the humans are beginning to notice. Their scientists and forensic experts have the tools and the technology now, not to mention all the books and films flaunting our secrets! In the beginning, it was easy to get rid of the ones that got too close, but now your brother is making it impossible to do so without drawing *more* attention from the humans. They take murder very seriously, if you hadn't noticed." Enhard took a sip of his drink and waved away the waitress who hovered far too solicitously for her own good.

"On top of that, Lucian's disregard for our treaties with the witch clans and his obvious acts of provocation including the murder of a high priestess, have drawn their censure. Any personal alliance with a witch is forbidden. They are calling for retribution in blood, your brother's blood." Enhard put both hands in front of him placatingly, his voice harsh with regret. "I'm sorry to have to be the one—" he said, and stopped when Christian put a hand on his arm.

"I've known for a long time that Lucian's desires would cost him," he said. "I just didn't realize we could all pay the price. Have they agreed on a course of action?"

"Yes. If you fail to stop him, the Council will vote on execution."

"What are their terms?" He knew quite well that Lucian would have little chance if the Council went to a vote as, given their fear of Lucian, the outcome was certain.

"Surrender of the witch or warlock helping him," said Enhard. "And Lucian?"

"He will be spared at the discretion of the Council. If he pursues any additional act of aggression against the witch clans, or does not abide by the laws of the Council, the vote will proceed."

A muscle ticked in Christian's jaw. Enhard's face was sharp with pity. The situation had worsened in the last few months and given the state of the Council, Christian had little hope to save Lucian without a miracle. Lucian's desire for power blinded him to everything else, and the deadly lure of Le Sang Noir had poisoned that desire and turned it into manic obsession.

"Tell the Council that it is a witch they seek, a short, dark-haired, dark-skinned woman. See if it can buy some goodwill," said Christian. Now he knew why those bruises on the woman's arms in Lucian's house had disturbed him—they were cleverly done, fake markings. That, coupled with her authoritative attitude in a roomful of deadly vampires, should have been a giveaway. He was angry with himself for only just figuring it out even though there was probably nothing he could have done differently. Enhard glanced at his watch and Christian stood, putting on his coat. They embraced.

"Thank you for your candor, my friend. I will see what I can do to salvage this and save my brother from himself."

Christian got into the limo and instructed the driver to head for Lucian's apartment. He raked his hands through his hair, furious with Lucian for endangering their way of life, their family, and their very existence.

This witch helping Lucian puzzled him because he couldn't understand what she would have to gain by aligning with a vampire. Even if Lucian were successful in finding Le Sang Noir, her only aim would be to kill him just as his would be to kill her once Lucian had exhausted her aid. Christian's only hope was that their continued alliance along with the magical wards meant that Lucian *hadn't* discovered Le Sang Noir.

But just as he finished that thought, he realized he was wrong about the wards. Enhard had said they'd become stronger a day ago ... just in time for Christian's arrival in Paris. They'd been strengthened for *him*.

Victoria!

Christian's first call was to the airport. His pilot would have his plane ready to leave in two hours. The second was to Victoria, voicemail again! Frustrated, he snapped the phone shut. Before the limousine even came to a complete stop, he had jumped out and slammed into Lucian's apartment, palpable rage streaming from every part of his body.

"Lucian!" he roared as he tore through the apartment like a whirlwind with enraged inhuman speed, ignoring the shocked stares of Lucian's guests.

Yes, dear brother. Lucian's mental voice dripped with sarcasm. Christian found him in the master bedroom on the fourth level of the townhouse. He was standing in front of the bed holding a naked girl close, his lips rimmed in red and his eyes feral. The bemused girl swooned as Lucian tossed her unceremoniously onto the bed, licking the lips that had pulled back in a sneer upon seeing Christian.

Snack? he asked. Christian snarled so ferociously that the girl's eyes snapped open from her semi-trance, and she shrank back among the sheets, staring at them like the monsters they were.

"Out!" Christian barked at the girl as she stared at him with terrified eyes. It would be up to her to make it out of the house alive, which probably wouldn't happen. He gritted his teeth. "Wait outside," he said, his eyes fierce and compelling, and she obeyed. Christian turned his attention back to Lucian who stared at him, a mix of boredom and arrogant defiance playing across his features.

"The Council will issue an execution edict for you unless you surrender the witch helping you to uncover the prophecy." At Lucian's stunned look, Christian smiled coldly. "Did you think they wouldn't find out? Magic use is carefully monitored. They know you are aligned with a witch. You are violating the terms of the truce, and they want you to stop. Surrender her and you live." Christian's voice brooked no disagreement. Lucian's eyes became manic as he stared at Christian.

"She is the key," he said. "I will not. I am so close that the Council's empty threats will mean nothing! They will soon be begging for me to spare *them*!" Lucian's eyes were demented, and Christian felt genuine alarm for his brother's state of mind.

"Lucian, Le Sang Noir is a legend. It won't make you invincible! Even if it could, your witch would kill you the minute she found it, don't you know that?"

Lucian's uncontrolled, hollow laughter echoed in the room.

"Kill me?" he said. "She won't."

"Why is she helping you?" Christian tried a different tack. Still, all he received in response was more of the same hollow, mocking laughter.

"Trust me, brother, and you can spare me the misplaced show of brotherly concern, there is no way she would kill me. Come on, ask me why?"

"Okay, why?"

"Let's just say, she knows who will lead the new world. In

return for her services, she will have whatever she desires," he said, laughing more at Christian's incredulous expression. "You would be surprised at how vicious she is, she's the one who killed the other witches, not me. I think she's a bit mad. Must have been why she was exiled." He smiled cruelly at Christian's shock. "My gain, though. Her services include a unique charm that can identify Le Sang Noir. Like I said, the Council will be on their knees in a matter of days," he said. "I suppose when Le Sang Noir is mine, I can dispose of her if I need to but I have a feeling that she will be quite useful to me in unearthing the weaknesses of the witch clans."

"Are you insane, Lucian? She is an exile for a reason!" Christian said. It was common knowledge that an exiled witch or wizard meant only one thing—mental illness. Normally they were stripped of the magical powers because they were so volatile, but it sounded like this particular witch had found a way to retain some of her magical abilities. That made her, and Lucian, very dangerous.

"So?"

"Where is she?" Christian said, suddenly realizing that on his way in, he had not noticed either the mysterious witch or Lena. Nor did he like his brother's coldly evil smile.

"Hunting," Lucian taunted with a meaningful smirk, and the air whooshed out of Christian's body.

"If anything happens to her—"

"What? I die? Get in line, brother!"

Christian turned on his heel and stalked out of the room. On his way out, he remembered the frightened girl who remained sitting on a settee in the hallway. He grabbed her by the arm, and her entire body pitched forward like a dead weight. Fresh red streaks stained her skin, and crescent-shaped gouges disfigured her limbs. She was dead. The scavengers had gotten to her.

Christian noticed a white face staring at him malevolently

from a doorway further down the hall, and he snarled. The face disappeared. Untold horrors lurked in every shadow of that house; things that made the most gruesome stories told about vampires seem like fairy tales. He felt a twinge of pity for the girl's wasted life but maybe it was for the best, she would have suffered far worse at Lucian's hands. He couldn't get out of there fast enough.

In the car, he tried Victoria's phone again and got a busy signal. Either her phone was dead or she still didn't have service. His next phone call was to Enhard to let him know that the witch was an exile. With any luck, the witch clans could use the information to narrow down possible options and to help to contain the situation.

The car drove onto the airfield as he stared impatiently out the window, knowing he could run faster and almost deciding to do it, when his phone rang. The number came up as private.

"Yes?" His voice was terse.

"Christian? It's me …" He collapsed back into the seat, his relief palpable. "Look I'm really sorry if you tried to call, I don't have any service here. I'm calling from a landline at the lodge with a calling card."

"I did try to call, several times," he said hoarsely.

"I was really worried that something had happened with Lucian when I didn't hear from you, not even a message," she said. "Is everything okay? What happened with the Council?"

"I'm sorry I didn't leave a message. Everything is okay, I'll explain later. I'm leaving, on my way back."

"Home?"

"Yes." He didn't want to scare her but he needed to make sure that she was alert and wary of possible danger. "Listen, Tori, there's been a complication. Remember the woman who attacked you in Canville? Well, she may be back. You need to be careful, stay with people at all times until I get to you. I will come for you, okay?"

His voice was urgent, compelling. He needed her to listen to him at all costs. He knew that the likelihood of Lena attacking in public was low, but he also knew how far Lucian would go to get what he wanted.

"Does this have anything to do with the barrier around you and the reason we can't communicate?" Victoria asked.

"Yes, it does," he said. "Promise me you'll stay with your friends!"

"I will."

"We're taking off now. I'll see you soon. Be safe, Tori."

"Bye, Christian."

EIGHTEEN

Snowstorm

VICTORIA WALKED BACK to the condo, relieved. Her phone had had no service and had been completely unusable. She couldn't believe how good she felt after hearing Christian's voice. Being so shut off from him for the last few days had been torture. She had tried to communicate with him mentally and all she'd sensed was a strange wall between them, a sort of impenetrable but flexible barrier, which meant magic. It worried her, and for good reason now that she'd spoken to Christian.

She went into her room and closed the door, where she sat on the bed and tried for the tenth time to summon her pendant. She couldn't believe that she had left it in Canville, and she cursed herself again for doing such a stupid thing. Leto would be furious if he knew. She'd put it in the music box at Christian's, and somehow it had been forgotten in the rush for the mountain despite Leto's *and* Holly's repeated warnings about always keeping it with her.

Victoria tried every place where it could be, but each time she performed the spell, all she got was a stinging headache and no amulet. She had learned from experience that to make the summoning charm work, she had to pinpoint the exact location of what needed to be summoned.

Foreboding rested like a weight in her belly but she refused to consider that somehow someone might have discovered and taken it. She felt naked without it, especially given what Christian had told her about that woman probably showing up again. And now, against his strict orders, here she was, *alone*, in the condo.

She heard the front door to the apartment open and close. She strained to hear anything, footsteps or voices, and almost jumped out of her skin when she saw the handle on her bedroom door beginning to turn.

"Who's there?" she said. The door swung open.

"Sorry Tori, it's just me. I didn't mean to scare you," Gabriel said, noticing her pale face. "Just checking to see if we are still on for this afternoon for snowboarding?" Although she was capable skier, Gabriel had volunteered to teach her to snowboard. She nodded and tried to be enthusiastic. At least she wouldn't be alone.

The afternoon was as briskly cold as the morning had been. She made it down several runs without falling a single time, even at some points outpacing Gabriel who said she was a natural before he zoomed past her showing off.

She felt exhilarated, the thrill of carving up the mountain was different from skiing, and it was addictive. Her thighs were burning as she got in line for the Sugarloaf superquad lift at the end of the Tote Road green trail that she'd just finished. Gabriel was nowhere to be seen, so she decided that she would try to find a trail a little further up that would bring her around closer to their condo on the east side of the mountain, located near the Lower Buckboard green trail.

As the superquad whizzed up the side of the mountain,

Victoria wished she had read the lift sign more closely—it seemed like they were going all the way to the top of the mountain! She got off the lift at the top and pulled her jacket closer to her, it was freezing. Reading the trail map board, she realized with a pang that the only choices were black or double black diamond trails. She tried to pick the ones that would take her closer to the east side and plotted out a path memorizing the trail names: Gin Pole to the Mid-Station Connect to Ramdown to Upper Buckboard, which would take her on a straight path to the condo.

The two girls who rode the lift up with her strapped on their boards and took off with a wave just as the lift behind her swung to a stop. She glanced at her watch. It was four o'clock. The sun left golden streaks along the deepening blue of the sky as it descended to the horizon. It was a beautiful view but Victoria couldn't appreciate it as nervous as she was. She took a deep breath after checking her helmet and goggles, and eased herself down the menacing black trail that would turn into a blue some distance below.

Arriving at the Mid-Station Connect, she tentatively maneuvered her way through the ungroomed areas that became even more treacherous where they connected with other double black diamond trails. The trees were thick and the path narrow. Her nervousness resurfaced, its icy fingers sliding into her bones. She had to fight the urge to point her snowboard downhill and throw caution to the wind just to get out of there as fast as she could.

It had started to snow, which seemed odd given the fact that the twilight sky was still clear. She brushed the flakes off her goggles. There was no wind, the trees were barely moving and the silence was deafening. Victoria realized that she was completely alone, just as she had promised Christian she would not be and just when her warning bells were all ringing like crazy. She expanded her mind to see if she could isolate the danger.

To her surprise, she felt the same pliable barrier she had felt around Christian while he had been in Paris, only this time it was around *her*! Slowly, she unclipped her right boot and stepped out of her binding. Staying alert and crouched low, she unclipped her left boot. She pushed against the barrier surrounding her like a bubble. It was the same, she was sure of it, and that could only mean one thing—*they* were here.

Taking a deep breath, Victoria moved closer to the intersection of the next double black diamond trail and only then noticed a single skier, tiny in the distance, heading down at breakneck speed— impossible speed—and generating a massive stream of powder, which was what she had felt earlier landing on her goggles. Victoria tensed, she could *feel* the sheer malevolence from the skier even as far away as he was.

In a cloud of snow, the skier skidded to a halt about forty feet away from her. Victoria felt the air shift. She feinted to the side just as a blast rocketed past her head. Magic! She gasped as she hit the ground and rolled left. Another blast melted the snow right where her head had been seconds before. She vaulted to her feet and crouched, unleashing a powerful blast of magic of her own, which the skier easily dodged. Victoria felt the air shift around her again and realized that the barrier was back. That meant that the skier couldn't use magic against her while the bubble was in place! Then again, neither could she.

Victoria could feel the blood boiling under her skin, begging her to release it, and she brutally forced it back. She needed to use her head and find out who the attacker was and what his purpose was. If she let the blood have its way, who knew what would happen?

The skier moved down about five feet and appeared to be watching Victoria intently. Then in an unexpected move, the skier pointed his skis downhill and started to come directly toward her as if for a physical attack.

Victoria realized that there was no way she could reattach her board and try to out-race the skier. She just wasn't that good, and since she couldn't outrun the skier in her boots, that left only one choice, magic, and if worse came to worse, blood magic. She pushed against the barrier and felt the same unyielding flexibility—it was incredibly strong magic, she thought, unwillingly impressed, but now also completely desperate.

In the seconds before the skier impacted, Victoria braced herself, digging her nails into her palms, and felt the blood fill her eyes as she let it loose, the magic bursting into the barrier in a blast so potent that it melted the snow at her feet instantly. The barrier exploded into emptiness as if it had been made of nothing but air, the atomic force of the blast knocking the skier head over heels almost a hundred feet *up* the mountain.

Victoria felt the ground beneath her feet rumble and alarm underscored the brief relief of having bested her attacker. The rumbling grew louder! She looked up the mountain at the ominous cloud of white that was rushing her way.

Avalanche!

Her breath caught frozen in her chest as the giant tidal wave of snow, triggered by the resulting shockwaves of her magic, bore down upon them. Victoria watched in horror as the snow covered the motionless body of the skier in a matter of seconds and headed toward her in a monstrous white cloud. Her mouth hung open in a soundless gasp, the fear decimating.

Think! Victoria told herself urgently.

The blood was still racing in her veins, but she felt curiously weakened, which she had never felt after magic use before. As her hands drifted toward her neck for the amulet that wasn't there, she realized that she was weak because without it, her complex spell had absorbed her own energy. She gritted her teeth and pulled herself together. Without the amulet, Victoria didn't know if she had the strength or the clarity to teleport off the mountain completely. But it was the only option she could think of.

She pulled her remaining energy into herself, surprised by the sudden rush. *Strange.* It was more powerful than she'd expected but she didn't have time to dwell on it. Victoria focused, clearly envisioning her bedroom in the condo. She completed the preparation process and started to cast the spell.

"TRAN—"

The blood in her veins whistled and Victoria froze. She *knew* that feeling—it was blood magic! And her blood's magic thrived on sacrifice!

Victoria's eyes snapped open in horror, and although the break in concentration didn't alter the spell, what she saw around her certainly did. Rows and rows of dead, blackened trees on either side of the trail in perfect symmetry around her, like the victims of a precise flash forest fire. She gasped. The teleportation spell slipped away from her even as a flood of white covered them.

Before the force of the snow hit her and sent her tumbling forward, Victoria did the only thing she could do—she grabbed her snowboard and braced herself, crouched and facing down the mountain with the board against her back. With the last remaining energy she had inside of her, she held strong to the earth building an invisible magical wall behind her. She felt the snow rush over and past her like a white river. Then the world darkened and disappeared completely.

Victoria knew she was still alive if only from the excruciating pain in her leg. She couldn't see a thing in the darkness but could hear the harshness of her breath in the small cave she lay in. She forced herself to breathe slowly knowing she didn't have much time before the oxygen in the tiny cavern disappeared. She needed to think. Fast.

The mountain personnel would have seen that there had been an avalanche, so once the snow settled, they would most likely send rescue vehicles for the few remaining people on the mountain. Victoria didn't know much about avalanches but she was hopeful that the trees would have dissipated much of the force before it reached the lower mountain.

Her leg was sticking out at an odd angle, obviously broken unless she had some other bendable ability she didn't know about. She didn't want to move too suddenly as she had no idea just how much snow she was sitting under, so she gingerly tried to shift her weight and winced at the sharp pain shooting up her leg. Victoria had no idea how long it would take to replenish her natural store of magic without killing anything around her, and she felt the panic surge in her belly. Then again, if it was a choice between her and a few trees, she could probably live with the sacrifice.

Victoria concentrated on healing her leg. The effort drained her, as she had to consciously prevent herself from taking any energy from the living things all around her. She could kill whole colonies of ants for a smidgen of energy, hundreds of birds, trees, *anything* that had life in it. The price of the blood magic was all the power in the world just at the cost of a conscience and a soul. Hers.

She took shallow even breaths as she felt her bones mending and her eyelids drooping. She just needed to close her eyes for a few minutes and everything would be okay, she thought wearily. Just a few minutes …

Victoria! Wake up! WAKE UP!

Stop it, Christian. I'm sleeping.

Wake up! You're not sleeping, you're dying! GET UP!

Reality came back swiftly and coldly after that. She had to get out of this mess before she did something really stupid, like going to sleep while buried under several feet of snow!

Christian? You there?

There was no answer and the sudden silence scared her. She concentrated on formulating a low energy heat spell that would melt some of the snow in front of her and just as she was feeling it starting to work, the ground beneath her started to tremble. Rescue snowmobiles, she thought gratefully, as an unseen force grabbed hold of her body and yanked her out of the snow, dumping her to the side.

She watched her cave implode in the dim glare of the trail lights, and taking deep gulping breaths of the sweet cold air, Victoria glanced around for her rescuers. She found herself face to face with the same skier who had attacked her earlier—a woman—only she was sans skis and no longer had a hat obscuring her face. She was very plain with brown hair and dark skin and wore a triumphant smile.

Victoria tried to free her arms but an invisible force bound them so tightly that she could barely move. The woman walked closer and stooped down near the side of Victoria's face.

"Don't struggle, the bindings will only use your own kinetic energy to tighten and strengthen," she said, her voice musical and unhurried. "One of my own inventions, very useful, no?" She laughed and the sound was chilling.

Victoria realized that even in her incapacitated state that this was her chance to find out who this woman was and what she wanted, and also to give her body a chance to recuperate. The woman glanced at her wristwatch, looking around impatiently; she was obviously waiting for someone. And from the looks of things, there were no rescue vehicles anywhere in the immediate vicinity.

"How did you find me?" Victoria said.

The woman laughed again and gave her a derisive look that plainly said she thought Victoria was an idiot. "Heat radiation."

"Who are you? What do you want with me?" Victoria asked. The woman ignored her pointedly, and spoke into her phone.

"Oui, quinze minutes," she said in French, and snapped the phone closed. Fifteen minutes for what? Victoria tried again.

"How could you have survived the blast?" she asked, injecting an arrogant tone into her voice to attempt to provoke the woman. It worked. The woman directed her black stare toward Victoria as if trying to gauge the question. She smiled cruelly and walked forward to reassume her position squatting beside Victoria.

"You are so young, and so stupid," she said. She looked at Victoria disparagingly. "I can't imagine why he could possibly think you are the one. Yes, you had one good trick, but not good enough to even save yourself, no? And now look at you. You are so weak, you can't even lift a finger against me."

As she moved to get up, Victoria saw the flash of a crystal and understanding surged through her like a warm flood. *That's* how she had been able to survive! Leto had told her that witches used crystals to store magical energy for protection, although unlike her own amulet, their stored magic could not replenish itself. Victoria gathered her strength knowing she had less than a few minutes before the unknown accomplice showed up, and guessed that she had enough inside her for a simple spell. She engaged her own sluggish magic and released a crude summoning spell toward the crystal she'd seen.

"Effero crystallus!"

She heard the snap as the woman whirled around panicked, at the exact same moment that the crystal spear-shaped pendant appeared in her fingers. Without thinking, Victoria took it into herself. Her body jerked as her hungry blood absorbed the magic like a sponge, the crystal turning immediately to dust in her palm. It wasn't her magic, but she consumed it like a starving beast, letting the raw power fill her, and still, she wasn't satiated even though it was more than she needed to escape. Her blood wanted *more*. It wanted it all—every last drop of the witch in front of her.

She shook her head once and her bindings fell off like paper. She stood up, her eyes burning like black coals and faced the woman who no longer looked triumphant. She looked very, very afraid. Victoria cocked her head to one side, like a cat studying a mouse, and watched as the woman calculated the odds of getting away. She was so easy to read, this little exiled witch, Victoria's blood thought patronizingly. But her magic had been so delicious, so much of the forbidden in there that it had been intoxicating.

The witch moved and tried to hurl a magic blast. Victoria deflected it lazily without even moving, and she watched the witch's eyes widen as a sudden cold understanding filled them, and she dropped prostrate to the cold ground.

"Please—"

Victoria's demon blood trilled, ravenous and inhuman. And while her smallest self screamed defiantly within her head, her blood rushed forward and claimed its prey. As the witch died, the taste of her death was heady like brandy burning through Victoria's body. Her blood sang victoriously. Despicably.

Victoria wanted to rip her skin apart and drain the poisoned magic out of her, its tainted evil fueling the darkest nature of the blood magic. She sank to her knees, delirious with sinful pleasure and sick with disgust at her own weakness, and clawed at her face and her stomach. Even as her blood healed the wounds of its own volition with the magic it had mercilessly stolen, she continued to tear at herself as if it assuaged the terrible guilt and self-hatred boiling inside of her.

She remained there until she felt familiar arms enclosing her in their tender warmth, Christian's voice against her hair, his lips on her temple, even as she struggled viciously against him.

"Don't touch me!" she screamed. "Don't touch me … don't touch me …"

CHRISTIAN REMAINED UNYIELDING, whispering against her hair until finally, inexorably she calmed, her body shuddering as she clung to him. He could feel the tightening of his jaw in violent response to the blood that had soaked through her clothing but he ignored it, stifling the urge viciously. The sound of her scream and the scent of her blood had all but done him in as he had raced to the top of the mountain.

When he had felt her slipping away earlier, Christian had almost lost it, especially as he hadn't been able to contact her right after their brief mental exchange. Holding her in his arms, her wild unhinged strength had been nearly impossible to contain, but he had held on.

Christian stood, taking her with him as if she weighed no more than a feather. With his free foot, he kicked fresh snow over the blood-spattered earth, knowing from the sounds lower down the mountains that the rescue crews he had seen would be heading their way. As he turned, Christian registered movement in the trees off to the left and his eyes locked with a pair of familiar icy blue eyes. Lena. She didn't move, just stood watching him and the gentle way he sheltered Victoria in his arms.

"Tell your *master* that if he comes after her again, he'll face me," he hissed in her direction.

Christian wondered how long she had been standing there, and whether the pile of ash-covered dark clothing lying on the ground was the remains of her witch friend. He glared at her ruthlessly, his lips drawn in a hard tight line, and turned away. He was gone in a second.

Christian held Victoria close against him as the limousine sped down I-95 to his house. While she slept, he telephoned Enhard.

"Enhard, it's Christian. The witch is dead."

"Did you do it?"

"No." He didn't elaborate.

"Good, that will help with your brother." Enhard paused. "Before you go, I spoke to one of the high priestess delegates after you left about Le Sang Noir. They call it the Cruentus Curse. What I learned may surprise you. She told me that its power can only be freely given, which means it can't be taken by force, nor can the witch who controls it be killed for it as the power will die with her. It's passed on to direct descendants and even then, it's sporadic. This thing goes back centuries, Christian, it goes much, much farther than we ever thought."

Enhard's revelations floored Christian. There was no way Lucian could ever possess its power, Victoria would never ever give it to him freely … unless he had something planned to force her to do so. The thought scared the hell out of him because he was familiar with Lucian's ruthless tactics. He would have to protect her at all costs. He stroked her cheek and felt her stir beneath his fingers.

Victoria's eyes opened and Christian's worried face swam into focus. Her body ached and she felt like throwing up. She could feel the memory of the witch's magic infecting her system like a virus. She didn't deserve to be touched. She was a monster, a hideous soul-sucking monster! Christian's arms tightened around her.

"Kiss me," she whispered, shamelessly taking the small comfort he offered. "Make me forget … please."

She pressed her open mouth urgently against his, tasting his hot breath, desperate for anything to offset the dark chill inside of her. Christian's entire body froze, his teeth the only part of him moving, and he ground his lips into a hard line. Victoria dragged hers from his suddenly unyielding ones and trailed them up his jawline to his ear. A muscle in his cheek ticked as she exposed the long delicate column of her neck to him.

Unable to help himself, he pressed his lips to her neck, drinking in the smell of her as his razor-sharp incisors shredded the inside of his mouth. His lips parted of their own volition and for one agonizing second, the taste of her sweetly forbidden skin invaded his mouth in a hot rush. He'd never wanted to give in to what he was so badly in that moment ... but all it took was one instant of weakness. Christian tore his lips away from the banquet of her warm flesh, tasting his own blood on his tongue and terrifyingly wanting more, a brutal reminder of what he was.

He held himself perfectly still as she rested her head on his shoulder.

"Are you all right?" he said hoarsely.

"No," she said. "My blood takes care of itself."

"Tell me," he said, stroking the backs of his fingers down her smooth cheek, his touch agonizingly tender.

"Christian," she said. "I'm ... I'm a monster."

"You are no monster." He laughed hollowly.

"But I am. Christian, I killed her. I killed the witch. And I enjoyed it, or the blood did, but it's still me." She spoke in a rush as if she wanted to get it out and looked away.

"Tori, she attacked you. You defended yourself and she lost. That was it," he said.

"You don't understand. I took her magic into myself, and even though it was filthy and cloying, I *liked* it. I liked the feeling of power, and when I killed her, I liked it even more! I loved it. It was so easy … I reveled in taking … the *taking* …" Victoria gasped, unable to finish. "The blood takes and *feeds* … and I am helpless against it."

Christian was quiet. He knew that she had only defended herself, and she was lucky that her blood had fought back. Lena would have been merciless if she had captured Victoria, and Lucian would have been far, far worse.

He understood her suffering more than she knew given the finite rules of his own hunger and the way it dominated every instinct. But he also understood her fear—the curse of Le Sang Noir was infinite power at unsustainable cost. Eventually, it would grow to control her if she gave in to it, as it had her ancestor, the duchess.

"You won't become her, Tori. You're nothing like her, and you're not powerless against the blood," he said after a long spell. "You know that. It doesn't own you. You control it, not the other way around. It's like my thirst—do you think it's easy for me when we're together when I can smell your blood calling to me every time we touch? Of course it's not, I have to fight to suppress it but I would never give in to it, I won't let myself," he said.

"I know. It's just … exhausting."

He watched her, the emotions playing across her face as she considered telling him something else that was obviously bothering her.

"The witch on the mountain seemed to know who I was, and she mentioned that someone else was interested in me, specifically a 'he.' It's Lucian, isn't it?" she asked.

"Yes."

"What are we going to do?"

"Nothing, for now. He will already know that his attack failed. Leave him to me. I will deal with Lucian." His voice shook with suppressed fury.

"Christian, there's something else." She paused. "I need my amulet. I forgot it in Canville. I tried to summon it but couldn't. It's … the key to controlling the blood. I can't find it anywhere." Her face was panicked. "If it has been taken, I don't know what—"

"I have it." Victoria's elated gaze snapped to his. "I put both in my safe at the house before I went to Paris, I know how much it means to you and I didn't want to leave it lying around. I'll get it for you."

"I'm so glad! Things got so rushed that I stupidly left it behind. You don't understand how close I came …" Her voice choked as she recalled what had happened on the mountain when the blood magic had taken over without the amulet's protective power restraining it.

There was so much that she didn't yet understand about the blood, the magic, and the amulet. The journal only had so many answers. She'd need to look harder to find some of her own before the blood destroyed her.

Victoria stared out the window at the brightly colored lights flashing by from houses decorated in the spirit of the season. It was Christmas Eve. Wasn't this a time when things were supposed to be happy and joyous? Instead, everything felt like it was closing in, a giant net she couldn't escape. The knot tightened in her stomach. She closed her eyes.

"I'm scared."

Christian stared at her drawn face as leaned her head against the window. They both had every reason to be afraid. Lucian was more than close … *too* close. Christian had barely made it in time to save her from the witch, with Lena lurking nearby in the woods. He didn't want to think about what would have happened if he'd been a few minutes late.

In Victoria's vulnerable state, Lena would have been merciless. The next time, neither of them would be so lucky. Now that

Victoria had killed the witch, the key to Lucian's grand plan, no doubt he would be furious. And fury drove people to do irrational, unpredictable things. Christian knew more than anyone how ruthless Lucian could be.

One thing was certain. Lucian would stop at nothing now.

NINETEEN

Happy New Year

How could one little ticket ruin everything?

Gabriel and Angie's unexpected Christmas present had astounded Victoria; a ticket to a New Year's Eve masquerade ball at the Rainbow Room in Rockefeller Center. It was an exclusive event by invitation only, and Victoria had argued that it was far too extravagant, but Gabriel had told her that it was nothing, a combination get well after her snowboarding accident and Christmas present. He had also told her in no uncertain terms that the tickets, courtesy of their parents, were not returnable.

Victoria had mentioned the ticket to Christian two days ago, and she'd been completely blindsided by his response. The minute she had said that it was going to be a masquerade ball at the Rainbow Room in Rockefeller Center, it was like he had become possessed, telling her in no uncertain terms that he forbade it.

The minute his patronizing words had left his lips, the room had become fraught with tension. She'd stared at him as if he'd been speaking a foreign language.

"Is this about Gabriel? Honestly Christian, get over it. Gabriel likes me but he knows that we're just friends, and that's all we are ever going to be. I do have friends other than you, you know, and just because he's asked me to a party in New York doesn't mean you need to go all Tony Soprano on me."

"It's not about Gabriel," he insisted fiercely. "I don't want you to go there."

"Then what is it about, Christian? These are my friends. Who do you think you are anyway?" Victoria said hotly.

"Victoria, I do not want you to go to New York. And that's it."

"Then stop playing games and *tell* me why," she shot back.

"I do not need to explain my reasons to you. It should be enough that I've asked you not to go for your own safety."

She launched a glare in his direction. "*You don't need to explain your reasons to me?*" she repeated in a shrill staccato, advancing on him enough that he'd stepped backward. "Let me explain something to you, Christian. You are not in the nineteenth century any more. In this world, guys don't get to order girls about. I don't know where you think you are or *who* you think you are, but you cannot tell me what I can or can't do. I am going to New York. And *that's it.*"

He'd stared at her with a pained look as if she'd slapped him, and then said quietly, his voice weary, "Fine, do whatever you like, then."

Victoria had left his house enraged, announcing that she was going to do exactly that. She hadn't seen him since.

Now standing in the guest bedroom of Gabriel's parents' opulent Upper East Side Fifth Avenue townhouse, Victoria was still shaken by the memory. Truth was, she knew that she was angrier at Christian for actually letting her leave yesterday without making contact with her, than she was that he had forbidden her to go to the party. After the wonderful few days they had spent together, she missed him.

A knock on the door interrupted her thoughts, and Angie poked her head in.

"Hey, Tori, the limo's going to be here in about an hour, okay?"

"Thanks Angie," Victoria said. "Thanks again for letting me crash here. I was more than happy to stay in a hotel."

"It's no big deal and you know Gabe, once he makes his mind up, it's a done deal. My parents aren't even here, and they don't care who stays here anyway," she said. She smiled awkwardly. Even though things were much better between them, Angie still wasn't big on small talk.

Victoria glanced at the large box on the bed and sighed as she removed the gorgeous dress, staring at it in awe. The ball was black tie and she had walked Fifth Avenue for hours trying to find something suitable. Maybe it was the rotten timing of waiting until the last minute, but the only dress options seemed to be either huge swaths of taffeta or pearl-encrusted contraptions. Frustrated, she'd decided to take a break when she received a call from Angie saying she'd had a package delivered to the apartment.

In complete surprise, she had taken the large box to her room and opened it to find the elegant red silk dress. She didn't recognize the designer but the box said Bergdorf Goodman, an exclusive luxury department store in Midtown. There was a single rose along with a note that said "*vraiment désolé*" in Christian's elegant script. He was sorry—sorry enough to send her a gorgeous dress to wear to a party he didn't want her going to in the first place.

Victoria dressed slowly. The lustrous, jewel-toned crimson of the dress was the ideal complement to her olive skin and draped her long slender body perfectly. She felt beautiful wearing it knowing that Christian had selected it for her. The strapless bodice was form-fitting with a ruffled bow-tie trim under the bust before flaring out in folds toward the hem. She had chosen to wear her hair in a simple, smooth chignon with Christian's rose tucked in the fold at the top of the knot. The effect softened the severity of the sleek hairstyle.

She left her makeup simple, with dark mascara emphasizing her wide green eyes, a dusting of tawny blush on her cheeks, and barely glossed lips. The overall effect was startling. Even her amulet seemed to shine more brilliantly red because of the dress.

At the very last minute before she left the room, she turned around and slipped the ring Christian had given her for Christmas on her finger. He had surprised her with his own extravagantly heart-wrenching gift; a magnificent vintage swirl ring inset with diamonds that extended to her first knuckle. When he had said it had been his mother's, Victoria had been overwhelmed. Despite her recent vow to never wear it again, deep down she knew that there was no way she wouldn't have worn the ring.

Angie popped her head in and her eyes went wide. "Wow Tori, you look amazing!"

"Thanks. So do you."

Angie was wearing a slinky gold spaghetti strap number. Her dark hair had been blown out, and she looked glamorous. Her matching gold and black sequined mask was daring and racy, the perfect complement to the dress.

"I don't think I would have recognized you, Angie, if I'd seen you at the party. You look so different."

"Thanks! Everyone's already here, so shall we?" she said, flushing with embarrassed pleasure and moving toward the door.

Victoria picked up the reddish gold Venetian mask that had accompanied the dress. It was a lovely half mask with red and gold feathers curling up behind her right temple, and golden chains dangling below them from the back of her ear to her cheekbone.

Everyone was waiting in the foyer of the apartment when

Victoria and Angie went downstairs together. Gabriel looked very rocker-glam in a luxurious velvet blazer with ruffled tuxedo shirt and lean tailored jeans, and his expression was one of frank admiration when he saw Victoria. Charla was stunning in a green Grecian-style gown. She embraced Victoria as if they hadn't seen each other in months, and was effusive in her comments about Victoria's dress.

There were four other people in the foyer; two seniors from the ski trip, Katie and Mike who were both really nice, and two other young men that Victoria didn't know. Angie introduced them as Taylor and Wyatt, both of whom she and Gabriel had grown up with. Since Angie seemed to pair up with Taylor, Victoria smiled as Wyatt extended his arm with a gallant bow.

As they headed to the waiting limo, Victoria noticed Gabriel staring at her. His expression was speculative and … greedy. It made her feel uncomfortable. Wyatt's arm curved around her waist and Gabriel's eyes narrowed, a flash distorting his handsome face, but when he noticed Victoria watching him, he smiled and abruptly went outside.

Sometimes Victoria felt that Gabriel's moods were too erratic. She had tried to read his mind, but it was like reading the same old book with the same story. What she saw *was* what she got. Still, she couldn't shake the feeling that he was hiding something.

The limousine headed down Fifth Avenue toward Rockefeller Center as they popped a bottle of Cristal champagne and started the first of many toasts to the year. The streets of New York were alive with throngs of happy, laughing people, and the limousine crawled along amidst the traffic.

Victoria had heard a lot about the famous Rainbow Room as well as its unparalleled view, but nothing prepared her for the amazing sight of New York City laid out in all its gold and white light glory with the Empire State Building gracing its skyline. It was magnificent. In the restaurant, she felt like she was in a different world! People were dancing and milling about, dressed in their finery with their faces covered in unique and exquisite masks. Golden cloths and elaborate centerpieces adorned the tables, and the music from the live band filled the room.

Gabriel waved her over to their table, which was already covered in champagne. They certainly wasted no time, Victoria thought as he handed her a glass, and pulled her over to the other window to show her the view.

"I like your Phantom of the Opera mask, it's very distinctive. It suits you," she told him.

"You look spectacular tonight, Tori, I meant to tell you at the apartment but didn't get a chance to. That dress is amazing."

"Thanks, Gabe," she said.

"Dance with me."

"Maybe another time," she said pointedly, as Charla came bearing down on them, and proceeded to drag Gabriel out to the dance floor.

One of the things that Victoria loved was people-watching and tonight was unquestionably the night for it—she had never seen so many beautiful people in her life! Still, as much as she was enjoying herself, Victoria felt like a part of her was missing. She'd secretly hoped that since it was a masquerade, Christian could have attended incognito and been there to toast the New Year with her. Victoria bit her lip, knowing that it was her own fault he wasn't there, but it was too late now. She sighed, her eyes roving the room, desperate to distract herself.

Suddenly her breath stopped. Her eyes traveled in reverse to the pair of familiar steel gray eyes that stared piercingly at her from across the sea of tables and gyrating bodies. She'd already taken a step toward him before even realizing that she had done so, the pull of him magnetic, and she could no more stop herself as she could still her beating heart. He made no move to come to her, just stood watching her as she made her way toward him. He looked unbelievably handsome in a black suit and dark silver mask that obscured half of his face. But Victoria would have recognized those eyes anywhere.

Her smile faltered as she got closer and still he seemed unresponsive, except for the unflinching steel gaze focused on her. Victoria hesitated, struck by his coldness but she supposed she deserved it after their argument. She hadn't even had the graciousness to thank him for the dress. The next move was definitely hers.

She took a deep breath as she closed the last few steps to stand in front of him, the strappy gold heels she had worn putting her eyes on level with his chin.

"I'm really glad you came. And I'm sorry too," she said. She peeked at him through her lashes and he was still staring at her, his expression unreadable. Taking another deep breath, she tilted her face up and pressed a kiss to his lips. At first he was unresponsive, then suddenly his lips softened and he wrapped his hand around her waist, hauling her closer and claiming her lips in a bruising kiss.

Victoria froze. Something was terribly wrong. She pushed against him, and he held her tighter. Fear uncoiled in her chest as she pushed away with all her strength and stumbled backwards, staring at him, her eyes wide with alarm.

"Christian?" she said.

"No, but now I can certainly see what all the fuss is about." His tone was insolent.

"Lucian." Victoria's voice was flat even though her heart was racing with panic, her hand unconsciously fluttering to her neck. Lucian noticed and smiled a very white, toothy smile. She dropped her hand immediately, which made his smile even wider.

"What are *you* doing here?"

"I wouldn't miss it for the world. I'm one of the sponsors of this year's event."

Suddenly everything became crystal clear in Victoria's head as she understood why Christian had reacted so violently when she had told him of the party. She wished he had just trusted her enough to explain it to her, but then she realized with a rush of guilt that she hadn't given him the chance.

Lucian was still watching her, and she was glad that her mask at least partially covered her face, although she wished that she could see his more clearly. It was uncanny how much he and Christian looked like each other.

Victoria glanced at her friends at the far end of the room, and looked back at Lucian, who was still watching her with a speculative, calculating expression. In that single look, she could see exactly what Christian had meant when he had said his brother was ruthless and would stop at nothing to get what he wanted. The amulet burned a warning against her chest as her heart pounded rapidly and she shivered, knowing intuitively that he was very, very dangerous.

He stepped toward her and she tensed, poised to attack, but he smoothly removed two glasses of champagne from a passing waiter, and handed one glass to her. Victoria knew she had to be calm even though every instinct was screaming for her to run away as fast as she could. She looked at him evenly.

"Well, it was nice to meet you," she said.

"Yes," he agreed, "it was very nice to *meet* you." His suggestive reference to the stolen kiss set her on edge, and her temper flared.

"I am sure you enjoyed our … *meeting* far more than I did. I can assure you I found it indelibly distasteful." Lucian's eyes hardened.

"Shall I remind you how distasteful you find me?" Victoria blanched at the sheer menace in his tone but before she could even move to step away, Lucian grasped her arm. She winced in pain. He leaned in, his eyes glacial. "Don't even think about it, your neck would be in my hands before you took another step."

"And you would be dead before you could flex your fingers," she said with scathing contempt.

Lucian stared at her in reluctant admiration, her eyes flashing and defiant. He was impressed, but that didn't mean that she didn't need to know her place. He squeezed his fingers around her arm and watched her eyes dilate. He squeezed harder.

Victoria felt like she was going to faint from the agony. As Lucian's face swam out of focus, she tried to pull herself together to step outside of the pain. She could only think of one thing.

Christian.

I'm here.

Relief flooded her body like a wave as her eyes swept the room and fell on the tall figure near the entrance. His face was a mask of freezing rage, and Victoria could see that even beneath the edge of the demi-mask, his lips were clenched so tightly that they were a white, fierce line. He was at her side in a flash, removing Lucian's fingers like they were twigs. Victoria could have sworn she had heard a crack but Lucian's expression didn't change.

"You touch her again, and you will spend a decade growing a new hand. That I promise you."

"Relax, brother," Lucian said. "No harm done, just introducing myself to your new ... friend."

"No harm done?" Christian said, holding out Victoria's arm bearing red welts from his fingers.

Lucian didn't answer but grinned cruelly. Victoria saw

Christian's hands clench uncontrollably at his side, and she knew that Lucian was just trying to push Christian's buttons. It was working.

She pulled her hand out of his and as she did so, she saw Lucian's gaze settle on her fingers. His look was one of bitter disgust as he noticed the ring.

"I see you have now completely dishonored the Devereux legacy, Christian. Our mother's ring? To a filthy witch?" The derision in his voice was unmistakable.

Christian's muscles tensed reflexively and Victoria grasped his hand.

Christian, please. She squeezed urgently. *Please.*

Hearing the desperation in her thought, he forced himself to calm down. He had never felt such terrifying, furious rage—he wanted to rip his own brother apart, let him heal, and do it all over again! Make him bleed in an endless cycle of unforgiving pain! People were starting to make a wide berth around them as if they could feel his wrath. He leaned in.

"You come near her again Lucian, and I swear I will kill you," he said in a silky, ominous voice. "I will do nothing to stop the Council. I will no longer protect you. Go ahead on your absurd search for Le Sang Noir and when you find it, may it bring you peace or death, or both." He paused and kissed Lucian on both cheeks. "But I am done, brother."

Lucian's expression was inscrutable as he watched them walk away. He turned as a waitress walked past him.

"Drink, sir?" she asked with a coquettish smile. Lucian smiled back, her eyes glazing over in complete submission.

"Yes, thank you. That would be just perfect," he said, his terrible teeth lengthening as he escorted her to a side door.

ON THE FAR side of the room Victoria leaned against Christian. He felt so warm and strong; all she wanted to do was to melt into the safety of his embrace.

"You look beautiful, just like I knew you would," he said.

"Thank you," she said, flushing. Christian leaned toward her and held her face between his palms. Victoria stared at him, she could hardly believe that she hadn't seen the differences between him and Lucian—they were like night and day. It was as if a part of her subconscious had wanted to see Christian so badly that she'd been blind to what was now so glaringly obvious. As identical twins, Lucian's beauty was also ethereal, but his beauty had a dark edge to it. He was colder and harder, more vampire than man, whereas Christian was the reverse.

Christian looked at her intently, brushing his thumbs against her soft cheeks beneath the edges of the mask.

"I should have come with you. I'm sorry," he said.

"No, it's my fault, Christian."

All of a sudden the noise in the room started to escalate, and they realized that it was five minutes to midnight. The countdown in Times Square had already started.

"Say goodbye to your friends and meet me downstairs in a half an hour. It's almost midnight, and they are looking for you. It's a black limousine parked across the street on the corner, right in front. Don't worry about Lucian. He won't hurt you." Christian kissed her fingertips and melted into the crowd. Victoria wanted to run after him but forced herself walk toward Gabriel and the rest of her friends.

"TORI!" Charla screamed at the top of her lungs. "Where've you been?" She hugged Victoria and then started hugging random people walking by. Victoria raised her glass in anticipation as they started the countdown.

"Ten … nine … eight … seven … six … five … four … three … two … one! HAPPY NEW YEAR!!!"

It was a magnificent firestorm of blinding color as fireworks exploded in the sky all around them, and confetti littered the ballroom. Everyone was kissing everyone else. Gabriel kissed her quickly on the mouth, the intense expression in his open eyes conveying far more than the chaste kiss, but the contact was so brief that she didn't have time to dwell on it. Wyatt also kissed her, which was disgusting. She needed a napkin after he was through. Angie and Taylor were locked at the lips, only interested in kissing each other.

As Victoria stood next to Charla and Gabriel watching the last of the fireworks, her eyes met Lucian's across the dance floor. He inclined his head and raised his glass in a toast. Victoria noticed that he looked distinctly less pale and felt disgusted. She didn't understand why the idea of Christian feeding didn't repel her, but looking at Lucian and knowing he had just fed, repulsed her completely. She felt like throwing up.

He watched her knowingly over the rim of his glass as he sipped his champagne, his lips red, and winked. Victoria stared back, her expression flat, and then looked away. She could swear she heard him laughing, and the sound chilled her.

All she wanted to do was to get to Christian. She was just thinking about the best way to make a graceful exit when Angie and Taylor announced that they were heading out. Charla and Gabriel exchanged a knowing look as they danced, and Victoria jumped at the opportunity to say that she would walk out with them, and catch a cab back. After waving to Charla and Gabriel, and saying goodbye to a crestfallen Wyatt, she followed Angie and Taylor out.

Victoria could feel Lucian's heavy stare boring into her back but refused to give him the satisfaction of acknowledging him. She left without a backward glance.

Outside of the building, they parted ways and Victoria waited until Angie and Taylor were out of sight before getting into the long black limousine across the street.

"Where are we going?" she asked, as she removed her mask. Then she stopped and stared at Christian. "Don't tell me you have an apartment here too?"

He smiled sheepishly. "Yes. Sorry."

Victoria laughed. "Well, I guess after a hundred odd years, it's only natural that you should collect several homes I guess."

"We could just drive around too. I know you are supposed to be staying with Angie, so I don't want it to be awkward for you."

"I doubt that anyone will be in any frame of mind tonight to worry about my whereabouts. I'm really glad that you came, Christian, although it's too bad that we didn't get to countdown the New Year together."

"We still can ..." His eyes smoldered. "Five ... four ... three ... two ... one ..."

And suddenly Victoria was the recipient of the sweetest, hottest kiss, and she forgot how to breathe. The fireworks started all over again. They couldn't get enough of each other. Maybe it was because of Lucian, maybe it was because of their fight, it didn't matter. Everything disintegrated into that one moment when their lips met ... love, regret, forgiveness. It enveloped them, its intensity suffocating, until Christian carefully extricated himself.

The minutes collapsed into seconds, their raw breaths harsh in the silence. She reached forward and he flinched, his face feral as he grappled with the change that tore through him. Stricken, she looked away, her attention drawn by a couple kissing on the side of the road. She sighed, touching her lips in unconscious mimicry.

I want more ...

The thought was fleeting but cracked like a gunshot in the silence. She'd thought it aloud to him. Christian felt his heart constrict; he had known that at some point it would come to this. He moved closer, as close as his shattered senses allowed.

"I know you do," he said. "And I'm sorry. It's too dangerous. I could hurt you."

"But I know you, I know you wouldn't. You didn't before, remember?" she said. He could barely hear her, her voice was so soft. She was still staring at the couple.

Christian closed his eyes. She couldn't possibly know what she was asking. Or maybe she did.

"Tori, remember when you said you couldn't control the blood's hunger, and how it consumed you?" She nodded. "Well, that is my fear, that one day *my* hunger will overtake my control, and I will lose you."

"You won't," she said fiercely.

Christian smiled. "Your faith in me is humbling. Unfortunately, my faith in myself is not as strong. I could hurt you without meaning to. What's that saying? The road to hell is paved with the best intentions? I, more than anyone, know how true that is. And I won't lose you Tori, I can't ..."

Victoria was silent. Chances were if he bit her, he would die, and they both knew it. It was a somber truth. Their relationship was utterly impossible! Yet even as she thought the words, she knew that there was no way she wanted to be without him.

She felt guilty for making him feel bad about something that neither of them could circumvent. It was painful and frustrating for them both but sometimes she just wanted ... well, more. She wanted the heated embrace that the couple outside had, with just their feelings for each other taking over, without having to hold back or worry about one of them killing the other. She wanted to touch him, to hold him against her, to give herself to him in every way. She wanted normal, but she wanted normal with Christian, and that was just not possible, so the only remaining option was their impossible love, because it was with *him*.

"I'm sorry," she said.

"It's okay, Tori. It's hard for us both."

Poignantly Victoria remembered the night at his house when he had asked the question, thinking the words he hadn't been able to say out loud. She wrapped her arms around him and felt him dip his head to gently kiss her bare shoulder.

"Stay with me, Christian," she said.

"I will."

TWENTY

Gabriel and Angie

JANUARY WAS DARK and dismal with icy frost and mountains of unending snow. The brutal wind chill of negative twenty made it impossible to venture outside except straight to class and back. On colder days, students chose to remain in the warm library, the most central building between classes, and head home when the day was done. It didn't get any better over the next month with several punishing winter storms. It was not a pleasant time.

Between classes, Victoria passed the time in the library. She had barely seen Christian as he'd had to travel to Boston and Los Angeles for Council business. Whenever he was in town, she went to his place where they studied or played the piano or just read in companionable silence. It was the safest place for both of them, as she still hadn't the faintest idea how to broach the subject of their relationship with Leto.

She had rarely seen Angie and Charla either as they both had full class schedules that semester. She'd seen them a few times in the library and then only a couple other times at the bar, which had also been quiet. If it weren't for the standing project session that she and Gabriel had in the library on Thursdays, she would probably have gone stir crazy.

Somehow, they'd ended up in the same Calculus class despite Victoria having the sneaking sensation that Gabriel had already taken the class, and they'd been paired together for a class project. They usually caught up for dinner afterwards, and it had grown into something that she actually looked forward to.

Over the last two months, they had become good friends. She felt connected with Gabriel in a way that she didn't feel with anyone else, not even Christian. As she had discovered, they were connected by a similar experience. He and Angie lived with foster parents because their biological parents had died in an accident when they were children. The admission had floored her and opened a wound she'd thought closed.

"We were eleven," Gabriel told her, "and the police told us that it was just one of those freak electrical fires. Angie was at a friend's house. I tried to help them but the smoke was too much. I fell out a window and broke my leg. They died."

"I'm so sorry," Victoria said.

"Well, you do what you have to, right? Try to put one foot in front of the next and repeat." She knew exactly what he meant.

In return, she confided to him about her parents, something she'd only ever talked about with Holly and Christian. But they couldn't understand the hurt as Gabriel could because he'd been through something exactly like it. Talking to him had been cathartic. He knew her pain, her sense of loss, and her fear of being alone. Victoria realized that Gabriel's constant desire to succeed and prove himself stemmed from the death of *his* parents. In his mind, he'd failed them.

Although their friendship discovered its roots in a common

tragedy, Victoria found that she connected with Gabriel on many other levels. They loved the same music, the same television shows, and the same books and movies. It was a little uncanny, and Victoria had once joked to Gabriel that if she didn't know him any better, she'd think he was making it all up just to get into her good graces. He'd smiled and goaded her to "test him," which she'd done. He'd answered every single question, even ones she didn't know herself and had to Google.

"You are a total sham!" she'd teased him, unwillingly impressed.

"All part of my evil genius master plan," he'd joked back.

She understood him and Gabriel understood her. And as long as he was happy to keep it at friendship, she was fine with that.

Sitting in her warm chair and staring out the big glass windowpanes of the north library wall at the falling snow, Victoria saw Charla and a group of her girlfriends out of the corner of her eye, and sighed. Not that she didn't want to talk to Charla ... well, actually she didn't ... for some reason Charla had gotten very catty in the last few weeks, especially about the Thursday night sessions, which Gabriel had told her were Gabriel/Victoria only.

Although Victoria had made it clear that she was not interested in Gabriel, Charla had started behaving like a jealous, over-protective girlfriend. When she'd mentioned it to Gabriel, he had just told her to ignore it, but it was hard especially when Charla was with friends and wanted to put on a show. She had started walking through the library on Thursday evenings now just to make a point, and it was starting to wear on Victoria's nerves.

Glancing around to see if anyone was looking, Victoria did a quick invisibility spell as the group got closer, hoping that they wouldn't decide to sit near her. She'd left her books visible so it looked like an occupied spot. Fortunately, they walked past chatting loudly, earning them looks from the resident librarian at the entrance. Victoria glanced around again and took a deep breath making herself visible.

"Hey!" She froze and looked up to see Gabriel striding toward her. "I could have sworn I just looked here like a second ago and you weren't here. And then all of a sudden, there you were!"

"Um, I went to the bathroom, just got back."

"The bathroom on the *other side* of the building?"

"I literally just got back. You must be confused about how long ago you looked," she said resolutely.

Gabriel was still unconvinced, but he tossed his bag on the table and sat down on the opposite chair staring at her. His disconcerting expression was almost *knowing*, and it made Victoria feel paranoid. He hadn't seen her disappear and reappear, had he? He couldn't have, she had checked properly. Still, she berated herself for even doing magic in a library of all places! She was being careless and it would only get her into a lot of trouble that she didn't need.

She buried her head in a textbook and heard Gabriel chuckling loudly. She poked her head over the top of the book and gave him a black look. He laughed harder.

"You know, if you're going to pretend to read, at least have the book the right way up!"

To her chagrin, she realized that she did indeed have the book upside down, and burst out laughing at the expression on his face.

"Busted!" he laughed.

Cheeks flaming, she put the book down and decided to give him a partial truth. "Sorry, it's just that Charla and some of her friends walked by and it was really uncomfortable, so I was thinking about what I should do."

Gabriel shrugged. "Don't do anything, she'll come around. She's just being ... Charla."

"But it's uncomfortable, Gabriel, to have one of your friends think that you are after her boyfriend … because that *is* what you are, isn't it?" she asked. "You need to tell her that this is nothing more than what it is—two friends studying."

"Is that all it really is?" he said, pouting. She shot him a dark look, and he put his hands in the air in surrender. "Just kidding, I know, I know … you're 'not in a dating mode right now,'" he said, mimicking her consistent response to him on why they shouldn't date. "We're just study buddies."

"Be serious, Gabe," she said. Gabriel smiled; he loved it when she called him Gabe. She noticed him smiling and chucked a book at him, thinking he was still messing around. "Please, will you just do it?"

"Fine, I'll talk to her," he promised. "Now will you stop bugging me? I really need to study!" Victoria rolled her eyes at his dishonest comment, and turned back to her book, this time making carefully sure that it was the right side up.

They worked in quiet camaraderie for a few hours until Gabriel sat back and announced that he was hungry. They decided to head to the Black Dog to get something to eat there instead of staying on campus, and Gabriel drove. It was the first time that Victoria had been in his car and she was impressed. It was black and sporty with shiny chrome wheels and custom racing stripes. Given what she had learned over the holidays about their wealth, she wasn't surprised that Gabriel could afford such an expensive car. But rather than seeming ostentatious for a high school student, it suited him perfectly, she thought, as he got in and gunned the engine. He smiled at the sound, and she rolled her eyes.

They got to the Dog in no time at all. Gabriel drove fast, flying around corners at breakneck speed and screeching to a stop in the restaurant parking lot. She'd held on to the sides of her seat with white fingers and literally released the breath she had been holding for five solid minutes when they finally arrived in one piece at the bar.

"Well, that was the first and last time you're ever driving me anywhere!"

"Come on." He laughed. "That was me being careful."

Gabriel held the door open for her, and they waved to Tony when they were seated in a booth near the bar. As they wolfed down burgers and fries, a couple of his teammates came over and chatted for a while. Gabriel glanced at her apologetically but she smiled and nodded for him to continue with his friends. As he spoke, she studied him. There was so much more than met the eye with Gabriel. It was as if some hidden part of her identified with a part of him. She had tried to explain it to Christian but he wasn't exactly open to the discussion.

Christian did not like Gabriel, and though he'd been especially irritated that they'd been partnered together on their Calc project, he had never asked her switch classes or change partners. Christian seemed to think that Gabriel was after Victoria, and while she assured him that that would never happen, he still didn't trust Gabriel's motives where Victoria was concerned. He'd even suggested that Gabriel had somehow masterminded them being assigned as partners, which was ludicrous. No one could get away with something like that!

Gabriel was still talking to his teammates when she saw Charla and her entourage make their way to a table at the far end. Charla looked around as if she were looking for someone specific, and it was very obvious to Victoria exactly *who* she was looking for. Victoria looked down at the table when she felt the hostile gaze settle on them. She kicked Gabriel under the table. He winced and looked at her accusingly. Victoria inclined her head toward the bar. She saw the recognition in his eyes and looked at him meaningfully until he sighed, excused himself from his friends and stood up, walking over to Charla's table.

Victoria watched as he hugged and kissed Charla performing like a pro for their captive audience, asking her entourage very loudly whether they were getting his best girl in trouble. Charla beamed from the attention. Victoria kept her expression carefully neutral. She hated the pretense and had decided that she would leave just to make the point for the hundredth time that she *wasn't* interested in Gabriel. She was just getting her stuff together to see if someone could give her a ride, when a small figure slid in the booth opposite her.

"Oh, hey Angie, you look different," she said, suddenly noticing the short hair and the fact that Angie actually looked happy. Angie smiled dreamily.

"Thanks. Just trying a little something new," she said. "Taylor's coming up this weekend." Victoria's mind went blank and then she remembered in a flash. Taylor? New Year's Eve Taylor whom Angie had been making out with for hours? Angie's face turned pink with embarrassment, and Victoria grinned. Definitely that Taylor.

"That's really great," Victoria said, and meant it. "I didn't realize that things had gotten serious after New Year's."

"We kept it under the radar. I mean we all grew up together, so we didn't want it to be weird for everyone else," Angie said. "But since he's coming up this weekend, it won't be a secret any more, will it?"

"I'm really happy for you, Angie. You deserve it." Victoria hesitated for a second and then asked the question that had been bothering her. "Angie, can I ask you something? Does Gabriel treat you the way he does because of what you can do?" The happiness on Angie's face immediately dimmed and she looked sharply at Victoria. "I mean I know you said that he isn't like you, but is that it?"

"Why?" Angie was reluctant to respond and kept shooting panicked looks toward her brother. Even though Angie hadn't said anything, Victoria had her answer.

"Don't worry I won't say anything ..."

"Say anything about what?" Gabriel interrupted rudely.

"Nothing, I was just asking Angie to give me a ride home."

"But I'll take you home, Tori," he said.

Victoria smiled. "Don't forget you have a job to do, Gabriel, and taking me home is definitely not one of them. Pay attention to your girlfriend," she said, jerking her eyes toward Charla sitting at her table and casting furtive glances at them.

Gabriel knew he was beaten when he saw the resolute look in Victoria's eyes, and he sighed, resigned. "Fine, I'll call you later then," he said.

As they made their way out, Victoria was rewarded with a happy squeal from Charla as Gabriel grabbed her from behind and twirled her in the air. She and Angie waved goodbye, and Charla gave them a big grin on the way out.

The ride to her apartment was quick, and just as Victoria was thanking Angie for the ride and getting out, Angie put her hand on Victoria's arm.

"Look, it's really weird between Gabriel and me. It's hard to talk about when he is there and well, it's pretty obvious how he feels about me."

"It's okay, I understand, sorry I asked," Victoria said.

Angie still looked like she had something to say and Victoria waited, her hand on the door handle. "I meant to tell you before, but I just didn't get around to it." Angie paused and smiled awkwardly. "I saw those guys in New York with you. You know, the ones without any colors. The dead ones."

Victoria leaned back into the car seat and stared at Angie. She didn't say a word. Angie squeezed her hand on Victoria's arm.

"Look, it's okay. I didn't say anything but I was watching them for you. I know that one was Christian Devereux. I recognized him even in the white mask, but I didn't know the other one." Victoria could see that she was starting to get agitated.

"It's okay, Angie. I knew that you could probably see and was wondering if you did, so thanks for telling me," she said.

"I wanted to make sure that you were okay. It worried me when I saw that there were two of them. But you were fine because you came back." She smiled. "Anyway I just wanted you to know that I … that someone … was looking out for you," she said.

"I appreciate that more than you know," Victoria said, dazed. She felt absurdly grateful. "Hey do you want to come up for a minute? I could make some tea."

Angie was surprised but accepted the invitation. In Victoria's apartment, she was very complimentary even though Victoria knew her place was probably tiny compared to the one that Angie shared with Charla. Angie sat down on the couch next to Leto.

"Oh, you have a cat!" She giggled as if something occurred to her. "Of course you have a cat!" She stroked him a couple times before pulling her hand away as if his fur had burned her. Leto stared at her, his green eyes unblinking. "He's not *just* a cat though, is he?"

"What does he look like? I've always wondered. His name is Leto, by the way," Victoria said, bringing the tea and a plate of biscuits over.

Angie stroked Leto's silvery gray fur. He turned his head into her palm and purred but studied her with an intense look. "Lovely name," she said. "Do you know what it means?"

When Victoria shook her head, Angie continued. "It means

'*the hidden one*.' Leto was also the name of the Goddess Leto who gave birth to Artemis and Apollo."

"How do you know all this stuff?"

"I'm a sucker for Greek and Roman mythology," Angie said. She stroked Leto again, her eyes unfocusing. "His colors are so effervescent, there's so much silvery light that it's almost blinding." She squinted at Leto thoughtfully and then refocused to look into his knowing green eyes. He stretched and gave her his quirky cat smile, and she looked astonished. "Does he—" she began, and then stopped, confused.

"Does he know what you are, you mean?" Victoria finished for her as she sipped her tea. Angie nodded. "You already know the answer to that Angie, sure he does."

"Do you ... does he talk?"

Victoria nodded, staring at Leto for a brief moment. "He says in my world, you would be known as an Aurus. It's a witch term for someone who can see the true spirits of people." Victoria's eyes squinted as if she were listening to something more Leto was saying. "He says it's a very rare gift. Rare and dangerous."

In the space of half a second, Angie's eyes seemed to cloud over and her entire body tensed. Victoria wasn't surprised when she stood up abruptly.

"I'm sorry. I ... I have to go. I ... forgot that I told Charla I would pick her up later at the bar," she stammered. Two pairs of identical green eyes followed her as she raced out the door, almost stumbling in her haste.

Victoria watched her leave and Leto padded over to the windowsill, staring at Angie's disappearing taillights. Victoria scratched his head.

"What did you mean when you said her gift was dangerous Leto?" she asked.

Not just her gift. She is dangerous. Leto paused. *The gift is coveted by many because of the power it grants to someone who can use it to control others. An Aurus has no magical ability, which is why most of them are usually bonded to evil witches and warlocks who abuse their gifts for their own ends.*

"But she's human," Victoria replied.

You're human, Leto pointed out and Victoria rolled her eyes.

"You know what I mean," she said. "She's no witch, and I know she's not part of a witch coven under some other witch or wizard either. I read her."

She's hiding something. She has a mark of magic on her. Victoria immediately burned red and Leto shot her a sharp look.

"It could be me," she said. "She's seen me do magic at the bar."

You what? Tori! How many times have I said that you need to be careful! Leto hissed and flattened his ears.

"It's just a drink guessing game, Leto! And it's not like she doesn't know what I am," she said.

That's just the point, Victoria. When a witch or warlock uses magic, it makes a mark like a signature. Leto's tone was patronizing. Victoria gave an impatient nod, she knew that already. The signature really could only be used to determine the identity of the magic user so she didn't know why Leto was bringing it up. Angie already *knew* that she was a witch.

Leto stared at her with baleful eyes until she flushed again, before he continued. *For an Aurus, that signature is as obvious as if you gave them the blueprint of your magic, and that information can be used against you ... to control you, to hurt you, to kill you!* Leto's mental voice shook with barely concealed fury. *That's why they are so dangerous.*

"Oh," whispered Victoria. "But it was nothing."

Doesn't matter, it was still your *magic. Please Victoria, you need to be more careful. You must know that there's a lot more at stake here. People have killed for far less.*

The pointed reference to her unique blood and who she was made her feel suddenly very cold, and she wrapped her arms around herself.

"The thing is Leto, I'm just not sure what my purpose is. I mean I read Brigid's journal but I just don't know what it is that *I* am supposed to do." She wrung her hands in frustration. "I am not part of a coven, no one even knows who I am."

Patience, Victoria. Our destinies are not always known to us but still we must prepare for them.

"And is that what I'm doing? Preparing? Preparing for what?"

For who you are.

"But what does that *mean*, Leto? Who am I? Please don't tell me I'm someone like Brigid!"

You cannot change who you are, Victoria. But you can decide who you become. If that is similar to Brigid's path or someone else's, then that is your choice.

Victoria raked her hands through her hair. She knew that Leto was right, but she wanted someone to come out and tell her what she was supposed to be doing.

She had never spoken to another witch except for the one that had tried to kill her up at the mountain. How was she supposed to find others like herself? Christian had said that the Vampire Council was negotiating with the witch clans in Europe, which meant that covens had to exist there and here as well. She would ask Christian if he could find out anything further for her about the witch clans. Perhaps he would even allow her to accompany him on his next trip.

Aside from her loneliness, she worried almost constantly about how to control the blood magic. It only became ravenous when she engaged it, the day-to-day spells and incantations she practiced barely touching on the limits of her personal power. She rarely took off the amulet whose absence had caused her blood to go crazy when she'd killed the witch. She felt stronger knowing that she didn't have to give in to its blood lust as readily as she did without it.

Victoria knew what she had to do but was deathly afraid to do it—she needed to put herself into a situation where she had to actually *use* the blood magic, to get it into a frenzy so that she could have the opportunity to control it and *learn* to harness its deadly potency. Brigid's words resounded like a mantra in her head, the price of the blood was hers to set, *hers* to set.

And there was only one person who was strong enough that she could ask for help creating such a scenario.

TWENTY-ONE

The Fight

"ABSOLUTELY NOT!" CHRISTIAN said furiously. She could see the muscle ticking in his clenched jaw. Victoria had just finished explaining her plan to him.

He stuffed his hands in his pockets and stared at her, irate. What she was suggesting was completely absurd, she could be hurt or worse, killed.

"Christian, please," she said. "I need to do this."

"Not this way."

"Christian, this is the *only* way!" As he shook his head, turning away, she continued fiercely. "Don't make me find someone else. I'm sure Lucian would be amenable."

Christian whirled back around, his silver eyes flashing fire. "Don't you ever say that! Don't you know what Lucian is? He is a merciless killer!"

"Yes."

Christian swore under his breath. He was caught between a rock and a hard place because on the one hand, he knew that

Victoria was right to try to tame the manic desires of her blood, her birthright, but by having him attack her, he felt that he was tempting fate. He wasn't even sure that he could control himself if things got too out of hand. The siren call of her blood was still far too sweet. On the other hand, he really didn't want her running off trying to provoke someone else, like Lucian, who could really hurt her or worse.

"Damn it!" he said.

"Does that mean you'll help me?" she asked. Victoria knew that what she was proposing could put them both in a lot of danger. Something could always go wrong, no matter the preparation or precautions. Christian held Victoria's shoulders, noting the defiant resolve in her eyes, and sighed.

"Victoria, you cannot possibly know what you are asking."

"I'm sorry, Christian. I just don't know what else to do, and this seemed like the best way. I need you. You're the only one I can trust."

"So when do you want to do this?"

"Now," she said, waving her hand toward the glass doors leading into the garden. The sky was overcast and it was warmer than it had been during the last couple months, a balmy thirty degrees, not that that really mattered to either of them. Christian blanched.

"It's not that simple, Tori. I need to feed first," he said.

"Fine, go ahead and I'll catch up," she said, the words rushing out.

She didn't want Christian to spend any more time thinking because he would undoubtedly find a way to get out of it. Christian, in turn, felt that Victoria was being far too cavalier about the whole thing. That fact alone exasperated him even more, but his hands were tied. She was headstrong and willful enough to do exactly what she had said—attempt to provoke someone like Lucian, and there was no way he could allow that to happen.

"Fine," he said curtly, and left. As quickly as he walked out the back French doors, he walked back in and hauled her up against him, kissing her soundly, hard and fast. He looked like he had something to say but then decided against it, and kissed her again before stalking out, muttering under his breath.

Victoria exhaled in a rush. She knew how hard this was for him. She deliberated taking off the amulet but then decided against it because she didn't want to put either of them into any more danger than necessary. Without it, she knew she'd be at her blood's mercy. Victoria left the necklace on. She would only use it if she had to. She checked her watch and saw that Christian had only been gone ten minutes. That would be just about right.

Christian raced into the forest beyond the manicured lawn of his back garden. He let the fury that he'd felt after Victoria's request run wild, allowing the beast within him to go free. It didn't take him long to track and capture a young deer. He drank deeply for several long seconds, feeling the life flow through him like a tonic. A whisper of movement in the air pulled him from his semi-trance. He let the deer go slowly and before it could even stand up on wobbly legs to escape into the forest, he was flying with inhuman speed toward the threat. Unconsciously, mere seconds before he reached the target, he smelled that it was human, and he hesitated.

It was enough for Victoria to hurl a ball of energy toward him, which he dodged with practiced ease. His eyes widened as she threw another one viciously toward him. That one caught him squarely in the stomach, and he flew back ten feet crashing into a large balsam fir tree.

He shook off the blow and vaulted to his feet snarling. If she wanted to provoke him, she was doing a stellar job of it. Christian circled warily and leapt into the air to the right. He felt her shift off-balance. He rolled into a crouch and attacked her vulnerable right side sending her flying. Her head smashed against a rock and the smell of blood saturated the air. In a flash he was on top of her with his hands around her throat.

Victoria ignored the stab of pain, and for the first time, felt the blood start to boil in her veins. She invoked a teleportation spell and disappeared from his vice-like grip, appearing behind him.

"IGNIS CREMO," she shouted. Two giant fireballs flew toward him as the blood began its familiar song, her eyes blackening with rage. It fueled her like nothing ever did. Christian dodged her attacks, moving with unearthly grace as she teleported around him again and again. The air crackled, thick with dry electricity as the two combatants spun and parried with incredible speed and agility. She launched an ice blast at his chest and crowed in triumph as the jagged shards sliced from neck to chest, blood discoloring his shirt. Christian's wounds healed immediately, and he was a blur once more, parrying with a vicious thrust to her exposed back. She fell to her knees gasping as the bones in her spine shattered.

"CURO!" she cried, and obediently her spine was rebuilt and realigned.

The energy sparked like blue fire between her fingertips, her face flushed with exhilaration. She'd barely brushed the edges of her own power even with the complex healing spell. The blood was manic in her body; all it wanted was life, blood, sacrifice, especially now that it had been spilled. It had a life and an energy all its own, but it was her body and her mind … *her* blood. She was its master. Victoria needed to push it as far as she dared so that she could harness its energy, and for that, she had to be completely in control to take it to the brink and then pull it back. She *had* to know that she could make it obey her otherwise she would always lose to it and then it would always own her.

Christian feinted to the left, his eyes frenzied as he saw the blood pulsing beneath her skin, her face so delectably red, the *smell* of it, so seductively potent. He ran his tongue against his teeth, feeling their sharpness, and flexed his fingers. He raced toward her, at the last minute throwing himself left, exactly where he had seen her eyes shift in the nanosecond before, and he collided with her, smashing her to the ground with his left shoulder. He felt the air leave her body in a loud whoosh and saw pain fill eyes that were so black they looked like burning embers. His brute strength broke her arm easily as she tried to wrench herself from beneath him, and he could feel his mouth filling with saliva as her blood sang its seductive song daring him to take it. But Christian knew that the minute he bit her, it would be over. *He* would be over. She gasped, and Christian couldn't resist, he kissed her, silencing the soft muttering that had parted her lips, while she struggled beneath him.

Then Christian made the fatal mistake of looking into her eyes.

Suddenly he couldn't move a muscle. They smoldered with a terrible black anger even as her mouth returned his kiss. It was as if they were two separate beings, the sweetness of her mouth upon his, and the darkness of her terrible eyes draining the life out of him. Christian could feel her heart racing, the fury of her blood uncontrollable, and he knew that if she couldn't rein it in somehow, he would be lost. Already his hunger eviscerated him, he could feel the holes in his gut as those eyes, so blackly terrifying—hers but not hers, sucking everything from him, taking, feeding ... *killing*. He felt wetness on his face.

Somehow, she'd become the vampire.

Victoria could barely control the tremendous rush of the blood driving her to take every last bit of life from Christian. Its heat burned her eyes as she tore her mouth from the sudden blue coldness of his, her left arm hanging limply, and stared in horror at the rivers of red bleeding from his eyes, nose, and mouth. It pooled to the ground in a sticky, viscous river beneath him, and she could feel him writhing in pain above her. She knew she was killing him, and it sickened her as much as it thrilled her. Her breath came in shallow pants as the fear took root—the blood magic wasn't stopping! Helpless, Victoria saw the dullness in Christian's eyes and knew that he was growing weaker with each passing second as the blood drained from him like water through a sieve.

Her left arm ached, limp at her side, and Victoria forced the blood magic to heal the injury, directing its fury away from its consumption, from its inhuman desire for death. As her bones mended, she tried to coerce the powerful blood into submission. She gritted her teeth, focusing and pulling the power into her, compelling the beast. It rebelled, furious. She felt like she was splintering under its fury, every cell in her felt like it was on fire and growing weaker by the second. It was relentless! Oh god, she couldn't do it. She'd thought she could control something she barely even understood and now Christian was going to die because of her reckless stupidity. How could she have been so arrogant?

Christian was as pale as death and his lips moved in soundless agony. She could hear the one word echoing over and over in his head like a staccato as if it were the only thing keeping him conscious.

Blood. Blood. Blood.

The cold realization hit her then—she *wasn't* strong enough. Christian was dying! In desperation, she called out to the one person who could help them.

Leto!

Victoria, what's wrong? Leto's voice was alarmed.

Need … help … blood killing someone … Please …

Where are you?

No time ... please, Leto ... so weak ...

Invoke the amulet. Evoco. Do it now!

"Brigid, help me! Evoco Brigid! I summon you!" she cried, grasping the stone in her palm.

The amulet surged. Victoria's whole body jerked like a puppet on a string as Brigid's power lanced through her. She was so weak, she could barely hold her body upright and she collapsed on top of Christian's inert frame. The magic invaded every part of her. She felt Brigid's will subdue the blood roughly, forcing it to release Christian. Like a dog, it cowed before her, but still Victoria could feel its terrible power churning beneath its submission. Brigid's control was only temporary, she saw that now, but at least it had saved Christian.

He was alive. Barely.

Blood was the only thing that would save him. Brigid's magic swirled, waiting.

"Transeo," Victoria said weakly, focusing on their destination. Heat saturated her body as each cell responded to her unspoken command, and she pulled Christian closer. Then there was a flash of nothingness and then they were lying on the floor in Christian's den. Victoria quelled her immediate nausea, checking to make sure everything had made the transition, and screamed for Anton, hoping that he was somewhere in the house.

The concern on Anton's face was unmistakable as he saw Christian lying prone, his face and clothes covered in blood. Wordlessly, he looked at Victoria and left the room, returning with an armful of disposable blood bags, several pints worth. Almost an hour later, Anton was done. Christian was a lot less pale than when she had brought him back, and even managed a weak smile for her as she sat down on the sofa next to him.

"I'm so sorry," she said. "I almost killed you, you could have died …" She trailed off. She'd failed. The amulet had saved them both. She shuddered at how close she'd been to losing him.

Christian held her chin in his hand, stroking the reddened welt on the side of her temple. She winced, she had forgotten about that. When Christian had slammed into her, she had hit her head on a rock but hadn't really thought about it at the time or much after it until now.

He watched as she healed it, the welt disappearing as the skin repaired itself at the area of impact. He was amazed at how easily the magic flowed through her, like a natural extension of her breathing. The rapidity with which her wound had healed before his eyes was a true testament to her skills. He glanced at her left arm, which seemed to be perfect. From the little he knew about healing magic, a broken arm would take hours, days even, to mend properly, but she had done it in minutes. A small part of him still felt a shudder of alarm as he remembered *exactly* what she could do. Again, he felt that same unfamiliar emotion at the base of his spine. It was one he hadn't felt in a very long time.

Fear.

"Are you okay?" she asked, noticing his expression.

"I will be fine. Bag blood gives me a headache," he said evasively. "I keep it around for emergencies because it does what it is supposed to."

"So you can't live on it?"

"It's possible I suppose," he said, "but our strength depends on real, live blood. It's as much to do with the energy of the life-force as much as it does with the blood itself. I think if we existed on essentially lifeless blood, we would be more like … zombies, I guess."

Victoria studied his white face. Her blood had almost killed him. If anything, now more than ever she knew that she couldn't control it, and she couldn't risk putting him in danger again. She knew what she had to do.

"Christian," she began, "we can't … I can't do this." He stared at her, silent. She dared not look at him or there was no way she'd be able to say what she had to. "More than ever, now I can appreciate how dangerous this is, not just you and me, but my power over the blood. I thought I could do it, but I can't. And I can't protect you … from me."

"You don't need to protect me."

"But I do. You don't understand what happened out there. I failed, Christian. My blood nearly killed you and I couldn't do a single thing to stop it. It was Leto who saved you, he saved us both." Her eyes met his, pleading. "I have to protect you from it. And there's only one way I can do that. We need to stop."

"Stop what exactly?"

"This. Us."

"Is that what you want?" His voice was devoid of emotion.

"Yes." Victoria was proud of the strength of her voice because her insides felt like they were shattering into a million pieces. "I'm sorry I hurt you for nothing … thank you for trying to help me even though you knew how risky it was. I couldn't bear it if anything happened …" Her voice broke then and she drew a strangled breath. "Please understand. Goodbye, Christian."

Christian made no move to convince her to stay, watching as she walked out of the den and out of his life. What she was doing was for the best—he would only expose her to more danger than was necessary and despite the ache inside of him, he knew that she would be better off without him. She would be *safe*.

As she drove away, Victoria didn't allow herself to feel anything. It was over. She felt the gentle touch on her consciousness and was grateful for the interruption.

Hi, Leto.

Are you okay?

Yes, it worked ... what you said to do.

What happened? Victoria didn't really want to talk about what had taken place, but she knew that she owed Leto an explanation.

I'll be home soon. I'll explain then.

The minute she walked in the door, Leto pounced, his expression not allowing her any stalling. In a few succinct sentences, she told him about Christian and the events leading up to the fight, leaving the fact that he was a vampire for the end. She could feel a furious hiss ripple through Leto's body. His eyes were slits.

A vampire? Victoria, that is forbidden!

"I know, Leto." Her voice was emotionless. "It was a mistake. It's over."

And you think he's just going to let you go? Just like that? Leto was almost screaming.

"Yes."

Why, pray tell? He didn't bother to disguise his biting sarcasm. *They cannot be trusted. You are a fool.*

"Because I asked him to. And I am more of a fool for thinking I could control this curse than trusting a vampire, because that is what will kill me, not him!" Her voice shook as all the emotion she'd been suppressing burst free. She sank to the floor, her head in her hands, silent anguish shaking her body. *I am a monster.*

Victoria ...

Just leave it, Leto. It's over, and I'm tired. The only thing I need from you is your help, not your judgment. I don't have anyone else to turn to. If you can't do that, then please leave me alone.

Leto stared at her, silent and shaken.

What do you need?

I need to know everything there is to know about the blood. Victoria raised eyes that were like emerald chips to his. *And I need to know how to kill it.*

TWENTY-TWO

Misunderstanding

"GABRIEL, I TOLD you fifty times, I am not going to Cancun with you guys!" Victoria said. Gabriel made a puppy-dog face as he leaned on the table across from her.

"Well, what are you going to do then?" he asked. "Sit around here and freeze?"

"I am going to finish my project," she said with finality. Then her face softened. Gabriel had been her saving grace the last few weeks, and life had finally started to feel a little less surreal. His feelings for her hadn't changed, but little by little, she'd let herself open up to him. He was the only thing in her life that felt stable, and she clung to that like a lifeline. She wanted to give him a chance, and also to give herself a chance at a normal friendship with someone who genuinely cared about her.

"Look Gabe, I really would love to go, but I just can't this time, okay?" Gabriel's eyes narrowed, he knew that look and that voice.

"You only call me Gabe when you want something, don't think I don't know it, I've caught on to your sneaky tricks!" he said.

Victoria rolled her eyes. She absolutely did not want to go to Mexico with Gabriel and his entourage. She wanted to spend time alone with Leto doing some more training. True to his word, he'd taught her what he knew about the blood curse, and the more she'd come to understand it and how intertwined it was with her magic, the more she realized how difficult it was to control it, far less exorcise it. But everything she learned gave her more confidence that one day, maybe, she'd have a chance.

"I'm not going. *Gabriel.*"

Suddenly his face broke out in a wicked smile. "Sure you don't want to see me in my skivvies?" he asked. "Most girls would go to Cancun just for that, you know."

"Whatever, I've seen better," she said. Gabriel grinned and pouted like Ben Stiller in *Zoolander.*

"You know you want some of this blue steel," he said cockily, kissing his flexed arm. Shaking her head and embarrassed, she shot Gabriel a dismissive look.

"Stop it," she said. "I want no part of your blue … steel." Collapsing in silent giggles, the tears leaked from her eyes and she grasped her stomach with both hands.

"Stop playing. You can't resist me and you know it."

"Resist this!" And she tossed a book at him. Watching the librarian walking over with a thunderous look on her face, Victoria hastily gathered her bag and coat, and fled. She heard Gabriel running behind her as he caught up with her on the top of the library steps. Victoria squealed as he lifted her into the air and like a lunatic raced down the rest of the stairs with her in his arms.

"Put me down!"

"You deserve punishment for leaving me back there with that demented librarian!" he said, spinning her around until she begged for mercy.

"Fine, fine, but put me down first." Gabriel deposited her into an ungainly heap on the snowy grass and collapsed next to her breathless. When she had recovered her breath, she started edging away, trying to make her escape.

"Oh no you don't," he said, his eyes mischievous, grabbing on to her arm as he started tickling her. "Say you'll go!"

"Stop it, Gabriel. I can't go … stop!" She laughed uncontrollably as she felt for a handful of snow and stuck it down his neck. She bit her lips, her eyes alight as he sat back with a shocked look on his face. As she tried to scramble away, she felt him grab her leg and pull her back. She scrambled harder, giggling like a maniac. A few students sitting on a nearby bench watched the scene unfold.

Unprepared for the weight of him as he threw himself on top of her, the breath whooshed out of her in a surprised gurgle.

"Gerooff me!" she said, futilely trying to wiggle her way out from under him, the snow pressing wetly into the back of her neck. Gabriel shook his head and made a face, crossing his eyes and blowing out his cheeks, making her laugh again at his over-the-top silliness. As he stared into her flushed face, Victoria felt him start to move forward. Inches from her lips, he stopped as she stiffened, her eyes darting to the right.

Victoria froze as a dim shadow blocked the hazy light trying to pierce the overcast sky. Her eyes were wide, her laughter wedged in her throat. Gabriel turned to see who the distraction was, obviously annoyed that the moment had been interrupted. His dark eyes narrowed, registering who it was and then dismissed him as no one of importance as he continued to walk past with silent footsteps. But the moment had passed and Victoria rolled out quickly from under him, muttering something about getting to class and dusting the snow off her coat as she walked briskly in the opposite direction.

"What about Cancun?" he yelled.

She turned around, made a rude gesture with her fingers, and kept walking. She didn't miss Gabriel's cocky smile.

Victoria clutched her bag to her chest in complete shock. She hadn't seen Christian in weeks, and seeing him had been like a jolt to her system. Her heart was pounding as she remembered the freezing rage in his eyes as he'd walked by. He had barely slowed, but the minute his frigid silver eyes had met hers, it felt like time had stopped, the weight of his anger anchoring the two of them in an unmoving space. The unhidden pain in his eyes had floored her. Even though she'd ended it between them, she had never wanted to hurt him.

Christian? She waited several long minutes, but there was nothing. *Please Christian, I'm sorry. Please talk to me.* She waited, the silence echoing across the hollow chasm between their minds. *Please ...*

Not now, Victoria.

His mind was cold, empty and closed. Victoria wasn't naïve, she'd known that Gabriel had been about to try to kiss her. She had been about to stop him when she'd sensed Christian, and instead of pushing Gabriel off as she had intended to, her entire body had been frozen into guilty immobility, making the situation look far worse than it actually was. A part of her argued that she'd done nothing wrong anyway—she and Christian were over, and what she did with anyone else was her business. But she couldn't help the guilt she felt, knowing that she had hurt him so much that he couldn't even bear to talk to her.

She went to class but could barely concentrate, and slipped out in the last ten minutes, running toward her car. Victoria floored it to Christian's house and made it there faster then she had ever driven, skidding to a stop at the top of the driveway.

The front door was unlocked as it always was and she went

right in, letting her mind open in search of him. The house was empty. She opened her awareness and detected movement in the underground garage.

As she made her way there, her cell phone rang. The caller ID said it was Gabriel. She thought about ignoring it, but knew that he would keep calling her over the next hour like a stalker until she called him back. It would be easier to get rid of him if she answered. She clicked on the phone.

"Hi, Gabriel."

"Hey Tori, where are you? I waited for you after class and noticed your Mini was gone. So I swung by your place and you're not there ... where are you?" Victoria detected a slight edge in his voice but had no time to sugarcoat.

"Stalk much? Look Gabe, sorry I bailed, but I had to run an errand."

"So are you going to come to Cancun? Come on, Tori, it will be great."

"I really can't, Gabe. I would but I'm swamped right now," she said as she tried to find the door leading to the garage.

"Fine, I'll stay here too then," he said. Victoria knew that he would stay just to prove a point.

"I'm on my way up to my Aunt Holly's," she said. "Look, I have to go, talk later. See you, Gabe."

She disconnected the call before he could argue and hoped that he wouldn't do anything stupid like drive up to Holly's. Finally, she found the mahogany door to the elevator that lead down to the garage.

Christian's garage was more like an underground warehouse with huge high ceilings, fluorescent lighting, and about ten cars, several bikes, and a wicked-looking cigarette boat on a trailer, all lined up in neat rows. Christian was standing next to the '67 Shelby

GT 500 that he'd told her he was restoring himself. He had on a pair of faded blue jeans, smudges of grease on his face and hands, and he'd never looked more appealing. She steeled herself as he walked toward her, his face shuttered and demeanor wary, like a goaded lion. Victoria swallowed, unexpectedly anxious. Maybe this hadn't been the best idea.

"What do you want?" he said, his voice cold. At his tone, she lifted her chin.

"You wouldn't let me explain, so I had to find you."

"Explain what? There's really nothing to say, is there?" She flinched from the emptiness in his words.

"Christian, I know what you thought you saw, but it was nothing."

"Is that what you call it? He was going to kiss you."

"No, it's not what you think," she said, and then added, "besides what does it matter? We broke up, didn't we?"

"You're right. So *why* are you here, Victoria?" She stared at him to see if his eyes were as unfeeling as his words were. They were worse.

"I'm sorry, I shouldn't have come," she said, fleeing before the tears came.

Victoria drove back to her apartment, her fingers clenched in humiliation on the steering wheel. What was she thinking, going to Christian's house like that? They were over—she didn't owe him anything! The way he had looked at her, as if she were nothing, had hurt her far more than she'd ever thought possible. She screeched to a stop in front of her apartment, only just noticing the lanky frame leaning against the wall as she got out of the car.

"Did you *run* over here?" she asked, her heart racing at the sight of him. She steeled herself, guarding her mind … and heart. Christian's face was pained.

"Victoria, I'm sorry. I handled that badly. I was just ... surprised by your visit, that's all."

"Look, it's nothing. I wanted to explain, but you're right, there's really nothing to say, is there? We're over."

After several agonizing moments, he spoke, his voice carefully modulated. "Yes, we are, and I'm sorry I reacted the way I did. You have every right to be with someone like you, someone ... human," he said. "Someone you can hold and love without fearing for your life. Like him." She remained silent. "You should be worrying about school and parties and dates, not whether some monster is going to rip your throat out." Victoria flinched even as he continued. "You've moved on, and that's good."

The rational, sane part of her agreed with him, the reasons why they shouldn't be together were obvious—he was as much a danger to her as she was to him, and she'd nearly killed him when they'd been together last. Yet at his words, something inside Victoria cracked.

"That's just it, I *haven't* moved on," she cried, everything she'd been holding in suddenly exploding within her. "I haven't been able to let you go, even though God knows I have tried. And I hate you for doing this, for making me this ... *weak* ..."

"Victoria—"

"Please, don't."

Victoria.

Christian couldn't help himself. Her stunning admission crippled any resolve he'd had. He caught her shoulders and pulled her to him taking her lips in a desperate kiss. She couldn't help herself either, kissing him back with everything she'd boxed away in her heart, every single bit of emotion she'd suppressed since they day she had left his house. The kiss decimated her.

Victoria broke away, gasping. *What was she doing?*

"Please," she whispered, "just go."

With a searching look Christian left, and she almost collapsed against the building. She touched a finger to her burning lips. Her mind and body felt like two separate things. She couldn't even begin to process the feelings Christian's kiss had kindled. Her brain spun with dizzying intensity as forgotten emotions threatened to overwhelm her. Seeing him had been torture. Kissing him had been excruciating.

Suddenly across the street, movement caught her eye as a person stepped away from a dark car parked in the shadows. Victoria tensed, her body already preparing for attack, as the stranger's features became clearer in the light. Her stomach flipped and soured immediately.

"Oh, hi Gabe," she said, wondering just how long he had been there. Gabriel's face was cold, his normally open smile was grimly absent and his lips were a hard, flat line. He'd been there a while, she guessed.

"I thought you were going to Holly's?" he said.

"Gabe—"

"Don't Gabe me," he said. "I *saw* you! I saw you with *him*! Devereux." His eyes were twin discs of ice. "Is he your boyfriend?"

"No. Not my boyfriend," she said, conscious of being cornered near the narrow doorway. She had never seen Gabriel this upset and a hollow feeling started to spread in her stomach in response to his ominous tone.

"So what is he then that you can kiss him so ... passionately?" Gabriel said. "Or do you kiss everyone like that?"

"No, he is ... was a friend ..." she said her voice shaking then trailing off at the vicious glare he sent her way. "Gabriel, I don't know what you want me to say."

"*Devereux*?" he hissed. "Is that why you got so weird earlier?"

Victoria flushed and stared at the ground, and the silent admission of guilt seemed to make Gabriel even more incensed. "I changed everything for *you*. And you're with *him*? And you lie about it to my face!"

He was right in front of her, his face dark and menacing and for the first time since she had known him, Victoria felt afraid, as if he could really hurt her without thinking twice about it. The corrosive hatred that she usually saw directed toward Angie was now directed toward her in unbridled measure.

"Gabe, please," she said. "I'm not with anyone. I have always told you—"

"Told me what? That you're just 'not in a dating mode right now'?" His laugh was bitter. "Obviously you are, just not with me, right?"

"Come on, Gabriel, you're my friend, you know that."

"Friend? Is Devereux just your friend or is he a friend with benefits? Or does he just take what he wants? Is that what you like, Tori?" he said, as he ran his fingers down the side of her face. Victoria flinched, her heart in her throat. She didn't want to have to hurt Gabriel, after all he had just seen her kissing someone else, but if he threatened her, she would have no choice. His hands slid down her jaw and closed around her neck slowly. His eyes were full of malice and every muscle in his body was coiled as tight as a spring. He wanted to punish her; she could see it in his eyes.

"Gabriel, you're hurting me." Her hands clawed against the fingers holding her neck in an unyielding grip. "Stop it, please."

Gabriel's hand seemed to tighten of its own volition as his face darkened in response to her pleading, daring her to take matters into her own hands. Just as she was drawing upon the energy to free herself, his grip slackened, and she ripped his hand off her neck, shoving his chest with both hands. He staggered back a few feet, but what scared her most wasn't the expression on his face after she had pushed him, it was the way he looked at her, as if she were nothing, as if she no longer *existed*.

Gabriel backed away slowly watching her with open loathing before he abruptly turned toward his car. Without a backward glance he jumped in and sped away, the tires screeching in protest against the asphalt and leaving black tracks in their wake.

Victoria slid down the side of the wall, her body shaking from the shock of the confrontation. That was something she had *never* expected, not from Gabriel of all people. His cold, almost inhuman rage had scared her. The virulent look in his eyes had chilled her to the bone, leaving her with little reservation about how he felt about her. She shivered remembering the look on his face as he had walked away. Hate barely did it justice.

He despised her.

TWENTY-THREE

Vulnerability and Rage

Victoria didn't get out of bed even though the sun was streaming through the windows and she knew it was mid-morning. She buried her head under the covers, giving in to the only sanctuary she had left.

She opened bleary eyes several hours later as Tony left a desperate-sounding message on her answering machine, checking to see if she could work an emergency shift that night. She squinted at her watch, it was three in the afternoon, and as much as she wanted to, she knew she couldn't stay in bed forever.

At least at the Black Dog she'd be able to distract herself and not focus on what had happened with Gabriel or with Christian. She showered and dressed, missing Leto terribly. His gift for comfort would have been useful, but they hadn't exactly been on the best of terms since he'd found out about Christian. She'd been the one to suggest that they take a break and he stay at Holly's. She concentrated on healing, taking slow long breaths as she dressed, wishing fervently that she could just go back to bed instead.

Tony gave her a grateful smile when she arrived. The Dog was short-staffed again, but it wasn't too crowded, she noticed thankfully, as she hopped behind the bar. Her stomach sank as she registered who was in the far right corner. Seriously, if she had noticed his car out front, she wouldn't have thought twice about calling Tony from the parking lot and canceling. But she knew that she couldn't leave him stranded now that she was already here. Victoria bit her lip and put her head down. She had a job to do.

She tried to pass the time joking with the other people in the bar as best as she could, but she couldn't shake the sour, sick feeling that rested in her stomach. Every time she heard the loud laughter from that corner, she had to force herself to not look in that direction. Even Tony noticed that she wasn't her usual jovial self and came over to ask her if she was all right.

"I'm fine, just a little stomach bug I think," she said. "Don't worry. I'll still be able to help you out."

Distracted by his parting comment about his special cure for stomach bugs involving Jagermeister, a loud peal of laughter drew her attention and her eyes flicked over automatically. They locked with a pair of cold black ones and her heart froze in her chest at the hatred she saw reflected there. She couldn't pull away from Gabriel's stare, and in slow motion she watched him pull a willing Charla onto his lap and kiss her, all while staring at Victoria.

It was ugly, sordid. She felt sick, her breath coming in short silent gasps—she could *feel* his lips on hers, the violence of them grinding into hers, bruising and punishing. He smiled.

Victoria dragged her eyes away with considerable difficulty, grasping the top of the bar for support, as she felt curiously weak and almost drained from the effort it had taken to pull away. Black spots danced in her head. She sank to the floor, assuming that it was stress from the shock of yesterday's confrontation with him.

Without warning, a wave of nausea overcame her. She started retching as she ran for the employee's bathroom. She splashed some water on her face and heard the door open as she wiped her face with some paper towel.

"I'm fine, Tony, just need five minutes," she said, not bothering to look up.

"Really? I wouldn't quite say that you're fine."

Victoria's head snapped up warily. She didn't know how much more she could take before she cracked. She gritted her teeth and swallowed, her throat dry.

"This is the employee's bathroom," she said in a flat, emotionless voice. Gabriel nodded smiling. It was an ugly smile, much the same as the one he'd worn earlier.

"I know, so it's not like we'll be disturbed," he said, stepping closer. "So was that good for you?"

"If you're talking about the grotesque thing with the kiss that you did, then no," she said, swallowing the bile stinging her throat. His eyes narrowed.

"Grotesque, was it? Does Devereux do it better then?" He stepped closer and Victoria braced herself for attack, not taking her eyes off him. "Shall we have a demonstration and compare?" Gabriel suggested with a hideous grin, stepping forward at the same time and grabbing her upper arms with brute force before she could move away.

"I wouldn't get any closer if I were you," said a silky voice at the door. Both Victoria and Gabriel automatically turned in the direction of the menacing voice.

"And what are you going to do about it, Devereux?" Gabriel said. Victoria's eyes were wide as she silently pleaded with Christian to not lose control.

Please Christian, not here. He's not worth it. Please …

Every inch of his frame was tense with barely restrained fury. She knew he could kill Gabriel without even breaking a sweat. Salvation came from an unexpected source as Tony's rounded bulk filled the doorway, shouldering past Christian and wielding a baseball bat nonchalantly.

"He's not going to do anything, but I am," he said coolly, tapping the bat in his left hand. "We can do this the easy way or the hard way." Gabriel's eyes narrowed and a muscle clenched in his jaw. Tony noticed and smiled. "You can make my day, kid. The cops are on their way. Your call."

Gabriel raised his hands in the air and grinned, the smile nowhere near his eyes.

"Sorry, it's just a little misunderstanding. I'll leave," he said.

Tony didn't look convinced but Victoria nodded to him to let Gabriel leave without a scene and Tony allowed Gabriel to walk by.

As Gabriel walked past Christian, Gabriel glared at him from head to toe. The threat in his body language was unmistakable. What Christian had on Gabriel in height, Gabriel made up for in sheer bulk, and the mutual dislike that flared between them was intense. Christian didn't bat an eyelash and Victoria remained frozen until Gabriel sauntered out into the bar. By the time they came out of the bathroom a few minutes later, Gabriel and his entourage had already left.

"What made you come?" she asked Christian.

"Just a feeling that you needed me," he said, and then silently, *did something happen last night?*

Gabriel saw us ... kissing. Her gaze fluttered from his lips to the floor. *He was ... angry.*

I sensed something after I left but I thought it was because of me. When I felt it again just before, I knew that something wasn't right. So I came to find you.

"Tori, you okay?" Tony asked, interrupting their silent exchange. She nodded, managing a weak smile. She closed her eyes as a wave of dizziness overcame her and she sagged against Christian.

Tony met Christian's eyes above her head.

"Can you take her home?" he asked.

"No problem," Christian said.

Christian pulled up to her apartment, and neither of them made any move to get out, sitting silently in the car. She leaned toward him, her heart in her eyes.

"Thank you, Christian. I'm glad you came and … I'm glad you're here now," she said softly. "I need to tell you something."

He turned to face her, his voice quiet but compassionate.

"Victoria, this doesn't change anything. What you did was the right thing. We can't be together. We shouldn't. That kiss was—"

"Don't even say it," she said. "Don't you understand now? I don't want anyone else! I've been lying to myself all along. Christian, how could I be with anyone else other than you?"

"You should be with someone like you, young—"

"Someone like Gabriel? We both saw where that got me."

"Victoria, this cannot be good for you no matter what you think you know. I am still a danger to you in every possible way. I can't be with you, and you shouldn't be with me. We are from different worlds, and what we were doing was not only reckless, it was wrong." His voice was dead, and if Victoria hadn't seen the agony in his eyes, she would have believed every hateful word that had left his lips. But she knew what he was doing—he was *pushing* her away.

"I already fear for my life just because of who *I* am, you think adding a little inconsequential vampire to the equation will change any of that?" She paused and her eyes went strangely blank as if something had occurred to her. "Or is it that you just don't want *me*?" she asked in a strangled voice.

"How could you possibly think that?" he said. "It's not you ..." He reached for her hands, and she pulled back, her face cold but her eyes bright with suppressed tears.

"That's it, isn't it? It's me. I'm just too young, too stupid, right?" she said. "I could never be as beautiful as that blond vampire woman, could I?"

In that instant, the obscure memory became clear, the one that had eluded her ever since she had first seen the blond woman— she had seen her when Christian had first let her go into his mind, into *his* memories. She was someone who had been close to him! More than close. Of course! The hot rush of understanding was like a blow to her stomach. They'd been *lovers*.

Christian couldn't help it, he started laughing, a derisive, humorless sound that echoed horribly in the car. "What does Lena have to do with anything?" he said, his confusion genuine.

"Nothing," Victoria said, jealousy exploding into every part of her. "Except that she's just beautiful and perfect *and* a vampire ... everything I am not and everything you could possibly want, so perfect for you. What was I then? Some kind of toy?"

"Victoria ... please ..."

Christian didn't know how to respond to her comment about Lena as it had come from left field and he had no idea what prompted it. He held his hands out toward her and Victoria leaned away, her eyes flashing black fire.

"You're upset and you're not thinking clearly," he said, as if he were speaking to a skittish horse. Her eyes narrowed.

"Don't patronize me, Christian. I've never been clearer about anything in my life. But you! You can't even fight for what you want, even when it's right in front of you. Go ahead. Push me away if that makes you feel better about your own choices. Make this about me. And run back to your perfect little vampire existence without some gauche *child* like me screwing it up."

"Tori, that's not it at all. I can't give you what you want. Every time we touch, we have to think about how long the moment is going to last. We both hold back because we have to. You don't deserve that. You deserve someone who can love you without reservation, without fear of hurting you, someone within the rules."

"What do you know about what I want?"

"You told me, remember?" His eyes were gentle. "In the limousine on New Years Eve?"

"You know what I meant! It's not *this* or whatever you've decided is *best* for me!"

"You said you wanted more. I can't give you that, Victoria."

"Did you give it to *her*?"

Victoria stared at him, her eyes narrowed to slits as torturous thoughts of the beautiful woman kissing Christian spun wildly through her brain. They had been lovers, something she and Christian might never be!

"Victoria," he said. "Lena is no one important." Her eyes flared and he knew instinctively that he had said the wrong thing. For a moment, Christian felt real uncertainty as he stared into her black, black eyes. He could smell the sweetness of the blood, the magic amplifying its heady fragrance a hundred fold, and he could sense its wildness simmering just beneath her hard-won but fragile control of it. "I didn't mean—"

"No one important?" she said. "Is that why she is in so many of your memories? Don't lie to me! What do you *want*, Christian? Do you know what it is you want?"

Fight for me, please. Fight for us.

I can't, it's too dangerous. You could die.

I won't. We live by our own rules. Say the words, Christian.

The crossroads loomed. He felt it in her voice, she would let him go, if anything to save her battered pride, but there would be no going back. Pride would offer no second chances.

"What do you want?" she repeated.

Christian swallowed, his eyes tormented. He could never let her go.

"You. It's always been you."

The moment froze in time as her eyes grasped his, searching for truth in their depths, and Victoria let out the breath she'd unconsciously been holding. She didn't know who took the first step but it didn't matter as she slid into his arms, and then they were holding each other so tightly that neither of them could breathe. It felt like coming home.

They stood there for an eternity, neither of them noticing the lone figure standing in the darkest shadows across the street, silently watching, his face contorted with rage.

TWENTY-FOUR

Romeo and Juliet

"ARE YOU SURE I look okay?" Victoria asked. Christian assured her that she did, and they walked down to the waiting limousine. "I can't believe I am going to meet a witch priestess!" she said. "I can't believe I am in Paris!"

The unexpected trip had arisen after an urgent call from Enhard the night before that the Council was being convened at Lucian's request. After the scene with Gabriel, Christian hadn't wanted to leave Victoria alone in Canville even if it meant risking exposure to Lucian. The last two times he'd left her alone, both times she'd almost been killed at the hands of his brother.

At least in Paris, he'd be able to protect her and with Enhard's unknowing help, he'd arranged a meeting for Victoria with the Witch Clans. Her presence in Paris would be under the guise of meeting others like herself, and under his protection because of the recent slew of vicious attacks. As a royal and Council advisor, his position was unassailable. It wasn't the most foolproof plan, but it was the best he could do on short notice.

When they had arrived, she had immediately fallen in love with Christian's apartment on Boulevard Saint-Germain, the evening bustle of the busy street making her as excited as a small child. The two-bedroom apartment was simple and tastefully furnished with old-world charm. It boasted a lovely balcony that overlooked the Seine and the glorious Eiffel Tower luminously draped in golden lights, holding court over her city. Paris was already living up to every expectation she'd ever had and she'd barely been there a day.

The limousine pulled to a stop at their destination in La Défense. They walked into the ominously beautiful obsidian tower and took the elevator to the very top floor. Victoria was awed by the opulence and the magnificent view.

The same beautiful receptionist greeted Christian who had met him before and she extended the same lush invitation as she had the last time. Victoria's eyes narrowed and Christian chuckled under his breath at her jealousy.

"Relax chérie, she's paid to do that."

"Well, she didn't come on to me, so obviously she's not doing her job properly," Victoria said. Christian laughed.

The receptionist ushered them into a small room set up for an informal meeting with deep armchairs around a small coffee table. There was a buffet table at the end of the room covered with an assortment of fruit, bread and cheeses.

Victoria tried to get comfortable as Christian stared at her from beneath a heavy-lidded gaze. He could appreciate why she was nervous, but despite it, she looked lovely, with her thick blue-black hair pulled back off her face and secured in a neat chignon. She had chosen to wear a plain white shirt with a ruffled collar and a black pencil skirt. The overall look was austere, but somehow made him want to kiss her thoroughly and demolish that tidy, proper hairstyle.

"Why are you glowering at me like that?"

"Because that little chignon of yours is driving me crazy," he said honestly, which forced a surprised laugh from her chest. "And Catholic school girls look the same in any era," he added with a grin.

Victoria laughed again. "Perv. I decided jeans weren't appropriate, so I borrowed this skirt from Charla. Considering she's four inches shorter than I am, I'm surprised it fit."

"Well, you look beautiful."

"Merci monsieur, so do you."

Victoria had been so overwhelmed earlier that she'd hardly noticed Christian's appearance. Clad in an immaculate dark navy suit, he looked like he'd just stepped out of the pages of a business magazine, some kind of young tycoon. She couldn't decide which look she liked better. He looked just as good in jeans and a T-shirt as he did wearing a jacket and tie. Her gaze flicked to his. His silver eyes were still smoldering unsettlingly.

Victoria shivered in delicious response dragging her eyes away. She was just about to reprimand him for staring at her in such a suggestive manner when the door opened and an attractive dark-haired man walked in.

He introduced himself as Enhard and embraced Christian warmly. Christian then introduced Victoria. When he said pointedly that her name was Tori, Victoria noticed that Enhard started visibly, his eyes snapping to Christian's who nodded imperceptibly. Enhard smiled with genuine pleasure, engulfing Victoria's hands in his own and telling her that he was honored to meet her. Victoria was taken aback by his effusive greeting but when she looked at Christian, he just smiled.

What's that about? she asked silently.

Nothing really, I just told him a little about this wonderful girl I had met.

She was staring dreamily at his face when she realized that

Enhard had asked her a question, a smile on his own face at her diverted expression.

"Sorry?" she said, turning red. Christian pretended to study his fingernails but she knew that he was laughing inside at her embarrassment. She glared at him.

"Did you have a pleasant trip?" Enhard asked, his voice mellow like butterscotch. Victoria felt like she was going to melt from the tone of his voice. What was *with* these vampires and their ability to charm the senses!

"Yes, it was fine, thank you," she responded with a winsome smile. She felt the gentle brush of his mind on hers that was undoubtedly intended to have been unnoticed, and responded with an answering touch of her own, leaving him in no doubt of what she was. Enhard's eyes widened as he whirled to face Christian.

"She's … a witch!" he accused.

Victoria tensed in response to the almost angry tone of his voice.

"Yes," Christian agreed, his face implacable.

The reproach in Enhard's expression was obvious. If she had simply been a human, it would have been acceptable. But Victoria was a witch. Their shared history was far too dark, and centuries of hate meant that no relationship between witches and vampires would be tolerated.

Victoria could feel the palpable change in the air as Enhard regarded her in stunned silence. She stared back just as fiercely until Enhard looked away, noticing that Christian had moved to stand behind her. She leaned into the length of his body and absorbed the strength he offered. His hand caressed her lower back in slow soothing circles.

"The meeting will start shortly in the main conference room," Enhard said, the warmth gone from his voice. "The High Priestess is already here." He left the room without a backward glance. Victoria was stung by his frigid manner, but Christian squeezed her hand reassuringly.

"Don't worry, it's about me, not you," he said, leading her across to the Council room where Enhard was waiting near the doorway.

"Christian, do you have a minute?" Enhard asked.

"Not right—"

"It's okay, Christian. I'll wait for you inside," Victoria said.

"Christian," Enhard began the minute the door swung shut behind Victoria. "I can't even begin to guess at what the Council will say to this. You are flouting ancient laws and this little flirtation—"

"It's not a flirtation. And if you think I give a damn about what the Council thinks, then you really don't know me at all," he said.

Enhard was quick to back down from the veiled fury in Christian's voice, and he sighed. The Council would not tolerate it should they realize Victoria was a witch, and despite Christian's considerable power, he would not be able to save himself. Or her.

"Does anyone know?" Enhard asked.

"Lucian does, I imagine."

Enhard gasped, his eyes flying to Christian's. His face was whiter than Christian had ever seen it.

"Then today will be even worse than I imagined. You know your brother has long craved your complete exile from your House and coveted your birthright. My fear is that he has called this meeting to discredit you with the Council ... because of her. He will use this to destroy you," Enhard said.

Christian didn't bat an eye. He had guessed that Lucian had had some sort of ulterior motive but now, everything fell into place like missing pieces of the puzzle. Lucian had *known* that Christian would not leave Victoria behind, and something he intended to do or say in that room had something to do with her.

He regretted that Victoria was already inside but there was little he could do at this point to remove her without drawing more attention to them both. He would have to deal with Lucian—and the Council—if Enhard's speculations proved correct.

Christian met Victoria's eyes reassuringly where she was sitting near the back of the room as he walked in with Enhard. Victoria noticed his eyes narrow as he stared at her, sensing that something was different about her, and it was her turn to smile reassuringly at him.

It's a non-detection spell. If it works so well for you, then it should work for anyone looking for Le Sang Noir.

Christian shot her a puzzled look. *This space is warded against magic.*

Yes, I can sense the wards. She frowned in concentration. *But my spell is fine.*

The meeting was called to order interrupting their silent exchange, and Victoria looked around the room. It was as beautifully decorated and furnished as the other room had been, with spectacular floor to ceiling windows looking out onto the city of La Défense.

There was a long glossy cherry-wood panel table at the end of the room that curved in a semi-circle, where twenty people were seated, obviously the Council. Enhard sat at the same table. The Council members ran the gamut of age, but they all had two things in common, their fierce mysterious beauty and pale white skin. It was difficult not to stare.

The rest of the room was divided into two sections, similar to a courtroom set-up with two other rectangular tables at the head of each of the sections. She recognized Lucian at one of the tables talking to a tall woman whose face she could not see, but who seemed vaguely familiar. Victoria remembered their last encounter with unease. As if he had felt her discomfort, he turned toward her, a disturbing, triumphant smile playing on the corner of his lips. His cold stare made her flesh crawl.

She looked away, distracted by two new attendees who had been ushered in by the helpful receptionist: a petite pretty woman and another older man. They were not vampires, which she could sense immediately and her breathing quickened as she guessed who they were. They were introduced as the delegates from the witch clan, Grande Prêtresse Aliya and Monseigneur Fardon. Aliya had soft blond hair and looked surprisingly young. The older man had a lined face and white hair. They both sat after bowing respectfully toward the Council.

With their entrance, the tension in the room became almost solid. Despite the fact that they were invited guests, the mutual enmity was, at best, thinly veiled. It was Victoria's first taste of the hostility that Christian and Leto had often spoken about, and it shook her.

She was surprised to see Christian sitting just to the right of the Council panel on a raised dais with two other empty chairs. Despite how young he looked, he radiated authority and everyone around him treated him with deference. It disconcerted her a bit because she had never seen Christian in this light. He was the leader of a House after all, she told herself, but still the thought niggled in her head, it wasn't just that he was treated with deference by his own House, he was treated like that by *everyone*, including the Council members. She tucked the thought away as Enhard, Council speaker, called the meeting to order.

Christian sat tensely in his chair waiting for the moment when Lucian would make his end-game clear. The minute the meeting began, Lucian's body language changed and he became alert, ready, and predatory. This farce of a grievance was only for show and Christian knew it the instant he saw his twin brother's calculating expression. This had been a pretense to get Christian here along with the representative factions of the witch clans, just as Enhard had feared.

He glanced at Victoria, realizing even more that her presence may have been Lucian's main focus. Her face was pale but composed, and she'd never looked more beautiful or fragile. He took a breath and nodded to Enhard to commence.

Lucian stood, his bearing arrogant as he faced the Council. He barely looked at the witch and wizard sitting to his right, his distaste for them evident, even to Victoria. He addressed the Council.

"My Lords, you have threatened me countless times with your contempt for my actions when I only seek to better our future. Yes, I concede that people have died, but that is the price of power." Lucian's voice echoed into the room and Victoria could see the clenched fingers of the petite witch on the arms of her chair. He turned to address Aliya and Fardon, his voice carelessly insolent. "But let's get to the point. You got what you wanted, your traitor died. By another witch's hand no less."

Victoria suddenly felt the world tilt at Lucian's words and her gaze locked on Christian. His jaw was clenched, and she could sense that he was furious. Lucian, now performing for a suddenly captive audience, turned to face her, his face twisted with an evil cunning smile.

"There's your killer right there." And he pointed straight to her.

Victoria felt all eyes in the room boring into her. Now it was her turn to grasp the arms of her chair with bloodless fingers. Through the haze, she felt Christian gently brush her mind giving her strength even as she could feel his restrained wrath beneath it.

The amulet stung the skin of her chest as the stares converged upon her and she fought the urge to flee.

Enhard cleared his throat. "Lord Devereux, what is this about?"

Lucian faced him his face a mask of cold rage. "My point, *my lord*," he said, "is that you censure me for seeking a better future when *he* seeks to destroy us all." Lucian spat the last words viciously staring at his brother with venomous eyes. Christian remained unmoved, his face chiseled from granite. The Council members muttered among themselves staring from Lucian to Christian and back again. The witch and wizard remained silent though their attention was clearly centered on the two brothers.

"Ask him," Lucian jeered. He indicated the woman sitting beside him. "Lena has seen his disgrace with her own eyes."

As Victoria heard the name, her eyes snapped to the woman who turned in slow motion, her eyes connecting with Victoria's. The malice in their ice blue depths was obvious, and Victoria recognized her as the woman who had attacked her as well as the one from Christian's memories. She felt her blood surge.

"My Lord Devereux is correct," Lena said. "His Grace brings dishonor to both our worlds by his … affiliation with this witch."

The whispers in the room became deafening. Victoria could feel the heavy weight of the stares of the witch and the wizard boring into her on top of the dozens of eyes already locked onto her. She sat coolly, her head high even though her skin was flushed.

"Lord Devereux, this is a grave accusation!" cried a Council member, supported by vocal affirmations from several others. Lucian's ferocious scowl silenced the Council member who had spoken and the vampire shrank back, cowed. Lucian's lip curled in ominous fury as if daring any of them to speak again. They did not look at him. The tension in the room thickened like quicksand.

Suddenly Christian stood and the room became still. "Cease," he commanded. "Lord Devereux is correct in his statement." Dead silence followed his statement amidst shaken looks. Enhard seemed physically pained. Christian continued. "She is under my protection as Lord Devereux's companion has attacked her twice now. Given the strained relationship between our societies, I thought it best to take her under my protection. Our laws do not forbid this."

"If by *protection*, you mean something else entirely, then I will say she is surely well *protected*," Lucian said, his insinuation clear. The room twittered in response. Christian's hands clenched at his side, and Victoria knew that it was time. He couldn't do this alone, not without her help. She stood, walking to the middle of the room and commanding everyone's attention.

"My Lords," she said, addressing the Council, "I confirm that I have been attacked twice by this woman and threatened once by Lucian Devereux himself. In fact, the *protection* of His Grace," she said, echoing Lucian's sarcastic emphasis as well as Lena's strange formal address to Christian, "is the only reason I stand here before you today."

Victoria didn't mean to consciously do it, but her sincerity was delicately and cleverly amplified by her magic. The Council nodded in unison, some even sitting forward in their seats at the unexpected power of her simple words. She heard the soft gasp of the blond witch sitting behind her, and could feel their startled glances. Compulsion on one person was not something easily done—it took immense skill and concentration to magically sway conscious thought. Compulsion on a roomful of vampires in a space warded against magic was another thing entirely.

"But I saw him with her!" Lena said. "He wants her!" Christian turned but Victoria beat him to the punch.

"Of course he does, he *wants* me to be safe from you," Victoria said, deliberately misunderstanding her words and diffusing Lena's poisonous exclamation. Lena opened her mouth to argue but Christian's crisp command pierced the room.

"Leave us, please," he said quietly. Victoria was amazed that everyone left without so much as a whisper in deference to his command, and the room emptied until it was just Lucian, Lena, Enhard, herself, and Christian. Lucian had told Lena to stay which seemed to anger Christian. He turned to him. "You forget your place, brother," Christian said.

"And you forget your duty!" Lucian said. "She is a witch!"

"That didn't stop you from wanting her, did it?" Christian's retort was just as quick. Victoria noticed the stunned look that flashed across Lena's face. "And why is *she* here?" Christian said, indicating Lena. Lucian looked at him coldly, spitefully.

"She is, after all, your Companion, is she not?" he said, his eyes glittering.

Christian glanced at Victoria, seeing shock crack her composure. "Lena chose another path, Lucian, you know that and she knows that," he said, but Christian knew the intended damage had been done. Victoria refused to look at him. "What do you want, Lucian?"

"You know what I want."

"I have already given you control of the House of Devereux. Anything more is impossible, you know that," he said.

Christian stared at Lucian, knowing exactly what was going through his head; there was another alternative, the right of succession. Lucian wanted the title Christian held as the first-born Devereux son. But Lucian was too cowardly to fight him in a fair fight, and he was afraid of the combined strength of the Council and the sway they held over the six other vampire Houses. Lucian believed that if he controlled Le Sang Noir, then he would have complete dominion over Christian and over all the Houses.

Challenge me then, Lucian, Christian silently said. *Take what you think is rightfully yours.* Slowly and with open loathing, Lucian stared at him.

Another day perhaps, brother. The time will soon come, that I promise you.

Lucian turned on his heel and sat insolently in his chair. Christian did not respond to his barely veiled threat and after a few moments, he signaled Enhard to bring in the Council. He wanted this over with quickly, so he could turn his attention to Victoria. He could already feel her anguish consuming her.

The Council members resumed their places, and as the meeting came to a close, Victoria slipped out the doors feeling Christian's eyes follow her exit. She went to the small room they had been in when they had arrived and collapsed onto a chair. Christian had a *companion.* She didn't have to be a vampire to know what that meant.

The very same woman who had tried to kill her, the one that she herself had said would be perfect for him. She felt sick with jealousy. Christian had made someone. He had loved someone enough to have made them a vampire. He'd made *her.* Hot tears leaked from her eyes as she sat hunched over. After everything they'd been through, the betrayal was crippling.

Hearing voices, she hastily composed herself, standing just as Enhard escorted Aliya and Fardon into the room. Without looking at her, Enhard explained courteously that they had wanted to meet the witch responsible for the death of the traitor. It was the last thing Victoria needed, but she forced herself to be civil and introduced herself. When she touched the woman's hand, the spark of energy between them did not go unnoticed, and Fardon eyed her with sharp interest.

"It's good to meet you," Aliya said smiling, her voice musical. "Do you mind if I ask how you ..." Victoria knew what she meant even before she finished her sentence. They wanted to know how she had killed the witch.

"I'm not entirely sure how, but I destroyed a crystal necklace she had," she said evasively, trying to avoid reliving the ugly memory of the witch's power running through her veins. Aliya nodded as if the simple explanation made sense.

"I see how that could be effective, considering that she was an exile and forbidden to wield magic," she said. "Are you self-taught?"

"My ... familiar helped with my training."

"And the compulsion in the meeting room? Where did you learn that?" Victoria was startled. "Don't worry. Some of us have natural gifts." Aliya smiled again, and Victoria felt her discomfort recede as quickly as it had come. Aliya's gift was clearly her ability to control emotions.

"You're a high-priestess?" Victoria asked. "You seem ... young."

A smile. "I am entering my fourth century as the liaison for relations with other societies, like the vampires, so not *that* young."

"And him?" Victoria asked, indicating the silent man at Aliya's side.

"Fardon is a Seer," she said. "He sees the unconscious mind of a person, and their true intent." At Victoria's confused look, she continued to explain. "A witch or wizard, or vampire for that matter, can block their conscious mind with the proper training but the unconscious part is more difficult to veil, just as it is also more difficult to interpret. Fardon sees what is hidden." She waved a hand to indicate where they were. "Which is also why he is here with me. If the vampires meant us harm, we would know it even before they did on a conscious level. We can't use offensive magic here, but we can teleport if we need to leave quickly."

Victoria nodded. It made sense that the vampires would have their own protective wards in place to inhibit a magical attack from the witch delegates. Smart.

"And what do you see then, with me?" Victoria directed her question at Fardon, who smiled at her boldness and then frowned soon after, his eyes widening.

Aliya was right, Victoria couldn't distinguish between her conscious and unconscious, but her *blood* certainly could. She let her energy flow, following the guidance of the blood magic, and kept her mind a blank slate. The harder Fardon focused, the more elusive what he was searching for became. She could feel his mounting frustration and smiled inside.

"I see nothing," he said after several minutes. He exchanged a baffled look with Aliya who had put a calming hand on his arm as if she'd also sensed his frustration. She watched Victoria circumspectly.

"That's impossible," she said slowly. "No, not impossible, but it would take a very accomplished witch to block Fardon. Not many can thwart his Seeing ability. And yet you do so effortlessly … and untrained …"

"Maybe there's just nothing to see," Victoria said.

Fardon frowned. "There's always something to see!"

Victoria remained silent, and they stood staring at each other, at a curious impasse until a knock on the door interrupted them.

Christian walked into the room without waiting for an answer, clearly looking for Victoria. He took in the scene right away— Victoria's discomfort, Fardon's interest, and Aliya's frustration. As soon as Victoria saw him, he didn't miss the immediate darkening of her eyes or the walls that fell into place over them. He cursed Lucian's earlier revelation for the hundredth time.

"Will you please excuse us?" he said to Aliya and Fardon.

As Aliya left the room, she looked at Christian with a shuttered, speculative expression as if she had detected something transpiring between the two of them that had made her suddenly uneasy. She frowned but left as he'd asked.

Christian closed the door. He stared at Victoria where she sat on one of the chairs staring into space, steadfastly refusing to look at him.

"Tori, please talk to me," he said. "It was a long time ago, and it ended a long time ago."

"Why didn't you tell me?" Her voice was a whisper.

"Because it doesn't mean anything. You have to believe that."

"She still loves you, you know," she said finally, looking him in the eyes. "And I can never compete with that, Christian."

"Compete with what, exactly?" he said, detecting a strange finality in her voice.

"That she is a vampire, like you, that you gave a part of yourself to her. She is who she is because you *chose* her. She will always have that piece of you ... that I won't." Victoria pressed her hands to her face, her torment apparent. Christian knelt at her feet and took her hands in his. She tried to pull them away, but he held on tightly. "She doesn't want to let you go, I saw it in her eyes."

"Victoria, that doesn't matter. Do you know why?" he asked. "Because *I* let *her* go a long time ago. I don't want her. I want you. I love *you*."

"You *love* me?" she echoed dumbly.

"What do you think this is all about?" he asked. Victoria turned her face away, unwilling to look in his eyes, knowing what she saw there would be her undoing. She shook her head in angry denial, refuting his gently given words.

"No. You were right. What we are doing is wrong. There's a reason for the laws," she said, bleak. "They hate us ... they hate *me.*" And then fire flashed again for an instant in her eyes as she remembered something else. "And I can't believe you never told me you're a stupid Earl or whatever!"

"A Duke. My father was the cousin of the King of France. Remember? I did tell you that he was the Duke of Avigny." As he said the words, Victoria remembered that he had said that, but at the time she had been more concerned with what had happened to him to make him *what* he was, rather than details about *who* he was. She nodded. "Well, that same title has passed to me and its royal lineage is recognized in our world," he said.

"And Lucian?"

"He has other titles, but as first-born, I inherited this one. Although it means little to me, and I would give it up in a heartbeat if I could."

"Couldn't you?" she blurted out.

"Only by dying."

Victoria blanched at his response, knowing that Lucian would be more than happy to have him dead.

"It doesn't matter," he said. "Don't you know by now that I do as I like? Tori, I gave you my mother's ring because it is my pledge to you, not to anyone else … to you. It doesn't matter to me what the rules are in my world or in your world, I only care about us and *our* world because anywhere that is, is where I want to be. It's the *only* place I want to be," he said, desperately willing her to believe him, to trust him.

He could see her on the verge of it, just about to grasp the hand he offered, when suddenly the door swung open and Enhard walked in, taking in the scene of Christian, a vampire royal, kneeling before Victoria.

His glacial response was all Victoria saw, and the tiny flicker of warmth struggling to stay alive between them abruptly faded, her expression deadening in seconds. Christian clenched his jaw swallowing his ire at Enhard's untimely entrance and whispered, "Please Tori, *trust* me."

"I can't, Christian." Her eyes closed in distress. "I'm sorry." She couldn't even look at him, knowing what she would see in his face.

Tori ... please.

I can't. We are impossible. It has always been impossible. No matter what we tell ourselves, there can be no happy ending for us. We are just another tragic love story waiting to be written.

Before Christian could even guess at her intent, he saw her grasp her amulet and she disappeared before his very eyes. He was left holding air as her hands vanished, leaving nothing but a cold memory of their presence. She had left him, he thought desolately, and he sank back to the floor his head in his hands. Enhard looked completely shaken by Victoria's unexpected exit, but the sudden lifeless expression on Christian's face troubled him far more than her startling vanishing act.

"Christian?"

"I'm sorry, Enhard." Christian's voice was like a staccato. "I can't let her go."

"You can't be serious, Christian. You do know what this means, don't you?"

"I don't care what it means." His words were hard, final, implacable. "I won't live without her."

TWENTY-FIVE

Betrayal

VICTORIA HAD MANAGED to teleport herself without any lasting damage to Holly's house. It was the only place she could think of besides her apartment, and she did not want to be alone. Leaving Christian had been one of the hardest things she had ever had to do. Her heart felt like it had been cleaved into two pieces, the other half abandoned halfway across the world.

On top of that, teleportation over three thousand miles had left her utterly drained, physically and mentally. She'd had to depend on some of the energy in her amulet to complete the transfer but even so the actual shaping of the spell had required a colossal amount of her own energy. If she had given herself time to think about it, she probably wouldn't have done it.

She lay on her bed shivering in a cold sweat, trying desperately to keep the post-traumatic nausea at bay, and struggling to figure out what she could possibly say to Holly to explain her sudden arrival. She checked her watch realizing that it was almost five a.m. No wonder the house was so dead quiet. Victoria pulled her blankets up to her neck. Her eyes were so heavy she could barely keep them open. She wondered groggily where Leto was for a second before darkness overtook her and she fell into a black, dreamless sleep.

When Victoria awoke many hours later, the sky was still dark and she flew out of bed at first, having no memory of where she was in the blackness of the room. The alarm clock's red numbers said it was seven in the morning, and everything came back to her in a sudden rush. She had to take several deep breaths to stop the rush of hysteria from settling in. She'd slept more than twenty-four hours. Victoria rubbed the sleep from her eyes and walked to the landing.

"Aunt Holly? Anyone home?" There was no answer. She poked her head into Holly's empty room and noticed that the bed had not been slept in. Was Holly away? She peered down the stairs. The entire house was shrouded in darkness, and Victoria felt the first stirrings of unease at the abnormal quiet.

"Illustro," she said, walking downstairs as all the lights turned on with her low command. She froze in horror at the state of the kitchen.

It was like a whirlwind had crashed through it. There was broken china strewn everywhere. The table was flipped onto its top and several chairs lay in a haphazard heap to one side of the room. Newspapers and magazines that had been in a neat pile on the kitchen counter littered the floor.

Victoria felt panic build in her body, and she opened her mind to search for Holly, at first in the house, then in the immediate surroundings, then in the town. She was nowhere to be found. Victoria pulled out her cell-phone and dialed Holly's number, and heard the answering ring coming from the kitchen drawer. Holly never left her phone at home!

Fretfully, she chewed her lips until she felt a sharp sting and the salty taste of blood filled her mouth. Where was Leto? If something had happened, he would have contacted her. The strange sense of foreboding grew and she repeated the same mental search for Leto. This time she sensed something faint in the back garden. She raced out there without thinking.

Leto!

He lay at the edge of the icy stream, his mangled body frozen and near death. She skidded to a stop across the remnants of snow and cradled his ice-covered body gently, noticing the funny tilt of his neck as if he had been strangled. She sensed that he was still alive. Barely. Blood flecked his silver coat. Victoria took him inside and wrapped him in a warm blanket. She said an incantation over his body and tried to infuse him with some of her own energy but he remained unresponsive.

Victoria's panic escalated. In mounting alarm, she decided that she would call Holly's friends to see if Holly had gone on a vacation that they would know about. It was then that Victoria saw the flashing light on the answering machine. The sense of foreboding grew as she pressed the button, skipping older messages. Her heart sank as she found the one she had somehow known was there.

Charla's recorded voice was tinny and cheerful, and the message was clear.

"I have that homework assignment you need. The quiz won't be too painful if you study carefully. Call me and I'll give you the details. Also don't try to ditch class because it'll count against your final. They say it's going to be brutal."

Victoria's blood pressed against her skin in scalding hot fury. Despite Charla's cryptic message, Victoria knew explicitly what she meant. How could she not? There was no reason for Charla to call Holly's house about homework assignments because they weren't in any of the same classes. Victoria replayed the message, her hands clenching and unclenching futilely, "It's *going to be brutal* ..." She checked the date of the message. It was two days ago.

With shaking hands, praying she wasn't too late, she picked up her cell phone and dialed Charla's number. She answered on the first ring.

"Hi Tori, I was wondering when you were going to call. I was getting a little worried about holding this homework for so long," said Charla, laughing hysterically as if she'd made the funniest joke.

"Where is my aunt? If you've hurt her—"

"You'll what?" Charla's voice was businesslike now, all trace of humor gone. "Put a hex on me?" She laughed. Victoria sank to the floor ... Angie. Charla heard the dead silence on the end of the phone and laughed again. "Oh yeah, Angie spilled the beans about your little secret. So you try anything and your homework gets dusted, okay?"

Victoria's blood surged like a tidal wave inside of her. "What do you want me to do?" she asked.

"Oh Tori, don't be so dramatic. We're in Manhattan and the party's just beginning so get here already, okay?"

"Where?"

"Grand Central Station, lower level. We'll find you."

The phone clicked off and Victoria hurled the answering machine off the table. Charla had tortured Leto in cold blood and to her he was just a cat. She didn't even know if Holly was okay. Victoria wanted to call Christian so badly that her body ached with it, but she steeled herself. Getting Christian involved was the last thing she needed to do. Holly was her priority.

She focused inward and tried to find Charla. Nothing. Angie. Nothing. It was like they weren't on the planet as if they'd vanished completely. The anger in the pit of Victoria's stomach turned into fear, and she jumped to her feet. She had no time to lose.

Without thinking, she held Leto and teleported to her apartment, the effort knocking the breath out of her. She realized that she hadn't quite recovered from the last time. After a few minutes, she threw on a pair of jeans and a warm turtleneck, and grabbed the keys to her Mini. She would have tried to teleport but there was no safe arrival site that she could focus on clearly, and too many variables could make it disastrous.

"I'll be back, Leto. I love you. Everything will be okay, I promise you," she whispered before leaving.

As she drove, she thought about Charla and the whole unbelievable situation. Victoria couldn't figure out the reason behind it. Was it some roundabout way of Charla hurting Holly to get to her? Because of Gabriel? It was the only thing she could think of that would possibly make Charla do something so unspeakable. Still, no one would be that vengeful over a boy, would they? Charla's words ran through her mind, "I can get a little Ted Bundy crazy where Gabe's concerned," and Victoria felt herself go cold. She stepped on the gas.

She made the trip to New York in six hours, the clock on the dashboard saying two p.m. just as she was pulling off the Henry Hudson Parkway onto 125th Street. The streets were packed, typical for a Tuesday afternoon with yellow cabs threading violently in and out of the traffic. Buses droned by, trailing black clouds of noxious gases, and busy pedestrians peppered the sidewalk.

As another driver almost side-wiped her, Victoria pulled the car to the curb, and centered her emotions. All she needed now was an accident. It was proving more difficult to navigate New York City than she thought, so she decided to ditch her car in a long-term parking lot on 125th and Park Avenue. She took the subway downtown.

When the train pulled into the 42nd Street Station stop, she walked slowly into Grand Central Terminal from the subway and waited on the lower level near the circular train information center, her heart pounding so loudly it felt like it was going to jump straight out of her chest.

She saw Charla at the same moment that Charla saw her, and wondered how she had known that Victoria had arrived. No doubt that sneak Angie was slithering around somewhere, doing Charla's dirty work, and had been watching for when she arrived. Charla was dressed in dark jeans and a white sweater, and walked with arrogant purpose.

Her pretty face was marred with spite as she walked up to Victoria. "Don't think about trying anything unless you want that old woman to die," she said. "I know your tricks and there are people watching to make sure you don't do anything stupid."

Victoria's face tightened. She wanted to rip the skin off Charla's smug face. She dug her nails into her palms to suppress her rage. There would be time enough when Holly was safe. She could feel the blood racing and knew that she would give it freedom soon, no matter the cost, she thought rashly. It churned in response.

"Come on, don't just stand there," Charla said, as she walked into the entrance to Track 114. Victoria frowned and followed her. Were they going to get on a train and leave Grand Central? Charla walked quickly down the platform ignoring the Metro North train that was waiting on the side of the platform and Victoria trailed behind, trying to work out where they could possibly be going. They descended the stairs toward the end of the platform and walked toward a long escalator.

"Why are you doing this, Charla?" she asked, trying to memorize the way. "What did Holly ever do to you?"

"You think this is about Holly?" Charla laughed, the sound chilling.

"Why are you hurting her if it's about me?"

"You just answered your own question, don't you think?" Charla said. "Come along, we don't have all day. The old lady looks a little peaked," she added maliciously. Victoria gritted her teeth and prayed for self-control. She had pegged Charla all wrong.

Near the 47th Street and Park Avenue exit, Charla finally stopped at an elevator where she inserted a key and, to Victoria's surprise, pressed the down button. Victoria wondered briefly whether she could overpower her and maybe take control of her mind to find out where Holly was, and then thought the better of it. If Holly got hurt because of her rash behavior, she wouldn't be able to forgive herself. She couldn't risk Holly's safety until she could use magic to get them both out.

When the elevator stopped, she followed Charla down a dark musty corridor lit by a string of industrial bulbs and entered a cavernous room with vaulted ceilings. The door swung shut behind them, and Victoria noticed that they weren't alone. A person in a black coat stood at the far end of the room.

The worn floors were marble and there were no windows. It didn't smell musty like the corridor had. In fact, it looked well used, and was quite architecturally dramatic, with faded but beautiful murals on the ceilings and huge crested plaques with medieval weapons hanging on the walls. Antique furniture dotted the far ends of the room, but the most of the floor space was uncovered. Victoria noticed that there were several other doors at the back of the room where the man remained standing.

She glanced around for Holly, expanded her awareness. Curiously, she couldn't make it respond. She tried again and failed. She thought she heard low laughter.

Victoria looked Charla full in the face, displaying no panic despite her pounding heart. "Where is Holly?" she said, enunciating each word. Charla ignored her and walked toward the man in the middle of the room. "Charla, where is Holly?" Victoria repeated more forcefully. Charla turned around, a strange expression on her face, a curious mixture of envy and hate, which she quickly masked.

"Holly, Holly, Holly … where is Holly?" she mocked. "Holly is fine." Victoria clenched her fists.

"If you've hurt her—"

"Yeah, yeah, keep your pants on," Charla said. "Don't worry, your precious Holly is safe. We made sure to take good care of her."

"Where is she?" Victoria repeated.

"Oh my God, are you deaf or just plain dumb?" Charla said. "She's here, you're here, everyone's here. It's our own private party." Victoria resisted the urge to scream and clenched her jaw, staring pointedly at Charla. "Oh, get over yourself, *Tori*, you really think we would hurt your stupid old aunt? She's over there." Charla jerked her head toward a door on one side of the room.

Victoria wanted to smash the smile off her face, but she didn't know if she was bluffing about Holly. Her eyes flickered to the silent figure still standing motionless halfway across the room. The amulet burned under her turtleneck.

"Show me," she said coolly. Charla threw her hands up in exasperation.

"You have legs, go see for yourself," she said with another shrug of her shoulder.

Victoria walked toward the side of the room, keeping her eyes on Charla. When she reached the tiny room that was little more than a cell, her knees almost gave out. Holly lay slumped in an armchair. She was unhurt and looked like she was sleeping. Victoria swayed, dizzy with relief.

"Holly?" she whispered.

"She can't hear you. Drugs." Charla studied her manicure. "I didn't want to waste them on her but—"

Victoria couldn't take it any longer. She summoned her energy, feeling it at the end of her fingertips like electricity, and focused coldly on Charla's monstrous face before releasing it without a second thought.

Nothing happened.

She could feel it crackling at the tips of her fingers and she tried again. Not a hair on Charla's head moved. There was sudden slow laughter from the person in the middle of the room, and he turned in agonizingly slow motion. He walked toward her his mouth twisted in a cruel smile until he was standing in front of her. Charla draped her hand around his waist and kissed him ardently on the mouth.

"As promised, delivered with a kiss," she said, as she rested triumphant, malevolent eyes on Victoria.

"Gabriel?" Victoria whispered in disbelief. She couldn't believe it. Was this about *Christian*?

He didn't respond, just stared at her with a strange expression on his face. It wasn't quite anger, more like irritated disappointment, and it made her feel as if she hadn't fulfilled some hidden expectation. She pulled the energy within and tried to teleport to Holly to get them both out. Her magic was responsive, willing, but still nothing happened. The slow, deep laughter erupted again from Gabriel's mouth, and Victoria felt the first tremor of anxiety run through her.

Something was wrong. Terribly wrong.

"That's not going to work," he said.

"What are you talking about?" she asked, summoning up a bravado she didn't feel.

He stroked her cheek, and she swatted his hand away furiously. "Now, now, no need to be nasty. I meant your magic's not going to work. This place," he said, indicating the cavernous room, "is warded specifically for your magic." Victoria stared at him in disbelief as he smiled calmly. The smile faded as suddenly as it had come, and his lips twisted in a cruel grimace.

"*My* magic on the other hand works fine. Ictus torqueo!"

Victoria gasped painfully, doubling over at the severe, stabbing pain in her belly. His hand moved again, and she sank to the floor clutching her middle with her arms. It felt like someone was twisting a burning knife in her stomach.

"Stop, please," she said.

"Make her beg, Gabe!" Charla said, her voice echoing in the room. She crouched down to whisper viciously in Victoria's ear. "You should have seen what he did to your cat." Malice glittered in her eyes.

Some demons were human.

Victoria bit her lip as she forced herself to stand, looking Gabriel in the face and seeing the terrible truth reflected there. He had known *exactly* what Leto was, even if Charla had not. She felt a rage like she had never known boiling inside of her and she gritted her teeth, pushing against the wards. She was rewarded with another magical knife twist that sent her gasping to the floor. She concentrated on healing and discovered with relief that the magic *within* her worked just fine; it looked like Gabriel hadn't counted on that! The pain subsided but she made sure that she didn't show it, remaining stooped on the floor.

"What did you do to Holly?" she gasped. "What drugs? She could die."

"Relax, it's just a mild sedative. She'll be fine," Gabriel said.

"If anything happens—"

"Oh, watch out Gabe, she's getting upset!" Charla taunted.

Charla didn't have time to react when Victoria vaulted to her feet, propelled by instinctive rage, and punched her in the mouth with all the force she could muster. Charla went sprawling backwards. Victoria felt a curious satisfaction as she saw blood spurt from the corner of Charla's lip, and she could have sworn she saw the beginnings of a smile on Gabriel's lips. He was enjoying this. She started to turn toward him and saw him shake his head, smiling slightly and moving his index finger back and forth in warning.

"EVINCIO," he said, and her arms fell obediently to her side, the magical binding charm holding them securely in place.

Victoria couldn't move, not even when Charla got up, her bleeding face murderous, and slapped her several times. She tried to keep her expression blank in spite of the sting of the blows. Her blood helped unbidden, assuaging the painful areas almost immediately. Charla moved in again.

"Enough!" Gabriel said, and Charla backed away. "Get her phone. I don't want her getting any other ideas," he told Charla, who removed the cell phone from Victoria's pocket roughly.

"Don't think you're going to need this, sweetie," she snarled, as she smashed the phone on the floor. "Gabe, wrap this up. I'm bored."

"Give me one minute," he said. Charla walked away sourly, and Gabriel moved to stand in front of Victoria. "Aren't you sad you didn't choose me after all? What a marvelous couple we could have made, witch and warlock hand in hand."

Victoria noticed the flash of naked pain on Charla's face as she turned back at his words. Still second best, she noted—that would explain the fleeting look of envy she had seen on Charla's face earlier. Charla was human. Gabriel was a warlock. Now she knew who really held the cards.

"I would have made the same choice even knowing what you are," Victoria said. She saw his eyes harden.

"Even knowing what *you* are?"

"Especially knowing what I am." And then as if she couldn't help herself, she asked the question. "How did you know?" Gabriel laughed.

"Angie!" he shouted, and one of the doors in the back of the room opened. Angie skulked in and refused to look at Victoria. Gabriel slapped her on the back roughly, and she flinched from the pain. "Did you know that my *sister* can see who people really are?" he said. "Her gift!" He looked at her with undisguised loathing. "Born without magic, but somehow given this incredible ability ... what a waste. She should die, but she's proved herself useful." Angie didn't raise her eyes but Victoria could see her shoulders trembling.

Gabriel turned to Victoria. "Don't you want to know why your magic doesn't work?" he asked.

"I'm sure you're going to tell me," she said, refusing to give him the satisfaction of knowing that she wanted anything at all from him.

"My little sister here can identify your magic, but I'm sure you knew that already." He smiled. "We can do so much more than just control your power, you know," he said. "She knows it all, the information of its entire makeup."

"I'm still not sure I know what you want from me, Gabriel."

"Come now, let's not play games, Tori. I want the Cruentus Curse."

Victoria faked derision. "Please, don't tell me you believe in superstitions now, Gabriel," she said. He smiled again.

"Angie told me who you are Tori, those black lines are pretty distinctive. So you can stop pretending, because it is trying my patience!"

His cold words sent a shiver of alarm down her spine but she knew she had to pretend she wasn't afraid. "So what now?"

"The million dollar question," he said. "You know what I want,

Tori."

"I will never give myself to you."

"And I will kill everyone you ever knew, ever loved. Holly will be the first. Then I'll finish off your familiar. It was my pleasure to toy with him," he said. "But her end will be worse, far worse. And Devereux will die an excruciating death."

"It's too bad I'm not with him." Victoria almost smiled as Gabriel looked into her eyes and read the plain truth in their depths. The slow pleasure that dawned across his face made her feel almost sick, but some small part of her still felt comfort that at least Christian would be safe. She would find a way to protect Holly too. Charla and Angie were on their own if they were with Gabriel. Victoria noticed that Angie had looked up at her briefly as if she'd said her name aloud.

Angie. She saw the frail shoulders shake and realized that Angie could somehow hear her words even in the warded room. *I know you can hear me. Please don't let anything happen to Holly. Please ...*

Charla chose that moment to re-enter the room even as Gabriel shot her a look of displeasure. She sat on a chair staring pointedly until he sighed and walked over to her. Victoria seized on the opportunity that had presented itself.

Angie, I know he forced you. I know you are my friend, and that you are good. Please help me. Don't be ruled by Gabriel. Please don't have Holly's death and my death on your conscience. Help me. You're not like them. I know you're not. Victoria was going all out, she had nothing to lose.

Angie raised tear-filled eyes to Victoria, and her mouth moved soundlessly. Victoria struggled to understand the words and as she saw Gabriel turn and start walking back, she grew desperate.

Please, Angie. Find Christian. His number is in my phone. Get the SIM card. Please, you have to try.

Gabriel wasn't stupid, he had picked up on something, a sensation maybe, but he was far too arrogant to even consider that his magic-less sister could hear thoughts from another witch. Still, he kicked Angie roughly, his blow sending her flying.

"Stop your sniveling, I can hear you from here. Get out of my sight!"

Victoria suddenly realized what irked Gabriel. He despised Angie because he feared that Angie's gift made her more powerful than he was, and he hated that. He hated needing her, and knowing that everything he had accomplished had been because of her, because of *her* gift. Victoria saw his intent clearly. As soon as he was sure of the blood curse, he was going to kill Angie. He wouldn't need her anymore once he had Victoria's power. Gabriel gritted his teeth and half raised his hand like he was going to do it right then and there, and Victoria's stomach dropped.

"Gabriel, why couldn't I tell what you were?" she said, trying to distract from Angie. He turned slowly, an arrogant smile spreading across his face.

"I know you tried. I felt it the last time. But it's like painting a picture that you want someone to see. Easy enough to convince anyone, if you know how to do it."

"And Angie? How did you do it with her?"

"She's weak. It was easy to remove any thoughts about us other than the usual mundane things," he said, as Charla walked over and draped herself around him.

"I'm hungry, Gabriel," she whined. "You promised to take me out for sushi." She stared at Victoria. "Not so scary after all are you Tori, all trussed up like a pig." Victoria's urge to inflict pain hadn't gone away.

"What do you get out of this Charla? He doesn't want you, you know. You're not like him, like *us*." She spat the word like a dart, and it found its target easily. "You're human, nothing but a means to an end, so enjoy it while you can because it's not going to last." Charla's face had turned a hideous splotchy red color, and her eyes blazed with hatred.

"It's going to last because you're going to die. Painfully!" She raised a hand to hit Victoria, and Gabriel caught her arm in mid-flight.

"Stop," he said. Charla's face grew even redder, but she tossed her head, giving him a look of disgust and stalked off.

"You're right, you know," he said almost lovingly to Victoria. Her skin crawled. "It *is* about us, and you'll come to your senses soon enough. Think long and hard about whether you want Holly's death on your conscience because her life is in your hands, Tori." Gabriel hauled her by the arm to one of the small rooms at the end of the big hall and shoved her into it. With an enigmatic expression, he stroked her face and the bile rose in her throat. "Would it be so bad? You and me? We were a couple, weren't we? We could be so good together."

"I trusted you, Gabriel," she said. "How could you do that to Leto? To *Holly*? She's a person, not some pawn in whatever game you're playing. You can't just hurt people to get what you want."

"Why not? My power gives me the right to take whatever I want. If you appreciated yours more, you'd agree with me. We're the same, you and I."

"I'm *nothing* like you," Victoria hissed. "I would never hurt my friends."

A cold, calculating smile. "Wouldn't you? What about your friend, the one you told me about? Brian? Brett?" The smile widened into something that no longer resembled a smile. "Or your parents …"

Victoria's eyes flashed fire. "Don't you dare—"

"Don't I dare what? You know exactly what happened in that car and why you survived and they died. They died because of you and you know it. You did what you had to do, just as I did."

"It was an *accident*!"

"Was it, Tori?" he taunted. "Didn't you want to punish your parents for putting your grandmother in that place? *Didn't you?* You killed them when you made the car run off the road."

"No, that's not what happened!" she said, backing away her hands outstretched as if warding off something horrifying.

"Yes. It. Is." He snapped the words through his teeth. "Face it. We are the same, Tori. You know why?" He leaned in. "I set the fire." Victoria's eyes widened. "I set the fire because they were going to send me away, and they weren't exactly talking Hogwarts." His mouth twisted into an inhuman grin, a rictus grin. "So I killed them."

A stifled gasp drew her attention as Angie clapped a hand to her mouth, her face frozen in horror.

"You're a monster," Victoria whispered.

"Am I? All's fair in love and war, Tori." His voice turned hard. "Make your decision."

"I'd rather die than be with you."

"That can be arranged. Don't push me, Tori. You won't like the result. Your cat was just a taste of what I am capable of. What did your friend Tony say in the bar? We can do this the easy way or the hard way. You decide." He paused, his voice almost gentle. "Think it through and you'll see … you don't have a choice."

The echoing of the door closing was ominous in the silence, like the toll of a death bell.

TWENTY-SIX

Blood and Magic

CHRISTIAN STARED DULLY at the ringing phone. The caller ID said "private number." He stared at the flashing screen for several seconds before flipping it open.

"Hello?" a voice said, "may I speak to Christian Devereux please?"

His voice was dry and curt. "Who is this?"

"My name is Angie, I'm a friend of Tori's," she said. At the sound of Victoria's name, Christian clenched the phone so tightly that he almost crushed it.

"Do you know where she is?" he rasped.

"I can't talk long but she's in danger. She asked me to call you. Meet me at sixty-eighth and Madison tonight in New York at midnight and I'll explain. I know you have no reason to trust me but I'm begging you to. I got your number from her phone. She needs you. I'm sorry. I have to go. He'll kill me if he finds out. Please come."

The call disconnected.

Christian stared at his cell phone with unseeing eyes. He'd come back from France a day after Victoria, and ever since then, he'd been haunted by the feeling that something was wrong. He'd gone to Victoria's apartment, and when he'd seen Leto, his heart had dropped to his feet. Christian had gently brushed his mind, finding nothing but pain-filled, glazed green eyes for his efforts.

It was at that soul-destroying instant that Christian's world crumbled, because he knew that Leto's unresponsive deadness, could only mean one thing—something or someone very powerful had hurt him on the *inside*.

Until Christian had received the phone call from Angie, he'd even considered enlisting Lucian's help! In his momentary panic at not even being able to communicate with Victoria mentally and after seeing Leto's crippled state, he had been teetering on the brink of revealing to Lucian that Victoria was the witch from the prophecy just so that Lucian would want to find her.

Christian had never been more terrified in his life that something unimaginable had happened, and he didn't care that Angie's mysterious call could possibly be a threat. It was the only lead he had after days of waiting. He would follow it even if it cost him his undead life.

Christian arrived in the city in not much time at all, and waited a block away from where Angie had told him to meet her. He recognized her as she walked to the corner looking for him, glancing at her watch and looking around as if she were afraid of something … or someone. Christian observed her carefully for several minutes to see if she was alone.

Angie paced and glanced at her watch again; it was ten minutes past midnight. As she turned around to leave, she found herself face to face with a leather-clad, white-faced Christian Devereux. Angie stepped back, her eyes wide and her hands automatically at her throat, but Christian ignored the instinctive response and waited for her to make the first move.

"It's not safe here," she said, starting to walk down Madison Avenue.

"Where is she?"

"Gabriel," she said. Christian stiffened immediately. "He's holding her captive." Christian felt the rage in him boil just from hearing the name.

"Can't she get out? Use her magic?" he asked, earning a swift look from Angie.

"No," she said.

She stopped walking and pulled Christian into the shadow of a building. "Did Tori ever tell you anything about me?"

"No. Why?"

"I was the one who told Gabriel about her, about what she was," she said. "I'm not a witch like Tori or a warlock like Gabriel, but I can see what people are."

Christian grasped her arm roughly as he whirled her to face him. Angie winced as if the movement were painful. His face was harsh in the darkened shadows.

"Hang on a second. First of all, Gabriel is a *warlock*?" Angie nodded reluctantly. "And you can see what people are? What does that mean? Can you see what I am?"

"Yes," she said. Christian wanted to hear her to say it.

"What am I?"

"Undead."

In an uncanny silence, they stared at each other under the black sky. Christian's expression was unfathomable. His mind raced at the power this girl would hold in the supernatural world. In the wrong hands, her gifts could be catastrophic. Angie remained nervous, as if she expected Gabriel to come racing around the corner at any moment. She kept shifting, her movements restless and agitated.

"Does Gabriel know about me? What I am?"

"No!" she said. "You only came into the picture when he saw the two of you together. He was in such a terrible rage. It lasted for days and days. You d … don't understand how he feels about her. He thinks she belongs to him. You took something from him that he thought was his. He asked me what you looked like and whether you were a threat to him."

"And what did you say?"

"I lied." For a minute her dark, mousy face looked almost proud that she had bested her warlock brother by successfully concealing her mind from him.

"Why?"

"It was my fault that she got into all of this. He saw her do an invisibility spell in the library, and he forced me to tell him what she was. He was attracted to her before that, but the fact that she was a witch made him ecstatic. Gabriel thought they were meant to be." She took a deep breath. "And then you came into the picture. He was so angry after that night at the bar that he went up to her aunt's place looking for her when she didn't show up to class." She trailed off, staring into her palms. Christian realized that she was crying. "That's how he got her to come to New York. He kidnapped her aunt."

"He *kidnapped* Holly? What does he want, Angie?" Christian knew the answer even before Angie gave it but he had to know.

"How much do you know about Tori? About her power?"

"I know enough." Angie raised tear-filled eyes to his.

"Gabriel knows who she is. He wants her. He wants her power for himself." Angie was sobbing now, the words running into each other. "I told him. I'm so sorry. I didn't have a choice. He was going to kill Leto and I knew he would. You don't know what he's capable of. He killed our parents. I think I knew it all along but when he said it to Tori, I knew I couldn't protect him or lie anymore."

"Did Tori know that you knew about me?" he asked.

"Yes, I told her. We were friends, sort of," Angie said softly. "She asked me to get you. She said 'find Christian,' and so I did." Angie was unprepared for the brilliance that illuminated Christian's eyes.

"Where are they?" he said, his voice choked.

"She's being held in a cell underground. I can take you to her," she said. "Don't worry, he won't hurt her. He wants what she has too badly. It blinds him to everything else." Angie noticed his indecision. "I'm not lying, please, you have to trust me."

Christian knew that he had no choice but to trust her. If she deceived him, there would be hell and more to pay. He brushed her mind quickly with his feather-light vampire senses, and apart from her anxiety at being discovered, he could detect no deception. He did see something else though. Without speaking, his eyes softened, and he pulled her toward him gently. She winced. Christian caught the scent before he saw the crimson streaks seeping through her light-colored sweater, and he stared at her, his question obvious.

"Gabriel," she said hollowly. "I tried to protect the cat." His jaw clenched into a hard line. It was all he could do not to break something right then and there. "It's okay. It's not the first time. I've endured worse from him over the years. Everything heals … eventually." Her eyes were downcast. "And it's no more than I deserve."

"Angie, no one deserves to be treated as you've been. You give yourself too little credit for the courage you've shown tonight. I am indebted to you."

Color rose in her face at the unexpected praise. "It's this way," she murmured, flustered by his startling kindness.

Christian followed Angie down Madison Avenue keeping to the shadows. It was clear that she was terrified of Gabriel, given his anger and what he had done to her, repeatedly it seemed. His fury surging to dangerous levels, Christian kept himself under tight control. If Victoria had been hurt, he wouldn't be accountable for his actions.

They reached 47th Street and Christian saw the entrance to Grand Central, but it was dark and the doors appeared to be locked. He looked at Angie, eyebrows raised.

"Not here. The entrance is around the block," she said, walking past the doors. They walked across 47th Street toward the East Side and then Angie made a sharp right turn onto Lexington Avenue. Slatted between two buildings was a small, dark alleyway with greasy black steps disappearing down into the darkness. Angie glanced around and then climbed down the steps. Christian followed.

The air was rank with the smell of decay combined with the hot stench of the sewers and the subway trenches. Angie pulled out a small flashlight that cast a thin light down the gloomy tunnel, and Christian's vampire eyesight adjusted naturally to the darkness. About halfway down the tunnel, Angie, who'd been counting quietly under her breath, stopped and pushed against a nearly invisible metal door. It swung open, creaking loudly in the silence and she jumped nervously, looking over her shoulder at Christian's wary, white face.

"It's just down here," she said, her voice harsh in the quiet. "This is another entrance, not the one that Gabriel knows. I found it looking at the rats one day."

Christian stared down the hallway and noticed the glow of lights toward the end. He walked on silent feet toward it. "What is this place?"

"I think it used to be some kind of secret meeting room in the nineteen thirties. The floor in the main room is marble, and there are paintings on the ceilings," she whispered back.

Christian wasn't surprised. New York City was full of secret meeting rooms and buildings located in unlikely places, and he himself had been in several of them over the decades. This one, however, was new to him. He stepped past Angie and walked stealthily down the corridor, noticing that at the first light-bulb there was a large wooden door. Angie remained in the darkness, her part finished for now, and he could hear her moving slowly back the way they had come.

He pushed open the unlocked door. The room was dark and empty but was just as Angie had described with its murals and marble floors. He sensed no movement and peered into the gloom. He crept silently into the room, keeping his back to the edge of the wall and letting his vampire instincts take over to get the scent of her blood. He was rewarded with the barest hint of it toward the back of the room. Relief flooded him like a river, and Christian rapped gently on the door to the room where the scent was most potent.

"Tori," he said, louder than he'd intended. He heard sounds on the other side of the door but still couldn't detect her presence other than the faint smell.

"Christian?" she said in disbelief, as if expecting a trick of some sort. The wards were so powerful that he could barely hear her even with his heightened senses.

"It's me. Angie found me like you asked her to," he said. Christian couldn't hear anything on the other side and he wasn't sure if she had responded or not. "I'm going to try to open the door."

The minute Christian put his hand on the handle, the shock sent him flying ten feet across the room, his hand burned black from the lightning bolt hex on the door. He watched as it repaired itself almost immediately and bounded back unhurt to the door. "There's some kind of spell on it," he said, forgetting to whisper.

"Well, of course there's a spell on it, *Devereux*," said a mocking voice. "Isn't that sweet, coming to rescue your love?"

Christian whirled around, furious with himself that he had been caught off guard. He straightened his spine and shook it off. He had no qualms about fighting this warlock. He had fought worse battles over the years and some whip of a boy wasn't going to get the better of him, no matter how powerful he thought he was.

"Gabriel," he said.

Gabriel walked toward the middle of the room watching Christian as if he were trying to work out how he'd gotten in there. Christian stayed still but ready, a tactic honed by countless decades and numerous duels.

"Don't you know by now that she's out of your league, Devereux?" Gabriel said, his tone deliberately insolent. Christian didn't answer. "Cat got your tongue?"

Christian remained unfazed, watching him carefully. Realizing that his strategy wasn't working, Gabriel tried something else. "Tori, your boyfriend's here," he shouted.

With a wave of his hand, the solid door became transparent, and Christian could see Victoria's worried face as she stood in the doorway, her hands up against the now invisible door. Their eyes connected for a split second just as Gabriel started laughing horribly, drawing their stares. He wiped mock tears from his eyes.

"You're no Romeo, Devereux," he said. "And she's definitely not your Juliet. Not by the time I've finished with her anyway." Despite his control, a muscle began to tick in Christian's jaw. "Enjoy the show, Tori. I'm certainly going to," Gabriel said to Victoria, just as he did the hot knife trick in her belly. She leaned against the door gasping. Her eyes were glued to Christian's, and Gabriel's rage erupted at their shared look. He twisted his hand again viciously and she fell, clutching her stomach but still not making a sound, defiant to the end. Christian restrained his fury.

"Do you know what I am, Devereux?" Gabriel said, making conversation as they slowly circled each other. "Do you have any idea what you're up against? No, of course you don't. You can't win, you know. She belongs to me now. So I ask you, is she worth it? Is she worth losing everything? Is she worth your *life*?"

Christian ignored his taunts and his unruffled silence irritated Gabriel more than anything. Gabriel's face contorted.

"Malus cremo!" A ball of black fire flew from Gabriel's outstretched hand. Christian who had been expecting it, dodged with unexpected speed to the right as it exploded into the side of the wall. Gabriel raised an eyebrow, his face registering surprise at Christian's lucky guess.

"Know what that is, Devereux? That's magic. Like I said, you can't win. She's a witch too, did you know? Or did she lie to you just like she lies to everyone else?"

Christian forced himself not to look at Victoria. He'd wanted to tear Gabriel apart with his bare hands when he saw what he had so viciously done to her. He did not want to show any weakness for her because he knew that Gabriel would use that against him without hesitation.

She, for her part, had not even made a sound watching them circle each other like two lions as if she'd come to the same realization.

Christian spared her a glance. Her eyes widened, alerting him to the danger just as Gabriel teleported, appearing behind him and lunging for him with a long curving knife. Christian swung out of the way just before the blade sliced through where his chest had been. Gabriel teleported again, and once more, Christian eluded his attack.

Gabriel was breathing heavily. "You're either born under a lucky star, Devereux, or tonight's just your night." Christian stayed silent. "So much for this physical stuff!" Gabriel cried and parried with a stunning spell that blasted a hole in the wall as Christian leapt out of the way. Gabriel screamed in thwarted fury.

"CORPUS DISCIDIUM!" he shouted. But like its counterparts before, the death spell missed its intended target as Christian vaulted out of the way, moving so quickly that he was a blur. Christian watched as the powerful spell pulverized an armchair, and his gaze moved to Gabriel, who was panting heavily.

Christian smiled with provoking mockery as if to say "bad luck mate," and Gabriel gnashed his teeth in frustration. For the first time, Gabriel looked confused and furious as if he couldn't fathom how his opponent kept getting the best of him. In aggravated rage, his gaze locked on Victoria and something ugly kindled in his eyes.

He teleported again, but this time it was into Victoria's cell. He grasped her by her hair and kissed her wetly on the mouth. She fought him, clumps of hair coming loose in his hand and scratching at his face with her nails. His mouth curled. He backhanded her across the face, and she stumbled back, her head colliding with the wall. Victoria slid to the floor, barely conscious. Gabriel regarded Christian through the transparent door and smirked before teleporting back into the main room.

Game on.

Christian was livid. The fury drove through his muscles but despite its intensity, he knew that he had to be careful. Gabriel was a *warlock*, a powerful warlock if his offensive magic was any indication. Christian waited, his fury simmering.

"I'm going to have to teach her how to do that correctly," Gabriel said, wiping his lips with the back of his hand.

"What? Have her scratch your face off properly you mean?" Christian said, unable to resist the jibe. Gabriel's fingers went automatically to his face where he felt the slight sting where she had scratched him. Little hellcat. He lunged toward Christian with the knife and at the same time summoned his energy, blasting a ball of energy exactly to where Christian leapt.

"Noceo!"

The force of the physical attack spell threw Christian off his feet and slammed him against the wall. The sharp crack of bone echoed. Christian's body slumped to the ground and he pulled himself to his knees just as Gabriel appeared, brandishing the knife like a conquering hero. Christian let Gabriel haul him up, pretending to be insensible from the blow and waited for it. Sure enough, Gabriel's next action was predictable and he sliced him from shoulder to waist with the knife. Christian heard Victoria's muffled scream and saw Gabriel's eyes grow giddy with success.

"Your luck just ran out," Gabriel hissed triumphantly. Blood darkened the light blue shirt in an unerring line, the material billowing open. He was so busy waiting for the sounds of agony that his eyes barely registered that the sheared skin was rapidly knitting itself together until the white expanse of skin was smooth and unmarred as if it had never been slashed. He raised incredulous eyes to Christian's silvery, feral gaze that was not at all insensible as his lips pulled back over glistening white long, sharp incisors in a ferocious snarl.

Vampire!

"My turn," whispered Christian. He swung his arm with inhuman speed, smashing Gabriel's head so hard that it snapped to the side and his body tumbled back into a faded club chair. Christian whirled and pounced on him before he could even get up. He grabbed the fallen knife and carved Gabriel's face from hairline to lip.

Gabriel screamed in agony, kicking savagely to lessen Christian's hold and screaming a fire curse at the same time. Moving with incredible speed, Christian dodged the spell with some effort and spun around to land just to Gabriel's left, the curse exploding like a Molotov cocktail against the wall behind him.

The blood leaking down the side of Gabriel's face drove Christian mad—he could feel the hunger and rage obliterating all conscious thought as he twisted Gabriel's arm up behind his back and sank his teeth into Gabriel's neck. His blood was so unexpectedly sweet, forbidden as it was to vampires that the shocking taste if it befuddled Christian's senses briefly, and the blow to his head caught him off-guard, sending him spinning.

Christian sprang to the side in a low crouch wiping his mouth with the back of his hand. No wonder it was forbidden for vampires to bite them, their blood was like a rich elixir infused by magic. Gabriel glared at him, sneering as he said a spell that healed the oozing tear on his face and the wound on his neck.

"Touch me again, you filth, and it will be the last thing you do," he seethed.

"Surprised, warlock?" Christian said. Gabriel scowled, the stunned shock on his face evident. His eyes flickered to Victoria's. Hers, however, showed no surprise. Gabriel's face turned black with rage as the realization hit him.

"You *knew*? You knew about him?" he spat at Victoria. "You

knew what he was all along and you still chose that *animal* over me? You would defile yourself and who you are with *him*? You disgust me. When I'm through with him, you're going to pay for your disloyalty to your own kind … and to me."

He flicked his hand and a slight murmur of his lips made her skin blister fiercely as if it had been doused with lye, and a second flick of his wrist made the door became opaque. Her scream echoed through the door. Gabriel's lip curled in a sneer as momentary rage cracked Christian's composure.

"Don't worry, that was just a teaser of what awaits her when I'm done with you." He smiled. "I like the sound of her screaming, don't you? Shall we hear it again?" he said, starting to wave his hand to inflict more pain on Victoria. Christian moved so quickly that Gabriel had barely registered the movement until he was right in front of him.

"Do that again and I promise it will be the last thing *you* do," Christian said, echoing Gabriel's threat. In one swift motion, his fist crunched into Gabriel's face, the force of his blow shattering the bones beneath it as Gabriel's body flew backward across the room. Gabriel gurgled something in mid-air, buffeting himself magically as he landed safely on the ground. He spat a mouthful of blood to the floor.

"Curo!" The spell reformed Gabriel's battered face in seconds. "Try again, vampire!" he snarled. He launched a table from across the room at Christian who leapt over it like a cat, his supernatural reflexes blinding as he soared toward the wall and grabbed one of the plaques as he flew by, fireballs bursting into the ground behind him. Grasping one of the swords from the plaque, Christian rolled toward Gabriel, deflecting the energy bolts flying his way with the blade of the weapon.

Gabriel lunged and teleported as the sword swung in a low arc, its tip drawing blue sparks as it crashed into the floor right where Gabriel had been. In that instant Gabriel reappeared behind him with the second sword from the plaque moving toward Christian's neck. Christian's senses tingled. With an unearthly impulse born from generations of vampires before him, he tilted his sword backward, grasping the hilt with both hands, and thrust it in violent precision behind him. The blade slid into something thick and heavy.

Gabriel stumbled backwards, the trajectory of his own sword shifting as his blade sliced wetly through shoulder bone and tissue, tearing a fiery path down Christian's back, just missing his vulnerable neck. Christian rolled to the side, the pain all-consuming as his body fought to repair the wound.

He could feel his strength waning but he would never give up, not while he had an ounce of fight left in him and not while Victoria was still locked defenseless in that room. With effort, he stood, watching as Gabriel weaved unsteadily on his feet. The gash on his own back struggled to close, his healing impeded by his hunger and the lack of blood to repair his injuries.

Gabriel's face contorted into a grimace as he inched the sword out of his stomach. Like Christian's strength, his magic was also becoming weaker. He had already tapped into the reserves of the sapphire ring on his finger.

"CURO," he gasped, trying to heal himself.

Everything would have been so different if Victoria had only seen reason. Her limitless power would have been his, and he could have ended this in an instant. Her stupid infatuation with this animal had been the sole reason that they weren't together. Gabriel's eyes glittered as if struck by a moment of genius. He knew *exactly* how to bring the vampire down.

"You'll never be good enough for her, you know," he said. He was unprepared for the soft response.

"I know."

"You *know*?" Gabriel repeated. "If you know, why don't you leave? You don't belong in her world, just like she doesn't belong in yours. What you're doing is a disgrace to her."

"That's her choice," Christian said.

"So what do you intend to give her, vampire? Death? Exile? No family, no *children*?" he said. Christian didn't answer, but Gabriel saw the hesitation in his eyes.

"Is that what you want her for?" Christian asked. Gabriel smiled a cold, evil smile.

"Of course I want her for other things as well, like her delectable body for one," he said, watching Christian's increasing rigidity. "But when I'm done with her, there will be others."

"You will destroy everything that she is just to punish me?" Christian asked. Gabriel's eyes were black and icy. Hearing the unbridled emotion in the vampire's voice made him shake with rage.

"Not just you," he said, "her too."

Gabriel flicked his wrist, and in the space of a second Victoria magically appeared next to Gabriel, her arms bound at her side. Christian lurched painfully to his feet.

"Try anything and she dies," Gabriel said, as he hauled her roughly against his side, his fingers pressed against her throat. Victoria gasped at his rough stranglehold and Christian started visibly.

"Is this what you want, vampire?" Gabriel asked, kissing her temple and running his face along her cheek. "Or how about this?" He tilted her neck to the side and kissed it roughly.

Ignoring Gabriel's taunts, Christian stared at Victoria, searching for any signs that she'd been hurt. She seemed fine although there was something about her eyes that didn't seem right, almost like she was confused. Had Gabriel put some sort of control spell on her? Her smell was off too, but that could also be because of the wards. He'd barely been able to smell her blood earlier.

Gabriel drew his attention again as he turned Victoria in his arms and kissed her passionately on the mouth. Christian expected her to at least try to fight him like the last time, but when he saw that she was actually kissing the warlock back, it almost drove him to his knees. She had to be under some sort of spell, she *had* to be!

He watched as Gabriel murmured something to her, caressing the side of her face, and she lifted her luminous green eyes to Christian's. They were filled with naked pleading.

"Christian, if you truly love me, you'll let me go. I don't belong with you," she said. "Please, just let me go. I want you to let me go." She stared at him head on. "I don't love you. I could never love you."

"You've bewitched her, Gabriel. I *know* that that's not her talking," Christian whispered. "She would never want that. She would never say that!"

Something about the eyes …

"Well, then you leave me little choice, because I'll never let her go to you," Gabriel said.

In horrifying slow motion, before Christian could even guess at Gabriel's intent, Gabriel's fingers pressed against Victoria's soft smooth throat. Her eyes widened as she stared at Gabriel in betrayed shock followed by sorrowful understanding, a slight smile curving her perfect lips. Brief remorse etched his face but there was nothing she could do, captive as she was to him, as his fingers tightened and the life slowly drained from her body.

It happened in seconds but was enough for Christian's howl of agony to resonate against the cavern walls as he hurled himself through the air in blind rage toward Gabriel.

Whether it had been ill-timed or he had been too overwrought to think clearly, Gabriel's stunning spell caught Christian squarely in the chest and he fell to the floor, his body wracked with violent spasms.

He could hear Gabriel's footfalls as he walked toward him, but all he could see was Victoria's lifeless body across the room. He didn't even care that Gabriel was moving purposefully toward him, he would welcome death. It didn't seem possible, but he had seen it with his own eyes. His chest felt like it was splintering into tiny, unrecognizable shards, suffocating him with each gasp of breath. It wasn't possible …

Victoria was *dead*!

Gabriel kicked him with a booted foot hearing the satisfying crunch as its steel tip met ribs and broke them.

"Arrogant, filthy vampire," he said. He bent down and looked into the glazed gray eyes, and swinging the silver knife he had found on the floor in a low arc. "Minuo," he said, methodically slicing Christian's face, arms, and chest, watching the dark blood flow out of the body and the cuts futilely trying to heal themselves. The wounds would continue to bleed from the parasitic bleeding spell he'd cast until there was nothing left. "It won't be long," he said to himself, as he watched the blood pooling beneath the body.

Now it was *her* turn.

Gabriel said a word, waving his hand as the door to her cell became transparent, and watched as Victoria's face froze in horror, taking in the impossible sight of her own body lying on the ground and watching as it transformed before her eyes into Charla's motionless shape. A glamour! Charla was dead, Victoria could see that clearly. Why had Charla been in her body? Had Gabriel used the glamour as a trick?

Her breath caught, and she desperately searched the room for

Christian, her eyes falling on his limp form and the terrible blood that soaked his clothes. He was motionless. A soundless scream parted her lips as she clutched at her amulet. Was he dead?! Gabriel moved to stand in front of her and Victoria glared at him with such a noxious hatred she could taste it in her throat. He read her expression easily.

"He's not dead yet," he said. "But whether he dies a quick and painless, or slow and agonizing death is your decision." Gabriel watched her expectantly. "You know what I want."

The door went solid.

Victoria sank to the floor, the pain suffocating her. She would give Gabriel what he wanted if it would spare Christian's life. That was no decision. She would give her life in a heartbeat for him.

But she didn't know whether Christian was alive or not. All she had was Gabriel's word and he was a scheming, calculating liar. There was no way she could trust him. The piercing fear that he had in fact been lying and that Christian was possibly already dead, gripped her in its jaws. Victoria rocked back and forth her arms around her knees, nails digging into the soft flesh of her palms until she felt the skin break. Her own blood smeared on her hands.

Time wound back onto itself.

Renewed clarity filled her. Strength saturated her. Power overwhelmed her.

Blood magic.

As before, whenever her blood was spilled or a sacrifice received, the blood magic came alive. It mushroomed inside her like an atomic explosion. Without hesitation, she channeled its power through the wards between her and Christian, moving through the maze until she could feel his faint consciousness. He was so terribly weak that he didn't even know she was there. She read his mind quickly and saw in horror that he thought she was dead. Her heart ached.

Christian?

Nothing in his mind even registered her presence; it was like he was already dead inside. He needed blood, and lots of it … just like the last time Anton had saved him when the blood magic had almost killed him. Victoria shivered at the memory. As much as she wanted to go to him, she understood that trying to save him on her own could be disastrous.

Gabriel was still out there, she could feel it. He wouldn't leave Christian's side, he was far too careful for that. Although her power over the blood magic had grown, there was no guarantee that she could control it, face Gabriel, and save Christian *and* Holly at the same time. Her arrogance had cost her dearly the last time and she wouldn't make that mistake again, not with Christian and Holly's lives hanging in the balance.

Victoria didn't know whether Gabriel would indeed keep Christian alive as he had said, but she was banking on the fact that as long as Gabriel knew that she would never give herself to him without Christian's life as an exchange, then she had a little time and something to bargain with. She needed to get to the one person who could help her, the one person who cared for Christian as much as she did.

Enhard.

He was the only one powerful enough to protect Christian if she failed. If she invoked her blood's deadly power and lost control, then Christian too would be at risk. Enhard could get Christian to safety should anything go wrong.

The blood magic swirled, cognitive. Every shred of her wanted to teleport into the main room where Christian lay so weakly on the marble floor and whisk him away, but she didn't trust herself to control her blood. And she could never leave Holly.

Gabriel was powerful, and cunning, if the last few days had taught her anything. Underestimating him would be her downfall. The only solution was to go for help.

She wrapped her consciousness around Christian, willing him to hear her.

Don't give up, Christian.

The slight flutter could have been her imagination but she grasped it as hope. She would do whatever it took, she vowed fiercely, *whatever* it took.

TWENTY-SEVEN

Paris Revisited

ANGIE? ANGIE, I *hope you can hear me. You're in danger. Gabriel knows you helped Christian. Get away if you can.*

Victoria hoped that Angie would be able to hear her. She wouldn't want her to come to any more pain from Gabriel's sadistic ways, and she knew without a doubt that her brother would punish her severely for what he would consider to be unforgivable disloyalty.

Despite Charla's cruelty and duplicity, Victoria couldn't believe that Gabriel had killed her so heartlessly when her only mistake had been to fall in love with *him*. He had used her and then abused her in the worst possible way, murdering her while she had been helping him. He was sick and twisted. Victoria knew that she would have to be the one to end him.

She looked around her small prison, looking for a weapon, anything she could use to cut through her skin. She needed to spill her blood, and a lot of it, for Victoria intended to invoke the blood craft she had been born with, something she should have done even before Christian became involved. But she'd been afraid—afraid to release the blood magic and not be able to control its terrifying power. She'd almost killed Christian the last time! Now, she had no choice.

After a frantic search, she disconnected a thin wire she'd found behind the rusty radiator in the room and inspected it critically, touching its sharp ends. With some pressure it would do. She sat in the middle of the room and pulled her energy into herself, commanding her blood into action. She could feel it surging through her body waiting for the release it would soon be granted, and she awarded it decisively, digging the thin wire across her wrist and severing the skin with barely any pressure. Brackish dark blood spurted out and she felt the magic of the blood craft suffuse her as her blood welled from the wound. It was sacrificial blood.

Murmuring a word, she healed her wound and felt the magic soaking her soul, until her eyes were black with it and her body trembled. It was almost too easy, the binding wards falling before her fingertips like they were air, and the confidence it gave her made her think for a second that maybe she could take Gabriel on her own. But she knew that would be her destruction. She was well aware of the risks that came with invoking the blood magic's devastating power—it would take advantage of any weakness, including pride. She needed to be smart and stick to her plan.

As the amulet warmed at her breast, Victoria belatedly realized that she could have used the amulet to release the blood—after all, that was the purpose of its sharp edge, she realized with dawning understanding. It made sense … sacrifice to summon the blood magic. She took a deep breath and closed her eyes. Holly first.

"TRANSEO," she said, and the room disappeared into nothingness; the power of the word combining with the power of the blood was consummate. Victoria's mind envisioned the room two doors down where she'd seen Holly. Before she could even take a breath as her body re-materialized, she grabbed Holly and teleported again, this time to Christian's home in Canville. Holly would be safest there under Anton's care.

The third and final time she murmured, "TRANSEO," holding the destination clearly in her head, she emerged in Christian's Paris apartment. Victoria felt none of the normal effects of the teleportation. In fact, she felt even better than she had when she had left earlier.

Unable to teleport safely given her unfamiliarity with the building, she took the metro to La Défense and entered the looming black monolith that was the Tour Areva. She went to the top floor without hesitation, expanding her awareness, searching. She found what she was looking for in the boardroom where they'd had the Council meeting. Without knocking she walked straight in, and found herself face to face with seven furious vampires. The leader stood slowly and stared at her with incredulous surprise.

"Enhard," she said by way of greeting. She stared coolly at the other six vampires watching her with varying degrees of shock and fury. After all, she had just entered their haven without having been invited. Remembering that Christian's life hung in the balance, she moved toward Enhard and was immediately surrounded by four snarling vampires. "Wait!" she said. They ignored her, their faces feral. She was the enemy.

"CONFUTO," she said, waving her hand. Incredibly they all froze, unable to move. She could feel their shock and hatred burning through her as she walked toward Enhard whom she had left free of the hold charm. She knew that they were stunned that she had been able to use magic against them in their own space. Too bad it wasn't warded for blood magic. Knowing she had to be careful whom to trust, she turned to Enhard.

"I need to speak with you privately," she said urgently.

Just because she had put a hold charm on the other vampires didn't mean that they couldn't hear what she was saying. Enhard stared at her and then nodded. She released the charm, and the vampires exited staring at her with caution. She waited until they were alone before beginning. Enhard stared at her, guarded but curious as to her intent.

"Enhard, I need your help," she said. His dark eyes reflected their surprise. "Christian is in great danger and I know that he is considered a royal—" She had barely finished the sentence when he jumped to his feet. She could read the alarm in his face.

"You know of Le Sang Noir? What my people call the Cruentus Curse?" she asked. At his nod, she continued. "Well, it's real." Enhard's face remained unmoved. Victoria took a deep breath and looked him full in the face. "I'm the one you've been looking for."

Enhard's went from surprise to disbelief to shock and finally to anger. "What do you mean?" he snapped.

"How do you think I was able to do magic here, in this place?" she said. Enhard still looked unconvinced. She sighed; she had expected this and there was only one way to prove it to him beyond the shadow of a doubt. "Do you have a knife?"

Victoria did not want to take out the amulet even though she was there requesting Enhard's help. That was private.

"Are you serious?" he said. "You do remember what I am, what we are here?"

"Yes. A knife, please."

Enhard reached into a drawer and handed her a small pocketknife. Without hesitation, Victoria ran it across her palm, the black blood welling. She healed it immediately and watched Enhard as he struggled for control, his eyes bright and wild. It was a losing battle she knew, her blood was like an aphrodisiac even to the most seasoned vampire, and she was unsurprised when he bounded over the table in one leap snarling hungrily. Victoria wasn't worried, she'd been under a shield charm since she had entered the chamber—he couldn't touch her. Still, she didn't prolong his agony and reached out to gently touch his hand.

"Vicissitudo normalis," she said, watching as his glistening, sharp teeth retracted and his wild eyes calmed in immediate response to her command. He stared at her in incredulous silence.

"What did you do? Am I human?" he asked, running his tongue against his blunt teeth and still smelling the blood but feeling no answering, immediate desire.

"No, not really, I just took away your hunger temporarily," she said. "My blood would have killed you had you taken it. But it was the only way I could make you believe that I am who I say I am."

Victoria explained what had happened with Gabriel and finally to Christian.

"Do you have any proof that what you say is true?" Enhard said.

"Call Lucian and ask if he can reach Christian. He'll know."

She waited as Enhard made the call and watched as his face darkened. He shut the tiny cell phone and stared at her. "He said that Christian is fine."

"He's lying!" Victoria said. "Enhard, listen to me. You know our secret, I love Christian, but I also know how you feel about us, and yet here I am in front of you asking for help. You want to see Christian with your own eyes, here!"

Victoria grasped Enhard's face and shoved the images of her last view of Christian into Enhard's head, not even knowing beforehand whether it was possible or even dangerous. She just did it, demolishing his walls like tissue paper, and watched as knowledge followed by horror crossed his face. She pulled back and he slumped in his chair.

"We must be quick. Tell me what you need me to do," he said weakly, after he had regained his composure.

A plan in place, they made their way to the lobby. They would meet in New York at Enhard's home. In spite of the precious added time, Victoria didn't trust herself to teleport Enhard safely. If anything happened during the transfer, all would be lost. She needed him, and she could only pray that Christian would hold on.

"How fast can you get there, Enhard?" she asked, her face worried.

"I will fly."

Victoria calculated the distance and time in her head, panicked. "But that's seven hours if we're lucky!"

"No, you misunderstand me, I can *fly*," Enhard said calmly. Victoria looked at him, confused, until comprehension dawned.

"Oh," she said. "I didn't know you could do that."

"I will meet you there in an hour," Enhard said. "Do you have transport?" Victoria lifted an eyebrow, and he inclined his head at her silent jibe. She would teleport from somewhere safe. She entered the elevator.

"Thank you, Enhard." His face remained inscrutable.

Victoria allowed herself to breathe the minute the elevator doors closed. It had been nerve-wracking to try to convince a vampire predestined to mistrust her every word to help her, but somehow she'd done it.

The elevator stopped on the fortieth floor, and as the doors opened, the heat of her amulet scorched her chest. Her eyes snapped to a pair of slate-gray ones. The shock of recognition was followed by the immediate souring of her stomach as Christian's twin brother stepped in.

Again, she was struck by the similarities between them, although each time she saw Lucian, their resemblance became less and less pronounced. Their height, coloring and eyes would always be the same, but Lucian's face was narrower and colder, and his hair was shorter, emphasizing the harsh angularity of his face. Victoria knew in no uncertain terms the danger she was in from the minute he crossed the threshold. The elevator felt suddenly very confined. She felt the steel handrail digging into her hips. Lucian smile was filled with malice.

"Well, isn't this a charming surprise," he said. "So to what do we owe the honor of your presence in Paris?"

"Why did you lie about Christian?" she countered. A good offense was a better defense. He smiled wider.

"I didn't lie. I said he was fine. And he is fine, for now anyway," he said. "But you know more about that than I do, don't you? Where is my dear brother then?"

"As if I would tell you."

"I could make you, you know," he said.

"You could try," Victoria shot back.

Her defiance and complete fearlessness threw Lucian for a loop. All he had to do was take one step and her neck would be in his hands, and he would be ready to tear her limb from limb. Yet here she was openly taunting him and being excessively bold about it, her green eyes flashing fire. He liked it. When he finally got rid of Christian, maybe he would keep her as his own private entertainment.

He pulled the stop button in a smooth motion and the elevator lurched to a sudden stop. Her hands gripped the rail, white-knuckled.

"So why are you here, Tori?" He said her name with a caress, and it sickened her just like it had the last time he had used that suggestive tone at the masquerade.

"It's not really any of your business, is it? After all, you won't even help your own brother. You disgust me," she said. His eyes widened at her arrogance. "For everything between you and Christian, if you were in danger, he would be the first person at your side, just like he was the first person here when the Council wanted to kill you. He saved you from that fate." The bored expression on Lucian's face incensed her, but when he finally raised his eyes to hers, they were filled with a simmering, dark hatred.

"That's one of my brother's greatest flaws. His need to *save* people who don't need saving," he said. "I, on the other hand, leave the cards to fall as they must."

"So you would just let him die?"

"If it is meant to be, who am I to stop it?" He looked at her with hooded eyes.

"I'm sorry you feel that way," she said, staring at him with undisguised loathing, wanting nothing more than to escape his cloying presence. She glanced at the control panel, releasing the stop button with a quick thought. The elevator whirred to life. Lucian smiled his despicable smile.

"Why in such a hurry? Care to stay for a bite?" he asked, grinning widely, his teeth gleaming and sharp.

"Trust me, Lucian, you won't like what you get," she said. "And I don't want to hurt you." Lucian laughed, a deep full-throated sound that echoed in the elevator.

"You ... don't ... want ... to ... hurt ... *me*?" he repeated with staccato-like mockery. At that precise moment the elevator glided to a stop on the tenth floor, and they stared at each other in the charged silence. As if things couldn't get any worse, Lena walked in, her face the picture of surprise at its unexpected occupant. Lucian looked even more infuriated by her untimely entrance.

"You did say to meet you on ten," she said, addressing Lucian and eyeing Victoria with barely veiled distaste. The venom from their last encounter before the Council hung thick in the air, and Lena's flawless face with its ice-blue eyes, generous lips and white-blond hair taunted her with its perfection. Victoria stifled her jealousy, knowing that she was in a very small space with two hostile vampires who would kill her without a second thought if she faltered for an instant.

Christian *loved* her, and that was all that mattered.

"Lena," she acknowledged.

"Baroness, actually," Lena returned coolly.

Lucian had settled back into his teasing humor after the passing flash of annoyance had disappeared. He'd enjoy watching Lena have her way with her after he was done. The witch had been stupid to come to Paris without his brother's protection, although Christian had certainly seemed incapacitated when he had checked. Before they broke her, he would find out exactly where Christian was and save himself the legwork of trying to locate him to ensure his long-awaited demise.

"Tori and I were just discussing dinner plans," he said to Lena.

Lena's eyes narrowed. She had warned Lucian about this witch's abilities and still he didn't listen. His arrogance would cost him. She glanced at Victoria, whose skin was flushed as if she'd just finished running a marathon, even though her breathing was slow, calm. Lena couldn't see why Christian was infatuated with her, this woman-child. She was quite ordinary, with the exception of her eyes, which were an unusual emerald color.

Victoria turned from Lucian to Lena, her look measured. It was at that same moment Lena realized that she had been mistaken about the color of Victoria's eyes. They weren't green at all … they were jet black.

"Lucian," Victoria said carefully, watching them both, "if you try to hurt Christian in any way, I will forget my promise not to hurt you because you are his brother."

Lucian was incredulous. He couldn't believe that she was still threatening him. Why he ought to kill her right there! His glance dropped to his mother's ring gleaming on her right hand and anger flooded into him, fueling his rage. With inhuman speed he lunged toward Victoria but to her magical, blood-inspired senses, it looked like he was moving in slow motion. She let him get within inches of her.

"CONFUTO," she said, as she'd done with the other vampires. Lucian's body froze in mid-leap. Lena snarled but she found that she couldn't move either. Victoria's blood boiled and without thinking, she almost said the words of death it whispered seductively.

Careful, she warned herself, the blood would kill deviously and without conscience, and losing control to it was the one thing she could not afford. She tore her eyes away from Lena with effort.

For the first time since he'd met her, Lucian looked at her with new awareness. Too late. She leaned forward and touched his face, feeling his muscle flex beneath her touch. "Like I said, because you are his brother, I'll be generous, but come near him, Lucian, and I won't be this kind," she said.

She could see the rage, the hatred and the new fear burning in his eyes. He wanted to hurt her so badly that she could smell it. Slowly, unhurriedly, she took out the pocketknife she had used with Enhard, and Lucian's eyes narrowed. "It's not for you, don't worry."

Victoria repeated the cut, slicing diagonally across her palm, letting the blood pool in her cupped palm. She knew they could smell its heady scent in the confined space and she was careful not to let a single drop fall. Lucian's body strained against the magical bonds and his eyes were feral with uncontrollable hunger, as were Lena's. Victoria smiled and said, "TRANSEO."

As before, her body melted into the air and the last thing she saw was Lucian's enraged face as he lunged into open air just where she had been standing.

Lucian stood in the elevator, clenching and unclenching his fists. The hunger was so fierce he could barely control himself.

He had never been so deliriously happy in all his life.

"Did you see it?" he said. Lena stared at him confused.

"The blood?" she asked. When he nodded, she continued. "I could barely stand to look at it. The smell alone was like nothing else I have ever smelled, it felt like my stomach was eating itself I became so ravenous. Why?"

"It was as dark as I have ever seen."

"So?" Lucian glared at her obtuseness.

"Le Sang Noir … it's her."

TWENTY-EIGHT

Clash of the Titans

VICTORIA HOPED HER Mini would still be where she'd left it in the parking lot at 125th Street. If not, this would end up being one of those teleportation jumps gone tragically wrong. She didn't have a choice because it was the place she knew in New York that had the lowest variability risk. She couldn't go to Angie's apartment because that would be too dangerous, and there was no way she could just pick a spot in the city and hope for the best, far too risky.

"TRANSEO," she said.

When she opened her eyes, she was sitting in the freezing cold interior of her car, and she breathed a slow, grateful breath. She hopped on the express number five subway train and switched to the local number six train to get to the address that Enhard had given her. She hoped that Enhard would have already arrived.

Time was running out. Victoria had stayed close to Christian via the tenuous tunnel between their minds that she'd kept open despite the risk of discovery. After a time, the effort for the portal had become mindless and she barely had to think about holding it open, it was just another thing that the blood magic did naturally.

Although it had been a matter of hours, the magical wounds that Gabriel had inflicted were doing what they were intended to do, and the accelerated blood loss coupled with Christian's lack of a will to live, left him weak and floating in and out of consciousness. He was still alive but his desire to die worsened his weakened condition. He had no fight left.

The few times that Victoria had reached him when he had seemed more conscious, he had treated her voice like a figment of his tortured imagination, and kept saying how sorry he was that he hadn't been able to save her. The more she tried to tell him that she was alive and well, the more he struggled against her, convinced it was Gabriel playing some inhuman game.

Enhard was waiting in the foyer of his apartment, his face brooding.

"We have to hurry. We don't have much time," Victoria told him. "I ran into Lucian in the elevator after I saw you in Paris, and he knows who I am. I had to invoke the blood magic to teleport away from him. Now that he knows, there's nothing else standing in his way. He'll be here, I can feel it." Enhard's face whitened even though that piece of news did not come as a surprise to him. Lucian would do whatever it took to take everything away from Christian.

Realizing that the stakes were higher than ever and that there was no margin for error, they combed through the details of the plan. They would sneak in the way that Angie had brought Christian. With any luck, Gabriel would have assumed that Angie had used the first entrance. No doubt he would have already discovered that Victoria and Holly had gone, but if he hadn't, that would be an added element of surprise. Once they got in, the main objective would be to get Christian out safely. The plan had many, many holes but it was the only option they had to save him quickly and in short order.

Victoria brushed Christian's mind gently as they were leaving. *I'm coming my love*, she told him, *hold on*. She looked around the room through his consciousness and noticed that although the room seemed similar, it was different from hers and Holly's. She had no way of knowing which room it was. When the time came, she'd have to guess which door he lay behind and hope for the right one.

They walked briskly downtown and Victoria glanced sideways at Enhard. It had been a risk going to him for help, but she really had had no other choice. There had been a fifty-fifty chance that Enhard would help, given how he felt about Christian's relationship with her, but she had bargained on the strong paternal bond that he'd had with Christian winning out in the end. And it had.

"I know you don't approve," she said, "but I love him."

Enhard didn't break his stride at her softly spoken words but she could see his face tighten and knew that he had heard her. A few moments passed before he spoke.

"My mentor was a vampire called Valerius. He met your ancestor, the Duchess toward the end. From what I have seen in his memories, you look very much like her. But you're different too, stronger ... worthy of the curse you bear." Enhard raised a hand and placed it on her shoulder, squeezing gently. "He loved her, I think, but he died for it." Victoria looked at him.

"As I would for him," she said quietly.

In the exact moment that she said the words, Victoria realized something. She hadn't been able to control the blood when she'd challenged Christian at his house because she hadn't understood it fully even then. But now, it was all so clear. It was an epiphany of epic magnitude, yet she'd known it all along—it was Brigid's legacy!

Love was the answer.

Her mind scanned through the last pages of the journal

remembering what Brigid had written, "the price of the blood's magic had always been mine to set! I lost the one thing that could have saved me … love." Her son's unfaltering love and her love for her granddaughters had been her saving grace, her one chance to salvage her humanity and control the blood curse. And she had conquered it and died doing so, but she'd done so on *her* terms. For the first time, Victoria felt hope that she would prevail.

They reached the entrance on Lexington. The metal gates to the alley were closed, most likely because it was in the middle of the day, but Victoria swept it with her mind just to be sure. Empty. Victoria kissed the ring Christian had given her and touched her amulet. She would need all the strength that both had to offer as she pulled the grates open and walked down into the darkness.

"Specto," she said. Her eyes acclimatized magically to the enveloping dark. She glanced around at Enhard and knew that he'd have no trouble with the darkness. He nodded for her to continue.

They crept to the door and Victoria scanned again; the room seemed to be empty but she couldn't be sure. Gabriel was nothing if not resourceful. Chances were, he already knew that she was there but she was hoping that he wouldn't be prepared for Enhard, which would give them a slight advantage. Indicating that Enhard should remain in the shadows for a few minutes before following, she invoked an invisibility spell and stole into the room. She felt the alteration as the protective wards within the chamber negated the simple spell of her own magic, and she gritted her teeth. *Push forward*, she thought. She didn't want to engage the blood magic unnecessarily.

The room was still in a shambles from Christian and Gabriel's fight, and she moved noiselessly to the doors in the back, her senses alert and her mind searching for Christian. Suddenly, every cell froze as she felt the delicate shift in the air.

"I knew you'd be back," Gabriel said.

Victoria turned, her features composed. Gabriel stood flanked by three people she didn't recognize, two older guys and a girl. Behind him, stood Angie, and Victoria almost gasped aloud in horror—her face was covered in purple bruises, her lips puffy with one eye swollen completely shut. She held her head down and shielded her face with her hair. Victoria's face must have reflected her horror because Gabriel smiled grimly.

"That's what happens when you defy me," he said, his tone hard and menacing. Victoria straightened her shoulders.

"Is that supposed to scare me, Gabriel?" she said. Victoria raised her hand and Gabriel laughed.

"Remember, your magic doesn't work here."

"Oh, is that why Holly and I were able to get out?" she said, and was rewarded with the barest flash of unease in his eyes, which he quickly masked.

"No matter, it won't help you this time. And if you try anything your *boyfriend* dies," Gabriel said. He nodded to the three people beside him and they fanned out. Angie remained where she was, motionless. Victoria watched the other two warily. "Oh, and in case you were wondering, they're warlocks and she's a witch so you may as well give in now, and I will honor my promise to you. Devereux can go."

Gabriel feigned sincerity, but Victoria knew that he would never let Christian go, just as he would stop at nothing to control her. She smiled coldly, she could already feel the blood hotly pressing against the inside of her skin, tingling. It was ready. *She* was ready.

"Where is he? How do I know he's even alive or still here?" she asked. Gabriel nodded toward Angie and she walked obediently to the last room, opening the door where Christian lay slumped in the back corner, his hands bound behind his back. Victoria's heart lurched upon seeing his beautiful face, so deathly pale that her knees almost buckled. The wounds on his shirtless body were deep oozing lacerations and she could see the poison infecting the grayish flesh beneath them. It was a spell of sadistically evil proportions. Her hands clenched in a rage so terrifying that her entire body shuddered with it; she didn't even have to draw blood, it came on its own as she brushed her nose, the blackly red smear shimmering on her fingertips.

The time had come.

"You really should be afraid you know," she whispered. "Obscurum!" The entire room was plunged into darkness. In the seconds it gave her, Victoria dispatched the other witch with an energy blast so powerful that her entire body imploded into nothingness within moments.

Victoria could feel Gabriel's wards pulsing outwardly against her, trying to force her magic into obedience, but the blood-craft was far more powerful, especially now that it had already received one death with such ease. She felt its power churning wildly within her and she reined it under control.

"Iacio!" A heavy chest hurtled toward her. Victoria watched it in slow motion as if it were being hurled underwater.

"Impedio," she said, and it came to a dead stop just above her head. She twisted her hands and it rocketed back the way it had come, dispatching its owner with a wet crunch. Her blood whistled, gleeful. She spun to her left trying to get closer to where Christian and Angie were but was immediately blocked by three fire bolts that flew past her head. She whirled around, brandishing her hand in Christian's direction and shouted, "Protectum!" At the very least the shield spell would protect them from getting hit by the blasts in the cavern.

Through the hazy darkness, Victoria could see the two

warlocks circling her, one on each side. Gabriel's face contorted with anger and he screamed a lethal pain spell. "Excrucio!"

"Corpus venenum!" roared the other warlock at the same time. Victoria barely had time to use a shield charm against Gabriel's spell, diffusing it completely, before blasting a lightning bolt in return. In the seconds that she saw the bolt send him flying backwards into space, the corporal poison spell from the other warlock hit her dead center in the middle of her body. Curiously, she felt nothing at first and then she realized that her blood was boiling hot, bubbling like lava as it absorbed the most brutal part of the spell. Still, she staggered backwards, a sheen of sweat coating her forehead as her skin glowed red.

"Curo," she said, and felt the immediate cure eliminate the rest of the poison. She could see the warlock who had delivered the spell staring at her with newfound trepidation. At the very least, the poison spell should have knocked her unconscious. Instead, she was barely afflicted.

Victoria inclined her head in gracious challenge, recalling the poison spell he'd cast and flung it back toward him. The warlock blanched and dove out of the way. It missed him by inches. Working her way backwards toward Angie and Christian, she noticed that Enhard had silently entered the room, staying out of sight, and she whispered a non-detection spell to help shroud him in secrecy.

The darkened room was clouded with smoke and dust from the menagerie of spells flying back and forth, and Victoria moved stealthily, searching for Gabriel. She didn't want him anywhere near Christian. Inching herself toward the back, she leaned against one of the walls and edged to the right feeling her way along the cold stone, kicking through the debris that littered the floor.

Just a few more steps, she thought.

Without warning, a dust-covered hand snaked out from her

left and grasped her by the throat. Victoria kicked wildly but her captor jerked her against him, his forearm braced against her neck.

"Not so tough now, are you?" the warlock said, his breath hot in her ear. Victoria flung her head back connecting with the bridge of his nose and the soft tissue of his cheeks, and she heard bone break as his arm tightened convulsively, blood spattering from his nose onto her back. "You'll pay for that," he screamed. "Excrucio!"

She barely had time to react before her blood reacted in her stead, deflecting the blast of the pain spell and rebounding the curse onto the man holding her prisoner. A high-pitched scream burst from his mouth, and she could smell the singed flesh of his blistered arm as he ripped it away from her incandescent skin, staring at her like she was a demon. His skin peeled off in sheets as the pain spell was magnified a hundredfold from the blood magic.

Victoria could taste her blood's metallic desire in her mouth, clamoring for its reward. She gave it. The warlock's face distorted in horror as her eyes metamorphosed from luminous green to darkly black, and her lips shaped the death spell.

"Mortis omnino," she said, watching as his mouth, eyes, nose, and ears bled rivers of red, as his internal organs collapsed. What was left of him folded like string to the floor. Victoria's blood sang and she swayed unsteadily, feeling drunk with its power.

"Illustro!" roared a voice from the other corner of the room. The lights came on blindingly. Victoria's bemused gaze registered that Gabriel had Angie's neck in his hands, his face black with suppressed fury. Christian lay unmoving on the ground to the right of them, about fifteen feet to her left just inside the doorway of the small room. She searched for Enhard and saw him crouching behind a chair, and imperceptibly nodded for him to try to get closer to Gabriel.

"What makes you think I care about her?" she said. Gabriel

laughed wildly.

"Oh you should care, Tori. Have you forgotten so carelessly what she does? You think your new magic is safe from her?" he said shaking her body like a rag doll. "That's all she's good for."

"My *new* magic, Gabe?" Victoria mocked with a grim smile. "Don't be naïve. Do you really think the Cruentus Curse can be controlled? And did you honestly think that I would come here alone?" She saw his eyes widen and he looked around calling her bluff. She took an imperceptible step closer toward Christian and met Enhard's eyes.

"LIBERO!" she shouted, freeing Angie from Gabriel's grip at the same moment that Enhard leapt from his hidden crouch straight toward him, and knocked Gabriel to the floor.

Gabriel looked stunned even as Enhard snarled and tore at his body with ferocious blows. He rolled away and jumped to his feet only to be knocked to the ground again by Enhard, who was lightning fast, his attack unpredictable and fierce. Before Gabriel was even able to gasp a spell, Enhard had him flat on his back or on the defensive, physically running away from him. Enhard moved so swiftly, he was a blur!

Victoria rushed to Christian's side. "Christian," she said, cradling his head in her lap and caressing his face, "can you hear me?" He moaned. She could see his teeth fully extended beneath his lips and she knew it was because of his constant state of unconscious hunger. They were sharp and white and still lethal. Angie crouched near to them and her face was lined with concern.

"Is he going to live?" she asked.

"He's alive but he needs blood, lots of blood," Victoria said. Angie stared at her for a moment and then hesitated.

"He can have mine. I'm human. I mean, not a witch … sorry … I mean …" she said, suddenly unsure of what she had offered.

Victoria was amazed at her generosity even now after her own considerable injuries at the hands of her brother. She couldn't believe how badly she had misjudged Angie; she was stronger than anyone she knew.

"No Angie, but thanks for offering. He would probably kill you, he's so hungry that he wouldn't know how to stop," Victoria said. "I don't even know if he's too far gone for either of us to help him."

But Victoria knew that there was only one way to save Christian. She knew what she had to do. She would have to invoke the blood magic, all of it, just as she'd done the last time when they'd fought in the woods near his house. But this time, she would win. She would control it. She had to.

Love was the answer.

Victoria looked out into the main room as Enhard and Gabriel circled each other. Enhard was far too quick for Gabriel's spells to even find a target and Gabriel was far too powerful at self-healing for Enhard's physically punishing attacks to have any lasting effect—it was almost a stalemate but they circled each other in a cautious unchoreographed dance, each waiting for an opening. She stared at Angie and then reached out her hand.

"Curo," she said, squeezing Angie's fingers and watching the marks on her face fade and the swelling disappear. "Get away from him, Angie. He will only bring you ruin, and you deserve so much more than that." The tears leaked unbidden from the corners of Angie's eyes. Christian stirred, and Victoria knew that she didn't have much time.

Christian? Can you hear me? She waited, her heart so tight it was impossible to even breathe. *Please, Christian ... come back to me, wake up ... please ...*

His eyes fluttered but did not open. Victoria summoned the

blood magic, pulling on the energy from the amulet, and went as deeply as she ever had into Christian's mind, searching for his subconscious, that silent part of him that she knew would remain as alert as anything else. The part that Fardon had said was always there.

I'm ready, she said. She almost jumped out of her skin when it responded.

Ready for what? Conversationally, as if it had known her all her life.

For you to take me into you.

Silence, pondering. *What will I become?*

I don't know. Victoria hesitated. *Will you accept me?*

Always.

Victoria stroked his face. None of the books or the journal had said what could happen if she did what she was going to do. For all she knew, they would both die, but either way, Victoria knew one thing—she owned the blood and she would make it bow to her will. She was her own master, and her love was the key. That's what the journal had been saying all along. She had to trust herself.

She stirred, inhaling deeply and pulled Christian close, removing the amulet from her neck. Angie's eyes widened as Christian's teeth grazed Victoria's neck.

"Maybe you should turn away," Victoria said, and Angie gladly obliged, turning her attention to the ongoing battle in the main room. The blood rushed wild in Victoria's veins as if it knew what she was about to do.

"Soporo," she whispered, and it quieted automatically. She kissed Christian's cold lips and drew the barely discernable blade of the amulet across her right wrist, wincing at the sting.

"Cruentus renovo!" she said, willing the blood magic to heal him as she pressed her wrist to his lips. Her heart was racing—

her gamble could kill him instantly.

The pressure was soft at first and then stronger as he clamped her hand to his mouth and drew her strength into him greedily, desperately. She brushed her free hand against his hair and his silver eyes opened, staring into hers with luminous faith. She could see the recognition and every emotion he'd ever had since they had met flash through their liquid depths. Victoria was bleeding her life into his mouth and willing him to live, willing him to live for *her* ... for them.

"Desino," she gasped, commanding him to stop as her wound closed on its own. She shook her head to clear it as Christian fell back, his lips rimmed in black. She could see the color flooding his skin, the new blood overtaking his ravenous, empty body, and he bucked against its foreignness. His wounds healed instantly as the new blood forced the poisons out, and still he writhed in silent transformation. Angie had scooted herself to the edge of the room, her eyes wide with fear and confusion, and when Victoria looked worriedly at her, she wrapped her arms around her knees rocking back and forth.

"What is it, Angie?" Victoria asked, watching as Christian continued his painful metamorphosis on the floor. She'd known that it wasn't going to be easy.

"You should see what's happening, it's unbelievable," Angie said, trembling uncontrollably. "It's like everything that is you is going into him and right now he is in complete upheaval. His very nature is fighting against it ... everything dead ... against everything so vibrantly alive! It's the most chaotically beautiful thing I have ever seen," she said, excited and terrified all at the same time.

After several tense moments, Christian sat upright and stared at Victoria. His eyes were bright, unsure but so incredibly knowing, it made it suddenly hard to breathe. And time stopped along with her breath when he crushed her to his chest and kissed her with the fierce, aching tenderness of a starving man too long deprived. She tasted a tangy sweetness on his lips and knew it to be her own blood. It electrified her more than she'd ever thought possible. They strained toward each other for what seemed like an eternity, bodies trembling and blood on fire, until he finally lifted her face to his, his thumb brushing the fullness of her cheek.

"Tori ..." His exquisite voice was like rough velvet and she almost wept at the sheer beauty of hearing it again. "What did you *do*?" Her throat choked at his inane question, he knew exactly what she had done, but she knew what he meant. He meant how.

"I didn't know if it would work, but it did. I controlled the blood magic. I did it this time." She was overwhelmed at the power that lived within her, and the magnitude of what she'd done. Christian had been on the verge of death one second and now he was completely rejuvenated in a matter of minutes after consuming barely an ounce of her blood. The same *poisonous* blood that could kill and destroy everything in its path, she had magically commanded to save him. And now he was awake, and alive. Victoria touched his face, emotion clogging her throat, and noticed that his once clear silver eyes were now rimmed in black, startling and unique ... a part of her now part of him.

A sudden crash from the room next door had them all on their feet. Enhard had just leapt off the wall to smash into the marble floor just where Gabriel's head had been, and there was a hole in the floor where his foot had crushed through the marble. They were circling each other again, and Gabriel was repeating something over and over in a monotonous chant. It was very dark magic. Victoria knew it as certainly as she knew herself—she could feel it sucking the energy from the air around them. She raced into the middle of the room.

"Enhard, get down!" she said, blasting a stunning spell toward Gabriel, which his shield spell easily deflected. In the split second before Gabriel's spell left his fingers, Victoria noticed something crouching in the shadows ... Lucian. He met her eyes and stood.

"INCENDO MALEFICUS," Gabriel shouted.

A low warning scream tore from her throat, just as Gabriel released the yellow-rimmed black fire that had formed between his hands at the exact same moment Enhard looked toward the doorway, drawn by the movement there. Lucian stood there like a statue, silent and detached, his white face calculating. That millisecond of distraction was Enhard's undoing.

The black fireball hit Enhard squarely in the middle of his chest and engulfed his body in black demonic flames. He didn't even flinch even though the dark spell would have been excruciating. Instead, he looked across at Christian, linking eyes with his and bowed. Then he looked at Victoria and did the same. She bit her lip watching impotently as he closed his eyes and was incinerated within seconds.

"NO!!!" The agonized roar was from Christian, a blur of movement as he grabbed Gabriel in a choke-hold, crushing his windpipe until his face went gray. With colossal strength, he flung Gabriel's body as if it were made of air against the wall, the sound of wetly crunching bone echoing in the cavernous room.

Gabriel fell to the ground gasping nonsensically, his splintered bones irreparable. Blood seeped into the floor beneath him and he gurgled helplessly. Christian fell to the ground where the only remnant of Enhard was a black smear on the marble floor, and touched a closed fist to his forehead in reverence to the man who had been like a father to him.

Christian rose after several minutes, suddenly cognizant of the newfound fluidity of his movements. He could sense the old hunger in him but it did not bother him at all; in fact, he was strangely oblivious to it. He stared at his hands, flexing them and feeling their new tensile strength, the extraordinary blood flowing in his veins from the tips of his fingers along his arms through his chest and throughout his entire body. His insides felt like they were gilded with light, Le Sang Noir tracing a fiery phosphorescent path everywhere it touched inside him, transforming, metamorphosing. Powerful.

He looked incredulously at Victoria. Christian didn't know how she had done it, but from sheer force of will, her deadly blood had fed him and saved him when it should have killed him. It was *impossible.*

Victoria remained silent, her eyes glued to his. She knew that if by some horrific chance, the blood turned him into something worse, she would be the only one who could kill him.

TWENTY-NINE

Bloodspell

"WELL DONE, BROTHER," Lucian said, pulling up from his slouch and walking into the room clapping loudly. "You have saved the day as always!" The sarcastic amusement in his tone was evident. Christian looked merely curious that Lucian was even there, and Victoria stared at him with wary distaste. Lucian's saccharine tone irked her. She knew why he was here; he had come to finish his brother off, and he had also come in search of her … to fulfill the prophecy that haunted him.

She watched in slow motion as he walked over to Gabriel's inert body and pressed his booted foot to his throat. He was still breathing. Locking eyes with Victoria, his face was cruel as he stepped with all his weight, breaking Gabriel's neck in seconds. The wet sound of crushed flesh and bone echoed in the room. Gabriel did not move. Lucian smiled with savage pleasure.

"No!" Victoria shouted. "You are sick! You really are a monster!"

"He attacked my brother."

"Strange that you weren't worried about your *brother* when I came to see you in Paris," Victoria said. "I warned you, Lucian."

"Warned me not to help my brother? You forget yourself," he said. Victoria looked at him with distaste.

"I can hardly forget that you were the one saying that if your brother was meant to die, then so be it. I also can't forget that you tried to kill me," she said, watching Christian's reaction out of the corner of her eye. She was not disappointed. He whirled in a fluid twist, his silver eyes like diamond chips and Lucian involuntarily backed up a step.

"What's this?" Christian asked, carelessly, like he was asking about the weather, but a muscle began its familiar movement in his jaw.

"Do you know what she is, brother?" Lucian said. "Of course you do, you played me for a fool and I listened to your song and dance about the prophecy not being about her, and that her blood was poison! You *knew* and you lied!"

"I did not lie, Lucian," he said. "Her blood was poison."

"You still protect her?" Lucian was snarling now. His overwhelming desire for Le Sang Noir impeded his better judgment, and his eyes were starting to go wild at Victoria's nearness, feeling the heat of the forbidden blood that surged so sweetly beneath the surface of her flushed skin. Such torment ... he could barely concentrate. It was so strange that he had never noticed it before until she had deliberately revealed it to him in Paris, and now it was like a tempting secret suddenly naked and exposed.

Christian watched Lucian, knowing the signs of the change intimately. He glanced around the room. Angie had wedged herself into a corner staring at them with unfocused frightened eyes as if she were watching something totally different in her head. She had moved Gabriel's body away from where Lucian had been standing and he lay just a few feet away from her. Her fist was pressed against her mouth as if to stop herself from screaming. Victoria was silent.

"Lucian," Christian said.

Lucian's long, lithe body started to lope with a familiar grace as the hunger spread through him, and he fought to control it. It was a losing battle.

"Lucian," said Christian roughly. "Snap out of it!" He tried to grab Lucian's shoulder and Lucian backed away ever so slightly, only to continue his frenzied shifting. "Lucian, that's what it does. I have seen it ... it lures you in and then it kills you. Trust me."

"Trust you?" Lucian's laugh was hollow and completely devoid of any humor. "I *never* should have trusted you. You couldn't stand to see me more powerful than you, that's why you hid it from me!" Christian looked at his brother's twisted face in stunned surprise.

"Is that what you think I've done? Saved you from a deathly mistake so that I could be more *powerful* than you?" Christian said slowly. Lucian's eyes were over-bright, and the truth of his feelings was clear as he glared murderously at Christian. "I *left* so that you could have the power you craved, to rule the House of Devereux as you wanted, not because I wanted to be more powerful than you!" Christian's body was rigid with disbelief at his brother's complete and utter hatred toward him. "We are *brothers* ..."

Lucian laughed humorlessly. "We are the furthest thing from brothers there ever was. Mother worshipped the ground you walked on. You were always the first. I only have the House because you left—"

"For you!" Christian said.

"You took Lena, you hid the prophecy from me, and now, *her*—"

"Lena?" Christian looked at Lucian like he was demented. "You have Lena!"

"But she has always wanted you, she was always yours, she still is!" Christian's eyes flew to Victoria's knowing that the turn in conversation would not be easy for her. Her face was inscrutable but he could see her white, clenched fingers.

"Lucian, what happened with Lena happened. I can't change the past. And if you wanted her so damned badly, you should have gone to the Council yourself," he said. Christian sighed and raked his hands through his hair. "What is this really about, Lucian? Le Sang Noir? You really think it's the answer to everything?"

"Yes." Lucian's voice was sulky.

"Well, it isn't, just ask her!" he said, looking over at Victoria.

It was entirely the wrong thing to do, and Christian cursed himself as soon as he said it. When he had been speaking to Lucian, he had unconsciously redirected Lucian's attention to himself and away from Victoria, but the second that he'd pointed toward Victoria, everything pivoted onto itself.

It was as if all the air had been sucked out of the room.

Lucian snarled, dropping into a feral crouch, transformation complete as he became the hunter … and his prey was Victoria. Christian shoved her behind him, and a low fierce roar tore from his chest as he faced his brother.

"Don't do it, Lucian," he growled. But Lucian didn't hesitate as he leapt with all his strength right at Christian, his hands connecting with his chest as they both went flying.

Christian barely had enough time to shove Victoria out of the way as Lucian snapped his teeth perilously close to her neck. He was unfamiliar with his newfound strength and she catapulted backward, her head cracking against the marble. She lay motionless on the cold floor, a thin trickle of dark blood dampening her hairline. The scent alone was enough to drive Lucian into a feeding frenzy as he whirled toward its source.

Christian twisted his body, wrapping his leg around Lucian's waist with enough leverage to flip him over, and held him down with the weight of his body. Lucian snarled even more ferociously as the terrible hunger clawed its monstrous way out of him; there was nothing human left inside of him. He threw a knee up into Christian's gut with brute force, heard him grunt in response, and then kicked with his other leg sending Christian somersaulting head over heels.

Lucian was on his feet in minutes, his teeth gnashing together in sheer rage at being thwarted, but the minute he turned to spring toward her motionless form, a bodily missile tackled him from behind. They rolled along the floor in a flurry of blows, their arms moving with silent and furious invisible speed. Christian sprang to his feet just as Lucian leveled a blow to his head that shattered the marble floor.

Christian was holding back because he wasn't sure that he could control the liquid heat inside of him, licking at his vampire senses like flames. Lucian lunged and landed a wallop that snapped Christian's head sideways. Christian answered with a vicious uppercut to Lucian's jaw and the crack resounded through the room as his jaw dislocated.

Within seconds, Lucian had re-aligned it and it healed into place even as he dived growling, his sharp nails slicing Christian's exposed chest. The wounds healed as expected and Christian swung around to counter his bloody attack, but Lucian was backing away slowly, watching him with an incredulous expression, his nostrils flaring. His eyes flicked from Victoria's still form to Christian in disbelief.

Confused, Christian looked down at his chest and touched the thin lines of blood that had welled along where Lucian had scratched him, a telltale blackly-red color smearing on his fingertip.

He smelled it too, different now but still the same underlying cloying heady scent.

Lucian's incredulous expression had transformed to one of accusation and then his face hardened into a mask of freezing rage. Christian hesitated in shock as his vampire instincts responded to the sight of the blood that was his but *not* his. The hesitation cost him dearly as Lucian spun with inhuman speed and snatched Victoria's body to his.

He held her in front of him, his fingers around her slim neck as her head lolled unconscious to the side.

"You liar!" he snarled. "You took her blood, I can smell it in you."

"Lucian, don't!" Christian said. "I didn't take it. She gave it to me but she altered it first—" He couldn't finish because Lucian had started laughing uncontrollably, the sound harsh and terrible in the silence.

"Come on, Christian, face it," he said. "She's going to die and I am going to take her blood, same as you. We both wanted it from the minute we saw her, you just got to her first." His smile was cruel.

Christian could see Lucian's terrible teeth lengthening even more as his face contorted into a terrifying grimace, leaning over Victoria's exposed throat, his eyes never leaving Christian's. Christian half lunged and Lucian shook his head in warning, dropping his mouth an inch closer to her neck.

"Don't fight it, Christian," he said. "I want you to enjoy this."

In that moment, something burst within Christian. He didn't recognize it but it flooded his stomach and his heart with wild energy. It raced unhinged along his limbs tingling like tiny bolts of electricity responding to an unspoken command and pooling purposefully and then flowing back out again. Christian swallowed hard as the pulsing power took complete ownership of his limbs, and he felt a shiver of fear for what was happening, so devastatingly silent inside of him. Was this what Victoria talked about when she spoke about the energy of the blood?

It couldn't be …

CRUENTUS PROTECTUM, it whispered in her voice. Defend the blood.

In a moment of sudden clarity, Christian realized what he had to do. One glance at Lucian, a hair's breadth away from Victoria's neck, and he made his decision. He let his walls fall.

Christian flinched as the strange magic slid into his consciousness. Its touch was curiously familiar. It felt like Victoria, the silent part of her that stared at him, shyly wondrous when she thought he wasn't looking, the quiet bit of her that tucked her hair behind her ears self-consciously whenever she saw him looking at her, and the calm side of her that lay curled up trustingly every night she fell asleep in his vampire arms.

He would trust it, and trust *her*, just like she'd always trusted him. He didn't fight it when it captured his conscious mind, wild with intent.

Blood magic.

Lucian's elongated fangs were at the skin of Victoria's neck when Christian stared at him, their silver eyes locking, only Christian's weren't silver any more … they were the silvery black of a moonlit sky, and Lucian's eyes widened in bewilderment.

"CONFUTO," Christian's lips said, only it wasn't his voice, it was a whisper soft musical sound that took shape in his mouth. And Lucian obediently froze, staring at him in astonishment. "LIBERO," the voice continued, and Victoria's body floated gently down to the ground where she softly stirred but did not awaken. Lucian's eyes widened even more until he couldn't even bear to look at his brother. And still the voice continued in its musical softness,

"CURO!" Lucian stared at Christian completely at a loss for words, he couldn't even move.

Release me, Christian! Lucian thought to him angrily, and then he paused. *How is this even possible, you can't do magic! You're a vampire! And what the hell is wrong with your eyes?*

It's the blood ... it's in my head, everywhere. Christian's voice was full of wonder but strangely calm. His mental voice sounded like his usual tone even though the voice that had come out of his mouth had distinctly not been his.

The blood? Lucian's response was skeptical.

Her blood in me, it's protecting her. From you.

That's impossible! Blood is not alive, it can't think for itself!

There are many things that are possible in this world, brother. And Le Sang Noir is one of the greatest of them. And as if he couldn't control himself, he continued his voice wondrous. *You wouldn't believe the energy, the magic. It's so alive!*

Lucian's eyes were unimpressed, imprisoned as he was by Christian's incantation in the first place. But the awe in Christian's voice brought back the feelings of righteous anger that Christian had taken the gift of Le Sang Noir while he himself had been deprived of it.

What happens next? Lucian asked flatly.

Christian didn't respond. He'd completely surrendered to the power of Le Sang Noir. The blood surged in his mind like a live being. This blood curse had a strength and power that seemed to thrive on sacrifice. He didn't even want to imagine what allowing the little bit that was inside of him to kill Lucian would do. Protecting Victoria had been the sole reason he had allowed it into his mind, it was something he had inexplicably understood, but now that she was safe, a vague sense of unease curled up his spine.

The blood surged in his head channeling most of its magic

into the last healing spell it had directed at Victoria. It still had not released Lucian and he stared at Christian with a furious intensity. Christian could see the fear in his eyes behind the deliberate look of hate-filled defiance. Victoria stirred and Christian's heart lurched as he rushed to her side, for the moment forgetting his brother, stroking her forehead gently. Her eyes opened and she smiled as she focused on him—they were the color of warm jade, and for a moment Christian was mesmerized, lost in their balmy liquidity.

"Do you know your eyes are black," she whispered.

"What?" he said automatically, and then realized that Lucian had also mentioned something about his eyes earlier.

The blood heaved again and he felt its energy start to amass once more, just as it had before each spell it had recently cast. It threw him for a second before he realized exactly what was going to happen. His gaze jerked to Lucian, and he saw the answering panic reflected in his expression. Christian's breath came in small raspy gasps, the potency of the blood's desire was overwhelming— he wanted to *kill* Lucian like he had never wanted to kill anyone, not even at the most ferocious demands of his hunger as a just-turned vampire. The desire for his death was eviscerating.

"Tori!" he said, gasping. His voice was desperate, and Victoria became instantly alert to the alarm in his tone.

"What is it?" she said.

"Your blood inside me healed you but now it wants to k … kill Lucian!"

Christian was on his knees grasping his stomach in unbearable pain, forcing himself not to look at his brother. Victoria looked completely shocked, and then touched her head, realizing that a spell that hadn't been of her own making had healed her head wound. She could still feel the remaining tackiness from the blood that had congealed in her hair, and she looked at Christian, recognizing that the healing spell had unbelievably come from his lips. And now it was her blood that held him darkly captive … it had been in his eyes, wanton and blatant.

Now it wanted sacrifice, vengeance!

Christian's face was covered in a damp sheen of sweat as he battled to not even look at Lucian, whose own expression was one of unconcealed dread.

"Sᴇᴄᴛᴜᴍᴄᴏʀᴘᴜs," Christian whispered, and Lucian screamed in agony, the pain intensified by his complete inability to move. Victoria's face was frozen in horror as she watched the veins in Lucian's neck bulging from the fury of the offensive spell intended to disembowel its victim. She could see the blood trickling from his nose. Where had that spell come from? Her blood was lethal even when it wasn't inside of her, probably even more so somehow knowing that it was outside of her normal control!

"Lɪʙᴇʀᴏ," Victoria shouted, after a worried glance at Christian still clawing the floor and his belly, and Lucian, finally released from his magical prison, backed away his eyes wide and gasping as his body automatically regenerated.

Despite the fading pain, Lucian clenched his jaw as the enthralling allure of her scent had not diminished in any way. Still, he moved away even further, watching intently as she crouched next to Christian's heaving body. Christian's face was strained, the veins in his head and throat standing out in clear relief as he violently struggled for control.

"Run," he said. *Run, Lucian!*

Lucian didn't need to be told twice. After an inscrutable look at the two of them, he vanished in moments and the cavernous room was empty. They were alone. Victoria looked around, noticing that Angie had also gone, and hoped that she had gotten to safety.

Christian was hunched over, pain evident in every rigid line of his body. Even though Lucian had left, the blood still sought vengeance against the aggressor who had threatened it, and its will was incredibly strong despite the fact that most of its strength had been used to restore Victoria. It was awe-inspiring and terrifying, and Christian's body strained with the effort to contain its vicious will.

He couldn't believe the force of its control and though he fought it with every shred of his own vampire strength, Christian did not feel any lessening in its desire for punishment ... for sacrifice. It was rampant within him, fueled by its own desires and infecting his senses with its taste for death. Christian felt the soft touch of Victoria's hand and drew a deep, shuddering breath.

Victoria realized that her blood only recognized one master and even though it flowed temporarily in his veins, there was no way it would obey him. He had no power over it. With some terror, she knew that the blood magic would probably destroy Christian the more he fought against it, and would attempt to dominate him completely or kill him, whichever came first. Victoria squeezed his shoulder and focused, delving into the power of the amulet. She would have to kill the blood before it had a chance to do either.

"Cruentus immunis totus," she said, her voice unwavering as she spoke the words to exorcise the blood curse. She grasped his hands. The power surged from the amulet through her body to his, and she felt Christian's body heave responsively, his skin growing fiery hot to the touch as the rogue blood struggled against its own execution. His shoulders convulsed spasmodically and within seconds, he retched, regurgitating a thick, blackly red mass that was almost spongy in its consistency. It was revolting.

Christian fell back as the blood lost its alluring luster and rapidly congealed as it died. The syrupy scent of it lingered heavy in the air. Depraved, Christian still felt his darkest nature still involuntarily craving it like an addict. He looked away with effort. All he wanted was to get as far away from it as possible.

"We need to leave," he said, trying not to breathe as he pulled her to him.

"Yes," she said, as her legs gave out from beneath her and she grasped his shoulders for support, the room starting to spin. That last spell had been intense despite the amulet's help, and her knees buckled. Christian hooked an arm under her legs, cradling her against his body. She buried her face in the contours of his neck as they made their way out.

"Where are we going?" she said, as they exited to the quiet and deserted street level of the alley.

"We'll go to my apartment. It's near here," he said.

At CHRISTIAN'S APARTMENT, Victoria felt shattered and confused. Other than a destroyed secret room, there was no visible evidence that any of the events had taken place. Everything seemed entirely too surreal—Gabriel's betrayal, Charla's murder, Enhard's death, and Christian's own possession by her demonic blood.

Surreal was the only word to describe it, and a part of her kept waiting to wake up from what she felt must be an impossible dream. But it wasn't a dream. People had died. She had killed some of them. Even Gabriel was dead. Her blood trilled softly and she shivered, turning toward the only comfort she knew.

"Will you stay with me?" she asked.

"Yes," Christian said, depositing them both on the sofa. "For as long as you need."

Forever, she thought.

Victoria nestled against his side and within minutes, he could hear her deep, even breathing. She was childlike in sleep, barely resembling the fierce fighter she'd been earlier. He frowned at the dark smudges under her eyes and rubbed his thumb across her cheeks as she sighed in her sleep, burrowing deeper into his side.

Memories of the night assaulted him, and Christian's head swam with unwanted images of Enhard as he bit back the hot wave of agony that filled him. He took several steadying breaths, and was unprepared for the sudden potent scent of Victoria's closeness.

It was unexpected. It was intoxicating.

It was *torture*.

The craving of his body for her blood was not unfamiliar, but what sickened him, was that despite knowing its demonic power, he *still* wanted it with a fervor that he could barely control. He remembered its thick, rich taste as it had flowed over his tongue and into the back of his throat like an elixir, so *pure*, that it had healed him in seconds. He had never dreamed of anything like it. Christian sighed wearily. He'd accepted the blood magic into himself knowing that it had been the only way to save Victoria from his brother. But its possession of him had been consummate.

He wondered if he could ever forget it. Or escape it.

THIRTY

Graduation

WHAT SHOULD HAVE been a fun and carefree time at year-end seemed forced and empty. The last few weeks had been overwhelming, and busy.

The news had broken across Windsor that Charla and Gabriel had been killed in a terrible hit-and-run accident while they were in New York, and the school had held a service on their behalf. Angie had been inconsolable, and the loss of her brother and her friend, despite their ultimate treachery, had only really hit her when they had all returned to Canville.

Victoria had closeted herself in Christian's house. She couldn't bear to be alone, especially at night when she was assaulted by horrific images of what had happened, and she'd only been able to get through finals with Christian's help. After the dramatic, life-changing events in New York, finishing high school seemed anticlimactic.

Angie's foster parents had let her return to campus despite their adamant wishes for her to remain with them in New York.

Angie had told them that she'd called 911 when Gabriel and Charla had been hit while running across the street after a late-night party, but the paramedics had been unable to do anything to save either of them. The deception had been essential to protect not only Victoria's identity, but also those of the vampires. Christian had made a call that same night to recover the bodies from the underground room. It was amazing to see the power of The Council. It had been a tragic but necessary façade, and somehow the police report corroborated Angie's story.

Victoria sighed, curling up on the sofa while Christian lit a fire in the fireplace as the temperature had dipped a bit since earlier in the day. She didn't want to think about what Christian had done to make that happen. It seemed that the supernatural world had its fingers and connections everywhere ... more so than she'd ever imagined. She wondered if she would ever get used to being a part of that world—the world that existed in the shadows on the periphery of human reality. For better or for worse, she was a part of both now. She sighed.

"Are you all right?" Christian asked quietly, joining her. She nodded leaning against him. He inhaled the strawberry smell of her shampoo with the heady scent of *her* flickering beneath it. His longing for her, and her blood, had only gotten stronger. All he wanted to do was to bury his face in her neck and take and take until he couldn't take any more, even *knowing* that her blood would consume him, consequences be damned. He shifted uncomfortably.

"Have you talked to Holly?" he asked, resorting to conversation as a suitable distraction.

"Yes, earlier today. I don't know if I ever told you that my grandmother had confided to Holly about us, about me. She knew. But she wasn't prepared for Gabriel. None of us were." Victoria faltered, the sense of betrayal still keen. "She says Leto is doing much better too. I think the magical therapy I did might have actually worked, thanks again to the blood magic," she said. "I think it will take him a while to come to terms with you and me though. Overcoming centuries of hate will take time." She smiled wryly. "Did you talk to Lucian?"

"Briefly. He's as well as can be expected. The Houses are convening next month to elect the new member to replace Enhard." His eyes clouded.

"I'm so sorry, Christian," she said.

"It's okay. Time heals everything, and that's one thing I have plenty of." Victoria wished she could erase the sadness etched in his face. She smiled brightly.

"Speaking of Enhard, did you know that he could *fly*?"

Christian looked at her, knowing she was trying to make him to remember the good things, the happy things, about Enhard. "Yes. He was over eight hundred years old. At that age, vampires can fly or shape-shift. There are very few left as old as he was."

"He told me about Valerius and Brigid," Victoria said quietly. "He said Valerius was his mentor. He must have hated her so much when she killed Valerius—almost as much as he hated me."

"He didn't hate—"

Victoria interrupted him. "Not at the end when he helped me. It was only his love for you that made him trust me. But I know that he was afraid of me, of what I am." She hesitated. "He was afraid that I would kill you, too."

Christian marveled at her perspicacity. As strong as she was, he knew the possibility was there that the blood could eventually control her and it scared the hell out of him too. It was a heavy curse, Le Sang Noir, or as she called it the Cruentus Curse, which she had explained to Christian meant bloodthirsty in their old language. It was an apt name. *Bloodthirsty.*

"Tell me what you're thinking," Victoria said.

"I was thinking about you, and about the blood," he said. He could feel her body tense but then immediately relax. "It would protect you at all costs right?"

"Yes probably," she said. "What are you worried about?"

"Me." Victoria sighed and looked up at his handsome somber face. "And … you," he admitted.

"Christian, we've been through this before," she said. He quelled her words by placing his finger against her lips.

"I know that, but sometimes fear is healthy. It's what keeps us alert and not seduced by a false sense of security because of who we are, *especially* because of who we are." He smiled sadly. "I don't want to lose you, Victoria …"

"You won't."

"Will you do me one favor?" he asked. When she agreed, he continued. "Will you put a protection charm on yourself when we are together?"

Victoria said nothing and bit her lip as she nodded once. Truth was she always had a shield spell in place whenever they were together, not because she feared him but because *she* didn't want to hurt *him*. Enhard had had a right to worry; she was every bit as dangerous as Brigid had been.

She sighed as Christian stroked her hair, lulled by the warmth of the fire and the rhythmic rise and fall of his chest, and closed her eyes, falling victim to the safety of his embrace as she always did.

Christian kissed her temple and felt her pulse immediately jump with life beneath his lips. Like a beacon, her blood soared, cognizant of its own seductive power and predatorily recognizing his weakness against it. He could hear it calling sensually to him with the tone of a forbidden lover and he sighed as he felt the tightening of his upper jaw. He'd fed earlier, but still it wasn't enough.

It was never enough.

He stood and stepped away putting several feet of distance between them, and stared out the window at the moonless night. Her scent curled around him. He sighed. Without any noise, he opened the French doors and stepped out onto patio, welcoming the cool air against his face.

Victoria heard him leave. She had reawakened the minute her treacherous blood started its tormenting song. Her heart wrenched at its duplicity. She closed her eyes, refusing to consider the possibility that he'd be better off without her, and without her blood tempting him every infernal second. Christian was right, they did have every reason to be afraid, but as long as they had each other and fought to protect what they had, then their love had to mean something.

Didn't it?

She leaned back on the sofa and stared at the ceiling, her fists clenched at her sides. After some time, she heard the sound of a violin in the next room, passionate and violent. Christian played to assuage something he too fought to express, his music giving voice to everything unsaid between them. Its cadence was harsh, the melody fraught with notes that sung of pain, and anger, and loss.

From Bach to Vivaldi, Victoria could feel him playing the runs faster and faster, whipping his bow at an impossible speed as if trying to exorcise something inside of him, the storm building and building and building, scale after scale, until it came to an exhausted, crashing halt.

Expelling a shaky breath, Victoria felt his spirit ease then as his strokes on the violin gentled into a more tender *Adagio*, soaring to something unbearably, poignantly sweet. It was music that only love could make, its language hauntingly beautiful, and one Victoria recognized—one that her mother had played to her father often.

It was a message … a promise … a love letter.

Christian was playing for her, weaving a spell she'd almost forgotten, one of beauty, and love, and unconditional hope. She felt a tear slide down her cheek as her throat constricted, the sounds of his raw emotions owning her completely, as she knew hers owned him, and telling her what no words could.

I will love you forever.

A few moments later, Christian returned to the room, closing the doors behind him. She felt the weight of the sofa shift as he sat down beside her, his smooth hand finding hers and gripping it like a lifeline. It was warm to the touch. Strong. He would be strong enough for both of them.

"Stay with me, Victoria," he said.

"Always."

The Bloodspell Playlist

These are some of the songs that I listened to while writing this novel. These particular songs influenced and inspired specific chapters or scenes, and whether I got stuck or was on a roll, I found myself replaying them over and over. Forthwith, the playlist:

1. *21 Guns,* Green Day (Metamorphosis/Inheritance)

2. *Bleeding Love,* Leona Lewis (At First Sight/Revelation/Falling)

3. *Breathe,* Telepopmusik (Discovery)

4. *Say It Right,* Nelly Furtado (Angst)

5. *Paralyzer,* Finger Eleven (Eye for an Eye)

6. *Bring Me to Life,* Evanescence (The Attack)

7. *Falling for You,* Jem (The Prophecy)

8. *The Hand That Feeds,* Nine Inch Nails (Paris: Christian/Lucian)

9. *Life In Mono,* Mono (Paris: Christian/Jardin des Tuileries)

10. *Road to Zion,* Damian "Jr. Gong" Marley & Nas (Paris: Christian)

11. *Stop and Stare,* OneRepublic (The Council)

12. *Savin' Me,* Nickelback (Snowstorm: Tori)

13. *Never Say Never,* The Fray (Happy New Year: Christian and Tori)

14. *Already Gone,* Kelly Clarkson (The Fight)

15. *Better In Time,* Leona Lewis (Misunderstanding: Tori)

16. *Blurry*, Puddle of Mudd (Misunderstanding: Gabriel)

17. *Always*, Saliva (Vulnerability and Rage: Gabriel)

18. *Glory Box*, Portishead (Romeo and Juliet)

19. *Missing You*, Jem (Betrayal)

20. *Pour Que Tu M'Aimes Encore*, Céline Dion (Blood and Magic : Christian)

21. *24*, Jem (Paris Revisited)

22. *Run*, Leona Lewis (Clash of the Titans: Tori and Christian)

23. *What About Now*, Daughtry (Bloodspell)

24. *I Don't Care*, Apocalyptica (Bloodspell: Lucian)

25. *Deliver Me*, Sarah Brightman (Graduation)

26. *Adagio in G Minor*, Albinoni (Graduation)

Acknowledgments

It takes a village, that's all I can say. I owe a ginormous debt of gratitude to the many people who helped me get this book off the ground and for believing in me even when I didn't believe in myself.

With all my heart I'd like to thank my husband, Cameron, whose support and love is unending, for never letting me give up (and for making sure the kids didn't go without bathing for days at a time while I was writing this book); Pam Sullivan, one part agent, one part editor, one part friend, for keeping me grounded and for all the laughter; my mother Nan for her unwavering faith and for helping me to find mine; my valiant first readers, Robert Stickney, Gian Gosine, and Amanda Davis, for their motivation, enthusiasm, and honesty; J. Mark Lane, attorney extraordinaire, for his expert and generous guidance; Craig Gordon for keeping me stocked in reading material and vampire paraphernalia; my brother Kyle for cheerfully enduring all of my questions on high school life, love, and lingo; the talented team at Langdon Street Press for helping to make this book a reality; and especially, my wonderful children, Connor, Noah, and Olivia for being so patient when mommy needed "just one more minute" to finish that chapter.

Finally, to my parents, who always encouraged me to think differently and fueled my hungry imagination with as many books as I could sink my teeth into, and to my beautiful family, whose love makes every breath worth more than I can possibly imagine, thank you for everything.

About The Author

AMALIE HOWARD grew up on a small Caribbean island where she spent most of her childhood with her nose buried in a book or being a tomboy running around barefoot, shimmying up mango trees and dreaming of adventure. She received a bachelor's degree from Colby College in Maine in International Studies and French, and a certificate in French Literature from the Ecole Normale Supérieure in Paris, France. She has also lived in Los Angeles, Boston, and New York City. She has worked as a research assistant, marketing rep, global sales executive, freelance writer, and blogger. A lover of other cultures and new experiences, especially of the culinary variety, she has traveled extensively across North America and Europe, and as far east as China, Indonesia, and Australia. She currently resides in New York with her husband, three children, and one very willful cat that she is convinced may have been a witch's cat in a past life.

Amalie Howard's debut novel, *Bloodspell*, evolved from a short story that took on an eerie life of its own, and is undoubtedly the result of a lifelong infatuation with witchcraft, vampires, and excessive amounts of chocolate.